RUTHLESS GUARDIAN
RUTHLESS HEIRS

SIENNA CROSS

Copyright © 2024 by Sienna Cross

All rights reserved.

No part of this book may be reproduced in any form or by any electronic or mechanical means, including information storage and retrieval systems, without written permission from the author, except for the use of brief quotations in a book review.

Paperback ISBN: 9798301789472

Cover Design: Covers by Juan

Interior Art: Samaiya Art

❧ Created with Vellum

To all the women who find it perfectly acceptable to fall for their controlling, possessive, slightly unhinged bodyguard…
~ Sienna Cross

PLEASE NOTE

This is a dark romance novel with scenes that may be triggering and sexually explicit in nature, specifically but not limited to pregnancy loss, violence and torture.

Ruthless GUARDIAN

CONTENTS

1. Valentino Mafia Princess — 1
2. Trapped in a Tower — 9
3. Handle the Pressure — 15
4. Time to Start Living — 22
5. My Damnation — 28
6. A Professional Distance — 36
7. A Lethal Combination — 42
8. The Perfect Candidate — 48
9. An Ounce of Freedom — 56
10. Dead and Buried — 61
11. The Stupidest Thing — 67
12. Cheers! — 74
13. My Fault — 81
14. Blackmail — 87
15. Finally Free — 93
16. Dark Memories — 99
17. A Security Blanket — 106
18. Unfettered Access — 112
19. Mr. Perfetto — 118
20. A Little Fun — 124
21. Shatter the Line — 132
22. Good Enough — 139
23. The Safest Option — 146
24. Pradas and the Pantheon — 152
25. A Friendly Warning — 160
26. A Full-Service Guy — 166
27. The Death of Me — 173
28. Hold On — 180
29. A Bad Idea — 186
30. Stupid and Desperate — 193
31. Duty and Desire — 200
32. If I Can't Have You — 208
33. What Do You Want? — 217
34. Impossible — 223
35. Cock Blocker — 229

36. Fratellino	235
37. The First Time	241
38. Clingy and Attached	249
39. You're Mine	255
40. A Fiery Blaze	261
41. Three in One Night	267
42. Punishment	274
43. You Belong to Me	280
44. Damage Control	288
45. Make Me Forget	295
46. My First Client	302
47. A Horrible Nightmare	308
48. The L Word	314
49. That Was Me	320
50. Coffee and Paranoia	327
51. Fool Me Twice	334
52. He Will Find Me	340
53. My Personal Hell	346
54. Beautiful and Violent	352
55. Burn It to the Ground	360
56. No Way Out	367
57. A Vow	376
58. For as Long as I Draw Breath	382
Epilogue	389
Also by Sienna Cross	399
Acknowledgments	401
About the Author	403

CHAPTER 1
VALENTINO MAFIA PRINCESS

I*sabella*

"Get down!"

I feel the subtle shift in the atmosphere—a tension that tightens the air an instant before gunshots explode across the swanky bar. Waves of gunfire follow instantly, shattering the rhythm of the night as screams erupt around me. I nearly choke on my martini as a big hand clamps over my head and shoves me beneath the high-top table.

"Stay down, Isabella, and don't move until I come back for you!" my bodyguard, Frankie, growls in my ear. He blankets me with his massive form for a long minute before he releases the gun at his hip and leaps back up to return fire. "Stay hidden, do you hear me?"

I nod, instinctively.

Bullets pepper the air, tiny missiles of death echoing over the pounding bass. The clink of glasses and bursts of laughter pervading the posh Manhattan bar are gone, replaced by blood-curdling shrieks.

My heart kicks at my ribcage, and I'm filled with the most overwhelming urge to scream myself. Why can't I just have one normal night? One night to celebrate my graduation from NYU with my friends.

"Shit, Bella! Are you okay?" Serena drops down to the ground beside me, her cocktail still clenched in her fist. Wisps of blonde hair fall across her bright blue eyes as she regards me. Guards now surround the table we're hidden beneath but still, her hand shoots out attempting to cover my head. I swat her away.

"Don't you dare, Serena. I'm not yours to protect. My life is no more valuable than yours."

"I don't know about that, cuz. I'm pretty sure your father would say otherwise."

"And I'm pretty sure your father would kill my father if you died trying to protect me."

She smirks, flashing me ruby-stained lips. "Touché. Let's just agree we're both incredibly precious then."

"Come on, huddle closer." I reach for my cousin, who also happens to be my best friend, and tug her beside me. Down on all fours in my sleek black mini-dress, I make a barrier of the surrounding chairs, and Serena pulls a silver handgun from her sparkly clutch. It's just another Friday for the Valentino mafia princesses.

Serena rises to her knees, her head nearly bumping the underside of the table thanks to that long torso of hers. She points the barrel through the slats in the chair and aims at the half a dozen men blocking the door.

"Maybe you shouldn't," I hiss.

"Why not? I can help and take a few of the guys out."

I quickly shake my head and strands of dark hair whip across my face. "What if you get one of *our* guys in the crossfire?"

Serena sticks out her bottom lip, pouting. "Fine…"

While Serena chooses to focus her talents at the shooting range, I prefer to work out my stress and occasional rage at the gym with hand-to-hand combat. Give me the feel of flesh and bone cracking against each other over a gun any day. Krav Maga is my current obsession, but I've taken classes in nearly all the martial arts since the day I could walk. *Papà* had insisted.

When your father is Luca Valentino, the head of the ruthless Kings, the most notorious crime syndicate in all of Manhattan, there's no such thing as being too prepared or a quiet girls' night out. It doesn't help that we chose The Velvet Vault, a bar owned by our cousin whose father, Marco Rossi, is the boss of a rival organization, the Geminis. The Valentinos and Rossi's may have found peace, but that doesn't mean every other criminal association in New York City doesn't want our parents dead.

And us, by association.

From beneath the table, I can just make out Frankie's black loafers, partially concealed by his dark slacks. Blood already splatters the leather. I blink quickly, chasing away the deep crimson staining my vision. Beside my guard stands a slew of Kings, our fathers' henchmen and our typical entourage. The barrage of missiles echo across the mostly empty bar, most of the patrons having raced out of here the moment the battle began.

I wonder if that gorgeous guy I met earlier at the bar got out alive. *Dio*, I hope so. The thought of the light in those piercing, velvety eyes going dim is just too terrible to consider.

"Bella!" A familiar voice surges through the chaos of ricocheting bullets. "Bells, where are you?"

"Down here," I whisper-hiss, waving my hand from under the tabletop.

Matteo crawls toward us, a gun clenched in each fist. My

cousin shoots a round over his head before holstering his weapons and turning his attention to us. Apparently, he has no qualms about accidentally taking out my dad's men. Then again, given the tumultuous nature of our fathers' relationship, I'm not that surprised. His dark eyes raze over me, searching for blood. I know the look, I've seen it in *Papà*'s gaze more than I care to remember.

"What the hell's going on, Matty?" Serena barks.

"Fucking Alessandro. He messed with the Russians last week so I'm guessing this is payback."

This lovely establishment is owned by our other cousin, Alessandro Rossi. Which is the only reason I'm occasionally allowed to frequent the place. Normally, no one is stupid enough to mess with the Geminis.

I guess all bets are off when the Russians are involved.

"Where is he?" I ask. "And where's Alessia?" Not that I'm a big fan of the female half of the twins, but she is my cousin—half-cousin—but still. From the Rossi side, Matteo is the best by far.

Matty shrugs. "Last time I saw Ale, he was texting Uncle Marco. And I have no idea where Alessia went."

Serena snorts on a laugh. "Calling Daddy to clean up his mess? Figures the cocky bastard would be a chickenshit when things got real."

"I know he can be an asshole, but he's blood, Sere." Matteo wraps an arm around me, tucking me into his side. Everyone in the family coddles me, Luca Valentino's *principessa*. Princess and heir to the Kings' empire.

"Speaking of blood," I add before peeking between Frankie's legs. My guard has been stationed in front of the table spraying the air with a continuous volley of bullets. "It's a good thing you didn't bring any of your siblings out tonight. Your mom would've killed you if anyone got roped into this mess."

"Which is exactly why I didn't tell any of them I was

coming here for our early graduation celebration." He presses a finger to his lips. Matteo has four younger siblings, the biggest family in the Valentino-Rossi crew ranging from Matty's twenty-four to Rex's twelve. I love the guy and all his brothers and sisters, despite who his father is.

"All clear!" Frankie's gruff voice puts an end to our casual conversation. It's a testament to the life we live, that the three of us can chat so nonchalantly while a full-on shootout resounds in the background.

After all these years, I've grown accustomed to the chaos. That, and I know Frankie has my back. He's been my personal bodyguard since the first day I left the penthouse without my parents back in grade school.

"Finally," Serena mutters, crawling out from under the table and pulling me along with her. "I better not have ruined my new Dolce & Gabbana dress, or I'm sending Alessandro the bill." She straightens to her full height, towering over me, even with my heels. With long, blonde hair and those ocean blue eyes, she looks every bit like her mom, my feisty Aunt Rose.

Matteo stands, leaning against the chair and runs a hand through his disheveled dark locks. "Don't worry, we're good for it."

"Where is Ale anyway?" I rise to my tiptoes to see over Frankie's broad shoulders. The rest of the Kings' men and the bar's security team are circling the bar, assessing the damage and righting fallen tables and chairs. At least there aren't any bodies. From our side anyway. I can't say the same about the Russians. I squeeze my eyes closed, avoiding their bloodied, mangled forms. They may be our enemies, but I've always lacked the bloodlust that's supposed to run through my veins.

"Over there." My guard ticks his head toward the modern glass bar that runs the length of the wall behind us. Or at least what used to be the bar. Shards of glass glisten across the black marble floor shimmering beneath the soft glow of lights.

Alessandro and Alessia pop up from behind it, and if it weren't for the bloody gash along Alessia's forehead and the crimson droplets dribbling down Ale's upper lip, I might have laughed. I've never seen my perfect cousin, Alessia, in such a state. Wild, wet curls tumble over her shoulders, her fuchsia dress splattered with an assortment of liquors from the mirrored shelves above. Ale is in no better condition, soaked from head to toe in his beloved alcohol. Above them, the rows of top shelf liquor bottles trickle pathetically, riddled in bullet holes.

"Fucking Russians," Alessandro growls as he throttles his gun and walks around the bar, glass crunching under his boots.

"This is all your fault," Alessia whines at her twin brother, wringing alcohol from her hair. "Pa is going to kill you for getting The Velvet Vault shot up like this. You know he hates when Gemini Corp gets drawn into the press alongside mob shit."

"It wasn't my fault," he mutters.

Serena releases a sharp cackle, her head falling back dramatically. "I'm sure you were the innocent one in all of this."

"Shut up, Serena. If this place closes down, where are you going to go trolling for your fuck buddies?"

"Oh, you wound me so. At least I can get some..."

"Alessandro, stop," I hiss. "Both of you, relax. Everyone's just on edge because of the shooting."

"And it's time for us to go, Isabella." Frankie moves to my side, squeezing my shoulder. "*Signor* Valentino is not pleased. And no one wants to see your father pissed."

I glance up at those dark eyes, the faint crinkle on the edges of the rueful smile.

Great. If The Velvet Vault closes, where the hell will I go for these brief moments of freedom? Unlike Serena who actually has her own apartment, it's not like I can bring a guy back to the penthouse I share with my brother and overbearing parents. *Papà* would strangle the guy before he set foot into the foyer. So much for my plan of finally meeting someone.

"Fine," I grumble.

Serena pulls me into a hug, then holds me out to arm's length and straightens the strap of my dress. "I'm sorry this night was a complete disaster. I never should have dragged you here. Tell Uncle Luca it was a freak incident that will never happen again."

"If he ever lets me leave the penthouse again."

"Isabella, it's time." Frankie motions to the entrance across the dancefloor, the thick velvet curtains hanging askew, and the matching velvet rope sprawled across the floor.

Matteo presses a kiss to my cheek, and Alessandro and Alessia offer half-hearted waves as my guard escorts me toward the door.

"He's never going to let me out again," I groan.

Frankie cocks his head and offers a reassuring smile. "Never is a long time, *piccola*." Little one. He's called me that for as long as I can remember, and now despite having just turned twenty-two and about to embark onto a long, difficult journey at medical school, when I hear the nickname, I'm that insecure little kid again hiding behind *Papà*'s looming shadow. Frankie tousles my hair and moves into step beside me as we cross the sticky dancefloor. I refuse to look down, preferring to ignore whatever it is I'm walking through. "Don't worry, I'll talk to him."

"Thanks, Frankie. Of all the bodyguards to be stuck with, you're the best."

He chuckles, the warm sound vibrating his barrel chest.

"I'm the only one you've ever had, *piccola*, so I sure as hell better be."

I step onto the red carpet, the soles of my Jimmy Choo's sinking into the plush material, and a shadow streaks across my peripheral vision. The velvet curtain glides back, and I'm greeted by the barrel of a gun.

A gasp slips through my clenched lips as time slows. Everything blurs but that hand on the sleek weapon, that finger on the trigger. A shot fires, and the scream dies in my throat.

CHAPTER 2
TRAPPED IN A TOWER

Isabella - One Month Later

Dropping the book into my lap, I stare out the floor-to-ceiling windows of my glass cage and blow out a breath. The deep greens of Central Park stretch out below, calling to me. What I wouldn't give to once again walk beneath the shade of the towering oaks.

My gaze flits over my arm, to the faint scar puckering the skin over my biceps. My chest constricts, a relentless ache squeezing my lungs. Not from the old bullet wound but from the memory of the man who gave his life for mine.

Fucking Frankie. Why did you have to be so damned noble?

If he hadn't jumped in front of me, I would be the one six feet under right now. Instead, he took the bullet meant for me. It sliced through his heart, tearing through bone and muscle and then sank into my arm.

Who the hell makes bullets like that?

I stare at the spot on my arm, and my lips curve into a scowl. I don't remember a whole lot from that night, but the little that I do remember haunts me. Mom had asked if I wanted the scar removed, as if a plastic surgeon could magically scalpel away the bad memories. No, I would keep the scar forever, a constant reminder of Francesco Bellini. It's stupid, but since the bullet went through him before piercing my arm, I like to think that a part of him is still with me, his blood mingling with my own.

Hot tears well in my eyes, and I blink quickly to force them back. I cried for days after his death, then for another week after the funeral. It's true what they say about not knowing what you have until you lose it.

I never realized how much I loved my faithful shadow until he was gone. I'd taken him for granted for years without ever truly thanking him. He'd given up everything for me.

Quick footsteps across the marble send my gaze spinning toward the hallway. Vinny appears with a backpack slung over his shoulder. My younger brother regards me in that quiet way he always does. "You good?"

"Of course." I offer him a cheery smile. "I'm a prisoner in a gilded cage. What could possibly be wrong?"

Rolling his eyes, he drops down to the sofa beside me. "You know, I'm sure *Papà* would let you leave the penthouse if you just chose a new bodyguard."

A knife in the gut would've hurt less. How can I replace Frankie? More than that, how can I choose the next man to die?

"Nah, it's fine. I'll just live in here forever, like Rapunzel, reading my books, trapped in this tower."

"Until your prince comes?" A lopsided smile curls his lips, and it's freaky how much he looks like our father. When *Papà* smiles, that is, which is a rare occurrence these days unless our mom is in the room.

At eighteen, Vincenzo Valentino, named after my mom's brother and dad's best friend who died, is everything I wish I could be. He's a real free spirit, who marches to the beat of his own drum, even when forced to live in the dark world we inhabit. He has the luxury of being the second born. Despite being born a female, *Papà* was adamant we stick to traditions naming me his heir, which is pretty fucking unfair considering Uncle Dante is the eldest brother and yet my father runs the family business, even if it is mostly in name only these days.

Vinny could have been pissed, could have fought for his position as eldest male, but he has zero interest in King Industries and even less in its underground dealings. We're the same in that respect, and despite my chosen career path, *Papà* insists one day I will take over the business, the legitimate side at least.

A doctor can still run a multi-million-dollar organization, principessa. *The Kings' empire must survive if we wish to.*

He's been trapped in this life for so long he truly believes there's no escaping it. Going to medical school is my way out, and God willing my father will live a long life and I won't be forced the take the reins of his legal or criminal empire any time soon.

"Well, I'm going to meet Jess for a coffee." He stands, his dark brow arching. "You sure you don't want to come? Dad can send Tony along with my guard. I'm sure even he would agree to that."

Tony has been *Papà*'s right hand man forever. He is like family and rarely gets his hands dirty in the dark side of the business anymore. I shake my head, sighing. I couldn't stand the thought of having more blood on my hands.

I lift my book and stick my nose between the pages. "I'll just live vicariously through my best book friends."

"Suit yourself, Bella." He hinges at the waist, light eyes fixing to mine. At eighteen he already dwarfs me, which is pretty embarrassing. "But you're going to have to leave this place eventually. And you will have to choose a guard."

I cringe at the thought, a surge of icy fingers dancing up my spine. "Maybe…" I whisper. But not today.

"Later, Bella." He spins toward the door, waving to Gerry on the way out, and I'm so damned jealous as I watch him casually cross the threshold.

I wish I could find the courage…

"*Buon giorno, principessa!*" *Papà* appears at the door juggling a tray of Starbucks and a jar of Nutella in one hand and a bouquet of calla lilies in the other, my mom's favorite. His dark eyes scan over me like some sort of harm could've come to me in the safety of our heavily guarded penthouse in the last twenty minutes since he left. He folds his tall form onto the cushion beside me, places the flowers in a vase on the cocktail table and hands over the Caramel Frappuccino with a disgusted twist to his lips before dropping the jar of my favorite treat in my lap. "Your coffee and breakfast…"

To *Papà*, if it isn't a legit Italian espresso from his old school stovetop espresso pot it isn't real coffee.

I take a sip, and a smile instantly melts across my face. *So good…* I barely resist the urge to pry open the jar of Nutella and dip my finger inside. But I'll wait until I'm alone to indulge.

My dad turns to me, something unreadable behind that well-crafted mask. He doesn't often wear it around his family, which has anxiety bubbling up deep inside. "Isa, your mamma and I have been talking and we feel it is time to find a replacement for Francesco."

I open my mouth to object, but he cuts me off, raising a hand.

"I know how difficult this is for you, and believe me, there is nothing I like more than having you under my watchful eye. But this is becoming unhealthy." He motions to the stack of books on the coffee table, then to the fluffy slippers beneath the couch before settling his wary gaze on my pajamas. "It's been a month, *principessa*. Frankie wouldn't want this…"

"How do you know what Frankie wants, *Papà*? How could you have any idea? How can any of us? Because he's dead and dead men don't speak, they don't think, their hearts no longer beat, lungs fail to function—" A sob builds in my throat, cutting off my manic rambling, and Dad jerks me into his chest.

His hand runs over the back of my head, and he whispers soothingly like he did when I was a silly child, awoken by a nightmare or terrified by some movie Alessandro had made me watch at their house. "I'm so sorry, Isa," he whispers. "I wish more than anything I could spare you from the dark parts of our legacy, of our grisly world." He holds me out to arm's length and spears me with those expressive irises. "But I must prepare you for what is to come. You will always be the heir to the Kings' empire and with it, comes responsibilities. I hope to protect you from it as long as possible, but I cannot do that properly without a guard at your side."

"I can't—"

"Yes, you can, and you will." He stands and ticks his head at the clock above the kitchen stove. "I have four candidates coming in today to interview with you. I've already vetted them all, and any one of them would make a fine choice. I hope that giving you the opportunity to decide on your guardian will help in the process, but if you cannot choose, then I will decide for you."

I jump up, my bare feet tingling against the cool marble. "No, I'm not ready," I growl. "And since when are you trying to get me out of the penthouse? My whole life you've wanted the exact opposite!" As a teen, I was never allowed to go to sleepovers, to the movies with friends, on dates with boys. Nothing.

"Because we're worried about you, Isa." Mom's voice echoes from the second floor. She pads down the steps, wet hair hanging off her bare shoulders.

My father's gaze pivots to hers and even in the midst of a fight, I see the fire in his eyes as he regards her. Even after all these years, he adores her. A part of me wants that so badly. Growing up with the most perfect, loving couple is damned intimidating. Even if I had the opportunity to date, would I ever find a love like theirs?

One thing is for damned sure, I never will if I don't leave the safety of these four walls.

I heave out a breath and drop down onto the couch. "Fine, I'll meet with the candidates, but if I don't like them, I'm not doing this."

Mom steps closer, and *Papà*'s arm instinctively curls around her waist. I'm not sure he even realizes he's doing it. He draws her close, nostrils flaring as if he's breathing her in. It's gross and sweet, and my heart aches a little more for what they have.

Steeling my resolve, I grab the books littering the coffee table and press them against my chest. "Let me know when the men get here, I'm going to get dressed."

CHAPTER 3
HANDLE THE PRESSURE

I*sabella*

"Are you married?" I stare at the quiet man in a black suit seated across the conference table in my father's office. He casts a glance out the window before returning his wary gaze to me. The imposing King Industries skyscraper towers over Midtown Manhattan, making it the perfect spot for my father's seat of power. The city sprawls out around us, the frenetic hustle and bustle completely drowned out by the thick glass windows. Refusing his eye, I glance down at his resume, scanning the black font. He's worked for a number of high-profile families, renowned senators, wealthy businessmen and even a famous pop star.

"I am," he finally replies, drawing my gaze back up to meet pale green eyes. "Happily, for ten years now."

Internally, I groan. I can't be responsible for making his wife a widow if something goes wrong.

"Kids?"

He nods again. "Three actually, the little one just turned five."

I rise abruptly, knotting my arms across my chest. "Thank you for coming, but I don't think it's the right fit."

The man stares at me, eyes wide for a long minute before one of the guards escorts him to the door.

I can feel *Papà*'s glare boring into me from the corner of the room. He hasn't spoken a word in the past three interviews, allowing me to take the reins. But I have a feeling his silence is about to come to an end.

So I spin on him, pre-emptively. "I know what you're going to say."

"Oh really, what's that?" He stalks closer, arms folded behind him.

"That I'm being too picky."

"Well, yes, that's one thing…"

"I won't choose a man with a family," I blurt.

"But Frankie didn't—"

"I know." And I feel awful for it. He dedicated his entire life to me and our family, without ever making the time to grow his own. "But at least, there were no kids to mourn his loss at the funeral. I couldn't handle that, *Papà*."

His head slowly dips, something like understanding in his eyes. "Isa, these men choose this life. It is no fault of your own. If it's not you, it's someone else they risk their life for."

"Then it's their guilt to drown in, not mine. I won't do it. I will not send one of these men to their ultimate doom."

My father draws in a steadying breath, then places his strong hands on my shoulders. "You are much too kind of a soul for this life, little princess."

A quick knock at the door sends my head spinning to the entrance. *Papà*'s executive assistant, Clara, pokes her head in. Her warm gaze flows over me, and a smile parts her perfectly red lips. The stunningly fashionable older woman is like a grandma to me, taking the place of the maternal grandmother I never met. "Mr. Ferrara is here."

"Are you ready?" My father lifts a dark brow.

"I guess I have to be, right?"

"I think you'll like this one, Isa. He's never been married and has no children, not to mention has an impeccable record. He should be the perfect match."

As much as I've been dreading this day, I can't deny the itch beneath my skin, to be free, to act like a twenty-two-year-old college grad again instead of an old recluse. "We'll see about that," I mutter, then stomp back to the conference table and sink into the high-backed chair at the head. I glance over my shoulder at Clara and return her smile. "Please, send him in."

Clara's grin widens, a glint of amusement sparkling in her eyes. "Of course, *principessa*."

I roll my eyes at the nickname, momentarily diverting my attention from the doorway. Again, I feel that prickle, the shift in the air that has goosebumps rippling across my arms. I lift my gaze and find myself ensnared by a pair of eyes as dark as the midnight sky. In an instant, I'm captive to that piercing, intense stare, as if the world narrows down to the space between us. A shiver of anticipation runs down my spine.

I've never seen a man so beautifully terrifying, his presence breathtaking and intimidating all at once.

And oddly familiar.

My breath catches in my throat, confirming my sentiment from a moment ago, as my gaze settles on the immense shadow darkening the doorway. I force my eyes away from his, down to that strong Roman nose and high cheekbones, to the dark stubble across his wide jaw, then travel further down. Good God, his shoulders are so wide he's forced to shift sideways to fit through the entrance. A black suit melds to his broad form, the sleek material like second skin. The hint of a tattoo peeks through the open collar of his pristine white shirt and suddenly, I must know what sort of art hides beneath.

I've never had such a visceral reaction to a man. Any man.

He stalks closer, and every nerve in my body tingles in awareness. I cross my legs, to extinguish the unexpected building heat, and fold my hands atop the mahogany conference table, reminding myself why we're here. I'm supposed to be interviewing him, not eye-fucking the man and imagining his naked, tattooed body sprawled beneath me.

He folds his massive form into the chair across from me and offers a guarded smile. "Good morning, *Signorina* Valentino." The hint of an accent laces his words, the smooth, deep timbre, a perfect match to the gorgeous man perched before me. "Thank you for taking the time to meet with me today."

Swallowing hard, I shuffle through the papers in front of me, trying my damnedest to remember what Clara had said his name was until I find his resume. Raffaele Ferrara. *Yes, that's it*! "Thank you for coming, Mr. Ferrara." I'm impressed with the coolness I manage given the sudden heat racing through every inch of my body.

I sit across from him, trying not to squirm, the sprawling boardroom doing nothing to temper the electric tension between us. The chandelier above the conference table casts a soft glow, accentuating the sharp lines of his suit and the undeniable presence he commands. I try not to linger on the sight of him, too aware of my wandering thoughts. Clearing my throat, I refocus on the task at hand.

"Mr. Ferrara, your record is impressive. Special Forces, then private security in some of the world's most volatile lands," I begin, scanning his resume while stealing glances at his hard expression. "What brings you to the doorstep of King Industries?"

Raffaele places his hands on the table, his posture a study in relaxed vigilance. "Protecting people is more than just a job to me, *Signorina* Valentino. It's a vocation. I'm here to ensure your safety, thoroughly. As to what brings me to New York specifically, I've grown tired of the endless travel in my stations abroad. I'm looking for a more permanent position."

The intensity of his tone tries to pin me down, make me feel secure, but it also pulls at the edges of my restraint. I lean forward, a playful smirk forming because apparently this man possesses some sort of magical power over me. I feel flirtatious, I feel alive for the first time in a month. And again, it all feels weirdly familiar. "Thoroughly, huh? Does that include tackling the dire threats of midnight chocolate cravings or extracting me from insufferably dull dinner parties?"

A spark of amusement lights up his dark eyes, briefly softening the steel in them. "If those pose a risk to your well-being, then absolutely."

My laughter cuts through the tension, sharp and maybe too raw. "My risks tend to be a bit more life-threatening than social faux pas, Mr. Ferrara." Though I wouldn't mind having him in my arm for a gala or two. The man would look devastating in a tux.

He doesn't miss a beat, his gaze locking onto mine with unflinching seriousness. "I'm fully briefed on the actual threats, *Signorina* Valentino. I heard what happened at The Velvet Vault last month. I assure you my dedication to your safety is absolute."

Some of the fire blossoming below wanes at the dismal reminder. And a flicker of a memory rises to the surface. It was *him*. He was the gorgeous guy I'd seen at the bar a month ago.

"I can guarantee something like that would never happen under *my* watch."

Something about his unyielding assurance makes me

pause and slightly pisses me off. As if Frankie had fucked up somehow. Shoving down the inappropriate thought, I rein in my emotions. There's a challenge in his eyes, an unspoken dare that I find both disturbing and exhilarating. I lean in closer, dropping my voice to a whisper so *Papà* doesn't hear. "But what if I'm the one who likes to bend the rules? I don't like cages, even gilded ones. How will you handle me then?"

His eyes narrow slightly, the corner of his mouth twitching in a semblance of a smirk. Does he remember me? "With respect, it's my job to keep you alive, not cater to your whims. However, I'll do my best to manage both."

The daring in his tone sends a thrill through me, a lethal mix of annoyance and attraction. I push back my chair slightly, sizing him up. "And if things get... complicated? Can you handle the pressure?"

"Complications are part of the job," he replies without hesitation, his voice low and steady. "I always keep my cool, *signorina*."

"Good," I say, a slow smile spreading across my face. "Because around me, things don't just get complicated—they explode."

"I can see that."

I get ready to stand, desperate to put some space between myself and this completely unexpected man. I wanted to hate him, planned on dismissing him like all the others, but I can't seem to keep my eyes off him. "One last question, or two, rather."

"Of course."

"Are you married?"

He shakes his head. "Forming meaningful relationships is difficult in my line of work."

I'm surprised by his candid reply, and by the twist of his lips, he seems just as stunned to have given it. "So no kids either?"

"No."

"Good." I bite my tongue, shaking my head. "That's not what I meant, I just prefer a bodyguard who isn't involved."

Raffaele nods once, sharply. "Personal feelings and attachments have no place in my profession."

"Right."

"Then we understand each other well, *Signorina* Valentino."

He takes my hand, his grip firm and resolute. The contact sends a jolt through me, challenging my resolve. As I let go, I can't help but wonder if I'm sealing a deal with a guardian or sparking a war with a man who might just be my undoing.

"Yes, I guess we do." Far too well possibly.

"I'll await your decision then."

My head dips and I press my lips together, not trusting myself to say anything else. Like can you start immediately? I can't help my traitorous gaze from trailing after his impressive form as he walks away, his confident stride a promise of the fiery dance to come.

CHAPTER 4
TIME TO START LIVING

I sabella

Nursing my morning cappuccino on the balcony, I draw in a deep breath as I take in the peaceful tranquility of Central Park below. Yesterday's trip into downtown had been the first time I'd left the penthouse since that night… The excursion had been as much exhilarating as it was draining.

Meeting those guards—and especially one in particular—had been a torrent of exhausting emotions. I want to be out there in the world living my life again, but the PTSD is real. It isn't the fear for my life, but the responsibility of another's. In my twenty plus years, Frankie was a constant and now he was gone because of me.

It sounds ridiculous, but I would have rather been the one to die.

I stopped fearing death at the ripe old age of six. I don't think I'd ever forget that day. *Papà* had come with Frankie to pick me up from school and instead of heading straight home, we took a detour to Central Park for ice cream. We were strolling around the boathouse when I felt it, that prickle of awareness I now understood was some long buried primal sense of self-preservation. *Papà* felt it too, and he slammed me to the ground an instant before a bullet whizzed by.

It was the first time I'd ever been shot at, and as I lay beneath my father, his body a human shield of blood and bones, an odd sense of calm crashed over me. "Everything is going to be fine, *principessa*," my dad whispered. "No one comes after my family and lives." More shots rang out and despite my father's big hand covering my eyes, I saw the man fall. Frankie stood over our attacker's panic-stricken face as blood poured from the wound in his chest. His face was contorted in fear as he begged for mercy, a gift he'd never receive. He must have known it too because I'd never seen such horror painted into an expression.

Frankie pointed the barrel to his forehead and with one quick pop, his head lolled back. The hard set of the man's jaw softened, and his eyes rolled back, then a slow smile crawled across his lips. He seemed so content, so completely at peace. After only six years of filling the small shoes of a mafia princess, I knew I would only ever achieve that level of complete serenity in death.

Squeezing my eyes closed, I force back the dismal images and sip my coffee. My parents fought so hard to keep me from the harsh realities of our brutal world, but despite their best efforts, the darkness crept in and annihilated the light.

The creak of the balcony door opening sends my head spinning over my shoulder. Rick, who's on front door duty today, holds the door open for Serena who rushes by with a coffee in each hand. When she spies my nearly full mug, she grumbles and drops the cups on the table. "Damn girl, how long have you been up? It's only eight in the morning."

"I couldn't sleep," I mumble. "So I'll be more than happy to take that second cup of coffee off your hands."

She smirks. "It's your favorite, caramel macchiato."

"And that's why you're my best friend." I lower my cappuccino onto the table and swap it out for the sweet goodness of Starbucks.

Serena plops down onto the lounge chair beside me and bumps her cup to mine. "Cheers."

I take a sip of the warm, caramel latte, and the turmoil in my gut begins to subside.

"So I heard you met with some guards yesterday…" She lifts an inquisitive brow. "Does that mean I'll finally get my wingwoman back?"

"Ugh," I grunt. "I'm not sure yet. They're only the first candidates I've met with and—"

Serena lifts a hand, cutting me off. "Oh, stop. I just so happened to stop by the office yesterday afternoon, and Clara already told me about that guy, Raffaele. Better still, she showed me the pic from his resume. Girl, he is sexy as sin and that security background? I'd let him shadow me any day. How could you not tell me about that delicious hunk of Italian man? Clearly, you need to pick him."

I force a laugh, even though just the mention of his name has heat blossoming below, and it has nothing to do with the latte wedged between my legs. I don't know why I don't mention seeing him at The Velvet Vault all those weeks ago. Probably because she'll think I'm crazy for remembering a random guy I never said a word to. "I'm not going to pick a guardian just because he's gorgeous," I finally reply.

"Ha! So you think he's gorgeous too."

"I'm not blind, Serena. I may have been stuck in this penthouse for the past month, but it doesn't mean I've forgotten what a hot guy looks like. And let's be honest, it doesn't matter how good looking he is, nothing could *ever* happen between us. You don't shit where you sleep or whatever that saying is. And anyway, *Papà* would literally cut off his dick if he ever lay a hand on me."

She clucks her tongue. "Fair enough. If you got caught…" A devious smirk curls her lips.

"Serena…" I grumble.

"What? Can you blame a girl for wanting her cousin and best friend to be happy? When was the last time you dated a guy?"

Never. "Um, junior high maybe."

She shakes her head, a satisfied smile kicking up the corners of her lips.

"You know how my father is."

"I do, because he's *my* dad's brother. Trust me, I've had to fight like hell to get past Dante Valentino's stubborn, pigheaded ways."

"Either way, nothing will ever happen with one of my guards. I can assure you *Papà* will be watching him like a hawk."

"Okay, okay, it's probably not the best idea to get involved with your guard anyway. And it totally explains why Uncle Luca picked Frankie for you. He was almost your dad's age." She shrugs. "But, I still think you should pick the beautiful bodyguard. At least he'd make great eye candy."

"Yeah," I mumble around another mouthful of the macchiato. "I'm just not sure I'm ready."

"Well, you better get ready, Bella, because I have *big* news, and I can't have you moping around the penthouse for my last few weeks in town. We need to celebrate!" She props her cup on the table and spins toward me, eyes shimmering with excitement.

"What? Where are you going?"

"Aunt Jia got me a job in Milan for the summer. With Dolce & Gabbana!" she squeals the last part. "It's only temporary, but if things go well, I could be moving to Italy permanently."

"Are you serious?" I leap up and pull Serena into a hug. Working for a top fashion house has been my cousin's dream for as long as I can remember. She attended the Fashion Institute in New York, just like our Aunt Jia who has her own clothing line and multiple boutiques across Manhattan. Jia is a fashion goddess as well as the head of the Four Seas, one of the notorious gangs of the Chinese Triad. It's a long story, but Serena has always idolized her despite our turbulent relationship with her kids, our cousins, Alessandro and Alessia. "That's incredible!" I shout as I spin her around. "I'm so happy for you!"

"I know. I am beyond excited. I can't believe it's actually happening."

We finally stop spinning, and a hint of sadness sneaks between the joy. "So when do you leave? And how long will you be gone for?"

"I fly out in two weeks, and I'll be gone until the end of the summer. At least." The corners of her lips quiver. "I'm going to miss you like crazy, Bella."

"Are you kidding me? You're going to be living a fabulous life in fucking Milano, while I'm stuck here in mafia princess dungeon. What am I going to do without you?"

"You're going to hire that sinfully gorgeous bodyguard so you can come visit me."

I roll my eyes. "*Papà* would never allow it, even if he did trust the guy."

"Well, one thing is for sure, you definitely won't be able to come without a guard. So do it, Bella. Just pull the trigger and pick one."

Pull the trigger... Frankie's bloodied form floats to the surface, and that guilt squeezes the air from my lungs.

Drawing in a breath, I push the grisly images to the far corners of my mind where I keep them tucked away. Instead, I turn my thoughts to *Papà*'s favorite quote by the great

Roman emperor Marcus Aurelius. *It is not death that a man should fear, but he should fear never beginning to live.*

I refuse to be that man, or woman in my case. My life may be predestined as the heir to the Kings' empire, but it doesn't mean I won't do my damnedest to try to live it. Or Frankie's sacrifice would be in vain.

"You're right," I heave out. "I'm going to do it. It's time to start living again."

CHAPTER 5
MY DAMNATION

R*affaele*

Fuck. I stare up at the soaring high rise across the street that houses the headquarters of King Industries, cursing first in my head then out loud. I keep the obscenities I grumble in Italian to avoid the pious old ladies climbing up the steps of St. Patrick's Cathedral. I've been sitting here like a *coglione*, a total asshole, all morning waiting for a call back after that interview with Isabella Valentino yesterday. Which makes no sense at all. I could have just as easily waited in the crappy motel in Queens. But then if she'd called, it would've taken me an hour to get here. And for some reason, that seemed too long.

Isabella Valentino.

The woman I'd seen at The Velvet Vault over a month ago. The woman who had left such an impression, I'd scoured the web until I found out who she was, which was what had compelled me to interview for this position to begin with.

My eyes slam shut in an effort to block her image from forcing its way into my mind, but since yesterday, she's been front and center once again. Why the hell had my cock leapt up like the damned Statue of Liberty at the sight of her?

I tear into the hot dog clenched in my fist, more ravenous beast than man. My temper boils at my own stupidity. I'd promised myself long ago I would never get involved with a client. I had made the mistake early on in my career, and it had cost me everything. A swirl of pain threatens its way up, but I take another bite of the lukewarm hot dog and swallow it down along with the incessant ache.

Now I have a strict policy. If I find the principal even remotely attractive, I walk away. It's as simple as that. Then why can't I seem to force myself off this step? I should have told her I wasn't interested right there on the spot. Instead, I was on autopilot spouting out the usual interview jargon.

Sure, Isabella Valentino is beautiful with those soulful sky-blue eyes that seem to pierce right into your darkest depths, but beauty isn't an unusual commodity to come across among the millions of women in Manhattan. But the reaction I'd had to her was primal. Despite my cool façade, I'd been overcome by the most insane urge to pick her up, throw her over my shoulder and find a cave to drag her into. And fuck her senseless.

I've lost my damned mind. Maybe all that time in the Middle East really has messed with my head. It wouldn't be the first time one of the VA docs mentioned it. I run my hand through my wild, dark hair and heave out a sigh. Perhaps joining the Army after years with the special forces unit of the Italian Carabinieri wasn't the smartest move ever.

The nightmares still linger, even now, years later. And I never want to go back. Private security is the only way forward, and this job babysitting the Valentino heir would have been perfect. If I proved myself guarding the great Luca Valentino's daughter, it would be no time before I'd get into the *capo*'s good graces.

But damn, that woman... That smart little mouth and those feisty comments. She was testing me already. Normally, I'd have no problem keeping my dick in my pants but there is just *something* about her.

A gleaming white Escalade stops at the light, the sun catching against the mirror and nearly blinding me. I glance up as it makes a U-turn, and the very blinged out vanity plate catches my eye. *Principessa*. Princess in Italian. Definitely not subtle. The corners of my lips twitch as I follow the SUV, first with my gaze and then with my feet, as it pulls up in front of the King's tower.

I dart across the street just as the crosswalk countdown begins. I sprint the last few feet and reach the sidewalk before a black BMW streaks around the corner and nearly runs me down. *Motherfucker*. Spinning at the asshole, I prepare to unleash a storm of my best Italian profanities when the familiar glint of the barrel of a gun peeks from a window.

"Get down!" I shout just as a guard slips out of the front seat of the parked Escalade and jerks the back door open.

Isabella slides out of the car, and my heart kicks at my ribs. "Gun!" I yell again, and this time, one of the guards reacts. "Black BMW!" I just grit the words out before shots explode over the cacophony, and the crowded streets of downtown Manhattan explode into chaos.

Screams ricochet across Park Avenue, the shrill cries muffling the rat-a-tat of bullets served by the Kings' security detail. Two men in suits huddle behind the oversized SUV, shooting over the roof. I jerk my gun out of its holster beneath my jacket and aim at the sleek black sports car. Stilling my racing pulse, I search for the calm, the inner silence that took years to hone despite the madness, the sprinting forms and steady wails. The BMW races down the street, weaving through traffic, followed by the steady spray of projectiles. With the pile up of cars, I can't get a clean shot of the tire which would be my target of choice. Knowing Luca Valentino, he'll likely want to question the fucker who tried to kill his daughter, or at least I sure as hell would. So instead, I aim at the passenger window, peppering the tinted glass with holes.

The car jerks to the right, then skids across the median before slamming into a garbage truck. The two Kings' men swarm the BMW, and a third man appears from inside the vehicle, planting himself in front of the door. Seconds later and a whole troop of guards spill out from the front doors of the building.

I'm overcome with the most overwhelming urge to stalk over there myself and shoot the asshole in the face, but I search for that calm once again. Not your job yet, *coglione*.

As the security team deals with the threat, I holster my weapon and march toward the Escalade. Before I get within two yards of the car, two massive guys block my forward movement. "I don't think so, *amico*." Friend, ha, that's laughable. The big guy lays hands on me, and I twist out of his hold so quickly, I nearly snap his wrist. I only restrain myself because of whom sits behind those tinted windows.

"Release him." A deep voice echoes from behind the door before the window glides open. None other than Luca Valentino stares up at me, dark eyes narrowed. And just beside him, his daughter. I fully expect to see fear in those brilliant baby blues, but an icy veil masks the expressive irises I observed only yesterday.

"You sure, *capo*?"

"Yes, Enzo, *Signor* Ferrara just single-handedly took out the threat while the three of you spun your wheels like *deficienti*. And by the looks of it, I should be requesting for him to release you. One twist and he'll have that arm in a cast for six weeks."

A smirk tugs at my lips as the big man's cheeks turn the rosy pink of a schoolgirl. I could likely take on Luca's entire security team. With my eyes closed.

Isabella peeks from around her father's broad shoulders and our eyes meet, then hold for a fiery instant. Her lips part, and I wonder if she remembers me or if she's as affected by me as I am by her. From the extensive research I conducted prior to the interview, I never found a single mention of a man in the beautiful heiress' life. Pushing the inappropriate thoughts to the furthest corners of my mind, I focus on the man in front of me, the one who will determine whether or not I get this job.

The job I should *not* take.

But now I'm invested. Because there is nothing that gets my blood boiling like taking out a scumbag who has his eyes on *my* principal.

Luca Valentino slides out of the car, straightens his tie and motions to the entrance of the impressive building. "Please, come with me, *signore*."

Signor Valentino turns before we reach the elevator bank and leads us through a metal door adjacent to the rear entrance. Isabella whispers something to her father, and I slow my footsteps, allowing them a modicum of privacy. The elder Valentino cocks his head over his shoulder, and his lips twist into a snarl.

"I promise we will find out, *principessa*," he murmurs as he holds the door open.

Princess… a little tongue and cheek if you ask me.

"Please have a seat." Luca motions at the small, nondescript room with two folding chairs encircling a plastic table.

I fold into the hard chair, and it releases a groan of protest beneath my weight.

Luca doesn't sit, instead he looms over me, his hand on

the butt of his gun which peaks out from beneath the waistband of his dark slacks. "That was quite a coincidence, you turning up at my building today at just the right moment."

Ah, now I see what's happening. "It was certainly lucky." I pause and twist my head over my shoulder to face Isabella. "For you."

"Do you mind me asking why you were here?"

I tick my head at the soaring turrets of the cathedral across the street. "Morning mass."

Luca chuckles. "I never pinned you as a religious man."

"It's not something I typically include in my resume."

"Fair enough." The elder Valentino glances at his daughter. "I am not a man who believes in luck, *Signor* Ferrara. I've worked my ass off to get to where I am today and luck had nothing to do with it. But it just so happens that my daughter and I were on our way into the office to have my assistant draft up the documents for your offer letter."

A twist of unexpected emotions whip across my insides.

"And after today's performance," he continues, "I'm convinced my daughter has made the right choice for a bodyguard." He pauses and fixes piercing irises to mine. "Assuming I determine you had *nothing* to do with this incident today."

"I assure you I did not. My clients' safety is of the utmost importance, and I would never orchestrate a stunt of that caliber merely to secure a job. I have a list of potential candidates awaiting an opening in my schedule."

Luca nods, lips pressed into a hard line. I've also done considerable research on the leader of the King's, and the man is no fool. He only wants the best for his daughter, and not to be cocky, but that's me.

"Well, we certainly wouldn't want to keep all those other clients waiting." Isabella's reply comes as a shock. She moves from behind her father and lifts that mesmerizing gaze so that I'm trapped in the endless blue. "Why would you choose me?"

The question lingers in the air, hanging like a charged silence between us. I meet her gaze, the intensity in her eyes both challenging and sincere. The answer comes easily, my voice steady despite the turmoil that her presence stirs within me.

"Because, *Signorina* Isabella, your safety isn't just another job to me," I start, carefully choosing each word. "I've worked with many, but your situation requires not only skill and dedication but a level of personal commitment that I'm prepared to give. You're not just another client on a list—you're a responsibility I'm willing to take on, fully aware of the stakes involved."

Isabella's expression softens slightly, the iciness melting into something resembling curiosity. Her father, Luca, watches the exchange, his scrutiny unwavering, as if trying to decipher the sincerity of my words.

"As you can imagine, I've interviewed quite a few capable men for the position," Isabella continues. "What makes you better?"

"I simply am better." I flash her a cocky grin, the one I've mastered over the years. It typically distracts women enough so that I can get my way, but Isabella's intense scrutiny doesn't falter.

It is a fair question, so I pause, ensuring that my response expresses my conviction because despite knowing this is a mistake, I want this job. "It's not just about protecting you—it's about understanding you. Knowing when to step back and when to step in. I don't see you as a task to be managed but as a person. And that will always make the difference in how I protect you. I'm not here to just guard a principal; I'm here to ensure that you live your life as freely and safely as possible."

Her look is penetrating, as if she's sifting through my

words for any trace of a lie. Luca's stance relaxes, a subtle nod indicating his approval of my answer.

"Very well," Luca finally says, breaking the tension. "We'll proceed with the paperwork. But let me be clear, *Signor* Ferrara, my daughter's safety is paramount. Any failure on your part will not be taken lightly."

"Understood, *Signor* Valentino."

As Isabella steps back, the hint of a smile touches her lips, and fucking hell my cock hardens at that one rare glimpse. And suddenly, all I want is a chance to prove my worth—to protect and understand her. So instead of walking away as I'd vowed to do, I find myself reaching for Isabella's hand sealing the deal that will likely lead to my damnation.

The brief touch is electric, her skin warm and soft against my rough palm. Her eyes lift to mine and again, I'm drowning in the sea of endless blue.

What have I done?

CHAPTER 6
A PROFESSIONAL DISTANCE

Isabella

"Welcome, *Signor* Ferrara. I'm pleased to see you again." Papà's voice echoes across the high ceilings of the penthouse foyer, and I slide to the edge of the couch cushion, a nervous energy rushing my veins. The sweet scent of the calla lilies on the coffee table do nothing to still the building anxiety.

"Always a pleasure, *Signor* Valentino. And please, no need for the formalities, call me Raffaele." That deep, rough tenor only quickens my pulse.

Relax, Bella. Raffaele is the one who needs to make a good impression, not you. I repeat the mantra over and over again, until the mad drumbeat battering my ribcage subsides. He's the one who must prove his worth as a bodyguard, and I just have to survive long enough for him to do that.

The shooting yesterday sure as hell shook me up, but it hasn't completely derailed me from the idea of starting to live my life again. It was a fluke… and it was handled. I smooth down the ruffles of the linen sundress, not used to the feel of actual clothes on my skin after living in pajamas for the past month.

The slap of heavy footfalls draws my attention back to the present, to the intimidating man stalking toward me. A black button-down shirt stretches across the broad expanse of his chest, neatly tucked into his dark slacks. For such a big guy, he walks with surprising grace, like a predator, fluid and focused. Every motion is deliberate and powerfully controlled, contradicting his size with the elegance of a panther on the prowl.

Raffaele dips his head when his eyes meet mine. "Good morning, *signorina*."

"It's Isabella, or Bella is fine too."

"I prefer *Signorina* Valentino if it's all the same to you. I find maintaining a professional distance helps to keep us both on task."

I rise, slapping my hands on my hips. I can feel *Papà*'s scrutinizing gaze observing our interaction. "So you expect me to call you *Signor* Ferrara?" Talk about a mouthful.

"I don't expect anything from you. You are my principal, my duty. You can call me whatever you're most comfortable with."

"What about Raf?"

A barely perceptible tendon flutters across his scruffy jaw. "If that's what you prefer, *signorina*."

Papà pivots, turning that measured gaze on me. "As you know, Raffaele has spent the last week with Tony, learning the ins and outs of our security protocols. I have every confidence in his ability to protect you, *principessa*."

I cringe at the silly childhood nickname, then heat rushes up my neck and diffuses across my cheeks when I catch the faint smirk spreading Raffaele's perfect lips.

"Well, I will leave you two to get acquainted." My father starts to back out of the great room toward the hallway that leads to his office. I'm not surprised he's chosen to work from home today, just like my mom coincidentally canceled her yoga session with Aunt Rose. They want to give me the semblance of independence while still keeping me on a short leash. Vinny is the only one who abandoned me for the morning, deciding today would be the one he'd start his summer internship at King Industries.

"Traitor," I mutter as *Papà* disappears down the hall.

"Excuse me?" Raf sears me with those star-flecked midnight orbs.

"Nothing." I saunter to the kitchen, in a lame attempt at nonchalance, and my new dark shadow follows. When I find the espresso machine empty, a curse escapes through my clenched teeth. Or maybe it's a blessing in disguise. "I need coffee." And Nutella. But I forgo my favorite morning treat today because all this inactivity has left me pudgy around the belly and with my shredded new bodyguard looming over me, the guilt is creeping in.

His dark brows twist as he eyes the elaborate machine. "Can't you make yourself one?"

"I thought maybe we could go out instead."

He reaches into his back pocket and pulls out a neatly folded piece of paper. "I'd prefer not to leave the penthouse until we've gone over the security protocols."

"I'm very familiar with the procedures, Raf. I've been living them for the last twenty years."

"Not like these, you haven't. After spending the week with Tony, I took it upon myself to tweak the protocols of my predecessor."

"Why?" I blurt, trying my hardest to keep my rising temper at bay.

Raf leans against the marble island, his mask of calm only more infuriating. "They were outdated and lacking, to be perfectly honest." He spreads the sheet out on the countertop, and I briefly scan the headers in neat type.

1. *Threat Assessment and Planning*
2. *Constant Surveillance*
3. *Secure Transportation*
4. *Personal Protection*
5. *Safe Environments*
6. *Privacy and Information Security*

The list goes on and on, the words blurring in the building irritation. "You had no right to change the way Frankie did things."

"On the contrary, I have every right." He pushes off the counter and steps into my space. "It is my duty to keep you safe, and I will do that to the best of my ability. It was impossible under the previous terms."

"You can't be serious? Frankie was an incredible bodyguard. He kept me alive for over twenty years, and you come in here on your first day and try to change everything? So you happened to be at the right place at the right time last week? It doesn't mean you're more capable than he was. Frankie gave up his life for me—" My throat tightens, the heat of unshed tears burning my eyes. I blink quickly to keep them from rolling over. The last thing I need is to cry in front of this man. Then he'll really think I'm nothing more than some spoiled little mafia princess.

The hard set of his jaw softens a touch, and he heaves out a breath. "I know how difficult it is to lose someone in this business. I am here to ensure that does not happen, for either of us."

I knot my arms across my chest and do my best not to pout like a sullen teenager.

Raf points at the bulleted outline, running his finger down the itemized list. "We can go over the protocols as I've set them forth and if there are any you have issue with, we can adjust."

Only five minutes with this man and I'm sure he has no

idea what the word adjust means. I'm going to kill Serena for convincing me to pick the hot one.

"Fine," I hiss out.

He pulls out one of the bar stools and motions for me to sit. Stubbornly, I remain standing and follow his finger tracing the text.

"What the hell is this? *Train the mafia princess in basic self-defense and emergency response protocols.*"

He grins, revealing a hidden dimple and despite my annoyance, my breath hitches a little at the sight. Why the hell did I pick the unfairly gorgeous bodyguard? This was such a bad idea. "What? I figured it would be beneficial for you to learn some basic combat skills."

"I'm not talking about that part, Raf. I mean the mafia princess bit…"

"That is what you are, isn't it, *principessa*?" His smirk only grows wider, and I have to curl my fingers into a fist to keep from wiping that smug smile off his face. Little does he know, *Papà* insisted I learned the basics in self-defense years ago.

"Don't call me that," I snarl. "I thought you were the one who insisted on keeping things professional."

The smile vanishes, replaced by the mask of the cold enforcer, the unfeeling guard. Again, only a short time with this man, and I've already begun to recognize his many faces. I guess it comes in handy in his line of work. "You're right, my apologies, *signorina*." He clears his throat and ticks his chin at the paper stretched across the counter again. "Anything else you'd like to go over?"

Stay close to the mafia princess at all times, especially in public or unfamiliar settings.

I read over the sentence again and again, each time only escalating my pulse. *At all times…* According to *Papà*, Raffaele is to remain with me from the time I wake until he tucks me in at bedtime. Despite the impressive eye candy,

I'm not sure I'll survive a day with this man let alone all my waking hours.

"Where do you live?" I blurt.

His steady gaze falters, flickering to the floor for an instant before returning to meet my own. "I'm looking for something more permanent as we speak."

Well, that is a non-answer if I've ever heard one. "My cousin, Alessia, is a realtor, maybe she can help." And it would give us an excuse to get out of this suffocating penthouse.

"Thanks, but I'll find something on my own."

I barely restrain the eyeroll. "Are you too much of a tough guy to accept help?"

"No, *signorina*. It's simply not proper to spend working hours searching for my housing."

"Then when would you find a place? *Papà* said you'll be with me all day. You can't live in a motel forever."

His dark eyes flash, and I clench my teeth to keep from grinning. Of course, I know where he's staying. *Papà* had the full background check done well before his first interview, and I've spent the last week learning everything I could about my new guard. Raffaele Ferrara, thirty years old, born in Rome, Italy, grew up in the Bronx before returning to his home country at sixteen where he served in the Italian Carabinieri's version of special forces. From there, the details are hazy which is typical for that line of work. Then he re-emerges in the private security scene and suddenly reappears a few months ago in Manhattan.

"I'll be sure to let you know when I get tired of it." Raf's voice draws me from perusing the mental file I've created.

"Suit yourself." I shrug. "Can we go get that coffee now?"

CHAPTER 7
A LETHAL COMBINATION

R*affaele*

Those piercing eyes bore into the side of my face, but I refuse to meet them, keeping my ever-vigilant gaze fixed on the rooftops surrounding the penthouse balcony. For multiple reasons. One—the *principessa* has been glaring at me incessantly from the moment I arrived today and informed her we were not ready to leave the confines of her parents' home yet. And two—because she's wearing a goddamned skimpy bikini that leaves nothing to the imagination. And trust me, I've got a fucking fantastic imagination.

As it is, I'm having a hard time keeping my eyes on the neighboring buildings searching for potential threats. This is exactly why I never should have agreed to this job.

Way too much temptation.

Not to mention distraction.

And in a job like this, it's a lethal combination.

"You know, the whole reason I hired you was to get my

life back. So that I could once again feel free to roam the bustling streets in the greatest city in the world." She pulls the ear pods out, depositing them in the small container, and Taylor Swift's latest hit blasts across the balcony.

"Oh, really? I thought you hired me to keep you alive." I shoot her a smirk, and she replies with a scowl. Even frowning, those pouty lips are so damned tempting. Shaking off the thought, I keep my eyes on hers instead of allowing them to drift down to the perfect swell of her breasts.

"Do they have to be mutually exclusive?"

"No, not necessarily, once I'm certain you'll follow my rules."

She sits up, swinging her legs around the lounger to stare up at me, those brilliant blue eyes ever challenging. "I've never been much of a rule follower."

"I can't say I'm surprised." Eyes up, *coglione*.

"What can I do to speed up the process? My cousin, Serena, is leaving town next week, and I'd like to spend some time with her before she goes."

"Invite her over here."

"Serena will be gone from the city all summer. She's not going to want to spend her last few days cooped up in my parents' apartment."

"As if this massive penthouse is the worst place to be…" I grumble. It's a damned good thing the *principessa* acts like a spoiled little brat sometimes. It helps to remind me we have no business ever being together. "And anyway, I thought the point was simply to spend time together."

"It is, but I'd also like to go back to some sort of semblance of a normal life."

"The curse of being a mafia princess."

She rolls her eyes at me, and damn, I wish I could fuck that naughty streak right out of her. She has no idea what that look of pure defiance does to me. Growing up the way I did has instilled a certain set of preferences in my sexual appetite. Not only do I stick to the hard and fast rule of no strings attached, but I also enjoy a little pain with my pleasure. It takes a particular type of woman to put up with it, and there is no doubt in my mind that this little princess would never agree to any of it.

Squeezing my eyes shut, I remind myself this entire mental argument is moot because I vowed *never* to involve myself with a client again.

"Surprise!" A shout has my head spinning over my shoulder like the god damned exorcist. A dark-haired male stands in the doorway, at least he does for the fraction of an instant I allow it, when the glint of a concealed weapon catches my eye. I'm moving before my brain can process it. I lunge at the guy, wrapping my arms around his as we crash to the ground.

He lets out a grunt as I twist his arm around and pin him to the marble.

"Raf!" Isabella screams, but I can barely hear it over the roar of my thrashing heart. Crimson taints my vision, pure darkness seeping into the edges. More screams ricochet through my mind and for a second, I can't distinguish the past from the present. "Let go of him! That's Matteo, my cousin." The words blur into an indistinct haze. Once I release the monster I keep hidden beneath layers of practiced charm, it's difficult to force him back into his cage of self-restraint. "Raf! Let go!" Dainty fists batter my back, jerking me from the brink of total meltdown.

"Give me the gun first," I growl.

"Yeah, sure no problem. Damn, relax, dude."

With my palms flat against the floor on either side of the cousin, I push up giving him an inch of space so I can relieve him of the weapon. Once my hand is around the sleek grip, I toss it across the marble floor.

"Now can you get off me, please?" Matteo grumbles.

I glance over my shoulder at Isabella who's shooting daggers from those sweet baby blues. "You sure?"

"Yes, I'm sure, you Neanderthal! I told you he's my cousin."

Pushing myself off the floor, I offer Matteo a hand and haul him up along with me. "He still shouldn't be able to stroll in here with a weapon." I cast a glare at the guard stationed by the door before I pick up the gun. It looks like I'll have to retrain the entire security team. Rule number one in Raffaele's guide to ultimate security: trust no one.

The guy's lips twitch as his eyes swing between us. "Guess you weren't exaggerating, cuz. He is a little overprotective."

"A little?" she squeals. "I haven't been able to leave my home since he started!"

"I told you, I need to ensure you will follow my rules before I'll risk your life out in the open."

"Oh, for the love of *Dio*!" Isabella drags her hands across her face before propping them on her hips, which only draws my attention to her sexy curves, then her bare torso.

"And put some clothes on, *signorina*. You have company."

Taunting me, she sashays toward the guy and hooks an arm around his shoulder. "This isn't *company*. This is my cousin Matteo Rossi. If I don't fire you first for driving me crazy, you should probably memorize his face. He's going to be over here a lot."

"You might as well send him pics of the whole dysfunctional family." The young Rossi lifts his broad shoulders.

I'm no fool, I know exactly who he is. Before securing the interview, I'd done my research on the entire Valentino-Rossi clan. It doesn't mean I'll allow a guy with a gun near my principal, no matter whose blood flows through his veins.

"He may not be here long enough."

I snort on a laugh. "Your father has already congratulated

me on my tireless efforts. I doubt he's too eager to see me go."

"Of course he isn't. He'd be thrilled to have me a prisoner in this penthouse just like he did my mom all those years ago." Shaking her head, she throws her hand up. "Forget I said that. Now, can I have a moment of privacy with my cousin? Don't you have some obnoxious list to make or something?"

I chuckle again, because the girl's got balls. I'll give her that. She doesn't find me the least bit intimidating like some of my past clients. Then again, I've never worked for the mafia. She's probably seen her fair share of daunting men.

"Of course." I stuff the gun in my pocket and tick my head toward the kitchen. "You'll get this back when you leave, Matteo, and I'll be right over there if you need me, *signorina*."

She rolls her eyes again, and my palm twitches. *Dio*, what I wouldn't do to spank that perfect ass. "So kind of you to give me so much space."

"Rule number seven: stay close to the mafia princess at all times."

"In public or unfamiliar settings," she barks back, and I'm impressed she's taken the time to read my protocols.

"*Especially* in public or unfamiliar settings," I counter. "That does not exclude familiar settings."

"You're completely *pazzo*." She's not wrong. You do have to be a little insane to be effective in this sort of position.

"And that's exactly why I'm so damned good."

Isabella spins on her heel, toting her cousin with her for the ride. My gaze trails her retreating form, the slender yet proud set of her shoulders, the slim waist and those curvy hips. That indecent bikini is going to send me to an early grave with a devastating case of blue balls.

Get her out of your head, *coglione*. Not only is she your

client and the daughter of a notorious mob boss who'd rip your cock off if you laid a finger on her, but she's also nearly ten years younger than you. She's a baby, and you have no right corrupting her.

Dio, but she'd taste so sweet.

From across the great room, I keep my eyes pinned to her, on the animated movement of her hands as she tells a story, on the way the corners of her mouth hitch at her cousin's jokes, in the insatiable spark of life in those darting eyes. Because it's my job to watch her. *Liar.*

As she chatters happily with her cousin, those sky-blue spheres occasionally flicker in my direction. Each time our eyes meet, that smile flips into a frown. Good. It's better if she dislikes me, sees me as too rigid, and resents my strict rules. In the end, it will simplify things for both of us.

CHAPTER 8
THE PERFECT CANDIDATE

Isabella

"I have to go, you insufferable man," I growl. "I need to pick up my final transcripts from the registrar's office at NYU." I'm about a second away from stomping my foot like a child with a tantrum. Not even a week with my new guard, and I'm ready to throw him off the balcony.

Worse, Serena is leaving in three days, and I haven't seen her once since Raffaele started working for me. I concocted this idea of meeting up on campus with her. She's throwing herself a massive going away party tomorrow night, and I'd hoped if my insane bodyguard met her today, he'd warm up to the idea.

Because I'm going with or without him. I don't care if I have to sneak out of the penthouse alone. I won't miss my cousin's big bon voyage party that I should have been the one to host.

He glares down at me, his arms pinned to the tight

black tee stretched across his massive chest. "I don't understand why they simply cannot email the paperwork to you?"

"It needs to be an official copy," I hiss. Sounds legit, right?

At this rate, I may just request to start medical school in the summer if only to escape Raf's overbearing clutches.

Soft footsteps round the corner, and Mom creeps into the kitchen, a lopsided smile already tilting the corners of her lips. She's been enjoying my torture way too much. "I think it would be a good idea for Isabella to get out of the penthouse for a few hours." She pretends to arrange the crystal vase filled with cala lilies as she watches us.

Thank *Dio*.

"See?" I cock a dark brow at the obstinate man dead set on ruining my life.

"But *Signora* Valentino, I have yet to surveil the campus and assess any threats prior to our visit."

"Isabella has attended NYU for the past four years, and there has never been an incident. It'll be a quick visit, right, sweetie?"

My head bounces up and down, and I try my hardest not to cringe at the *sweetie*. Sometimes I'm certain my parents still think I'm ten years old. It's this whole living at home thing. As soon as things settle with my new bodyguard, I'm having the talk with my parents. It's time for me to get my own place. I don't care if *Papà* sends a whole damned battalion of Kings to guard me, I need my independence or I'm going to lose my mind.

"Great, let's get going then, Raf." I tick my head at the door, and the big brute literally winces.

"Before we go, we need to go over the safety protocols for—"

I lift my hand up, cutting him off as I reach for my tote and throw it over my shoulder. "I'm very familiar with the rules. You've made me read and re-read them dozens of times. I promise I'll be the perfect principal."

"Somehow, I doubt that," he mutters under his breath.

I blow my mom a kiss and mouth a quick thank you as Rick holds the front door open for us.

"Have fun, you two!" she calls out.

Raf couldn't possibly look more miserable as he trudges out beside me, and I can't help the swirl of satisfaction that scowl brings with it.

My surly guardian jabs his finger into the elevator button, his jaw so tense it could crack diamonds, a silent testament to the storm brewing within. Ignoring him, I shoot off a quick text message to Serena.

She's going to stage a coincidental walk by right next to our favorite café. The trap is set, and I only hope my overprotective bodyguard doesn't ruin my perfectly laid out plans.

Our driver, Johnny, pulls over the Escalade right in front of the NYU administration building. But he can't park there which will force him to meet us around the corner right by the café where Serena will be waiting.

"Meet you at *Think Coffee*?" Johnny twists his head to the back seat.

"Sounds perf—"

"No. You can circle until we're ready. I'll call you on the com when we're walking out." Raf presses his finger to the sleek device permanently embedded in his ear.

Are you fucking kidding me?

"But I usually just park and meet Isabella—"

"Did I ask you what you usually do, Johnny?" Raf barks, cutting him off. "You shouldn't *usually* be doing anything.

That leads to sloppiness and predictability. If anyone is trailing the *signorina* they'll know exactly what to expect. Had I known we were going out today, I would have sent you the new protocols."

"Sure, whatever you say, Ferrara."

"No!" I finally squeal, whirling on the overbearing man beside me. "It's not whatever you say. I always grab a latte from *Think Coffee* on my way out. Johnny can meet us there."

"I never approved a stop on this little adventure. You said the registrar and that was it."

"I didn't think a coffee was such a significant detour!"

He reaches into his back pocket and pulls out the damned dictionary of lists and procedures. "Did you forget about rule number twelve? All outings must be approved ahead of time so that I have the necessary intel beforehand. I need a team to sweep the location before you go in."

"This is crazy! You are absolutely insane!" I shout. "It's just a café. We're not in the middle of a war zone. And besides, Serena is already there. I'm sure it's perfectly safe." I reach for the door handle, but he snatches my wrist.

"So you planned this?" he snarls. "You didn't have to come to campus at all?"

"Let go of me." I try to wriggle free of his hold, but his fingers are like a steel trap.

"How can I trust you to be out in public if you act like this?"

"Like *this*?"

"Like a disobedient child!"

"Maybe if you gave me an inch of freedom I wouldn't have to." I slam my free hand into his chest, and it's like crashing into a solid wall of muscle.

"Everything okay back there?" Johnny unbuckles his seatbelt and pivots to face us.

"No, it's not."

"Everything's under control, Johnny," Raf grits out as he

attempts to physically restrain me. He's a damned animal, pinning me down with the hard planes of his torso. The scent of musk and amber, sensual and warm invades my nostrils. I do *not* breathe him in because that would make me as insane as the man trapping me to the leather seat.

"If you don't let go of me, I'm going to scream."

He tips his head closer, warm breath skating over the shell of my ear. "Go for it, *principessa.*" His lethal whisper sends goosebumps spilling down my bare arms. "No one will be able to hear you through the bulletproof glass."

Two quick knocks send my guard's gaze swiveling to the tinted window. I blow out a breath as I make out the familiar blonde through the glass.

"Thank God," I murmur and finally succeed in shoving him off.

"It's Miss Serena Valentino," Johnny announces. "Should I unlock the door, Ferrara?"

"Of course you should," I shout at my traitorous driver. As soon as the click resounds across the vehicle, I jerk the handle and nearly leap out of the car. A steel band laces around my torso, and I'm stuck dangling in mid-air.

Serena watches, a flicker of amusement in those bright blue eyes we share as I'm hauled back into the back seat. "So this is what was taking you so long?"

"Let go of me, Raf!" I rasp out.

"I apologize if we kept you waiting, Miss Valentino, but your cousin did not inform me of the real plan today. As I was trying to explain to her, there are certain protocols that must be met—"

"If you say the word protocols one more damn time, I'm going to shoot you in the face." I make a move for his gun, but he twists his hips, and I nearly brush his crotch instead. *Merda.* Jerking my hand back, heat races up my neck, blanketing my cheeks.

I can feel his smirk without looking up. Oh, *Dio,* kill me

now. Serena, on the other hand, is grinning like mad, flashing those perfect teeth.

"Don't just stand there laughing, you jerk. Help me out."

"Oh, come on, Raffy, let the poor girl get her caffeine fix. I guarantee she'll be much easier to manage after the coffee." Serena leans against the open door, eyes twinkling in mirth. Raf's arm is still laced around me like a seatbelt made of flesh and blood. In a second, I'm going to claw that perfectly tanned and tattooed flesh.

And no, I'm not staring at the ink painting his skin in a gloriously dark and twisted pattern.

"If it's any consolation," Serena offers, "both Isabella and Matteo have frequented the café for years, which means their respective guards have cleared the location on numerous occasions."

"It hasn't been cleared by *me*."

"And *Dio* knows Raffaele Ferrara is a bodyguard god, the only one capable of properly securing any location." I roll my eyes so hard I hope only the whites show.

"Fine," he grits out, "but if anything goes wrong and your father kills me for it, I promise to come back to haunt you until the end of your days."

"Well, that certainly would be the worst punishment in the world," I counter, "to have to deal with you in this life *and* the next."

"Out of the car, *principessa*," he whispers the hated nickname before forcefully helping me out of the Escalade. "It won't be long so don't go far, Johnny." He barks the command before slamming the door shut behind us.

The familiar sounds of campus immersed in the chaos of the city surround me, and I heave in a breath. Until my shadow moves into step beside me, his looming presence stealing the moment of false independence.

"Now I understand why I haven't seen you all week."

Serena casts a glance over my head at the broody Italian marching next to me.

"And I'm not sure I'll be seeing you tomorrow night," I whisper.

"You have to, Bella. I won't take no for an answer."

"Well, good luck convincing this guy." I jerk my thumb over my shoulder.

"Convincing me of what?"

"Don't worry about it," I grumble. No point in poking the bear until I've had my latte.

As we walk the short block to the café, I can practically feel the tension radiating from the hulking beast beside me. His eyes never stop moving, a constant scrutiny of every sound, every soul that walks by. It must be exhausting.

Once we make it inside *Think Coffee*, the savory scent of roasted coffee beans fills my nostrils, and the rage begins to dwindle. Maybe Serena was right about my caffeine fix. As we wait in line, Serena chatters on about her big move, and I can't help the twinge of jealousy and sadness from sneaking in. I'm going to miss my best friend like crazy, and I am so envious that she's going to have this amazing experience without me.

As I sink into a pity party for one, I feel my guard twitch beside me. A hand lands on my shoulder, the touch lasting only an instant before it's ripped off and a scream ricochets across the café.

I whirl around to find my bodyguard's massive frame trapping a guy beneath him. Again. A wave of gasps echoes around us, and embarrassment steamrolls over me as I make out the wriggling form beneath. "What the hell, Raf? That's my Genetics professor!"

Pools of pure black stare up at me as he twists Professor Dykeman's arm behind his back. "He touched you."

"As normal people often do." I crouch down on the floor,

muttering apologies as I haul the overprotective asshole off the ground.

Thankfully the crowd begins to disburse, more interested in their morning coffee than my family drama. Serena watches the whole scene like it's the funniest thing in the world that my bodyguard just assaulted one of my instructors.

"I'm so sorry, professor." I throw Raf a scathing glare as my teacher from last semester rubs his wrist. "Are you okay?"

"Barely. Your boyfriend over here almost snapped my wrist."

I choke on a laugh. "He is *not* my boyfriend. This is my new bodyguard," I offer sheepishly. "He's a little overzealous. Again, I'm so sorry." Most of the staff are well aware of my situation. Though most think I have men in suits trailing me because of my father's legitimate business, few know the dark truth.

"Clearly," he mumbles. "I saw you as I walked in and wanted to share an exciting opportunity that I thought you would be perfect for." His light eyes bounce between Raf and me. "But perhaps, I was mistaken."

"No, please, what is it?"

"A colleague of mine from *Policlinico Gemelli* just informed me of a summer internship available to pre-med students with outstanding potential. One of the students dropped out last minute, leaving a spot open. The position is in Rome, and I figured with your Italian background, you'd be the perfect candidate."

CHAPTER 9
AN OUNCE OF FREEDOM

I sabella

"Oh my God, are you serious?"

"Well, I was until a moment ago when your guard assaulted me." He eyes Raf like he's a ticking timebomb and the slightest move could set him off. He's not exactly wrong from what I've seen so far of the volatile male.

I dig my elbow into Raf's side, and with an obnoxious grunt, he clears his throat. "I apologize for hurting you, but as I'm sure you understand, my client's life comes first."

Professor Dykehouse snorts, but at least he looks slightly more at ease.

"Why don't the two of you sit down to talk?" Serena leads us toward a table in the back with our coffees in hand. "I'll keep Mr. Impulsive in check."

"I don't think so," Raf snarls, "but I'd be happy to sit and watch while you discuss." He points at a table in the corner with enough seats for us all.

"There's not much to discuss honestly." My professor is still eyeing Raf like a wild animal who might strike at any moment, despite the apology, and I can't say I blame him. The man is intimidating as fuck. "I can email you all the information, and you can decide whether you'd like to take the opening. But you don't have much time, the program begins in two weeks."

"Yes, I would love that. Please send me all the details." I keep the rest of my thoughts to myself because I don't want to sound like a child. *If my parents will let me go.*

"Will do." He dips his head and turns toward the door, clearly eager to escape Raf's caustic stares.

Serena grabs my hands and squeals the moment my professor is gone. "You have to take it, Bella! This would be incredible, you in Rome and me in Milan, we'd have the most incredible summer."

Raf clucks his tongue beside me, the sound sending a wave of irritation all the way to my bones.

I whirl on him and hiss, "Do you have something to say?"

"Only that I wouldn't get your hopes up, *signorina*. It'll never happen."

"And why not?" I growl because I'm a total masochist. I know very well that my parents would never allow it.

"I think you know the answer to that."

"Humor me."

"Assuming you could convince your *Papà*, which is extremely unlikely, you'd never be able to persuade me. I left the corrupt streets of Rome long ago and have zero desire to ever return."

"Well, that's reason enough for me." I offer him my sweetest smile. "It sounds like a win-win from where I'm standing. I'd get to spend the summer in Rome and get a new bodyguard."

"Good luck with that, *prin*—" He cuts himself off when

he notices Serena's curious gaze, listening to every word that falls from his unfairly perfect lips. "Let's just get the hell out of here. I think I've had enough surprises for one day." He marches toward the door and holds it open for Serena, then me.

"And God forbid, we mess up your perfectly planned day and every orchestrated move."

He whirls on me, trapping me against the door and those dark spheres become nothing but endless night. "Listen to me, *signorina*, there are reasons behind those protocols and the utter control that governs my life from sunup to sunset, they are in place to safeguard *your* life."

There's something about his savage tone that has the hair on the back of my neck prickling. I remain perfectly still, pinned against the glass door for an endless moment, mesmerized by the flash of something feral in those eyes and the rapid rise and fall of his chest against mine.

"Are you two coming or not?" Serena pokes Raf in the shoulder, and he finally steps back, freeing me from not only his physical hold but that ensnaring, black gaze.

Of the two, it's definitely the most lethal.

"Please, *Papà*." I'm begging now, all sense of pride gone. I need this. Going to Rome on my own would finally give me the independence I so desperately desire.

My father stares at me from across his grand desk with Mom perched on the arm rest of his high-backed chair.

"Uncle Dante is letting Serena go to Milan, what's the difference?"

"You know Dante and I do not see eye to eye on many things. How we raise our children is one of them."

This is going nowhere. I've been begging since I got

home over an hour ago. "Come on, Mom, when you were my age, you were already living with *Papà*."

"That was different," she mutters.

"Because he forced you?"

She shakes her head, eyes glossing over as if she's remembering their turbulent past. My father is nothing but adoring and devoted to our family, but I'm not stupid enough to think he's a good man. And before he met my mom, for the second time in his life, he would go to any lengths to get what he wanted. Still does actually.

I slide to the edge of the chair and prop my elbows on the gleaming mahogany. "You say I'm to take over the Kings one day, but how am I to do that if you won't give me an ounce of freedom? I'm twenty-two years old and you treat me like a child. You were running an empire when you were my age, *Papà*. It's not fair." I bite back the last word, realizing it's not helping my cause. "It's not right," I amend. "Even Vinny gets to come and go as he pleases."

"It's not that simple, *principessa*." For some reason, from my father the childhood nickname holds a whole other connotation than when my testy bodyguard says it. "Sending you to another country means dispatching a retinue of guards along with you, men that I trust to protect you, and Raffaele has already informed me he is unwilling to go. We've only just hired and trained him, and I believe he's doing a wonderful job."

I snort, unable to keep the unladylike sound at bay. "We'll find someone new."

"And train them in two weeks' time?"

"You did it with Raf…"

"It took me weeks to vet the four men you interviewed, then there's the training time, which given his impeccable background, was much quicker than normal." He shakes his head and blows out a breath. "I'm sorry, but the only way I would even consider this is if you convince Raffaele to go with you."

"Are you kidding me?" I grind out. "The man is completely insufferable and suffocating. He doesn't leave my side, and he takes threats way too seriously. He attacked my damned professor for the love of all things!"

"We like that about him," my mom offers with a smirk. "He's nothing but dedicated. And besides, he grew up in Rome. He's already familiar with the layout of the city."

"Ugh, this is unbelievable."

"Give me a day to think on it, Isabella. I need to see if mobilizing my men across the world is even feasible in this short timeframe. In the meantime, see if you can convince Raffaele to your side. It would do wonders for your cause."

I barely bite back the slew of swears perched on the tip of my tongue. But cursing at my father would not be tolerated. Instead, I slowly rise, knowing full well who I'll find standing just outside the door to my father's office.

Begging Raf to come with me sounds worse than gargling cut glass. And here I thought the toughest part of today would be persuading my guard to let me go to Serena's party tomorrow night. Now I had to beg the man who makes my life miserable to continue in his tireless efforts all the way across the Atlantic Ocean.

CHAPTER 10
DEAD AND BURIED

R*affaele*

"Please."

"Don't beg, *principessa*, it's not a good look on you." *Lies.* There's nothing I would enjoy more than this woman on her knees. I pour a cup of coffee and casually lean against the counter.

Isabella pushes out her bottom lip, that pout so damned tempting as she glares up at me. Her arms are knotted across her chest, only accentuating her breasts, which are already spilling over her low-cut top. Why did I take this job again? Oh, right, I'm a fucking glutton for punishment.

"It's a small gathering with a close group of friends and family at my cousin's house. What could possibly go wrong?"

I take a measured sip from my mug then lower it on the counter, in an attempt to maintain my composure. I've never had a client who riled me up like this woman. "It's a going away party, you said it yourself. And from what I know of Serena Valentino, there will be nothing small about it."

"I am not your prisoner," she hisses. "And I will go to my best friend's party with or without your permission."

I bark out a laugh and erase the distance between us, trapping her against the marble island. "Don't push me, *principessa*, I am not your babysitter or your doting daddy. You will obey me or suffer the consequences."

Now she's the one laughing, tossing her head back so those long, raven locks dance along her bare shoulders. "You work for me, *coglione*." She jabs a perfectly manicured fingernail into my chest. "I was only being polite and doing my best to stick to your stupid rules."

I snatch her finger and jerk her closer, and a gasp parts those pouty lips. "Let's get something straight. I do *not* work for you, I work for your father. He may want you to believe otherwise, but he's the one that signs my check. So if you think you can boss me around you better talk to daddy dearest and tell him to add some more zeros to my pay."

"We'll see about that," she grits out. She tries to spin away, but I have her body trapped against the island and her finger squeezed in my fist. "Let go of me." Her eyes flash, that sea blue growing darker. And *cazzo*, now I'm getting hard.

So I take a step back, releasing her. The last thing I need is my client feeling my cock rubbing up against her stomach. "So you've given up on the trip to Rome already?" Anything to change the topic.

"Not at all. I'm only looking for a better solution than having you tag along with me."

"Good luck," I mutter.

"Oh, I don't need luck, Raf. I always get what I want." She shoots me one of her wicked smiles, the one intended to placate me and storms off toward her bedroom.

Tony's head appears through the sliding glass doors of the balcony, dark eyes pivoting to mine. "Hey, Raf, the boss wants to see you." The brawny Italian has been Luca's right-hand man for decades, which means he oversees all the security staff. He's a decent guy, but too old-school for my preferences.

Isabella's gaze swivels toward me for an instant before she buries her nose back in the book she's been consumed in for the past hour. Either that or she's ignoring me because of our earlier fight.

I march toward her and mutter a quick, "Behave," before I join Tony at the sliding doors. "You got her while I'm gone?"

Tony's dark brows rise, meeting his receding hairline. "You want me to watch her in the penthouse?"

"See what I have to put up with, Tony?" she mumbles under her breath.

"Isabella is not *in the penthouse*. She's out on the balcony, completely exposed. There are at least ten points in a fifty-yard radius that would be the perfect spot for a sniper. She's completely vulnerable out here. Do you want to explain to *signor* Valentino how his daughter got shot under your watch?"

"Uh, no…"

"Then park your ass out here until I get back."

Tony stares at me wide-eyed, but my expression is calm, resolute. I don't back down. Ever. I don't care that this guy has decades on me. If there's one thing I've learned, it's how to keep my principal alive.

"Fine," he finally grits out.

The hint of a smile plays across Isabella's lips. It's faint but I catch it because that's what my years of training have taught me. To catch every detail, no matter how insignificant.

"Don't miss me too much, *signorina*," I call out over my shoulder and catch a flash of her middle finger in the air as I slide the doors closed.

Tony's chuckle permeates the thick glass, and I can only imagine the sparkling review the little princess must be giving me. That's her problem, not mine. My only purpose is to keep her safe. If she hates me for it, it'll only make my job easier in some respects.

When I reach Valentino's office, the door is ajar, and he's sprawled across his leather chair, brows furrowed as he stares at the computer screen. A vase filled with fresh cala lilies sits on the corner of his massive desk, the delicate white flowers an odd contrast to the powerful man behind them.

"Knock, knock."

His eyes lift to mine, and he motions me in, then points at the chair across his elaborate mahogany desk. It reminds me of the one my own *papà* had all those years ago in Italy. Squeezing my eyes closed as I settle into the soft leather, I dismiss the unwanted memories of the past. They are exactly why I refuse to return to my motherland. Too much darkness, too many damned ghosts.

"Raffaele, I wanted to commend you on the work you've done so far. It's impressive."

"*Grazie, signore.*" I dip my head.

He heaves out a breath and strangles a pen in his fist. "As you know, my daughter has gotten it in her head to go to Rome for the summer."

"Mmm." *Please, don't ask me to accompany her.*

"Have you changed your position on the topic?"

I shift in my seat, sliding to the edge. "Honestly, no. While I am very happy under your employ, I've only just returned to Manhattan, and I'd hoped to remain here. I consider guarding Isabella a privilege and not one that I take lightly. I am not certain that I will be able to do that to my best ability in Rome."

"Why do you say that?"

Darkness seeps into the corners of my vision, and a familiar face coalesces, then that voice.

"Get the fuck out of my city, Raffaele. You are no longer welcome here."

"But Papà…"

"And you're no son of mine. You are a disgrace to the Ferrara name."

I blink quickly, shaking the dark memories from the forefront of my mind. "There's too much history for me there, *signore*. And I'd prefer to keep it dead and buried."

He blows out another breath and props his elbows on the desk, piercing me with fathomless midnight irises. Before taking this job, I'd heard all kinds of stories about the infamous Luca Valentino. But now, in this moment, all I see is a frightened father. "And there's nothing I can do to change your mind?"

I release a breath, the one I've been holding since I marched in. I already had a pretty good idea what I was walking in on. "I don't think so—"

"I'll double your pay. *Cazzo*, I'll triple it if that's what it takes."

"*Signore*—"

"Cut the bullshit, Raffaele. You know as well as I that I could force you into this. I don't want to do that because I truly believe that in order for you to be effective, you must want the position. Up until the Rome trip came up, I believed you did. I need the man that I met on Park Avenue two weeks ago, the one that was willing to jump into traffic to save my daughter. Are you still that man?"

I clear my throat, buying myself a few more seconds to think. Do I think the mafia king would make good on his promise to force me into this job? Probably. Would it involve threatening to murder everyone I know and love? Likely. It's a good thing I don't have many of those anymore. I knew very well what I was getting into before I signed on the dotted line.

"It's three months, Raffaele, and you'll be back in Manhattan. I promise to make it worth your while if you go willingly."

"Can I have a day to consider?"

He nods. "But no more. My daughter informs me the deadline is quickly approaching, and I hate to disappoint her." A bittersweet smile hitches up the hard line of his lips. "I thought I'd gone soft when I met her mother, but having a daughter, it changes you in ways you'd never imagine."

"I bet." I slowly rise, eager to finish this meeting.

"No wife or children in the cards for you, Raffaele?"

"No, *capo*. It wouldn't be fair in my line of work. If I can't devote a hundred percent of myself to the client, I'm not operating at full capacity. I could never do that with a family."

He rises, extending to his full height which nearly matches my own. He pins me in that penetrating stare. "And that's exactly why I want *you* in Rome with Isabella."

CHAPTER 11
THE STUPIDEST THING

Isabella

With one last glance in the mirror, I steel my nerves for possibly the stupidest thing I've done in my life. But for good cause, I remind myself. Missing Serena's going away party, or *Buon Viaggio* Bash as she'd touted it across social media is not going to happen. So fuck the consequences, and I am certain there will be plenty of them.

Running my hand through my perfect beachy waves, I attempt to slow my racing pulse. Then I smooth the oversized NYU sweats over my black mini dress. Totally unnoticeable. Everything will be fine. I'd convinced my parents and overbearing guard that Matteo was coming over to watch a movie, a totally believable concept as we frequently have movie nights in our home theater.

Moving away from the mirror, I pace the length of my bed before curling a hand around one of the ornate bed posts forcing an end to my agitated movements. The first stage of the plan is already in motion. Serena made accomplices of her parents without them being the wiser. My Uncle Dante and Aunt Rose were already on their way to a Broadway show with my parents. That meant half of the penthouse security went along with them.

Which would make my escape much more feasible.

The only problem is my ever-vigilant guard.

Reaching for my cell on the nightstand, I open the security app. Our home is constantly monitored through a series of hidden cameras. Vinny's room is empty; he's gone for the night with his guard to a friend's house. Flipping through the video feed, I stop at a familiar towering figure. Broad shoulders bar the entry to my room, those eyes flickering across either side of the hallway as if some crazed gunman is going to appear at any moment. I've been hiding out in my room for the past two hours getting ready for the party, and the man hasn't moved from outside my door.

Doesn't the *coglione* ever pee?

If I hadn't planned this diversion so perfectly, I wouldn't have made it a foot past Raffaele. Despite the elaborate plan, I'm not certain I'll escape. But I have to try because Serena will kill me if I don't at least make an attempt.

The sharp squeal of the doorbell through the security app sends the phone flying out of my hands. "Shit!" I squeak as my phone hits the floor with a smack. Dio, *chill out, Bella*. I get down on all fours and reach for my cell, then watch as Johnny opens the front door and Matteo saunters in. As expected, Raf doesn't budge.

I follow my cousin on the cameras as he offers Johnny a smile and a wink, then continues into the living area on his own. No one, except my paranoid guard, would expect anything nefarious from one of my closest cousins. With my heart tapping out a frantic beat, I watch as Matteo swings by the kitchen, opens the microwave, sticks something inside and gently closes it.

"Hey, Bells," Matty shouts, "are you coming out to greet your most favorite cousin or what?"

And that's my cue. Drawing in a deep breath, I tuck my phone into my pocket then grab my tote bag which hides my strappy stilettos and wrap it in a big fluffy comforter. Then I march toward the door, slipping on a mask of calm. I haven't quite mastered it, not like *Papà*. My mom says I wear my heart on my sleeve, but not tonight.

Jerking the door open, I fully expect to catch Raf off guard and drop him on his ass, but the man is like a jungle cat. He gracefully leaps out of the way and even manages to hold the door open for me.

"Your date for the evening is here, *principessa*." A wicked gleam lights up his dark irises.

"Don't be disgusting." I barrel by him, tucking my comforter beneath my arm.

A dark chuckle echoes behind me as I lengthen my strides to put some space between myself and my domineering bodyguard. Matteo stands in front of our home movie theater, in a pretty convincing pair of sweats.

In fact, my cousin and I are matching in NYU purple and white. Only Matteo could pull it off. He tugs me into a quick embrace with my guard looming over us.

"Is it really necessary for you to touch my client?" he grumbles.

I roll my eyes, shooting Raf a scathing glare before Matteo can answer. "What do you think he's going to do, shank me?"

My guardian shrugs, the picture of innocence. "You never can be too careful."

Matty opens the door to the dark room and dips into a theatrical bow. "After you."

I cross the threshold, and my shadow steps in stride beside me. Whirling around, I waggle my finger an inch from his Roman nose. "I'm sorry. You are not invited. This is a cousins' only night. Since you forbade me to go to Serena's party, you do not get to watch *The Princess Bride* with us."

"Oh, you wound me so, *signorina*." Raf motions a knife to the heart, his expression so melodramatic I barely suppress a grin. But I refuse to gift him that smile.

Instead, I slam the door in his face, ever so proud of myself. As soon as we're enclosed in the soundproof room, I whirl around to Matteo. "Are you sure you can do this?"

"Sure as shit." He grins as he pulls out his cell.

My cousin is kind of an IT whiz. He studied computer engineering at NYU and in just four years, managed to outsmart most of his professors. There isn't anything he can't hack, including my father's home security system.

Or at least, that's what he assures me.

"So how is this going to work exactly?" I murmur as his fingers fly over the keyboard.

"It's simple." He steers me toward the front row of the small theater and pulls me into the seat beside him. "I'm going to film us like this, then set it on a loop. So if your crazy guard decides to spy on us, he'll see us sitting right here safe and sound all night."

"So we'll have about two and a half hours." Luckily, Serena's apartment is only a three-block walk from the penthouse.

"Right."

"And the distraction?"

"Set to go off in about two minutes when Johnny heats up his nightly cup of Joe."

My lips slide into an easy smile. "You're brilliant, you know that, right?"

"I never could have done it without you and your intel." He pinches my cheek, the annoying habit one that he picked up from his father. My uncle Nico has always had an obsession with my cheeks since I was a kid. Now Matty does it as a joke.

Opening the security app once again, I toggle to the camera in the kitchen. "We do make quite the devious team."

Right on cue, a loud explosion booms through the phone's speaker.

Raf whips the theater room door open, his eyes wide and gun clenched in his fist. "Stay here and do not move."

"Will do." I shoot him a reassuring smile.

"And lock the door behind me."

So predictable. I rise, pretending to do as I'm told, and the moment he's out the door, Matteo springs up alongside me.

"Hurry, we only have a few minutes before he's back." Tucking my tote under my arm, I grab Matty's hand and drag him down the hallway to my parents' bedroom. *Papà* had taught me long ago never enter a room without calculating your exit strategy.

Thanks to my dad's paranoia, there are two elevators out of this penthouse. The one hidden in his room is a direct ride to the garage where Matteo's car is waiting. We race into my parents' bedroom and head straight for the secret exit.

My heart punches my ribs as the sleek elevator doors glide closed behind us. *Come on. Come on.* The security app always loses signal in the elevators, so we're flying blind. Just a few more seconds...

The elevator dings, and the doors slide open. I race out with Matteo by my side and find Jackson, Matty's younger brother at the wheel of his new ruby red BMW. It's a perfect match to his bright hair. "Damn, you guys took long," he grumbles.

"Sorry, my guard is kind of tough to shake. I didn't know you were coming to the party, Jax."

"I'm not. I'm just the designated driver." Though Jackson is nearly my age, he rarely hangs out with the cousin crew. Matteo says he didn't get the Valentino-Rossi gene, he's all

Vanderbilt like his mom, preferring to lay low than paint the town red with the rest of us.

The video feed comes back online, and I catch a quick glimpse of the guards filling the kitchen. Smoke darkens the frame, but I can clearly make out Raf with the fire extinguisher.

"Hard to shake is the understatement of the year," Matty mutters.

We pile into the car, and Jackson guns the engine. As we pass through security, I drop down behind the front seats as my cousins wave at the guard.

The moment we hit Park Avenue I heave out a breath of relief. We made it. "Holy shit, I can't believe that worked!" I cry out.

No sooner are the words out than a familiar voice blasts through the speaker on my phone. I glance at the camera, at the loop playing of Matteo and me in the home theater. Raf's voice booms through the speaker as does the pounding of his fists on the door. "Are you okay, Isabella?"

A hint of guilt creeps in at the fear lacing his tone. Am I imagining it?

Dismissing the insane thoughts, I press the speaker button on my phone as Matteo watches warily. "Relax, Raf, we're totally fine. What happened out there?"

"Nothing. A fuse ruptured in the microwave. There was a little fire, but it's all under control."

"Great, then I can go back to watching my movie."

"Unlock the door first."

"Nope, I don't think so. I like it better with you stuck out there."

"Isabella…" he growls.

"Come on, Raf, just give me this! You already ruined my night by not letting me go to Serena's party. Can't you just leave me alone for two hours? I'm perfectly safe in here."

He mutters a curse, the Italian expletive ringing out in the quiet car. *Dio*, if I get away with this, I deserve a prize.

"Fine," he hisses. "But I'll be right out here if you need anything."

"Great, thank you."

I release the speaker button and draw in a breath. "Damn, I can't believe I got away with that."

Matteo's lips melt into a beaming smile. "Tonight is going to be memorable to say the least."

CHAPTER 12
CHEERS!

I sabella

The banging bass vibrates off the floor-to-ceiling windows that form the walls to Serena's modern loft. Despite its large size for a Manhattan apartment, it's filled to the brim with writhing bodies, dancing to the hypnotic beats. I can't remember the last time I've been in a room with so many people. The DJ stands in the corner, spinning a mix of house and techno beats, perfect to get into the European club mood.

I strangle the stem of my champagne flute, scanning the mass of wriggling forms for Matty. He disappeared into the crowd a few minutes ago in search of another martini. I should have gone with him. Instead, I'm perched on the end of Serena's leather sofa as a couple dry humps beside me. *Get a damned room.* What are they teenagers?

The packed dance floor parts, and a familiar pair saunters

in my direction. "Oh, hey, cuz, I didn't think you'd be here tonight." Alessia sashays closer, wearing one of her mom's couture designs. It's a bright red sequined top, that hangs off her shoulders with sheer sleeves embroidered with Chinese dragons. Like all Aunt Jia's designs, it's gorgeous. And with Alessia's exotic mix of Italian and Chinese, she looks stunning as always. Alessandro, her twin brother, walks beside her, and a hint of unease tightens a knot in my belly.

The last time I saw Ale was the night Frankie was shot.

"Move." Alessia shoos away the couple with no qualms about PDA and sinks into the seat beside me.

"How are you feeling, baby cuz?" Her twin towers over me, his unique irises, one a brilliant blue and the other a dark chocolate brown, scrutinizing me.

"I'm fine. Thanks for coming to check on me, by the way, asshole."

"Sorry, Bella. Things were chaotic after the incident at The Velvet Vault." He drags a hand through his long hair. The wild dark locks nearly brush his shoulders now. "But I was thinking about you." Something darkens his expression, a twitch in his typically casual demeanor. Maybe he has been going through something…

"And Pa was pissed as all hell," Alessia adds. "He threatened to take the Vault away from him for that fuck-up with the Russians."

"No need to bore our cousin with all the details." His gaze swivels away from mine, taking in the array of female guests. "I need to get laid tonight."

"Unlike every other night?" Alessia smirks up at her twin.

Ignoring his sister, he reaches for my champagne and swallows it down in one gulp.

"Hey!"

"I need it more than you do, trust me."

"You have no idea what's been going on in my life, Ale," I hiss.

"Actually, I do. Matteo keeps us up to date on all your struggles with your new bodyguard, princess."

"I heard he's hot as fuck." Alessia's sharp gaze circles the room. "Where is he by the way? I was hoping to get an in-person peek."

That flare of guilt rises, but I swallow it down, wishing I had some champagne to wash it down with. "It's his night off."

"And Uncle Luca let you come here by yourself?" She lifts a perfectly plucked brow.

"Not exactly—"

"There you are!" Serena barrels through the crowd with a drink in each hand, tumbles of golden blonde locks trailing down her bare shoulders. She hands me the fancy cocktail before clinking her glass against mine. "To my best friend and blood, Isabella, who had to escape the clutches of her sinfully gorgeous but slightly psychopathic and overprotective new guard to be here with us tonight."

A grin crawls across my face at her ridiculousness despite my best efforts.

Matteo appears behind her a moment later with three drinks, completing our dysfunctional family circle. "I thought you said this was supposed to be a small party," he grumbles before taking a sip from his martini. "It took ten minutes to get drinks from the bartender." He hands one to Alessia and the other to Alessandro.

Serena shrugs. "What can I say? There are a lot of people in Manhattan that are sad to see me go."

"No one more than me." I clink my glass against my cousin's. "I'm going to miss you so damned much, Ser."

"Aww, you guys are just so sweet." Alessia's lips twist into a sneer. I love my cousin, but she's kind of a bitch, and even though we're close-ish, there's no one like Serena.

"Cheers to you, cuz, and the best damned time in Milano." I lift my glass, and the others all follow. "You are going to rock Dolce & Gabbana's world this summer."

"Cheers!" All our glasses meet in the center, the clinking barely audible over the booming sounds of the DJ.

After we've all taken our celebratory sips, the five of us disperse, the boys and Alessia moving to the dancefloor, while Serena and I flop down on the couch.

"So everything went according to plan with the escape?" She eyes me over the rim of the crystal flute.

"Surprisingly, yes. I guess Raf isn't as good as he thinks he is."

"Or maybe you're just that much better." She shoots me a wink. "I just hope this little impromptu late-night getaway doesn't worsen your cause."

"Only if I get caught." I grin and take another sip from my drink, some sort of fruity rum punch.

"Do you think your dad will give in on the Rome internship?" Serena squeezes my hand, eyes lifting to mine. "I don't know what I'll do without you for the entire summer."

"It's not my dad, but the hot bodyguard you made me pick that I have to convince. Great choice by the way." I roll my eyes and suck down another big gulp through the straw.

"It'll work out, I know it will. Mark my words, you'll be thanking me I forced you to pick Raffaele one day."

"Yeah, when he's dancing on my grave."

"Oh, stop it!" She gives me a playful shove before jumping up and hauling me along with her. "Come on, finish your drink so we can dance. This is your first time out in months. You can't just spend the whole night on the couch."

"I'm not really in the mood—"

She clucks her tongue, shaking her head. "It's my going away party, and you will do everything I say. Got it?"

"Now who's acting like the spoiled mafia princess?"

"It's my party, baby!" She twirls me around, and the brilliant red liquid nearly spills over the edge of my glass. "Now, let's go!"

Downing the remainder of my fruity drink, I drop the empty glass on the cocktail table beside Serena's flute and follow her onto the dancefloor.

Five cocktails later and I haven't left the dancefloor the entire night. Some guy grinds up against my ass, but I'm having too much fun to shoo him away. Serena's wiggling her booty across from me, dancing with some other guy who I think appeared when my dude did, so I assume they're friends. That and they keep high fiving each other over our heads. If I wasn't two sheets to the wind, I'd find it annoying as all hell.

But right now, the haze of booze has me all numb and tingly and for the first time in months, I feel free.

"I am so glad you made it, cuz!" Serena shouts over the pounding rhythm. "This night never would've been the same without you."

"I know! Me too." I reach for her hand and give it a squeeze, but the guy behind me, pulls me closer, pinning me to his torso.

"You're not going anywhere, baby." His warm breath skates across my ear, and goose bumps cascade down my bare shoulders.

Serena waggles her brows and mouths, "He's hot, go for it."

I shake my head, and the room spins ever so slightly. It's been forever since I hooked up with a guy and with my new shadow, who knew when I'd get another chance? Maybe I should keep an open mind. The alcohol is rushing my system, and a little release could be fun. Not that I would consider giving up my virginity to some random guy at a party, but I could do other things... I wasn't exactly a saint, I just hadn't dated much since I spent most of my life behind lock and key in my gilded penthouse tower.

The guy's fingers tighten at my hips before he spins me around to face him. Golden locks tumble over his brow, and vivid green eyes meet mine. Serena is right, he's good-looking with that California, surfer boy style.

He leans in, lips nearly brushing the shell of my ear. "I'm Jason, by the way. I figured I should introduce myself since I've been rubbing up on you for the past half hour." A boyish grin curls the corners of his lips as he retreats, holding me out to arm's length once again.

"Isabella," I whisper-shout. Then I throw my thumb over my shoulder and point at my cousin. "Serena's my best friend."

"Oh, gotcha. That's my brother, James, she's dancing with. I'm in town visiting him for a few days from the west coast. I guess they know each other."

"Let me guess, California?"

He nods and runs his hand through the blonde, curly tendrils. "San Diego. How'd you guess?"

"You just had that look."

"I hope you like that look." A warm smile lights up his face.

The copious amounts of alcohol I've consumed loosen my tongue. "I could get used to it."

He reels me in so I'm flush against his torso, and his hands roam my lower back. As he presses me against him, I feel his cock harden between us and heat flickers down my lower half. The music slows, the first ballad all night filling the air. Jason's hands settle along the small of my back, his long fingers just barely brushing the curve of my ass in my black mini.

His erection nudges my belly as we sway to the music, and my lower half lights up at the incessant rubbing. Okay, when was the last time I took time for self-care? Apparently, it's been longer than healthy because I'm suddenly horny as hell. I may be a virgin, but I own a vibrator and know how to use it. It's just been so long since I have.

Jason leans in again, so his lips are only inches from mine. "Do you want to go somewhere more private?"

CHAPTER 13
MY FAULT

Isabella

I glance over my shoulder and catch a glimpse of Serena in a lip-lock with James. It would be kind of fun to hook up with brothers. I'm definitely wasted or that would not sound so appealing. The errant thought flits through my mind, but I push it back, giving in to the warm haze of champagne.

Turning back to Jason, I quickly nod. "We can go to my room."

His hand wraps around mine, and he steers me through the crowd. "I thought this was your friend's place?"

"Serena's my best friend, actually. I spend the night here a lot, so she gave me my own room." Over the years, I've learned to protect my identity at all costs. The fewer people who know I'm the daughter of the notorious CEO Luca Valentino, the better.

Once we clear the packed dancefloor, I take the lead and guide us toward a long hallway that leads to the bedrooms on the first floor. Serena's room is upstairs in the loft. Though she did give me one of the spare bedrooms to keep extra clothes whenever I do sleepover, we usually sleep together in her massive bed upstairs.

Jason spins me toward him, catching me completely off guard once the chaos of the party begins to fall away. His lips crash into mine, and he shoves me against the upholstered wall in the corridor. Well, that's unexpected. He's a little sloppy, his tongue plunging into my mouth like he's on a mission to plunder every inch.

He presses his body against me, gliding his cock up and down my dress. It feels kind of good, but also a little too much since we're still in the hallway where anyone can walk by.

"Hey, slow down," I mutter against his mouth.

"But you feel so good, baby." He groans as his hand comes around to cup my breast.

Also, I hate that term of endearment. *Baby*. Maybe it's because I feel like I've been treated like one my whole life.

"I can't wait to fuck you—"

I shove him back, planting my palms on his shirt. "Excuse me?" I hiss.

"What? I thought that's what we were doing." He captures my lips again, mouth sucking my lower lip a little too eagerly.

"Get off!" I shout.

"Oh, come on, baby, you don't mean that." His thigh pushes my legs open, pinning me to the wall.

A flash of darkness streaks across my peripheral vision, and Jason's mouth is wrenched free of mine, nearly taking my lip with him, then his whole body is midair. I gasp as he hits the marble floor halfway down the hall an instant later. And a familiar form is hunched over him, bashing his face into the ground.

"Raf!" I cry out. My feet are moving again, the haze of

alcohol suddenly lifting. Where the hell did he come from? I sprint down the hall and slide to my knees.

Jason's head bounces off the marble, blood spewing from his nose and mouth.

"She said no, you *pezzo di merda*. Don't you know what that means?" Another crack as Raf's fist connects with Jason's nose.

"Stop!" I tug on my guard's arm with both hands, barely able to encircle his massive biceps. "You're going to kill him!"

"Good. That'll teach the fucker to listen when a woman says no."

He hits him again, now with his left fist.

"Raffaele, stop!" I shout again, doing my damnedest to haul him off the guy, but my best efforts achieve nothing. It's like a mouse trying to move a mountain.

"This is your fault, *principessa*," he growls as he hits him again. "What the fuck were you thinking sneaking out of the penthouse?"

"You're right, it's my fault." I kneel in front of him and cup his cheek, forcing his gaze to mine instead of the bloodied form beneath him. Those wild eyes meet mine, a tempest of rage crashing across the dark surface. "It's my fault, not his. You want to take this out on someone, take it out on me."

The hard line of his jaw softens, the desperate look in his eyes waning. His jaw ticks, that tendon feathering. "This is on me," he grumbles. "Fuck!" Then he's back on his feet, pacing the length of the corridor. "How the hell did you get past me? This happened on my watch. I'm the one responsible."

"Nothing happened," I whisper. "The guy got a little handsy. I could have handled it."

Raf barks out a laugh, that unhinged look back in his eyes. "That's what you think. You have no idea what was in that man's head. What he wanted to do to you..." His words fall away, and he swallows hard before dragging his fingers through his hair.

"*Merda*, what happened over here?" Matteo jogs down the hallway, eyes wide.

Before he reaches me, Raf lunges and pins him to the wall. "What were you thinking bringing her here? I should beat the shit out of you, too."

"Raf, no!" I jump on his back, wrapping my arms around his neck so I'm hanging off him like a freaking monkey. "Don't you dare hurt, Matteo. This was my idea. I forced him to help me escape." I cling onto Raf's back, tightening my hold around his neck until he releases my cousin.

He finally steps back, and Matteo sidesteps around my hulking guard. "*Dio*, what did you do to his face?" He stares down at the floor, and I'm too scared to look.

"Get Serena, she was with his brother." I slide down the length of Raf's broad shoulders, and my stilettos hit the floor with a smack. "We need to get him to the hospital."

"No," Raf snarls. "No hospitals. We'll call your father's personal medic."

"So you want *Papà* to find out about this?" I glance between Raf and the poor bastard on the floor.

"No," Raf finally grits out.

"Then just drop him off at the hospital."

"What if word gets out?"

"I didn't tell him my last name, you idiot. I'm not stupid." Wrapping my arms across my chest, I glare up at the insane man who's taken over my life. "Hopefully, he'll just think you're some jealous boyfriend or something."

He snorts on a laugh. "I wouldn't wish that on my worst enemy."

"Fuck you," I hiss.

"You wish."

Matteo appears with Serena a moment later, hauling

James behind her. "Oh, shit." Her eyes bulge out of her head as she takes in the bloodied man on the floor. Luckily, all the other attendees have been too busy with the raging party to notice the disaster down the hall.

James slides to the ground beside his brother, horror carved into his expression. "What the fuck happened to him?"

"He wouldn't take no for an answer." Raf's voice is deceptively calm, like the surface of the Hudson just before a storm, hiding the turbulence lurking beneath. "Now, I suggest you take your piece of shit brother to the hospital and forget this night ever happened, or I'll take my girl here to the precinct to press charges."

James stands, his pallor a sickly lime green. "But he wouldn't—"

"I saw it," Matteo interjects. "He was trying to force himself on her."

Serena whirls on James, venom in her voice. "Take your asshole brother and get the fuck out of my house."

"But—"

"Get out." She shoves him back so hard he nearly trips over Jason's unmoving form.

A lethal mix of embarrassment and a flood of warmth invade my chest. As fucked up as our family can be sometimes, I know they'll always have my back. Even when I'm the one that screwed up. Big time.

James hauls his brother off the floor, and I can't even watch as he practically carries his broken body through the crowd. This is all my fault. Why did I think I could have a normal night out?

"Let's go." Raf's thick fingers encircle my forearm as he drags me down the hall. "This night was a fucking shitshow."

"Yeah, because of you." I plant my heels, which is rather difficult in four-inch stilettos. "If you'd just let me come, none of this would've happened."

"You're wrong." His eyes flash and he jerks me closer, so his musky scent envelops me. "It would have happened all the same if I'd seen that shithead pawing at you."

"So no one can touch me now?"

"Not if they want to keep their fucking hands, *principessa*." He snarls my pet name an inch from my ear so only I can hear.

"Hey, hey." Matteo stalks closer. "I get that you're trying to protect her, but you can't manhandle her either."

Raf blows out a breath and releases me. His chest heaves, the manic rise and fall slightly disturbing. The mask of calm descends across his features, and the spasming tendon in his jaw stills. "You're right." He dips his head at me and motions to the door. "Please, *signorina*, may I escort you home?"

My gaze pivots to Matteo then Serena. At least we had a few hours of fun before everything went to hell. "Night, guys."

"Are you sure you'll be okay with your guard?" Serena asks. "He seems a little frazzled."

I barely suppress a cackle. Frazzled is putting it lightly. "Yeah, I can handle him."

Raf grunts before sliding his arm around my waist and escorting me rather forcefully to the door.

CHAPTER 14
BLACKMAIL

R *affaele*

Cazzo, I feel like absolute shit today. And I must look it, judging by the look on Ricky's face as I stalk through the entrance of the Valentino penthouse. After I'd gotten the little escapee home safely last night, I opted to sleep the remaining four hours in my car instead of driving all the way to the crappy motel in Queens and back which would have left me with even fewer hours to sleep.

More than the exhaustion after a terrible night in my cramped backseat, I'm pissed as all hell. At that asshole who dared to lay a hand on my client, at Isabella for attempting an escape and most of all at myself for allowing it to happen. And then for losing my shit when it did.

I thought I had a better handle on that rage…

Darkness creeps into the edges as screams ricochet across my skull like a pinball, bouncing off every corner with an increasing frenzy. Blood paints my vision, so much blood it stains my skin, digs beneath my fingernails and remains there for all eternity. Isabella is not *her*...

"Good morning, Raffaele." Mrs. Valentino offers a smile over her cup of coffee, jerking me from my murky past. Thank *Dio*, Luca is already gone for the day. I don't think I could face the man after my monumental fuck up last night.

If anything had happened to Isabella...

"*Buongiorno*," I echo back with a quick wave over my shoulder. I'm anxious to have it out with the *principessa* this morning. Given her intoxicated state last night, I assumed any attempts at a real conversation would be futile. Now, I'll lay into her for that incredibly stupid move she pulled. She has no idea how fragile life can be, how quickly it can be torn away.

"Isabella is in the gym," she calls out behind me.

"Great, thank you." I turn down another corridor of the sprawling penthouse. Despite never having been in the home fitness center, my steps are sure and quick. I've memorized every inch of this apartment. *And still the little princess got the slip on you.* A dark voice echoes across my mind, the deep timbre and thick accent markedly similar to that of my father. He never approved of anything I wanted to do; nothing was ever good enough.

And now every time I fail at anything, that damned voice worms its way into my subconscious, feeding the doubt and prodding the monster.

By the time I reach the gym, my nails are cutting into my palms, and it's taking every ounce of self-restraint I possess not to rip the door off its hinges. Instead, I suck in a breath and count to ten before opening the door. Loud music seeps through, interrupting my quest for Zen, and I jerk the door open a second later.

Isabella stands in front of a wall of mirrors in a sports bra and yoga pants that leave nothing to the imagination. I freeze in the doorway as she bends down, touching her palms to the mat and giving me a front row view of her perfect ass.

My hands twitch as I stride forward, my palms begging to spank that ass raw for disobeying me last night. Isabella is so damned focused she doesn't even notice me until I'm right up on her.

She peers up at me, dropping into downward dog. "Do you mind? I'm trying to relax."

"How can you relax with the music blaring like this?"

"It's soothing."

"Like a chainsaw."

The corner of her lip twitches, but she doesn't give into the smile. Instead, she continues her workout, completely ignoring me.

I crouch in front of her, getting right in her face so she has no choice but meet my eye. "We need to work on your awareness, *principessa*."

"I am aware. Very aware of how annoying you are." *So sassy*. She offers a sweet smile before switching positions once again. Cat pose or some shit where her back is arched and her ass sticks up, just begging for me to spank it.

Clearing my throat, I force my scattered thoughts to focus. "I just walked in on you a second ago, and you didn't even notice. What if I'd been sent to attack you?"

She twists her head to the side, skewering me with those baby blues. "I did notice. I was simply ignoring you."

"I hope you're not bullshitting me for your own sake."

Isabella rolls onto her back and glares up at me, her head nearly between my legs and inches from my hardening cock. Then she lifts her hips into bridge pose and my eyes instinctively chase to her tight-ass yoga pants and the hollow between her thighs. *Merda*, I can practically see the outline of her pussy. She's doing this on purpose to rile me up, I'm certain of it.

Dropping back on my haunches, I heave out a breath,

squeezing my eyes closed. "When you're done with your workout, we need to talk."

"It'll be a while." She thrusts her hips up, and fuck, all I can picture is my body blanketing hers, and my cock pounding into her.

Damn it, Raf, stop that. I've never been so turned on by a female I found so irritating. In an effort to keep my sanity, and my job, I reach for my phone and start scrolling funny cat videos. Nothing like hilarious kittens tumbling around to keep your mind off forbidden pussy.

As I pretend to watch the videos, I keep one eye on her at all times. It's not even on purpose; my duty has been ingrained so deeply it's second nature. And it's not even because of how badly I want to fuck her either.

A never-ending hour passes before she finally stands, reaches for a towel and wipes the beads of sweat off her forehead then slowly runs the terrycloth down her chest and across her tight abs.

There is no doubt in my mind that this woman is testing me.

Because what better way to get rid of me than telling Daddy I made a move on her. I'm impressed by her last-ditch effort. Today is the deadline to accept the residency in Rome after all.

"You ready to talk?" I grit out.

She huffs out a frustrated breath and plops down on the weight bench. "What do you want now, Raf?"

"We need to talk about last night, and all the reasons why it will *never* happen again."

"I learned my lesson, okay? I promise never to sneak out when we're in Rome." A smirk tugs up the corner of her lip and with those rosy cheeks and the glint of perspiration on her skin, she looks goddamned radiant.

"*When?*" I bark once I've stopped staring at her like a damned lovesick teenager. "You're out of your mind."

"I am not."

I stalk closer, arms pinned across my chest. "I already told you I'm not going to Rome."

"Oh, but you are, or I'll tell *Papà* about last night."

My pulse skyrockets as she innocently nibbles on her bottom lip. "You're going to blackmail me into this?"

"If that's what it takes." Her eyes lock on mine, a hint of mischief streaking through the ocean blue. "I told you I always get what I want."

"So tell him, and I'll get fired, big deal. There are tons of spoiled little girls out there in need of protection."

Her eyes flash, and a satisfied smirk crawls across my face. Only a few weeks with Isabella, and I know exactly which buttons to push. She's so easy to read, it's child's play really.

She rises, slowly unfolding to her full height, which is still a full head shorter than my own. But the way she glares up at me, you'd think she was twice my size. "Not only will you get fired, but *Papà* will make sure you never work in private security again. He has more connections than the freaking mayor, and no one will ever hire you again. If he allows you to live that is…"

"You've got to be fucking kidding me," I growl. "He can't—"

"He can, and he will. You're a smart man, Raf. I'm sure you know what my father is capable of."

"This is bullshit, *principessa*." I whirl on my heel as fury fills my gut. I stomp around the gym, looking for the punching bag before I lose my shit. The red canvas bag flashes across my peripheral vision, encroaching on the blooming darkness. I march toward it and let my fist fly. One punch, two, three, four. I lose track of the hits as it wobbles from the dangling chain. Why the hell did I take this job?

I broke my own damned rules, and now I'm being punished. Figures.

A soft hand on my shoulder stills my arm and stunningly quiets the rage. I spin around, chest heaving.

"It's only temporary, okay? Once the summer is over, you're free. It's not like I want you in my life any more than you want to be in it."

"You swear?" I hiss.

"I swear to *Dio*." She crosses her heart as her eyes remain fixed to mine. "I need this Raf. I need it more than anything. I swear I'll be on my best behavior."

"Somehow, I'm not sure you even know what that means." I blow out a frustrated breath because I'm so damned close to caving. Not just because of the threats, but because a tiny part of me actually feels bad for the mafia princess. That's how stupid I am.

"I'll follow all of your crazy rules and do everything you say while we're there."

"And you'll let me train you in some basic hand to hand combat?"

"I already told you I've been taking martial arts for years."

"Not from me you haven't."

She rolls her eyes so hard my palm twitches. "Fine, that too."

I mull over what I'm about to agree to for a long minute. I haven't been back to Rome in ten long years. Not since I walked out on my birthright. Fuck. The last thing I ever wanted was to return.

"Please, Raf." Isabella inches closer, pushing out her pouty bottom lip. "It's three months. What could possibly go wrong?"

She had to say it, didn't she?

CHAPTER 15
FINALLY FREE

Isabella

"I'm going to miss you so much!" From beneath the airplane hangar, I pull Serena into another hug before she steps onto the tarmac. The rumble of the jet echoes around us, a steady reminder that my best friend is about to leave me. My brother Vinny, and my cousins, Alessia, Alessandro, Matteo and all of his siblings have already had their turns. The entire Valentino-Rossi clan showed up for her departure, and next week, if all goes well, I'll be the one saying my goodbyes.

"Not more than me," Uncle Dante grumbles.

"You already agreed, Pa, no taking it back." Serena shoots her dad a grin. "Besides, it's only one year."

"Of course, we wouldn't take it back." Aunt Rose jabs her elbow into her husband's side then squeezes Serena's shoulder. "I'm so proud of you."

"Yes, of course, proud," her father adds. "And don't

forget, I'll be visiting often. There's a new business venture I'm considering in Milano—"

"No business talk today, D." Aunt Rose cuts him off with a deviously sweet smile. "Today, is about Serena and her accomplishments."

My uncle's lips press into a hard line. "Right, and I trust you'll be in good hands with Jia." He eyes his half-brother's wife, and I can't say the look inspires much confidence.

The twins' mom moves into step beside Serena after a steamy kiss with her husband, my uncle Marco. As unpleasant as it is seeing my relatives make out, it's kind of sweet to see how happy they all are with their spouses. It gives me hope that one day, I'll have what they do, in spite of the dark world we inhabit and the questionable ways in which some of those relationships started.

Speaking of that world, my ever-present shadow inches closer as if one of my family members were an actual threat.

"I can't wait to see you two in Rome in a few weeks." Serena winks as her eager gaze bounces between Raf and me. Then she leans closer and whispers, "I told you he was the right pick."

"Yeah, never mind the fact I had to blackmail him into going with me."

She shrugs. "Whatever works." She inches closer still, and murmurs, "And don't forget to get on the pill before you leave for Italy. Trust me when I say there is no way you're coming back home with that V-card still intact."

I nearly choke on a laugh. "I'll see if I can make that happen with my dark shadow in tow." Having Raf escort me to the gynecologist would be the ultimate embarrassment.

The pilot appears in the doorway of the jet and waves down Serena. "We're clear for takeoff Miss Valentino, whenever you're ready."

"Eek, I can't believe you're really doing this." A hint of sadness lingers in my tone despite my best efforts.

"Me either."

"You're going to kill it in Milano."

"Thanks, cuz. And I hope you don't kill anyone in Rome." She tosses me another wink before she pulls me into one final hug. "I'll come down to visit as soon as you're settled in."

"Promise?" I'm suddenly nervous, and it doesn't sit well. All I've ever wanted is to be free, to have an ounce of independence, and now that it's nearly upon me, I am terrified.

"Absolutely." Serena throws her designer carry-on over her shoulder and waves at all our family gathered beneath the shade of the hangar. "See you all soon! *Ciao!*"

I can't tear my eyes away from my best friend as she hurries up the steps in her chunky heels behind Aunt Jia. A mixture of excitement, happiness and fear jostle around my insides. I remain planted to the spot long after the door to the jet closes.

"Come on, *principessa*, we can't stay forever." *Papà*'s hand closes around my shoulder and steers me back toward the awaiting car. "You'll see Serena soon enough."

"In Rome, right?" I cock my head to the side and give him my best puppy dog eyes. After I'd gotten my reluctant bodyguard to agree, I'd gone straight to *Papà*'s office with Raf to let him in on the exciting news.

He was just as excited as I imagined him to be.

"Were you able to get the men you wanted on board for our Italian excursion?"

Because apparently one psychotic guard isn't enough, my father had to ensure he could attain another dozen guards as back up. As most of the King's operations took place in the U.S., he was hard-pressed to find a team in the motherland so quickly. *Papà* had emigrated to New York when he was just a kid, and though he had some connections in Italy, there weren't many he trusted with my life.

Or at least that was the story I'd gotten.

"Almost." He kisses the top of my head before steering me toward the limo. Raf cuts in front of us and opens the back door where Vinny and Mom are already seated.

"*Grazie,*" says *Papà* as he ushers me into the oversized backseat next to my brother, and Raf slides in beside me. I don't bother complaining anymore as to why my personal guard must be within inches of me at all times while Vinny's can remain within a normal distance. In fact, his guard rides in the car behind us along with my mom's security team. Tony, my father's right-hand man rides up in the front with our driver, completing the Valentino entourage.

As my parents slip into an easy conversation about my Aunt Maisy's next fundraiser, I elbow my brother in the side. I've barely seen him in the past few weeks since he started his summer job at King Industries. "How's it going at work?"

He lifts a nonchalant shoulder. "It's fine. Clara gives me all the grunt work, and I spend hours buried under stacks of paperwork, but I guess I have to start somewhere."

If I hadn't chosen to study medicine, the job would've been mine. A part of me still hopes that the role of CEO will fall to my brother one day. My father insists there's no reason I can't be a pediatrician and run the family enterprise, but it'll never happen. I know one day I'll be forced to choose.

Papà has been more than patient with me, allowing me to pursue my passion, but it doesn't take away from the ever-looming presence of my title as mafia princess.

"I still can't believe *Papà* is letting you go to Rome," he whispers.

"Same." I lean closer to my brother, and I swear Raf scoots along with me. "I won't really believe it until I'm on that plane, like Serena."

"I think he is actually trying to pull it off. I overheard him yelling at Tony yesterday about making it happen." He grins and curls his arm around my shoulders. "You've come a long way, big sis."

"You better come visit."

"You know I will, as soon as *Papà* gives me a day off."

"I'll be waiting forever then." I muss up my brother's dark hair, and my heart pinches. As much as I dread the idea of taking over the Kings, I'd never want it for him either. Vinny was named after our mom's older brother who was killed when he was around my brother's age now. He'd been involved in the family business too. The idea of losing him in such a tragic way has my throat tightening and emotion surging to the surface.

A volley of shots pierces the calm, and the giant limo swerves across three lanes of traffic. "Everyone get down!" Raf shouts as his massive body blankets my own, and I pull Vinny down beside me.

My parents are across the backseat, *Papà* pinning my mom to the floor as the shots ping off the bulletproof windows. I always wondered why we had to stay down if the glass is supposed to be thick enough to protect us. I don't dare ask Raf now.

"Who the fuck is shooting at us?" my father growls toward the front seat.

Tony's head appears through the opening, his expression pinched. "Some BMW is trailing us," he shouts.

"What color is it?" Raf calls out over my head.

"Dark, black or maybe navy." Tony rolls up the back window before turning to his own and shooting off a round.

"I wonder if it's related to the one that shot at us in the Escalade a few weeks ago." *Papà* mutters a curse.

"I thought Tony was supposed to find out who was behind that." Raf drags Vinny and me closer so he and my dad can continue their conversation over the barrage of bullets outside the window.

"He *was*," he growls. "The guys we picked up were hired

thugs, and they refused to give up their benefactor. Whoever it was, must have paid a shit ton of money to dare take a shot at *my* family."

Ricky swerves, cutting across another lane and speeds off the exit. The thundering spray of bullets falls away, and the massive male on top of me shifts his weight so I can finally breathe.

Papà springs up and rolls down the window between the back and the front seats. "Tony, I need you to find that *pezzo di merda* before the day is out or find a new fucking job."

"Sure, *capo*, I'm on it."

My father and Tony have been best friends for decades, and I'm certain this isn't a fireable offense, but it's a sharp reminder of how serious this situation is. Most of the big crime syndicates have been living in relative peace over the past decade. My father and my uncles went to painstaking lengths to ensure it.

So what the fuck is happening right now?

Papà helps Mom back onto the seat, and the rest of us follow suit. He ticks his head at Raf, eyes murderous. "Get everything ready for Isabella's trip. I want her out of the city before I burn it to the ground. It appears as if the long-lasting standoff in Manhattan has come to an end."

My heart leaps up my throat, a lethal mixture of anxiety and exhilaration battering my insides. I can't believe this is really happening. I'm finally going to be free.

CHAPTER 16
DARK MEMORIES

R*affaele*

I stare at the cracks in the ceiling, tracing the webbing along the dingy white plaster of the motel room as I count down the minutes before my alarm goes off. I've been awake half the night, a wicked storm of dread and unease brewing in my gut. Tomorrow, I return to Rome, the eternal city, the one I'd vowed never to set foot upon again.

What the hell was I doing?

I never should have agreed to any of it. I knew it the moment I strolled into that boardroom and those brilliant, soulful eyes latched onto mine, I should have walked away. If I'm being completely honest with myself, I felt the attraction long before that day, the night I saw her at The Velvet Vault, but I ignored it all the same. Now, it's too late.

Not only is my career on the line, and my life, but also, I'm like a pit bull when it comes to my clients. Once I'm invested, there is no walking away. And damn it, that little mafia princess will be my ultimate undoing. I can feel it deep in the marrow of my bones.

A streak of light seeps through the blackout curtains, and I hiss out another curse and roll over. My cell phone sits on the nightstand taunting. I've been putting off this call for days, ever since I agreed to this cursed trip. With our departure nearly upon us, I can't postpone it for much longer.

With a grunt, I reach for my phone and force myself to sit up. The crappy mattress squeals its protest, coils digging into my ass. At least, I'll finally be rid of this nasty motel. If I don't douse myself in cologne every morning, the scent of dampness and mildew cling to my skin all day.

I slowly scroll through the contacts, my finger finally settling on the least detestable option. With one quick glance at the clock, I confirm the time difference and jab my finger at the call button. The now foreign ringtone buzzes, different from the familiar one in the U.S. Every second feels like an eternity, and I'm an instant away from hanging up when a deep voice echoes across the line.

"*Pronto?*"

"*Ciao*, Giuseppe, it's me."

A string of curses vibrates across the line, and I can practically see my older brother's face as he spits them out. For a second, it feels like only mere inches separate us instead of an entire ocean.

"Are you out of your mind calling me? Do you know what *Papà* will say?"

"Yeah, I have a pretty good idea."

"Then why?"

"I thought you'd want to know that I'll be back in Rome in a few days."

"*Che cazzo fai, stronzo?*"

That's a good question, but the truth is I have no idea what the hell I'm doing. "It's a job," I hiss. "Don't worry, I'm not coming home."

"You'll be in Rome, *coglione*. That is home."

"It doesn't change anything. I'm coming with a client. We'll be there for a few months, and then I'm out of your life for good."

"Damn it, Raffa, are you trying to piss *Papà* off? Or just trying to get me in trouble?"

"I'm not asking you to get in the middle of this. I simply wanted someone to know in case word gets back to the *capo*."

"You know Antonio is running most of the operation now—"

"I don't care, Giuseppe. I'm not interested in any of it. *Papà* made his decision long ago. This was my courtesy call and the last you'll hear from me if all goes well."

"And if it doesn't?" A jagged edge laces his tone, raising the hair on the back of my neck.

"Is that a threat, *fratello*?" I growl.

"No, just a question, Raffa. I hope you know what you're getting into coming back here."

"I can handle myself."

"And your client?"

"Don't fucking worry about her. She's my responsibility."

"Oh, a she?"

"Yes, a she," I snarl.

"Do you think that's wise after—"

"Don't you dare say her name, Giuseppe, or I swear to *Dio*, I will reach across the phone and rip your spine from your throat."

"Relax, *fratellino*. I see you really have that temper under control."

"*Vaffanculo*," I grind out. "Fuck off with that temper bullshit. Like *Papà* was the best role model for keeping his cool."

"Clearly, or we wouldn't have turned out to be such well-adjusted men." A rueful chuckle slides out.

"I have to go. I have a trip to prepare for."

"Good luck, Raffa, I mean it."

"Thanks, *stronzo*." I press the call end button and toss my phone on the mattress. At least the worst part is over.

Now, all I have to do is make sure my client and my family never cross paths while we're in Rome.

Screams echo across my subconscious, the blood-curdling cries elevating my pulse. My breaths come in ragged pants, and I squeeze my eyes closed in a vain attempt to drown out the surfacing memories.

But it's too late.

I'm sucked into that room, the darkness crawling through every corner, the metallic scent of blood infiltrating my nostrils. And those screams, oh *Dio*, I'd never get them out of my head. They are permanently carved into my skull, much like my tattoo and the ensuing blood staining the back of my eyelids.

"Let go of her," I shout. "I'll do anything you want." With my gun clenched in my fist, I drop to my knees as he presses the knife to her neck.

"*It's too late*, figlio mio, *her fate is sealed along with yours*, traditore pezzo di merda."

"It's never too late, just please don't—"

A scream streaks across the chamber, ripping the air from my lungs. It isn't until I feel the tears running down my cheeks that I realize the guttural howl came from me. A fracture races down my heart, splitting not only my failing organ in half but my entire being. A pool of deep crimson inches dangerously close to my jeans as I kneel on the floor, stunned, immobile, numb. I drop my hands to the concrete and the blood seeps into my palms. She's still warm...

The scene blurs and retreats into the dark recesses of my tortured subconscious, to torment me another day. I blink quickly and sit up straight, trying to clear my mind of the horrible images that refuse to stay buried. Sweat trickles down my spine as I slide off the mattress and pace the tiny room. I'll never survive this trip to Rome.

Heaving out a breath of resignation, I march toward the bathroom. I need a fucking shower.

When I walk into Isabella's room, it looks like a bomb went off. Four suitcases are spread open on the plush carpeting and more clothes than line the racks at Barney's are sprawled across the bed, on top of armoires and spilling from the closet. It's the first time I've been granted access into her private sanctuary, and I can't help but take it all in. I'm typically dismissed at her door with a cold smile or contemptuous wave.

Beyond the chaos, I see bits and pieces of the spoiled little princess standing at the massive walk-in closet which could double as a bedroom for most. One entire wall is all shelves covered in glittering medals and trophies. From ballet to horseback riding, it seems the *principessa* has excelled in it all. Valedictorian of her graduating class in high school, high honors from NYU and an empty frame beside the first two diplomas. I inch closer and peer up at the tiny black scrawling at the interior corner of the gilded frame: *Isabella Valentino, MD*.

It seems as if my client has her entire future all planned out.

I continue to scan the room with her attention fully devoted elsewhere. Below the main trophy shelf, I find more awards, these lacking the typical gold-plated characters atop a pedestal. These instead are from organizations, charitable ones: Humanitarian Award from the Cancer Foundation, Community Service Award from the city of Manhattan, Angel Award from NYU Langone Hospital, Lifetime

Achievement Award in Philanthropy… the list goes on and on.

A frustrated grunt spins my attention to the little overachiever as she sits atop a Gucci suitcase trying to force the zipper closed. There is no way that girl earned all of these awards.

"Need help, *principessa*?"

Her upper lip curls into a snarl when I offer a hand. She tries and fails again to zip up the oversized baggage before her shoulders slump and she crawls off the suitcase, defeated. "Yes," she mutters.

"Yes, what?" I drop down beside her and lift a brow.

"Make yourself useful and close my luggage," she bites back.

"I'm not your butler, *principessa*." I slowly rise but her hand winds around my forearm, dragging me back.

"Please," she grits out. "I can't get it closed."

"Clearly. Because it's much too full."

She bats dark lashes at me, crawling closer on her knees. "You're telling me with those bulging biceps, not even you can zip it up?"

"I'm so thrilled you've noticed my arms. I work very hard to achieve these results." I shoot her a teasing grin as I cross those arms over my chest.

"Come on, Raf, just do it, please."

Oh, *Dio*, the sight of Isabella on her knees, begging nonetheless, have me instantly hard. It's like the woman's mouth has a straight line to my cock. And now I can't stop thinking about those pouty lips wrapped around my dick. *Merda*.

"Right. Out of my way." I circle her and drop down to the floor once again to drag the zipper all around the pricey suitcase. For what she probably paid for that thing, the closure better be indestructible. Once it's secure, I rise and meet a pair of blazing blue spheres, an unexpected glossy sheen opaquing their typical brilliance. "What's wrong?" I mutter.

"Nothing." She spins around and disappears into the closet once more.

A long minute later, she finally emerges, a hint of redness encircling those mesmerizing eyes. She was definitely crying… but why? She's finally getting exactly what she wants.

She keeps her back to me, gaze dipped to the mountain of luggage. "We're wheels up at seven tomorrow so make sure you're ready to go bright and early."

"I'm already packed. I don't have quite as much to bring as you do."

"Great."

"No snappy comeback? No comment about my all-black wardrobe?"

"It's not always about you, Raf." Without turning to face me, she saunters out of her room, leaving me in a stunned silence.

CHAPTER 17
A SECURITY BLANKET

I*sabella*

"It has to be here, damn it." With my eyes still filled with tears from the lengthy family goodbyes at the airplane hangar, I rifle through my oversized tote in search of those blessed little white pills. The rumble of the jet engine picks up, taunting. Shit. Shit. I can't fly without my Xanax.

"What are you looking for?"

The luxe cream interior and gold trimmings of *Papà's* private jet all blur in the background as panic starts to set in. My heart launches into a mad drumbeat, thrumming against my ribs like a frantic prisoner rattling the bars of a cage. My breaths grow shallower, and my chest starts to heave from the effort.

"Isabella, *cazzo*, what's wrong with you?" Firm hands clasp onto my shoulders, and the scene trembles for an instant before I focus on a pair of wary pitch orbs.

The jet lurches forward, and a scream sticks in my throat

as I grit through the rush of anxiety. But somehow, I stay put, anchored by the beast of a man sprawled in the leather captain's chair beside me.

"Isabella!" He shakes me again, and this time it's forceful enough that instead of the paralyzing fear, I focus on that unshakeable gaze.

"My pills," I murmur, nibbling on my bottom lip. "I can't fly without them."

The jet begins to move more quickly, the steady rumble growing louder by the second. "I hate to break it to you, *principessa*, but I think it's too late for that. We're going to be in the air in a second."

My fingers latch onto Raf's forearm, nails digging into his skin as we hurtle down the runway. "No, I can't do this…"

"Let me get this straight, you don't flinch about a shooting in the middle of Park Avenue, but you need medication for a flight?"

"Yes," I grit out. "Now stop being an asshole and find my meds!"

"Isabella, look at me." His big fingers clamp down on my chin forcing my eyes to meet his, which are steady and reassuring against the impending storm of panic. "You're safe. Focus on my voice, all right? You don't need pills. We're going to get through this together."

"I can't—"

"You can and you will."

I nod, my breathing shallow and quick. Raffaele continues, his voice steady and soothing. "Let's try to slow your breathing. Take a deep breath in with me, now." He inhales deeply, holding his own breath, then exhales slowly. "And out." His eyes hold mine, a silent promise of his weighty presence.

"Again, breathe in." I follow, and this time it feels a bit easier, my initial gasps beginning to smooth out into longer, more controlled breaths. "And out. Good girl. That's my good girl." A wicked grin tips up the corners of his lips, but I ignore it because for the first time in years since I've been aboard an airplane without being heavily medicated, it doesn't feel like my lungs are caving in. "Each breath in is calm, and each breath out lets go of the fear. You've got this, *principessa*."

As the plane levels off, Raf keeps talking, his words a lifeline as we soar higher. "You're much stronger than you give yourself credit for, Isabella. I've seen you handle situations that would break most people. This plane, this moment—it's no different. You own this experience; it doesn't own you."

My breathing steadies gradually, the panic receding as his calm certainty fills the space around us. His typically imposing and overbearing demeanor now feels soothing, transforming the cramped jet into a sanctuary.

Finally, I manage a small, grateful smile despite how weird it feels. "Thank you. I don't know what I would have done without you here."

"Always." An uncharacteristically gentle smile flashes across that scruffy jaw. "I'm here whenever you need me, no matter the situation or your opinion of me in the moment. It's my duty to protect you, whatever the cost. Don't forget that." His words wrap around me like a security blanket, easing the last remnants of my anxiety.

I sit back in the leather chair, leaning on the headrest. My fingers are still curled around his forearm, but not squeezing quite so forcefully. I consider removing my hand, but the plane dips for an instant, and my fingers instinctively clamp tighter around his skin. Refusing to give into the fear, I attempt a distraction instead. "How did you learn to do that?"

"The breathing exercise?"

I nod as his eyes chase to mine.

"As you know, I served in Italian special forces for a few

years before I got into private security. I found myself in some tense situations with my team, and it was a coping mechanism I learned from the start."

I can't imagine what sort of situations he was forced to endure. My knowledge of special forces extends to what I've seen on television shows. Not that my life has been a cakewalk either, but it must have been infinitely less stressful than running covert operations in foreign countries and putting your life at risk on a daily basis for fellow countrymen who don't even know you exist.

"What was that like?" We have an eight-hour flight ahead of us, and I would much rather spend the time distracting myself than focusing on the fact that we're flying over miles of endless ocean below.

"I'd rather not talk about it, if it's all the same to you, *principessa*." He leans against the headrest, closing his eyes.

I heave out a sigh, and my knee begins to bounce. The other bonus of the Xanax is that it knocks me out.

Raf's head swivels in my direction, peeking through heavy lids. "What's wrong now?"

"I can't sleep."

"It's a red eye. You're seriously not going to sleep the whole night?"

"Maybe a few hours, but I'm not tired yet." I doubt I'll sleep a wink, honestly. My insides are a twisted knot of excitement and anxiety. There is so much riding on this trip, I'm not sure I'll ever relax. Not only do I have to prove myself as an intern, but also as a capable adult who can survive on my own. It's all I've ever wanted, and now that I'm hours away from having it, I'm petrified.

"So what is it that you'd like to do?" he grumbles.

"Tell me about you, your family, your life? Anything really." In the past few weeks we've spent together, I've realized I know little about the man who is glued to my ass twenty-four hours a day.

"There's not much to tell."

"Raf," I whine.

"What? I'm not the biggest conversationalist."

"Yeah, I got that."

"And I don't like to share. As I said before, it's best to keep things professional."

I roll my eyes. "So if you tell me about your parents or siblings that's going to make it unprofessional somehow?"

"I'm not close with my family, okay? They're nothing like yours… When I left, I didn't have dozens of cousins, aunts and uncles filling up a hangar clamoring to say goodbye." His eyes slide closed again, but this time it doesn't feel like it's from exhaustion, but rather a way to block something out.

"Okay, what about a significant other?"

His lids snap open, and he shoots me a murderous side-eye. "I told you before, I don't do relationships."

"Ever? Aren't you like thirty-something? You've never had a girlfriend—or a boyfriend? I don't want to assume—"

He straightens in his seat, bristling. "*Cazzo*, Isabella, yes, I have at some point in my life had a girlfriend, and just to clarify I *am* into women. And I just turned thirty not thirty-something."

"There you go, you see? That's sharing." I toss him a smirk, and his dramatic eyeroll in return is everything.

"If you're so into sharing, then why don't you tell me something about yourself?"

"Well, you've spent the last month with me, so I'm fairly certain you already know a lot. Or you're not as perceptive as you tout yourself to be."

A chuckle escapes through the hard set of his jaw. "You're right. I do know a lot about you. I know that your favorite coffee is a caramel macchiato with an extra shot of espresso and one pump of vanilla coupled with Nutella spread on pretty much anything, that you enjoy sunbathing on your balcony, that you text Serena every morning when you wake up, that you nibble on your bottom lip when you're nervous and that the vein across your forehead pulses every time I call you *principessa*." A wicked grin slashes across his face, and there's nothing I want more than to rip it right off.

Just when I think he's being semi-tolerable.

"Any idiot could have gleaned that information after a month attached to my ass."

He inches closer, leaning across the arm rest so his breath mingles with my own. "Fine," he grits out. "How about this then?" He lifts a finger. "Your eyes crinkle slightly at the corners when you truly smile, not the fake one you give when you want others to think you're fine." A second finger rises to meet the first. "You twist a lock of hair around your finger when you're fully enrapt in one of those fantasy books you binge read." Another finger. "Your lips pull into a pout when you're unsure or hesitant about something." The fourth finger pops up. "Your footsteps slow when you're enjoying a moment, as if you're trying to fully soak in your surroundings. You do it whenever we walk through Central Park or around the campus of NYU." A fifth and final finger comes up between us. "And let's not forget the faint scent of gardenias from your perfume that lingers even after you've left a room, and how it's subtly different in the mornings compared to the evenings when it mixes with your delicate natural scent."

With his free hand, he extends a long finger tipping up my chin so my jaw closes. I'm staring with my mouth hanging open like an idiot. *Dio*, I never realized he paid such close attention.

His grin grows wider as I continue to gape at him. "And that's why I'm the best, *principessa*."

CHAPTER 18
UNFETTERED ACCESS

R*affaele*

My stomach dips, the slight jostle waking me from a fitful sleep. My eyes snap open as my heart lurches up my throat. It takes me a second to regulate my breathing as I scan the lavish interior of the jet. We're safe. We're aboard Luca Valentino's private plane on our way to Rome, not on a covert mission in the Middle East. I heave in a breath, and the moment of panic passes.

Soft breaths turn my attention to the head of dark hair splayed across my shoulder. Isabella sleeps peacefully beside me, the faint crinkle between her brows, which I hadn't mentioned in my detailed account of all her quirks, smooth now in sleep. Her hand rests on my chest, slender, delicate fingers stretched across my pec. I spend too much time watching her, memorizing every detail of her face. I tell myself it's an integral part of my job, but I'm fully aware I'm a fucking liar.

There's something about her... something that niggles at my flesh, a desire so raw and undeniable, it feels like a fire simmering just beneath my skin, waiting to burst into flames. The mafia princess has cast a damned spell over me, and this excursion to Rome will only intensify her hold. It was one thing when we were under Luca Valentino's roof, beneath his watchful eye, but now I'll have unfettered access.

We spent most of the night talking, something I was loathe to do. Keep it professional. Do not engage with the principal. My rules are everything. They are what make me one of the best damned bodyguards out there, and one by one, she's obliterating them.

And she doesn't even realize it.

A soft groan escapes her pouty lips, and my cock twitches at the sound. *Dio*, I want to be the one coaxing those moans from her, but in an entirely different scenario. Worse, it's not just my stupid dick that reacts to her, but an unfamiliar feeling fills my chest at the sight of her on my shoulder.

We fell asleep talking, and never even extended the seats to their fully flat position. We could have had a much better night of sleep, but instead, I remained upright, scared to move and wake her. She'd been so fucking nervous before we took off I wasn't certain I would be able to talk her through the panic.

But somehow, I did...

It's ridiculous, but maybe I affect her in a similar way. The thought is oddly satisfying.

The plane pitches forward as we begin our descent, and Isabella squirms beside me. Her hand falls from my chest, plunging down to my lap. And right on top of my hardening cock.

Merda.

As if she's felt it, her eyes jolt open, lifting to mine.

"Good morning, *principessa*." I offer a pleasant smile despite my cock screaming.

She must notice my unease or maybe she feels my hard-ass erection, but she doesn't comment. Instead, she jerks her hand back and sits straight up before running her other hand through her wild, dark locks.

"We'll be landing in a few moments."

"Oh, good." She turns away and wipes a dribble of saliva from the corner of her mouth, her cheeks flushing an enticing crimson. Once she's adjusted her top to keep her breasts from spilling out, she faces me once more. "Did you sleep okay?" she mumbles around a yawn.

Surprisingly, yes, despite the fully upright position. "Umhmm," I murmur. I hadn't been plagued by the incessant nightmares that typically haunt me. I tell myself it's because I slept so little, and it has nothing to do with the woman sleeping by my side.

"You?"

"Clearly." She motions to the wet spot on my shoulder that I hadn't even noticed. *Cazzo*, so much for my infallible observation skills. "Sorry about that."

I shrug as the wet warmth seeps into my skin. "It's fine, I have another one in my carry on. One of the hazards of guard duty."

Another lie. I've never allowed myself to fall asleep beside a client. Not since *her*...

"I'm going to freshen up in the bathroom, if you want to change out here." Isabella rises and grabs her designer duffle, tossing it over her shoulder.

"Sure, will do."

I can't help my traitorous gaze from trailing that perfect ass as it sways hypnotically in those tight yoga pants. *Fuck.* Squeezing my eyes closed, I force myself out of the chair and stretch my arms over my head. Even in a private jet, my long legs cramp after hours of not moving. Once I've gotten my muscles stretched out, I rifle through my bag for a new shirt. Not that Isabella's drool is that noticeable on a black t-shirt, but if she's changing then I suppose I should too.

I tug the shirt up and over my head as the door to the cockpit opens, and the flight attendant saunters out. Her gaze latches onto my bare chest, to the map of scars then to the ornate skull surrounded by red roses tattooed to my flesh. A cross is inked behind it, intersecting the skull, symbolizing a balance between life and death and the precious woman caught between the lethal dance. I got it the day after I lost *her*... Darkness creeps into the corners of my vision, threatening to pull me under, but a cheery voice hauls me back to the present.

"Good morning, Mr. Ferrara. Is there anything I can get you before we land in Rome?" The woman, Janey, I believe she said her name was, struts closer, a grin on her ruby red lips as she continues to blatantly ogle my bare torso. I'd only seen her for a few minutes when we'd been welcomed aboard and then again when dinner was served. She'd been a little flirty in front of Isabella but hadn't deliberately stared like this.

"Just some water would be fine." I swing my head over my shoulder, motioning toward the back of the plane. "But we should see what Miss Valentino would like."

"Of course." She inches closer still, her eyes fixed to my chest, or maybe it's the tattoo, but I can't help but get a *please-fuck-me* vibe from the woman. I wouldn't be surprised if she's provided all sorts of entertainment for VIP clients. Though Luca seems completely obsessed with his wife, one never knows what a man is like in private. "That tattoo is incredible," she whispers as her hand lifts to my chest. She traces the bold outlines and rich colors, her finger running a path along my carved torso.

Clearing my throat, I take a giant step back. Not only am I supposed to maintain professionalism with my clients at all costs, but also anyone on staff. "Thank you," I say, an icy edge to my tone that I'm hoping she'll pick up on.

But either she's clueless or doesn't care.

She closes the distance between us once again, her hand finding its way to my stomach and dangerously close to my belt buckle. She rises to her tiptoes and whispers, "I'll be staying in Rome for twenty-four hours if you want to meet up after you've dropped off your charge. I'm up for whatever you want, Raffaele…"

The bathroom door whips open, and Isabella pops out, her gaze immediately jumping to the woman's hand on my abs. Her mouth curves into a capital O, and those brilliant sapphire irises flash.

A long minute passes before the fucking stewardess releases me, and I can drag my shirt over my head. "Janey here was just asking if there was anything more we needed before we landed?"

"I bet she was." Her eyes narrow as she regards me for an endless moment, something like disappointment in her gaze. And it hurts like fucking hell. She slides between the flight attendant and me and dons that fake smile, not the one that makes her eyes crinkle in amusement. "I'll take a mimosa, Janey. And make it quick."

"Of course, Miss Valentino, right away." She spins on her heel and disappears behind the dark velvet curtain.

I remain frozen by the bathroom door like an asshole, no worse, like a kid who's been caught with his hand in the cookie jar only I didn't even get my damned cookie. Nor did I want it. Which is odd… and something I choose not to focus on at the moment.

Isabella stomps back to her seat and drops into the pristine leather. After a moment of waffling, I follow and dip into the seat beside her. "That wasn't—"

She lifts a hand, cutting me off. "Whatever it was or wasn't is none of my business, Raf. You're the one that said you don't *do* relationships. I guess that doesn't mean you don't *do* women in general."

"I'm not—"

She presses her finger to my lips, and her tantalizing scent fills my nostrils. It takes all my restraint to keep my tongue from snaking out to taste it. It's a heady mix of sweet gardenias and succulent strawberries. Does she fucking bathe in the stuff or what? "We'll be living in Rome for three months and we're both adults, free to date or screw whomever we want."

"I don't know that I agree with you there," I mumble around her finger.

Her dark brows furrow. "So you're saying you won't be dating?"

"No, I'm saying *you* won't be dating."

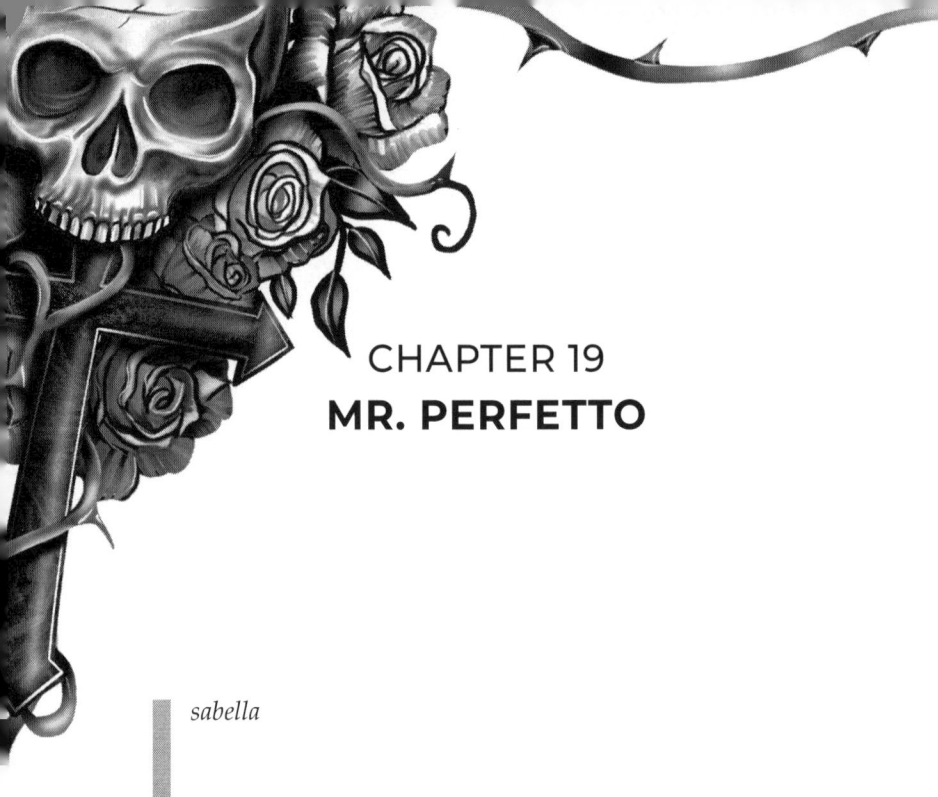

CHAPTER 19
MR. PERFETTO

Isabella

Why did I ever think allowing this stubborn, pig-headed man to accompany me to Rome would turn out well? My blood is boiling, fiery heat racing through my veins and not in the good way. We spent the entire ride from the airport arguing about whether or not I was allowed to date while in Rome.

Allowed? Are you fucking kidding me?

I did not get out from under my father's oppressive hold only to be squashed by Raf's. Trailing after the obsessive psycho, I stomp up to the building where I'm supposed to live for the next three months with our new driver, Salvatore, hand-picked by my father, following behind us with my luggage. I'm so pissed, I barely notice the beautifully intricate façade or the carefully manicured shrubs teeming with bright pink blossoms. The entrance is adorned with ornate cornices, sculpted reliefs, and arched windows framed by decorative moldings.

Raf jabs his finger at the call button on the aged stone wall.

"*Pronto?*" A gravelly voice echoes through the speaker.

I lose focus as I take in the gorgeous architectural details of the old Renaissance building. It's been years since I came to Rome with my parents. Unlike most of my friends from high school who got to backpack across Europe after graduation, I was forced to spend the summer with my little brother and parents touring the continent in luxury. I fully realize how bratty I sound, but I missed out on the normal experience, just like I did with practically everything growing up.

"What do you mean the apartment isn't ready?" Raffaele's furious growl jerks me back to the present. "Miss Valentino has arrived today, not tomorrow. What am I supposed to do with her now?"

The man across the speaker apologizes a hundred times over in both Italian and English as my guard tears him a new one.

Latching onto Raf's arm, I tug him away from the call box. "It's not a big deal, we can just stay at a hotel for the night."

"That will be difficult, *signorina.*" Salvatore pivots his gaze to meet my guard's feral one. "It's the beginning of *Estate Romana*, it's a four-month festival throughout the city featuring film screenings, theatre performances, concerts, special exhibitions, and more. Finding a hotel so last minute will prove challenging." He swallows hard as he forces out the last word.

"Fucking unbelievable," Raf grumbles.

"I would offer you my home," Sal continues, "but unfortunately, I live with my family in a small *appartamento*, and my hospitality would only extend to a cramped sofa."

"Thanks, Sal, I appreciate the offer, but there are

hundreds of hotels in the city." I pull my phone out of my back pocket and pull up my favorite hotel app. "They can't possibly all be sold out." I scroll through the endless list of accommodations and find... nothing. "*Merda.*"

Raf is pacing and cursing now, his perfect plan gone awry, and I've never seen the man so flustered.

"I know, I'll just call the professor who coordinated the residency at *Policlinico Gemelli*. I'm sure he can help us find a place."

"He better," Raf grumbles. "Let's get back to the car. I don't like being out in the open like this." I shoot him a super dramatic eyeroll because we are in one of the nicest parts of Rome, not downtown Baghdad, as he escorts me back toward the enormous black limousine. The huge car stands out like a sore thumb among the dainty European vehicles. I'll never fit in here if I'm forced to ride in that monstrosity all summer. I make a mental note to discuss that with my guardian once he's in a less murderous mood.

Once we're safely back behind the tinted windows of the limo, I find the contact information for *Professore* Ricci and pray he has an answer for us, or I'm afraid Raf might quite literally explode.

Thankfully, the residency coordinator answers on the second ring. "*Pronto?*"

"*Buongiorno, Professore* Ricci?"

"*Si?*"

"Hi, this is Isabella Valentino."

"Oh, yes, of course, *signorina* Valentino. Professor Dykeman spoke very highly of you."

Heat flushes my cheeks at the compliment. Dykeman is not one who gives out praises often. "Well, I just arrived from New York and unfortunately my apartment isn't ready. There was some confusion as to my arrival date. I tried to find a hotel, but the entire city seems booked. You wouldn't happen to have any insider tips, would you?"

"Ah, that is going to be a bit problematic with *Estate Romana* kicking off this weekend. But wait, give me a second, I will think of something." The click-clack of quick fingers striking a keyboard echoes through the phone line.

"Thank you, I really appreciate your help, *Professore* Ricci." I thrum my fingers against the supple leather of the backseat.

"Please, call me Massimo. We will be seeing a lot of each other this summer, and my full name and title would get quite tiresome."

"Okay, Massimo."

Raf sits beside me, tension vibrating from his entire form. His thigh brushes against mine, and I can feel the coiled muscle beneath his slacks. I whirl on him and mouth, "Relax."

"Ah, I've found something, *signorina*. It's likely not what you're used to at home, but it is clean and close to the center of town."

"I'm sure it'll be just fine."

"*Perfetto*. I will have my assistant, Carlo, make a reservation at the *pensione*, so the owner knows to expect you. Her name is Bianca, and she will be the most gracious hostess. I will text you the address now."

"*Grazie tanto*, Massimo."

"No need to thank me, I'm happy to help. I will see you on Monday at the *Policlinico*. If anything else should arise, please do not hesitate to contact me."

The moment I pocket my phone, Raf's enraged eyes meet mine. "So?"

"Relax, everything is under control." A part of me can't help the satisfaction at seeing my cool and collected bodyguard so unhinged. I guess Mr. *Perfetto* isn't so perfect after all. I cross the sprawling backseat and press the button that opens the window to the driver's portion of the vehicle. "I've got an address, Sal."

As I read the name and address to our new driver, Raf looms over my shoulder. A muttered curse squeezes through his gritted teeth.

"What's wrong now?"

He looses a frustrated breath and sits back on the seat as I buckle my seatbelt. "The area hasn't been scouted, the staff vetted... nothing. I spent days researching the area around the apartment, the owner, past tenants, etcetera."

"I'm sure everything will be fine. It's one night, Raf. What could possibly go wrong?"

"Well, *merda*." I stare at the tiny room with one queen size bed that spreads from wall to wall, and my heart just about hits the soles of my feet.

"*Mi dispiace, signorina*, but this is the only room available."

Yeah, I'm sorry too, because there is no way I'm sharing a bed with my bodyguard. And there's not even a couch.

Bianca stands beside me in the doorway, her long silver hair pulled into a bun, as I eye the closet-sized quarters. There's not even a private bathroom in the *pensione*, instead all the rooms on the floor share the one in the hallway. In all fairness, there are only six in the petite establishment, three on each floor, but still, that means sharing a toilet and a shower with strangers.

"No, absolutely not, this will not do." Raf drops our suitcases, then stomps around the room before letting loose on the poor woman in Italian.

I jerk him back when the little old lady starts to tremble. "Enough!" I growl, digging my fingernails into his arm. Once he's stopped cursing, I slam my palms into his annoyingly firm chest and shove him down on the bed. Then I spin around to face the woman once more muttering apologies. "The room will be fine, *grazie*." Then I pull a fifty Euro bill from my pocket and sneak it into her hand. "I'm so sorry about him."

Shaking her head, Bianca darts out of the room so fast my head spins. When the door slams shut behind her, I whirl on the big brute still muttering curses in Italian. "That was totally uncalled for."

"How can she expect us to sleep here?" He points back and forth between us like a madman.

"It's not her fault. We're lucky we're not spending the night in the limo."

"Maybe that's not the worst idea," he mumbles as he drags his hand through his hair. "It'll be more comfortable than the floor." He points at the sliver of space between the end of the mattress, the suitcases and the door.

I'm not even certain those broad shoulders of his will fit.

"You're right. You go sleep in the car, and I'll be right here." I plop down beside him, and stretch out, the jet lag starting to hit hardcore.

He snorts on a laugh. "Like I would leave you here by yourself, *principessa*."

"You're right... Bianca seems like a shifty one. You better keep an eye on her while I take a quick nap."

The ghost of a smile tilts up the corner of his lip, and I refuse to acknowledge the flutter of wings it incites low in my belly. Instead, I curl under the blankets and my head sinks into the pillow.

He blows out a frustrated breath and pushes up to his feet. "Sleep, *principessa*, we'll figure out the evening's arrangements later."

I barely hear the last part of his sentence as sleep takes hold, my lids so heavy I can do nothing but succumb to the darkness.

CHAPTER 20
A LITTLE FUN

R *affaele*

Sleep threatens to overtake me, my lids growing heavier by the moment, as I pace the small confines of the hotel room. With this quiet time to reflect, the guilt has started to set in. I'll have to apologize to Bianca later. I hate the feeling of lack of control, and clearly, I do not do well with surprises. The apartment not being ready was bad enough, but then to be forced to spend the night in this tiny room with Isabella is pushing my restraint to the limit. I shouldn't have taken it out on the owner of the *pensione*… Damn it, Giuseppe was right about my temper.

I heave out a breath, and my stomach rumbles reminding me I'm also starving. At this point, I'm not certain what I want more: to join Isabella in that bed for an hour of blessed sleep or a pizza. Shaking my head, I remind myself I can't have either.

My mouth waters, and I'm not certain if it's from the idea

of food or *her*. A curtain of dark hair is splayed across her pillow, her lips slightly parted in sleep. I watch, hypnotized, at the gentle rise and fall of her chest, at her perfect breasts straining against her pale blue blouse.

I've been watching her like a *coglione* for the past two hours as she sleeps peacefully, and it's absolute torture. Besides being sleepy as all hell myself, I've been swept with the most overwhelming desire to curl up beside her.

It has to be sleep-deprivation.

I do not cuddle.

I wasn't lying to Isabella earlier, I do not do relationships. That doesn't mean I don't occasionally fuck women… I'm no saint by any means. I need an occasional release like any man, and my rough palm doesn't always do the trick.

But with her… I'm suddenly inundated with all these *feelings*. Feelings I'd promised myself long ago I'd bury, never to see the light of day again. It is the only way to survive in this line of work.

A faint sound purses Isabella's lips, drawing my attention to the bed. She rolls over, and her skirt crawls up her thighs, revealing soft, milky-white flesh. A groan vibrates my throat as a hint of pink panties appear.

Squeezing my eyes shut, I force myself to turn around. Improper. Unprofessional. *Wrong*. With my cock already thickening, I compel my feet toward the window. Tourists line the busy streets just a stone's throw from the Colosseum, it's ancient crumbling columns standing proud against the brilliant sun. It's just past three in the afternoon and all the stores are opening once again, after the typical afternoon closures. The Spaniards aren't the only Europeans who take a mid-day *siesta*, even the eternal city comes to a halt for lunch. My stomach grumbles again, but at least my hunger for food turns my thoughts away from the other hunger coiling beneath my belt.

"What time is it?" A familiar raspy voice jerks my attention from the sights below. Isabella sits up, and a yawn escapes her pursed lips.

"Just past three."

She stretches her arms over her head and her blouse rides up, gifting me a sneak peek of skin. "Why'd you let me sleep for so long?"

I shrug. "You seemed tired."

"Now I'll never sleep tonight."

"Sure you will, just have a glass of wine with dinner, and you'll sleep like a baby."

Isabella's dark brow arches, the corner of her mouth lifting with it. "Are you trying to get me drunk, *signor* Ferrara?"

"I would never, *signorina* Valentino." But a smile crawls across my lips all the same. "Now get ready, I'm starving, and I haven't had real food in years."

"Real food?"

"Yes, you know, *Italian* food."

With an eyeroll that has my palm twitching, she slides to the edge of the mattress and laces up her sneakers. Once they're on, she slowly rises, pinning me in that wary gaze. "So where are you taking me for dinner? A romantic spot by the Colosseum?"

"Oh *Dio*, no. All they have around here are tourist traps. You won't find any real Roman food in this area. We'll have to go to the outskirts of town."

"Great. Is Sal ready to go?"

I shake my head at her, a grin creeping across my face. "It's our first night in Rome, the most beautiful city in the world, we're walking, *principessa*."

"I guess it's a good thing I have my sneakers on then."

I eye her oversized American shoes, and I must scowl because she saunters up to me and slaps her hands on her hips.

"What? What's wrong with my Hokas?"

"Nothing. If you want to look like a tourist... You might as well be waving an American flag as you walk."

A laugh tumbles from her lips and *Dio*, that sound kicks up my sluggish heartbeat. She twists her foot, eyeing the bright yellow and orange shoe. "They're not that bad, are they?"

"If you want to look like a real Italian, I'll take you to buy some more appropriate footwear tomorrow."

"Thanks, I think," she mumbles. "I'm not sure if I should be upset about you insulting my sense of shoe style or appreciative for the tip."

"Definitely the latter." I twist the knob and hold the door open. "Now come on, I'm literally going to eat my arm off in a second."

After a quick walk by some of the city's most iconic sights, the Trevi Fountain, the Spanish Steps, and St. Peter's Basilica, I'd really worked up an appetite. But I can't even focus on eating more with this tempting woman sitting across from me.

"Oh, *Dio*, this is heaven." Isabella slurps up the final bite of spaghetti carbonara with a groan, and I shift uncomfortably beneath the worn wooden table. The quaint *trattoria* is nearly empty, with only one other table occupied besides ours. It's exactly why I picked it.

Watching this woman eat has been a true testament of my self-control. I've never met anyone enjoy food the way she does. Every bite comes with a groan or a moan, a licking of lips or some other tantalizing gesture that has fire racing to my cock.

I finished my meal in record time and have spent the last twenty minutes watching her devour the pasta. I never thought the simple act of eating could be so damned sexy. I reach for the glass of wine and down a deep gulp. Drinking on the job is one of those hard and fast rules, but *cazzo*, being with this woman makes me want to throw all my guidelines out the damned window.

Just tonight. So I can sleep.

If I have any hopes of getting quality rest on the floor, I'll need to be knocked unconscious.

Isabella draws her glass to her lips and takes a healthy swallow of the red wine. A giggle snakes out as she finishes it and reaches for the bottle. The *second* bottle she ordered. Shit, how much has she had to drink? Not only have I allowed myself to indulge, but I haven't kept an eye on her intake of alcohol either.

In the past month since I started working for the Valentinos, I've only seen her drink that one time when she escaped the penthouse to attend Serena's party. Which means her tolerance cannot be that high…

The waiter appears, drawing my attention back to the present, holding a chilled bottle of limoncello. "Compliments of the chef." He offers Isabella a smile as he sets down the small glass and begins to fill it with the lemon liqueur.

"*Grazie.*" She smiles brightly at the young guy, and a twist of jealousy uncoils in my gut.

I place my hand over the shot glass before she can grab it. "I think you've had enough tonight, *principessa*."

"All I had was some wine. I feel totally fine." She winks at the waiter. "Don't I seem fine?"

"Oh, yes, you certainly do. *Sei bellissima.*"

"Excuse me?" I growl, rising to my full height and towering over the guy who had the nerve to call *my* client beautiful.

He cowers, taking a step back. "*Scusi.* I meant no disrespect, *signore*. I did not realize you were her boyfriend."

"He's not," she blurts. And for some damned reason, her words sting.

You're not her boyfriend, you stronzo. *You are her guard.* I repeat it over and over to myself, hoping it'll get through my thick skull.

While I'm distracted, she downs the glass of limoncello then licks her lips, eyeing me with a smug grin.

"For you, *signore*?" The waiter has balls to even dare offer.

"No," I bark.

"Oh, come on, Raf. Loosen up a little…" Isabella brings the cool glass to my lips and the tangy scent of lemon fills my nostrils.

"It's not a good idea."

"Fine, then I'll have it." She shoots it before I can stop her.

"Isabella, no more," I hiss.

"Who are you, my father? I'm twenty-two years old, Raf. You can't tell me what to do, or what to drink and most of all who to date." She eyes the young man again and bats her dark lashes. "I'm Isabella by the way, and you are?"

Oh, fuck no. I leap up so quickly my knee hits the bottom of the table and the entire thing rattles, sending plates and utensils scattering. This was a mistake. This is exactly why I stick to my rules, to my carefully calculated procedures, to prevent moments like these.

Dropping a wad of Euros on the table, I pull Isabella to her feet.

"What are you doing?" she screeches.

"We're going back to the hotel."

"But I'm not ready to go…"

"We're leaving anyway." I drag her to the door as she flails, and a handful of curious gazes flicker in our direction. "*Ci scusi. Mia moglie ha bevuto troppo,*" I call out over my shoulder as she tries to squirm out of my hold.

"I'm not drunk, and I'm not his wife!" she shouts.

Once we make it outside, she wraps her hand around a light post, halting us, and glares up at me, bright blue eyes ablaze beneath the lamplight. "I'm not going anywhere with you. Damn it, Raf, I was just having a little fun. We were at a freaking restaurant, why can't I have some fucking limoncello?"

"Because you're already well past tipsy and two more shots of limoncello will get you black out drunk."

"Maybe that's what I want. Did you ever think about that?" She twirls around the post, head back and eyes to the night sky. "It's our first night in Rome! I just want to enjoy it."

"Enjoy it in the daytime when you're sober, and we have our normal retinue of guards."

"Oh, my, God, Raf! You're going to drive me crazy." She tugs at the long locks of hair cascading down her shoulders. "I came here to escape, to finally have an ounce of freedom and you're making it impossible."

"I'm not here to cater to your whims, *principessa*. I'm here to keep you alive. Can't you understand that?"

She closes the distance between us and jabs a slender finger into my chest. "What good is being alive if you can't actually live?"

"It all trumps being dead." I bring my hands to her face, cupping her cheeks. I'm too close to her, but I can't stop myself. My head spins, a mad pounding in my skull a mixture of fury and the warm haze of wine. "Trust me."

She inches closer, her body flush against mine. Her tongue darts out, dragging across her bottom lip and a flare of lust widens her pupils.

Fuck.

My eyes latch onto hers, the fire building in those crystalline irises igniting something deep inside me. The most overwhelming urge to capture those pouty lips rolls through my entire body. Every fiber of my being screams to close the distance, to taste the promise of her breath mingled with mine, as the quiet Roman streets around us fade to nothing but the electric space between us.

Instead, I wrap my hands around her hips and haul her over my shoulder.

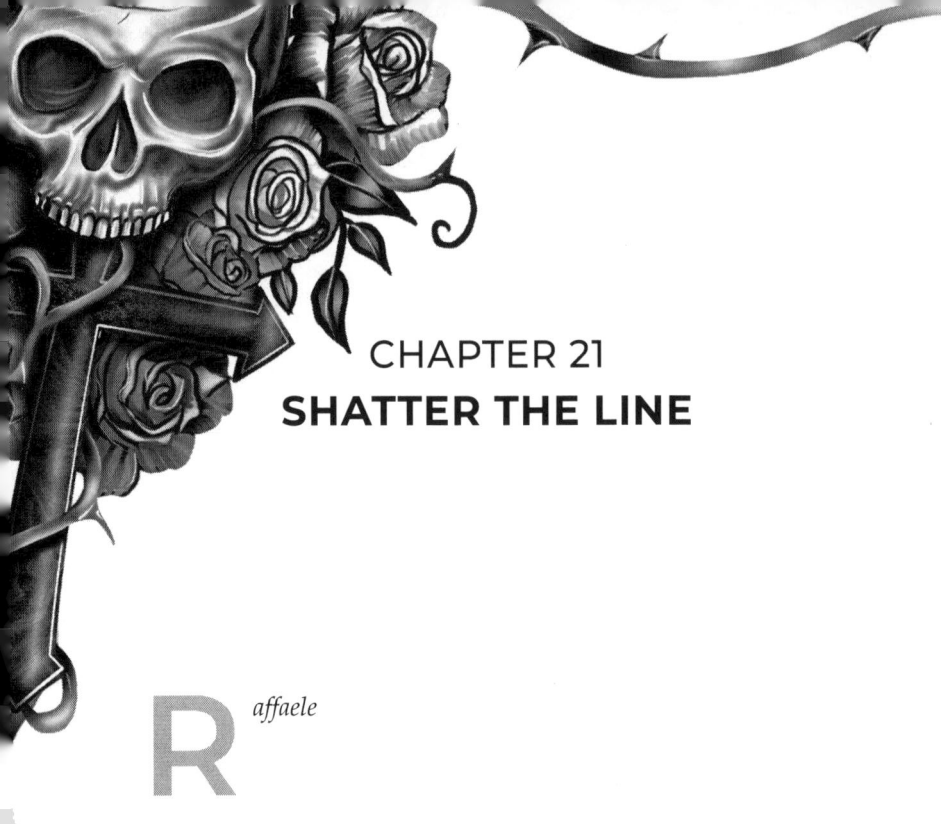

CHAPTER 21
SHATTER THE LINE

R *affaele*

"Put me down!" Isabella continues to pound at my back as we finally cross the threshold of the miniature hotel room.

"Gladly," I mutter and toss her onto the bed. She lands on all fours, her face crashing indelicately onto the pillow. After I'd been forced to call Sal to pick us up from the restaurant, I'd had to physically restrain her from running when we reached the *pensione*.

"I just want to see the Colosseo at night!" she whines as she glares up at me from over her shoulder. She's still on all fours, tight jeans wrapped around a perky ass that's just begging to be spanked.

Squeezing my eyes shut, I draw in a deep breath to slow the mad thundering of my pulse. Once the storm subsides, I open them again and my gaze latches onto a hair tie she's left on the nightstand. Dragging it over my hand, it just fits my wrist. I snap it, the slight pang like a bee sting. *Perfect.*

Hopefully, it'll be my answer to these damned inappropriate urges.

"We're going to be here for three months," I grind out. "We'll have plenty of time once I scope it out first."

"Ugh," she grumbles and rolls onto her back. Her fingers dig through a small pocket in her jeans, drawing my attention to a faint bulge.

"What's that?" I bark.

"Nothing." She slaps her hand over the spot.

"Isabella..." I stalk closer so that my legs brush hers which are dangling from the mattress. She crab-crawls backwards until she hits the headboard, and I follow her like a fucking idiot, crawling up the mattress until I loom over her.

Now pinning her to the bed and with those blazing blue irises peering up at me, the rage simmers, and I realize my monumental mistake. My cock is heavy, straining against my zipper as I brace myself over her. Isabella's pupils widen, her mouth curving into a tempting O as if she too has suddenly realized the compromising situation we've found ourselves in.

I attempt to push off, but her leg curls around my hip. "Stay," she whispers, the scent of limoncello swirling between us, and my heart halts mid-beat.

The word *no* is perched on my tongue, but for some goddamned reason I can't seem to set it free. I snap the elastic band around my wrist again.

"Isabella, I—"

Her gaze drops between the measly inches of space between our bodies and her hooded lids rise, along with the corners of her lips. Fuck. "Don't tell me you don't want this, Raf. I can see you do..."

I clear my throat, every muscle tense as I hover over her, fighting the urge to capture her lips and throw all my rules out the window. "It's a physical reaction, *principessa*, nothing more." I grit the words out, even as I feel the bitter lie in them.

Her head falls back on a cackle, and I stiffen over her. Once the laughter has finally died away, her eyes lock to mine once more. "So why can't this just be physical? I can barely tolerate you, and you've made your feelings about me clear. Just one night? To dispel the tension…" Her hand crawls up my torso, tracing the trail of abs then settles on my chest.

I'm so damned hard now I'm going to bust the zipper of my jeans.

Her free hand moves south, fingers dancing along my waistband so that her flesh touches mine.

Madonna, mia, I deserve to go straight to heaven for this. I snatch her hand away and pin it to the mattress. "No, we can't." The rough edge to my tone calls me out for the liar I am.

"Why?"

"There are countless reasons, *principessa*, but mostly right now because you're drunk," I growl, pissed at myself for getting into this situation.

"I am not." She rolls her eyes so hard only the whites show.

I release her hand then grab her ankle in an attempt to pry her leg off my hip. Her hold only tightens, and I'm impressed by her strength. And also, even more turned on. "Let go of me, Isabella. I don't want to hurt you."

She laughs again. "I'd like to see you try."

Now, it's my turn to chuckle. "If I wanted to, I'd have you incapacitated before you could blink."

"Wanna bet?" Amusement sparks across the brilliant blue of her irises. "How about this, if you can *incapacitate* me in under a minute, I'll never mention *this* again." She signals between us. "But if you can't, I get what I want."

"Which is what exactly?" My brow arches unbidden because this girl is just full of surprises.

Her shoulders lift, a faint crimson hue blossoming across her cheeks. "A much-needed release."

Cazzo, do I need that too.

Clenching my jaw, I consider the madness of this request. On the one hand, there's no way I don't win in this scenario. Maybe it will earn me some goodwill if I agree, and she'll be more amenable going forward. "Fine, you've got yourself a deal, *principessa*."

Placing my free hand between us as I continue to brace myself only inches over her, I motion to my watch. "Set the timer for sixty seconds."

She nimbly finds the app and hovers her finger over the start button. "Ready?"

"Always."

Her leg tightens around my hip, drawing me nearly flush against her. My cock rubs against her center, and I barely restrain a groan. Damn it. If only my hand wasn't occupied holding myself up, I'd snap that hair tie around my wrist again to control my maddening urges. Nothing like some negative reinforcement to rid myself of this highly inappropriate behavior.

She presses the button, and her other leg curls around my waist, then her ankles lock around me. Again, I'm surprised by the strength in her thighs, so much that I freeze for an instant. Then my entire body locks up when her hips rock up, rubbing against my cock.

"Hey!" I bark, "that's not fair."

"No one said anything about fair." She rocks harder, and fire surges at the tormenting friction lighting a blaze between us. "My Krav Maga sensei always told me there are no rules when it comes to escaping an attacker."

I lose precious seconds with this argument when I should be focusing on peeling her body from mine. Instead, my stupid thoughts are focused on finding a way to slip her pants off so I can bury my throbbing dick inside her.

"Stop that!" I hiss, and her stunned eyes meet mine. "I can't focus."

"What? The perfectionist bodyguard Raffaele Ferrara can't handle a little challenge?"

"This is cheating." I've never had to overcome lust and my traitorous cock when battling an assailant.

"Tick tock…" She eyes my watch as the timer counts down.

Merda, I cannot lose. Throwing my body to the right, I attempt to wrench myself free but she rolls with me, and we tumble right off the mattress. I hit the floor with a grunt, the tiny sliver of space between the bed and the wall barely wide enough for my shoulders.

Isabella straightens, straddling me triumphantly as the seconds continue to wind down. My hands clamp around her thighs, desperate to remove her as my cock strains against my jeans, shouting for her attention. I'm a second from prying her free when she starts to rock against me again, the tantalizing motion of her hips shooting fire from my dick, down my legs to the tips of my toes.

Cazzo, what is it about this woman?

I can barely stand her most of the time, but a few seconds of over-the-clothes action, and I'm like a horny teenager.

"Isabella…" It's meant to be a warning, but it comes out as a desperate, needy plea.

She rubs against me again, and a faint moan parts her lips.

Fuck…

Just like that, every last ounce of restraint dribbles away, and I *want* her to win. So I just lay there like a *stronzo* while she rubs herself against me, and the final seconds count down.

When the shrill sound of the timer goes off, her hips halt

their devastating circles and a shit-eating smile parts her lips.

"Told ya."

"Yeah, I'm the one that lost," I deadpan. I sit up, bracing myself on my palms. The new angle only drives my cock more firmly against her center and another breathy little sigh escapes. My guess, she's already halfway to an orgasm and embarrassingly, so am I.

Slowly, I lift my gaze to meet hers. "You won. Now what, *principessa*?"

The cocky grin falters as if the haze of alcohol has started to recede. She digs her fingers into her pocket and reveals a tiny bottle of limoncello.

Where the hell did she get that?

She pops the cork and downs the liqueur confirming my suspicions that her buzz was starting to wear away. After she swallows, she licks her lips and my damned cock twitches between her legs. "Just so that we're clear, this doesn't mean anything." She signals between us once more. "Since you won't let me leave the hotel room and we're stuck here together, I just figured we could have a little fun. It doesn't change the fact that you drive me crazy, and I can barely stand you."

"Damn, you really know how to turn a man on, *principessa*." A smug grin curls my lips. "And just so we're clear, you may have won the bet, but I will not be fucking you tonight." As badly as I want to…

Her victorious smile wanes, her slim shoulders slightly rounding. "But—"

I press my finger to her mouth because I already know where she's going with this. That pouty lip is a telltale sign. "I'm a man of my word, and I will give you the release you desire but fucking you, however pleasurable that may be for both of us, would go against every single one of my carefully thought-out rules."

"That's part of the reason I want to do it." A wicked grin slashes across her rosy cheeks.

"I'm not surprised."

"Then how is this going to work?"

"Simple, *principessa*. I'll guide you through it. I'll tell you where to position your fingers and exactly what to do with them." That rough edge is back in my tone as I imagine those dainty fingers sinking into her soaked pussy. I'm well aware this is such a tiny loophole in my rules, it's practically non-existent. Driving her to orgasm whether I do it with my fingers, my tongue or my cock is going to shatter the fine line I've desperately sought to create between us. I'm fucked, and I'm fully aware of it.

Lust flares in her eyes, and she reaches for the top button of her jeans.

CHAPTER 22
GOOD ENOUGH

Isabella

The warm haze of alcohol has nearly bled out of my system, replaced by the fiery lust consuming my lower half. Am I certain this is a monumental mistake? Yes. Will I undoubtedly regret it later? Also, yes. Will I stop the madness? Hell, no.

I draw the tight zipper of my jeans down, revealing a sliver of my lacey pink thong beneath. Raf's eyes become two pits of endless night as he traces the movement.

In spite of how much he drives me crazy, he's also sinfully delicious and this forbidden thing between us is only adding fuel to the sweltering fire. Not to mention the mere notion of compelling my stubborn bodyguard to break one of his precious rules is reason enough.

I'm fully aware I'm playing a dangerous game, but I can't seem to stop myself.

What if he *had* agreed to fuck me?

Would I really have wanted to lose my virginity in a crappy motel to a man who can barely stand me? That's a definite no. But a tiny part of me was banking on the fact that Raf would never do it. Despite his ability to drive me up a wall, he's a decent guy and honor is everything to this man. After a month with him, I'm certain of this, which is partially what made me run my mouth. That and the limoncello ravaging my system.

I'll never admit it, but he is right, those last two shots at the restaurant pushed me over the edge. But I'd had the entire car ride and fight with Raf to sober up. Enough, anyway. A slight buzz still surges through my veins and clouds the logic that would usually keep me from what I'm about to do.

"Ready?" Thick desire laces Raf's tone, and if I wasn't already soaked from the building pressure of his cock between my legs, I am now.

"Always." I echo his words from only moments ago.

A feral grin parts his lips, and his biceps strain as he braces his palms behind him, eyes locked to mine. "Give me your hand."

I hold it between us and his fingers wrap around my wrist, bringing my index finger to his mouth. He tugs it into his mouth, and his cheeks hollow as his tongue swirls around.

Oh, fuck...

When he's finished with that one, he takes my middle finger and repeats the spine-tingling process. An endless minute later, he releases my hand and positions it at the apex of my thighs. "Now, slip your index finger under your panties."

I do as I'm told for once in my life because the ache brewing between my legs is becoming impossible to ignore.

"Are you wet for me, *principessa*?" His pupils are so blown out, his eyes are nothing but endless spheres of black.

So of course I have to fuck with him. If he knew how badly I wanted him, his gigantic head would explode. "A little," I rasp. "But it could be from the cute waiter at the *trattoria*."

His eyes flash, a murderous expression carving into his jaw. "Doubtful," he grinds out. "Shall I check?" He lifts his thick middle finger and runs his tongue across the tip.

"No," I squeal before my traitorous mouth blurts the complete opposite.

"Now, find your clit," he whispers.

I find the swollen nub and nod slowly.

"Start circling with the pad of your finger. Do it lightly, like a good girl." He watches as my finger sinks inside me, raw emotion playing across the hard set of his jaw. "While you're doing that, take your other hand and slip it beneath your top. With two fingers coax your nipple into a hard peak."

I do as he instructs, and the pleasure begins to build and blossom, escalating my pulse. His scent invades my nostrils, the musky, amber fragrance a warm cloud around us. If I just close my eyes a little, I can imagine it's him, his finger instead of mine inside me.

"Good," he murmurs when a faint moan escapes. "That's my good girl."

Dio, I've always hated when men used that term, but with him it's hot as fuck. For once, I *want* to be his good girl.

"Now take your middle finger and slide it inside that dripping wet pussy while you continue to circle your clit."

I've never been so excited to do as I'm told in my entire life. This is certainly not the first time I've practiced self-care, but damn, it has never been like *this*. This is so beyond my normal realm of comfort.

"That's right, now fuck your finger and pretend it's my —" His jaw slams shut, tendon feathering beneath his five o'clock shadow. "Pretend it's whoever you want."

I want it to be him. The traitorous thought rises to the surface, but I keep it clenched between my teeth. Instead, I say, "hot waiter at the restaurant…" Because there's nothing I love more than riling him up. Despite that cool mask, I'm fully aware of the monster that lies beneath just waiting to claw its way to the surface. I recognize it well because I've been surrounded by powerful men with the same affliction. I dare say, I have my own beast I keep carefully locked deep inside.

A string of curses flees from Raf's thinned lips, and he bucks beneath me, attempting to stand. "Relax," I blurt. "I'm just messing with you."

"You should know better than to fuck with a man who's holding your orgasm ransom." The tension from his broad shoulders dissipates as that cocky grin stretches across the hard angles of his jaw.

"I'm pretty sure I could manage by myself just fine."

His hand closes around my wrist, stopping my movements. "Should we find out?"

"No," I whine as I grind against his cock, still rock hard beneath me. I'm fairly certain even if I didn't have use of my fingers, I could eke out an orgasm just from grinding against his hard length. "Can we just do this already?"

"Such a spoiled little mafia princess…"

A growl rips through my gritted teeth. "Fuck you," I hiss. Nothing pisses me off more than when he calls me that and judging by the stupid grin on his face, he's well aware of it.

"Oh, believe me, *principessa*, if you weren't my client, I'd bend you over the mattress and fuck you until you screamed my name. Your pussy would weep for my cock as I forced out orgasm after orgasm. You'd be walking like you just spent a week in the saddle after I was done with you…"

Again, his jaw snaps closed, as if he hadn't meant to divulge all the sinful thoughts he has about me.

Dio, if he knew I'm a virgin.

A chill skirts up my spine at the embarrassing truth. I would never admit that to Raffaele. He's likely been with countless women.

"Can we…"

"Yes, let's finish this." He presses my palm to my mound, keeping his hand firmly in place on top. His palm is rough and masculine, nothing like the handful of delicate NYU pre-meds I've hooked up with in the past. As he continues to exert pressure, he guides my fingers beneath my panties once more.

"In and out, in and out," he whispers, eyes fixed to mine. "One finger on your clit and the other thrusting in and out of that dripping pussy."

A moan escapes when he positions my free hand on my breast again, trapping it against his own.

"Feel how soft you are, how fucking perfect." The jagged edge to his tone only feeds the burning fire between my legs. "You're gorgeous when you're about to come, *principessa*. Your cheeks are flushed the most enticing shade of pink and your mouth is pursed into a perfect O…" He stops himself, but I can practically hear his thoughts. He wants my mouth on his cock and in this wild, forbidden moment, so do I.

The acceptance of the fact, even if it's only in my head batters my final walls of restraint. I feel my pussy clenching around my finger, and I rock my hips faster, harder.

"That's a good girl, come for me."

The corners of my vision darken with each ragged pant as a rush of pleasure crashes over me. My eyes close, finally free of Raf's penetrating gaze, and raw ecstasy pummels into me, wave after wave until stars dance across my vision.

"Fuck, Raf…" I groan as my head falls back.

His warm hands clutch onto my waist as I ride the swell

of endless pleasure. Never in my life have I had such a powerful orgasm. Not by myself and certainly not with any man.

With my legs still trembling from the heady rush, I finally force my eyes open and meet a pair of molten spheres of endless night. A satisfied smile tugs at the corners of his lips, and I'm fairly certain my grin mirrors his.

If he wasn't such a smug bastard, I might have thanked him.

"Was that the release you craved?" he whispers.

That and so much more. And still, as I feel him hard beneath me, it isn't quite enough. But this is a huge wall that came crashing down between us, and I know better than to push my luck. Not to mention the fact that once all the alcohol has left my system, I may be left with nothing but mortification in the morning.

"It was good enough." I shrug and zip up my jeans, then slowly fasten the button.

Raf clucks his tongue as he watches me, eyes wide, and I almost feel bad for him. Judging by his hard-ass cock, he's going to have a massive case of blue balls and without a private bathroom, let alone a private room, he's going to be shit out of luck. A wry chuckle breaks the building tension as he rises, adjusting himself. "That was way better than good enough, and you know it, *principessa*."

"Guess you'll never know." I plop down onto the bed and pull the covers down before crawling under them.

He watches me for a long moment before his gaze flickers to the door.

"Go shower, Raf. I'll be fine alone for a few minutes."

Indecision furrows his brow, and a long minute later he shakes his head. "It's fine. I'll wait until tomorrow."

I eye his tented crotch once more before burying my head in the pillow. Without looking up to meet his gaze, I whisper,

"You can sleep on the other half of the bed. I swear I won't try to take advantage of you in the middle of the night."

Another chuckle. "Don't worry about me, *principessa*. If you keep that up, I'll start to believe you actually care." A warm hand finds my forehead and tucks a few strands behind my ears. But with my eyes closed, I could have imagined it. "Goodnight, Isabella, sweet dreams."

CHAPTER 23
THE SAFEST OPTION

R*affaele*

Isabella's gaze is fixed on the bright pink blossoms dotting the shrubbery in front of her new apartment as I ring the buzzer. If the place isn't ready today, I'll lose my fucking mind. One night was bad enough trapped in that tiny space filled with her intoxicating scent. I would not be able to control myself for another one.

As it is, I'd broken one of my hard and fast rules. *Never get involved with the client.* Sure, officially, I hadn't touched her but it's a huge technicality. My life is all about control, precision, black and white, and already, I've strayed so far into the gray that the lines I once drew so firmly around my world are starting to blur and fade.

And what's worse, I want them to.

It's been a while since I've gotten laid, so yes, I'm hard up but it's more than that with Isabella. It has been from the start, which is what makes this so dangerous.

"No! Don't touch that," I shout as Isabella reaches for the pink flower.

Her eyes snap in my direction, and it's the first time she's met my gaze since last night. The usually chatty princess has barely said more than two words all morning. Does she regret last night?

"What? Why not?"

"Those are oleander blossoms, they're poisonous."

Her eyes widen as she scans the colorful bushes. "Then why is it blooming all over the place?"

"The flowers are indigenous to Rome, the locals know to stay away."

"So how poisonous are we talking here?"

"Even small amounts can be dangerous if ingested and can cause nausea, vomiting, diarrhea, even irregular heartbeats. In severe cases, oleander poisoning can lead to serious cardiac complications and even death."

"Okay, but I'm not going to eat it… It's just so pretty."

"Touching the plant's sap can also cause skin irritations and eye inflammation." Now I'm the one who sounds like a future doctor.

She snatches her hand back and tucks it beneath her underarm. "I still think it's a stupid idea to have them out in the open like this."

"Beauty often masks the deadliest of threats, *principessa*, like a rose concealing its thorns beneath velvet petals. You should know that." I offer her a wink, and she rewards me with a grin, the first one I've seen today.

The buzzer vibrates the air, unlocking the wrought iron gate. I push it open and step through, holding it for Isabella, then signal to Salvatore in the car to bring the luggage. Lively sapphire eyes grow wide as they scan the arched stone over our heads, adorned with decorative moldings and gold filigree. The walkway leads to a lush courtyard with a fountain in the center, two cherubs spouting water from their pursed lips.

Hedges of oleander and gardenias line the outdoor space, perfuming the air. Four doorways lead up to each of the wings of the classic Renaissance building. Climbing ivy decorates the ancient walls adding a touch of vibrancy to the old stone structure.

"It's beautiful," Isabella whispers as we walk to the doorway to the left, apartment two. The door whips open, and a little old man appears, whisps of white hair fluttering on a light breeze.

"*Benvenuti.*" He dips his head. "*Signorina* Valentino, *Signor* Ferrara, *benvenuti a casa*. My name is Ricardo, and again, I am sorry for the confusion yesterday." His accent is thick, grammar imperfect, but still, he attempts to welcome us in English. And I'm not surprised, considering Luca probably paid a shit ton of money to rent this place out for his daughter.

"*Grazie,*" she responds. "And please, call me Isabella."

"*Bene.*" He motions inside. "Come, I will give you the grand tour."

As expected, the apartment is luxurious, a blend of traditional Roman charm and modern elegance. The entryway is steeped in historical character with high ceilings, giving an airy, spacious feel to the room. Large, wooden-framed windows fill the space with natural light that offer scenic views of the bustling city on the eastern side and the lush quiet courtyard to our west.

After a quick tour of the modern kitchen, he leads us up a narrow, winding staircase as Isabella stares at every detail, completely entranced.

"There are three bedrooms on the second level." He points to the three doors and then the fourth and final one. "And the bathroom is over there."

Isabella saunters into one of the bedrooms that overlooks

the bustling city below, and I trail after her. An exposed brick accent wall adds a rustic touch to the sleek white of the chamber, the decorative crown moldings and trace ceiling accentuating its charm. "I'll take this room." She glances out into the hallway where Ricardo still stands. "Did we miss the bedroom downstairs?"

"No, *signorina*, there is no bedroom downstairs. Only three on this level."

I move toward the door just behind me and twist the knob. It opens into a second bedroom. Perfect. "I guess this one will be mine then."

"No way, absolutely not. *Papà* said I'd have some privacy, that it would be almost like we each had our own place."

Funny because that was not at all how Luca had described it to me. In fact, when I'd suggested adjoining rooms, he'd been thrilled. "Guess not." I shrug and march into the attached bedroom which is much like Isabella's only it faces the courtyard instead of out onto the streets. I'm not certain I love the idea that she's so exposed. Perhaps, I'll bring up swapping after Ricardo leaves.

"Unbelievable," she grits out and flops onto the bed.

"It's not what you wanted, *signorina*?"

"Oh, no, it's beautiful, Ricardo. I only wished for a little more separation between my guard and me."

"Ah, I understand." His knowing gaze flickers between us, and the hint of a smile curls his wrinkled lips. "Would you like to see the *terrazzo*?"

Isa pops up, her eyes alight once more. "Oh, yes."

"Come, follow me." Ricardo leads us up to the third level and opens the small arched door to the balcony. I have to duck to get out, but once I'm outside, my jaw nearly unhinges at the sight.

All of Rome is stretched before us, from the ancient columns of the Colosseum to the massive dome of St. Peter's

Basilica, the Pantheon's dome and oculus, the Roman Forum and Vatican Museums.

"Wow, *bellissima*," Isabella murmurs. "It's incredible." She walks toward the antique railing as she takes in the sights, mouth agape. "Forget my bedroom, I want to sleep out here every night." She signals toward the seating area with four lounge chairs, a table and a firepit.

"Not happening," I grumble.

She casts a quick glare in my direction before she circles the enormous space, scanning the view from all sides. Logistically, this will be a nightmare to secure. She's a sitting duck out here. I can already envision the princess sprawled across the lounger in a skimpy bikini pushing me toward a massive heart attack at the ripe old age of thirty.

Ricardo fills us in on the day-to-day information, housekeeping, trash pick-up and all the domestic mumbo jumbo. His words blur in the background as I create checklists in my mind, secure points of entry, and add to my list of protocols. Luca's team should be here shortly, and I need to ensure all my bases are covered.

Isabella's internship begins in only two days which doesn't give me much time to scope out and secure the hospital, *Policlinico Gemelli*. My guess is that Luca didn't share the extent of his security detail with his daughter. She's not going to be pleased when she sees the entourage of men stationed throughout her new workplace. But I didn't take this job to get her to like me, I took it to keep her alive.

And I would, no matter the cost.

"If you have any questions, I've left my phone number in the kitchen."

I blink quickly, returning my thoughts to the present as Isabella thanks the old man. After a hasty goodbye, he disappears down the steps and the *principessa* sinks into the lounge chair, stretching her long legs along the white cushion.

"I think I could get used to this."

"I wouldn't." I fold down onto the nearby chair and eye the adjacent rooftops. "We're too exposed out here."

"Relax, Raf, no one's going to try to kill me in Rome. No one even knows I'm here."

At least she's talking to me now.

The silence on the car ride over here was brutal. I'd much prefer her constant inane chatter to that. I feared there'd be consequences after last night, but it seems like she's simply going to pretend it didn't happen.

Which is fine by me.

It is the safest option for both of us.

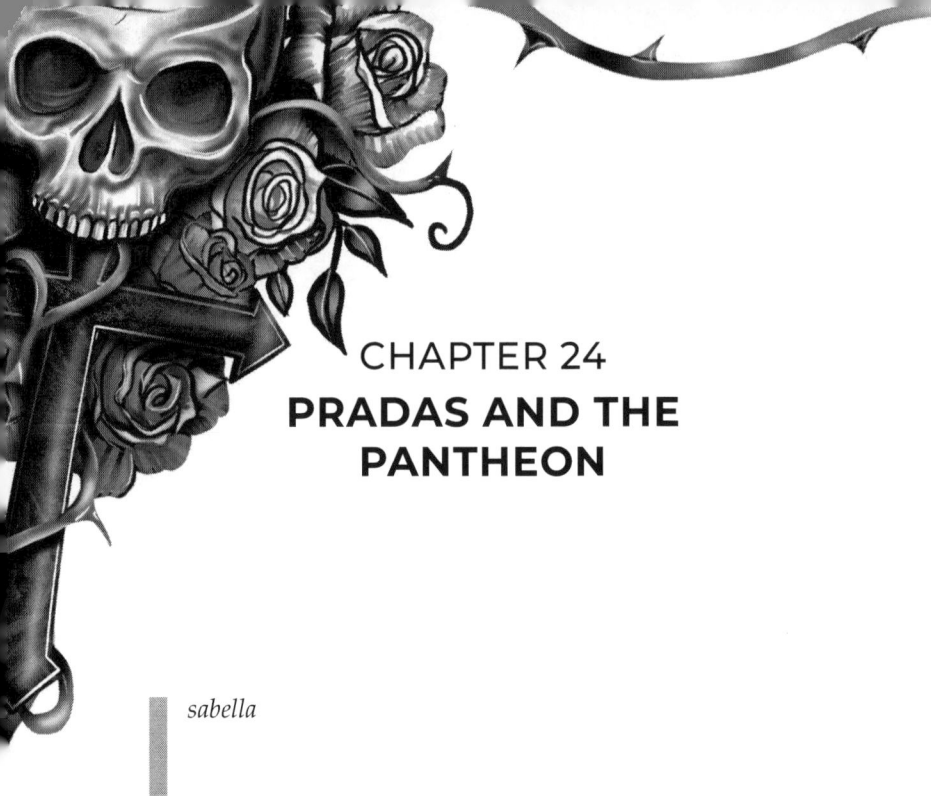

CHAPTER 24
PRADAS AND THE PANTHEON

Isabella

The first night in my new apartment in Rome was a success, despite the broody Italian in the adjoining room. But I refused to let Raf ruin my fun or my freedom. Tomorrow would be the first day of my internship and I vow to give it my all, which means today, I want to spend the day as a tourist, enjoying the historical sights.

I type out a quick reply to Serena and slide my phone into my back pocket. I've been texting with my cousin every day, but I have yet to tell her about the night at the hotel room. That feels like more of an in-person type conversation. She keeps promising to come visit, but we haven't quite settled on a date.

"Are you ready yet?" I call out into the hallway. I swear the man takes longer to do his hair than I do. He's been hogging the bathroom all morning. I guess it's true that you never really know a person until you live with them.

The adjoining door in my bedroom pops open, and I nearly jump out of my skin. "Damn it, Raf!" I screech. "What if I'd been naked?"

"I saw that you were dressed when I walked past your room a few minutes ago. You really need to focus on that awareness of your surroundings issue we talked about."

"I am aware. You just move like a damned jungle cat on the prowl."

A flicker of amusement lights up his dark irises, and instantly, I'm transported to the night at the *pensione*. The way his eyes bled lust as they watched me. The night I've banished all memories of and forbidden myself to think about. Ever. It never happened.

Dealing with it any other way is just too embarrassing. Clearly, I must have been drunker than I thought. What else would possess me to do *that* in front of *him*? Not to mention the fact I basically bribed him to do it. Any other man would have given into temptation and fucked me senseless, and I would've been drunk enough to go through with it. Then I really would've regretted the whole thing.

"Are you ready?" he asks, drawing me from thoughts that aren't supposed to exist.

"Yup, I just need my shoes."

"I've got that covered." He pulls out a pair of red sneakers from behind his back. My eyes go ridiculously wide as they land on the Prada logo along the side.

"You bought me designer sneakers? But how?" My thoughts whirl back to yesterday as we settled into the apartment. He never left my side for a second.

"I ordered them online and had Sal go pick them up this morning."

My heart staggers a beat, unexpected warmth filling my chest. My expression must show it because he runs his palm across the back of his nape, a rosy hue coating the warm caramel of his cheeks.

"It's nothing, *principessa*. Don't get all emotional or anything. I couldn't be seen walking around Roma with you in those hideous things." He ticks his head at my Hokas and all the warm and fuzzies vanish.

"Jackass," I mutter.

"Well, if you don't want them..." He hides the expensive shoes behind his back, and I lunge for him.

"I do want them!" I reach around him, encircling his waist as he steps back into his room. "Raf, give me the Pradas!"

"But I know how much you love those old, ratty things—"

"Raf!" I leap at him, sending us both staggering backward. He must have hit the end of the bed because the next thing I know he's falling and dragging me down with him.

We land in a heap atop the floral bedspread, my shiny, new sneakers trapped behind his back.

I pin the grinning *bastardo* to the mattress. "Hand them over."

"Only if you say please."

"Please, asshole."

"In Italian and drop the asshole part, *principessa*."

"*Per piacere*." I drag it out through my teeth, bastardizing the Italian with my best American accent.

He chuckles and lifts up, freeing my sneakers but also, rubbing his *hard* cock across my center. Heated, forbidden images of the night before flood my mind, and I freeze. He mutters a curse because he's clearly felt it too before snapping my hair tie around his wrist which he's commandeered as his new bracelet. And now I can't keep my gaze from dropping between us to his ever-hardening dick.

Merda, this man isn't human. How could anyone get turned on that quickly?

I scramble off and snatch my new Pradas before that heat pulsing at my apex reaches uncomfortable levels. He stands as I attempt to scurry back into the safety of my room, but steel bands lace around my bicep before I can get away.

"Wait." He spins me around, hauling me so close our noses practically touch. His musky, amber scent envelops me, forcing another round of memories from the hotel back to the surface. "Maybe we should talk about the other night…"

"No!" I squeal.

"Why not?"

"Nothing happened," I grind out.

His eyes flash, something unreadable streaking through the dark abyss. "Fine," he growls an endless moment later, and his fingers unravel from my arm.

"Now, let's just go for that walk, okay?"

He nods, and I skitter out of his room like a kid who got caught stealing candy from the grocery store. Why oh, why did I think getting drunk with my psycho bodyguard was a good idea?

The pitter-patter of cobblestones echoes beneath the soles of my new sneakers as Raf steers me down one of Rome's narrower streets, his hand light on my elbow. I can't decide if it's more to guide or guard, but either way, it chafes. Especially after that unfinished conversation I refuse to revisit.

"There," Raf says, nodding towards the Pantheon with its massive columns and domed roof standing proud against the sky. "Built by Emperor Hadrian around 126 AD. Originally a temple for all pagan gods."

I arch an eyebrow, glancing at him. "A bodyguard and a tour guide, Raf? Is there no end to your talents?"

He gives me a small, almost imperceptible smile like he's been doing all afternoon, the kind that doesn't quite reach his eyes. "I did say full-service security in my resume, didn't I?"

Laughing, I shake my head and let him lead me closer to the ancient building. "I'll keep that in mind." A whisper of heat streaks up my core at the full-service comment, but I shove it down and focus on the oculus overhead as we step inside. The sunlight streams through the circular opening, bathing the marble floors in a warm, golden light. "Imagine all the rain falling through there on stormy days."

"It couldn't have been pleasant. And still, did you know the great artist Raphael chose to be buried here because he was inspired by the beauty of the Pantheon? He said it was a fitting resting place for an artist."

I roll my eyes. "You made that up."

"Maybe," Raf admits with a shrug, "or maybe I'm adding to your dramatic story quota for the day."

I snort on a laugh. "The last thing I need is more drama in my life."

After we've circled the room, he leads me out the doors, dodging the dozens of tourists milling around the ancient rotunda. We've been walking all day, the history unfolding at my fingertips—complex, rich and utterly captivating. Much like my guard. And still there's so much left to see despite our speed-touring, so much about which I'm left wondering.

"The Trevi Fountain is next on our quick tour of the city."

The day has been a whirlwind, and we haven't even seen half the sights. We skipped the Colosseo and Vatican City because one could spend the entire day in either of those historical sites. Luckily, I'll be here for three months, and I'm hoping I'll have the chance for a little downtime.

My phone buzzes in my pocket, calling my attention to the unfamiliar Italian number. "*Pronto?*"

"*Ciao*, Isabella, it's Massimo."

Raf raises a curious brow, leaning over my shoulder. I

shove him off and move toward a quiet portico, away from the mass of tourists.

"Oh, yes, *ciao, professore*."

"Please, just Massimo, remember?"

"Right, of course."

"I just wanted to call and check in to make sure you were all settled in your new apartment?"

"Yes, it's all worked out. Thank you so much for that last minute accommodation. I really appreciated it."

"*Perfetto*. I'm in the center of town now, would you like to meet for a *caffè*? We can discuss your schedule before you start tomorrow."

I hazard a glance at my overprotective bodyguard who looms dangerously beside me. Likely listening in on every word. "That would be great, thank you."

"Where are you now?"

"Actually, walking toward the Trevi Fountain. I am spending the day enjoying the city."

"Good for you, Isabella. There's a café nearby where I could join you in about ten minutes. I'll text you the address."

"Great, see you then." I slide the phone back into my pocket and meet a pair of inquisitive eyes.

"Coffee with the professor?" Raf's dark brow arches.

"Yes. Is that a problem?"

"No, not exactly. I've already had all the staff of the university and hospital that you may have any interaction with checked out."

"Of course you did." I barely suppress an eyeroll.

"But I would prefer these sorts of outings to be pre-arranged so that I have the opportunity to have the location swept before your arrival."

"You're insane," I mumble as I pull out my phone. "Here's the address. I'm sure you can send *Papà's* goons ahead of us. I know they've been following us all day."

The ghost of a smile lingers at the edges of his lips. "Good girl, you've been paying attention."

Those two words and I'm back in that hotel room with his hand over mine as I finger-fuck myself into oblivion. *Damn it.* I squeeze my eyes closed, banishing the images, but when I finally open them, I meet pitch orbs and dilated pupils inches from my own. Clearly, I'm not the only one he's triggered with those two seemingly innocuous words.

Raf clears his throat and wraps his fingers around my upper arm, gone is the light touch on my elbow. He wants to show everyone around us that he's in charge, that I belong to him. The possessive hold is all at once infuriating and exciting. Because obviously, I've got issues.

A few minutes later, we arrive at the café, with the splish-splash of the iconic Trevi Fountain echoing just behind us. I make a mental note to come back so I can throw a penny in its mystical waters to be sure of a return to this magical city. Raf's fingers are still bruising around my upper arm as he leads me inside. An attractive man seated in the back stands, waving, and my guard's hold becomes punishing.

"*Ciao,* Isabella, *piacere.*"

My professor strolls closer with a warm smile. Dirty blonde tendrils of hair flop over his forehead, brushing his chic glasses. He's much younger than I imagined, probably around Raf's age. "*Ciao,* Massimo. Nice to meet you, too." He leans in and offers the traditional Italian greeting of a kiss on each cheek, and I can practically feel my guard fuming beside me. If he were a cartoon character, there would be plumes of smoke rising from his nostrils and ears. For some reason, the visual makes me snicker.

Raf leaps between us, extending a hand. "And I'm Raffaele, Isabella's bodyguard." Massimo winces as my guard crushes his slender hand in his big rough one.

"Raf," I hiss through clenched teeth.

"*Scusi.* Sometimes I don't know my own strength." He

finally releases him, and Massimo holds his battered hand to his chest.

"Not a problem," he mutters. "Of course *Signorina* Valentino's safety is of the utmost importance. Although, I am sure she will be perfectly secure here in Rome." Then he signals toward the table for two in the back. "My apologies, I didn't realize your guard would be escorting you."

"That's okay, he can stand." I shoot Raf a narrowed glare as we approach the circular table. It's the least punishment he deserves after nearly crushing the bones in my new professor's hand. "Right, Raf?"

"As you wish, *signorina*." He offers a savage smile before he pulls my chair out and plants himself behind it.

I settle into the seat and Massimo sits across from me, smiling pleasantly.

"You are going to love Roma, Isabella. I didn't know you were interested in the historical sights. I'd be more than happy to have my assistant arrange for a tour, and I would be honored to accompany you myself."

"Oh, thank you, that would be lovely."

"Wonderful, it's a date then."

Raf's hands curl around the back of my chair so his knuckles brush the exposed skin between the straps of my sundress. Again, that tension seeps from his pores clouding the air around me until it's so thick I can't breathe let alone focus on what Massimo's saying.

Oh, *merda*, what did I get myself into?

CHAPTER 25
A FRIENDLY WARNING

R*affaele*

I'm going to rip that fucking professor's eyes out if he doesn't control his wandering gaze. Since the moment Isabella arrived at the hospital this morning, he hasn't stopped staring at her. There are a dozen students in the program, but his flirty gaze remains locked on my client.

I press my arms tighter against my chest in a failing effort to restrain the mounting rage. Instead of focusing on him as he lectures the medical interns, my gaze pivots to Isabella. Her long, wavy hair is pulled into a ponytail, she's wearing minimal makeup and her favorite pink scrubs, and fuck, I get why the man can't take his eyes off her.

There shouldn't be anything sexy about scrubs and especially not paired with those brightly colored Hokas she's reverted to wearing for work. The standard uniform for medical professionals is usually oversized, with an unflattering coarse material, but on her? She looks tempting as all hell. The way those slinky pants cling to her ass, highlighting the perfect curves… If I were dying and she were my doctor, there'd be no better way to go.

Squeezing my eyes closed, I remind myself for the hundredth time to stop ogling my principal then snap the band around my wrist. I shouldn't have eyes on her, I should be scanning the perimeter for threats. Professor Massimo finally finishes his speech, and all the interns begin to shuffle around, dividing up into smaller groups of twos and threes.

Isabella rushes over, a beaming smile on her face. "I got the Pediatric ER! Just what I wanted."

"Congratulations. I'm happy for you." I force my mouth to slide into a smile. Of course the professor made sure she got her choice. The *bastardo* is doing whatever he can to win her over. After watching him flirt with her for over an hour at the café yesterday, his intentions were obvious, even if they weren't to Isabella. She's spent her life so damned protected she doesn't even realize when a man is clearly trying to seduce her.

"Then why don't you look happy?" She glares up at me, glossy lips puckered.

"I told you, I prefer to know these things in advance. Working in the ER means dozens of new patients walking in and out on a regular basis. It doesn't make for the best security scenario."

"Relax, Raf. No one is going to try to attack me while they're bleeding out. Especially not a kid."

I release a frustrated grunt as she spins away and follows two other interns down the sterile white hall. The halogen lights beam overhead, catching highlights in her dark hair as she moves. My traitorous gaze zooms in on her ass in those tight scrubs as she saunters a few feet ahead, swaying her hips at some invisible tune. One of the other interns, a guy from NYU, says something to her, but I'm too far away to catch it. Closing the distance between us, I move into step beside her.

The blonde guy glances up at me over Isabella's head and quirks a brow. I've already done a background check on all the students from the program prior to our arrival. I've also memorized faces and names.

"Don't mind him, Jeff, that's just my bodyguard," she explains. "He'll be following me everywhere."

"*Everywhere*," I grit out with a menacing smile.

Jeffrey Sanderson is from Tennessee. He graduated from Vanderbilt with high honors and was accepted to NYU Medical School only a few months ago. He comes from a good family, and so far, seems like a decent kid. But that doesn't mean I'll let this guy have free rein around Isabella.

The blonde offers me a half smile in return before they continue their conversation about molecular biology, and I zone out to focus on one of Luca's men standing at the end of the hall. Valentino doesn't mess around with his daughter's safety. He deployed at least a dozen of his own men on this little trip in addition to acquiring local help. They're working on a rotating schedule so that Isabella will have around the clock surveillance both at work and at home. Though I'll be the only guard staying inside the apartment, there will be a team stationed outside.

Isabella thinks it's overkill, but I appreciate the man's thoroughness. If I'd had a child, I would have done the same. Invisible strands of pain lace around my heart as the past attempts to surge to the surface, but I squeeze my eyes closed and tamp down on the rush of emotions. Losing someone you love has a way of changing your perspective.

I follow Isabella down another hall, the scent of disinfectant thick in the air. I've never been a fan of hospitals, the only times I'd ever been in one was to say my final goodbyes. That would not be the case this time around. I vowed to return Isabella to New York in one piece, safe and sound.

As we approach the entrance to the ER, a female doctor marches toward Isabella and the other two interns and begins yet another lecture. I take a step back, assuming my spot along the white wall. The main entrance to the emergency room is just behind the woman's back and another door is to her left, marked Pediatrics. The automatic doors glide open, jerking my attention over the doctor's shoulder as a dark-haired man strolls in.

My stomach bottoms out, hitting the soles of my shoes.

What the fuck is *he* doing here?

Bright green eyes flicker to mine before he ticks his head to the right, to a small alcove where the restrooms are. I slowly shake my head, but my stubborn brother sets his jaw in a tight line and motions to the same spot again.

With a huff of irritation, I press the com in my ear, and it crackles to life. "Aldo, I need coverage for Oleander for five minutes while I use the restroom." If I wasn't so pissed I would have chuckled at the new code name I'd come up with for Isabella inspired by the beautiful and deadly blooms that grow throughout the city.

"Sure thing, *capo*." The reply comes back almost instantaneously. Aldo has been with the Kings nearly as long as Tony. Both men are well into their fifties, but surprisingly fit considering their age.

Aldo emerges from the shadows an instant later and takes my place along the wall a yard from where Isabella stands, attention captured by the female doctor who is to be her mentor for the next three months. I don't bother to interrupt to inform her of my temporary absence. Instead, I circle around them and skulk toward the recess in the wall where the restrooms are tucked away.

I shove through the door of the men's room and lock it behind me. When I spin around, my gun is already clenched in my fist as I meet those familiar jade eyes. Despite it having been ten years since I've seen them in person, in some ways, it feels like only yesterday.

"What the fuck are you doing here, Giuseppe?" More importantly, how did he know where to find me? How to find her?

He holds his hands up, a spark of amusement in his light eyes as they lance over my gun. "Relax, *fratellino*, I come in peace."

I holster the weapon and take a minute to really look at my older brother. Those eyes, that quirky smile, they remind me so much of *Mama* my chest tightens. I don't often allow myself to think of her. She was taken from us much too young. Fucking cancer. Then I remember Giuseppe abandoned me, taking *Papà's* side when everything went to hell and grind out, "So why did you come?"

"A friendly warning that your return to Roma hasn't gone unnoticed."

"*Cazzo*," I hiss. "How did you hear?"

"Antonio has an inside man at the *Guardia di Finanza*. You know how important their role is in border control, particularly in preventing and combating financial crime and smuggling activities." He smirks. "*Papà* must have had your name flagged years ago." He steps forward, the grin twisting into something darker. "He's not the only one with insiders in the government, Raffa. You have to be careful…"

My thoughts flicker to the past, then I nod quickly, anxious to return to Isabella. "Thanks for the heads up." I start for the door, but a question nags at me. Spinning around before I reach the exit, I blurt, "What did *Papà* say about my return?"

Giuseppe swallows, his Adam's apple jogging down his throat. "We haven't told him yet."

I stand there for a long moment, the silence thickening between us. "It's probably better that way," I finally murmur.

"I'm going to monitor the situation, Raffa. If it becomes an issue, I'll have to tell him."

"Do whatever the fuck you want, Beppe." It feels strange, using the nickname we came up with as kids, but if he insists on using mine then so will I. For some reason, it feels like it levels the playing field. "You made your decision long ago."

He makes a move toward me, but I unlock the door and grip the handle, wrenching it open before he can get the words out, if he had any.

My father's betrayal was one thing, but both of my brothers? It fucked me up for a long time. Hell, maybe I'm still screwed up because of it.

I slam the door behind me and march out into the hallway, the steel bands around my chest relenting the moment I catch a glimpse of Isabella safe and sound, standing right where I left her.

CHAPTER 26
A FULL-SERVICE GUY

Isabella

The warm summer sun bores down on my bare shoulders, and I draw in a breath, forcing myself to enjoy this moment of peace. The first week at *Policlinico Gemelli* raced by in a rush of sleepless nights, endless cups of espresso and adrenaline. Every day swept me further into a whirlwind of raw emotions and a relentless pace. Even today, on my first day off, the staccato beeps of heart monitors echo through my mind, each one a reminder of the stakes.

My hands, once unsure and tremulous, moved with a purpose I didn't know I possessed a week ago. The small, trusting faces of my patients both break my heart and bolster my resolve; their resilience in the face of pain teaches me more about bravery than I could have imagined. I've barely had time to reflect, caught up in the immediacy of blood draws, comforting scared children, and decoding doctors' orders on the fly.

Despite the exhaustion that creeps into my bones day in and day out, a sense of fulfillment anchors me through the chaos. I know I am exactly where I'm meant to be. The thought is sobering and all together terrifying.

I draw in another breath and flip the page of the romance novel I've been pretending to read on the rooftop balcony for the last thirty minutes, but the words all blur in the swirl of thoughts ravaging my mind.

Would nine-year old Marcello be able to play *calcio* again after that broken leg?

And what about twelve-year old Graciela? Would that hole they found in her heart lead to another stroke?

All the patients' anxious faces tumble through my mind and their parents? *Dio*, speaking to them is the worst. As interns, we don't do the talking, but we are still forced to stand there and observe. To see their faces crumble, tears spring to their eyes, when the prognosis is bad, is pure torture.

My entire life I'd wanted to be a doctor, to heal instead of harm, and now, the reality of it is finally settling in. Would I be strong enough to endure it?

"What's wrong, *principessa*? That vein across your forehead is dancing the tango." The asshole smirks from his lounge chair, only exacerbating my annoyance as he tips his sunglasses up to perch atop his messy locks.

On a positive note, he completely distracts me from my existential crisis. "Shouldn't you be monitoring the perimeter?" I bark. "Since when do you ever sit down, let alone relax?"

"Today is my day off."

My eyes nearly bulge out of my head. That would explain the glistening abs and swim shorts. I've been trying my hardest not to ogle his perfect form, but I'd be lying if I said I hadn't been sneaking in little covert peeks whenever I have the chance. Besides the carved muscles, I've noticed at least a dozen scars. Bullet wounds, long since healed-over gashes from blades and who knew what else? *Dio*, what has this man been through?

In all the months since Raf started working for me, he's never taken a day off. And now I feel like the asshole because it never even dawned on me until this moment.

He ticks his head over his shoulder to a guard in all black standing by the door that leads downstairs. "Aldo will be covering for me today."

I eye the familiar man with the long nose and silver strands glistening through his dark hair. He's been one of *Papà's* men since before I was born. "Then why are you still here?"

He shrugs. "What can I say, I'm a work-a-holic."

"Obviously."

"So will Aldo be accompanying me to the party tonight?"

"What party?" He shoots up from the lounge chair and the seatback drops with a clang.

"I told you all the interns were meeting up for an aperitivo tonight."

"Shit," he mutters as he reaches for his phone. "I have it in my calendar for tomorrow night."

"The infallible Raffaele Ferrara made a mistake?" I gasp dramatically. "It cannot be!"

"It's this time zone difference, it's screwing up my calendar."

"Whatever you say." I shoot him a teasing grin because it's so rare to see him flustered, and I just can't help myself.

"Doesn't matter, I'll be escorting you tonight." He stretches back out across the lounger, and I can't help my eyes from trailing over the canvas of ink across his chest and the rippling muscles beneath. Since we've been living together, I've become intimately acquainted with his grueling workout routine. It's no wonder the man is sculpted like a Roman god.

Despite his best efforts at training me, my body is nowhere near his perfection.

"It's really not necessary," I finally squeeze out once I've unglued my eyes from his torso. Another night out with my wickedly tempting bodyguard while drinking sounds like trouble.

"It's fine, I can take a few hours off tomorrow to make up for it."

"Oh, good since I'll have my date with Massimo then."

He releases a string of curses that has Aldo flinching from the corner of my eye. "Never mind," he grits out. "I don't need the time off." He sits up again, resting his forearms on his knees. Despite his attempt at cool and collected, his foot is twitching, vibrating all the way up his muscled thigh. "Do you really think it's a good idea to get involved with a professor, let alone the the head of the internship program?"

"I never said we were getting involved," I bite back. I only used the word date to rile him up.

"Well, it's clear he wants to fuck you."

This time the gasp that slips out is entirely real. Not that I didn't notice Massimo flirting, but I hadn't expected Raf to be so blunt about it. "How would you know?"

"Because I'm familiar with the look." Those dark eyes raze over my bikini, drinking me in inch by inch. I squirm beneath that heated stare, squeezing my thighs to keep the unwanted surge of heat at bay.

"And what if I want to fuck him too?" The question spills out because apparently, I don't have an ounce of common sense or a sliver of self-preservation.

"Careful, *principessa*," he growls, deep and low under his breath so Aldo can't hear.

"What? You said you had all the students and staff checked out, so he's safe right?"

"Safe to be within your presence with me at your side."

He leans closer, scooting to the edge of the chair. "Not for his cock to be anywhere near you."

"Is my father paying you extra for this?" I hiss, matching his stance at the edge of the lounger. "Did he tell you not to allow me to date?" My father's overprotectiveness I've grown to expect and understand even, but my bodyguard's? This is just too much.

Mom knows about my virginal status, had she told *Papà*? Worst, had he told Raf? Oh, *Dio*, I'd die of mortification if he'd been sent to protect my purity.

"He didn't say it in so many words, no…"

"But?"

"But protecting you means keeping you safe from all of it, Isabella. I've told you before, I'm a full-service kind of guy."

"So are you going to fuck me then too?"

Aldo's wide eyes snap in our direction, and a rush of heat blankets my cheeks. *Shit*!

"Yes, of course, I'll tuck you in, too, Bella," Raf practically shouts in the guard's direction. Aldo's expression visibly calms, and he resumes his pacing of the rooftop's perimeter. Then Raf fixes his wild eyes on me, nostrils flaring. "Are you trying to get me fired?" he snarls. "You'll be on the first jet back to Manhattan, if you do."

"What good is being here if I can't do anything?"

"What do you mean anything? You go to work every day, I'm letting you go to the damned party, and I'll even let you go on your date with that snobby professor. But I'm with you at all times."

I shake my head, irritation heavy on my brow. "It's not fair, Raf. I deserve to have some sort of privacy." Lowering my voice still more I whisper, "And a sex life."

He heaves out an exasperated breath, dragging his hand through his hair. "You're going to be the death of me, you know that?"

"But what a way to go, right?" I toss him a smirk before settling back into the lounger and burying my nose in my book. I need to hook up with someone tonight, anyone to get Raf out of my head.

The twinkling lights of Rome reflect off the smooth surface of the Tiber River as we approach the designated meet-up spot, RiverBar. As the name suggests, the open terrace overlooks the river, offering stunning views of the water and the cityscape beyond. I'm so entranced by the beautiful scene, I pay little attention to the grumpy guard beside me.

He steps ahead of me, holding the door open and the swanky bar stretches out before me with artistic light fixtures and exposed brick walls. The atmosphere buzzes with energy, a familiar energy I haven't felt since that night at The Velvet Vault. For an instant, I'm transported to Manhattan, to my cousin's bar, huddled beneath the table as shots pepper the air.

Squeezing my eyes closed, I push back the dark memories of what comes next, refusing to drown in the pools of blood tonight. *Dio*, I miss them, my brother Vinny, Serena and Matty, even Alessia and Alessandro… They may drive me crazy, but there's nothing like family.

"You okay?" Raf's breath skates across my ear, jerking me to the present. He leans in, and a single finger laces around my own. The darkness recedes in the space of a heartbeat, his presence offering a depth of comfort that surprises me.

"Umhmm," I murmur, my eyes dropping to our entwined fingers. All this time and I've never mentioned that night at the club. Did he remember the few words we'd exchanged before the chaos began? One day I'd ask.

"Isabella, over here!" A familiar voice lifts my gaze to the archway behind the bar and the outdoor seating area. Massimo motions us over to a cluster of high tables and large comfy sofas right along the riverbank.

Raf unwinds his finger from my own, shifting his hand to the small of my back. With a gentle nudge, he steers me through the doorway. The outdoor seating area is a chic arrangement of minimalist furniture and subtle lighting coupled with smooth beats from the DJ, creating an inviting ambiance.

Massimo strides toward us, and I can visibly see Raf tense, from the sharpening of his jaw to the narrowing of his eyes and the sudden broadening of his stance. "*Ciao*, Isabella, so glad you made it." Despite my bodyguard's murderous glare, my professor nears, delivering the infamous double-cheek kiss. *Brave man.*

A deep growl vibrates the air, and it sounds like it comes from the darkest pits of hell, but judging by the ripple in Raf's throat, the animalistic snarl must have come from him.

Massimo laces his arm through mine and Raf's hand slips from my back and winds around my waist, anchoring me to his side. My professor tugs, but I'm trapped against a wall of unyielding muscle.

"Raf!" I hiss.

Instead of releasing me, he moves forward begrudgingly so that I'm now wedged between the two males like a damned chew toy.

Yeah, this is going to be fun…

CHAPTER 27
THE DEATH OF ME

R*affaele*

This *pezzo di merda* is going to die an excruciating death if he doesn't stop eye-fucking my client. I stand beside Isabella as the eager *professore* regales the interns about his thrilling new research project on immunotherapy. She watches him mesmerized, as if every word that falls from his mouth is pure gold. If he's such a damned good doctor, why isn't he a practicing physician?

"Ah, there you are, Carlo." The professor pivots his gaze to the young man approaching from my right.

I'd caught a glimpse of him an instant before from my peripheral. He doesn't look familiar which has my hackles raised. He's not from the medical internship program, and he's not on staff at the *Policlinico*, so who the hell is he?

"Students, I'd like you to meet my new assistant, Carlo Piemonte. He went through the same program at the hospital a few years ago."

The guy looks like he could be Massimo's younger brother with the same trendy wire-rimmed glasses and conservative button-down shirt and skinny jeans. Only where the professor has dark golden hair, his assistant's is a shade lighter. The young man is also a little taller with a slighter build. I yank my phone out of my pocket and shoot off a text message to Aldo with the guy's name. I need a background check ASAP. If Isabella will be spending time with Massimo, then his assistant must be cleared as well.

As all the students exchange pleasantries with the newcomer, the hair on the back of my neck prickles when he reaches his hand out to Isabella. "*Piacere.* A pleasure to meet you." Luckily, the contact is brief. Maybe because I'm glaring at the *coglione*, and he has an ounce of sense, unlike his mentor. "I hope your stay at the *pensione* was okay?"

"Oh, yes, thank you for arranging that, Carlo." Isabella gives him a sweet smile, the one she reserves for strangers in polite conversation. It's guarded and doesn't quite meet her eyes.

Thankfully, Carlo moves on to the next intern, and his arrival has put an end to the professor's monologue about malignant melanoma. Isabella's eyes flicker to mine as I watch the lanky assistant move through the crowd of students to join his mentor, Massimo.

"What's so funny?" she whispers.

"Nothing. I'm smiling because I'm glad it's over."

"Massimo's speech might be over, but the night has just begun." She lifts her flute of prosecco and clinks it against my sparkling water.

"As long as there are no more rousing speeches on the efficacy of the professor's novel immunotherapy in treating advanced melanoma, I suppose I could tolerate this get together a little longer."

"Don't be an ass," she growls under her breath. "That's important research he's conducting."

"I'm not saying it isn't, but does he really have to brag about it for over thirty minutes?"

A grin ghosts over her lips, and despite her best efforts, I coax out a smile. "It's interesting…"

"If you say so, *principessa*."

With an eyeroll that has my palm twitching, she gulps down the remainder of the prosecco and turns toward the bar. "I'm getting another."

"Do you think that's wise after last time?"

Her cheeks blush a tempting crimson, and my cock stands at attention at the hypnotic sight. I can't help my thoughts from wandering back to the night at the hotel, to the flush of her skin, to the curve of her lips, and to the stars that danced across her brilliant sapphire eyes as she came.

"Probably not," she counters, "but this time, I'm sure I'll find a willing participant." Her lips slide into a feral grin. She's provoking me, and I know it. But I'm too mesmerized by those pouty lips and sparkling eyes to stop myself.

I lean closer, so close, my nose brushes the shell of her ear. "You know very well I would have been willing if the circumstances were different."

Her eyes meet mine, darkening and defiant. "But nothing has changed, has it?"

I grind my molars, clenching my jaw before I snap the hair tie around my wrist. "No," I grit out. "I am your guard, and you are my client. If I am to work at the highest level of my ability, the lines must remain between us. My duty above all else is to keep you safe."

"Then I'll just have to find someone else to see to my *other* needs." She spins away, swaying that ass so provocatively that I'm biting my tongue to keep from running after her.

Fuck, there's nothing I want more than to be the one to satisfy her needs. I dream about sinking my cock into her pussy nearly every night now that we're under the same roof. I'd never admit to her how many evenings I spend lingering at our adjoining door just listening to her soft breaths as she sleeps.

Worst, it's becoming more than just a physical need. I've always been possessive over my clients, but what I feel for Isabella goes above and beyond. I don't even know how it's possible since she drives me insane, and most of the time I can't decide what I want more –to kiss or strangle her.

I watch her every movement at the bar, every twitch of her lips as the bartender tries to flirt. The girl is gorgeous, no doubt about that, but it's the air of confidence coupled with a touch of naivety and her refreshing youth that makes her truly attractive.

One of the other interns moves toward her, the blonde guy from NYU she frequently chats with. Jeff. He's just gathering his nerve to ask her out, I can feel it. Time to put an end to that.

I stalk up to the bar, downing the rest of my water so at least I have a reason to be there. Not that I need one. I'm her damned guard, right? Standing at the far end of the counter, I order another water and keep one eye on Isabella and Jeff.

She's fucking giggling. The guy is not funny. I've listened in on enough of their conversations to be certain of that. Damn it, is Isabella that desperate to get laid or does she really like this guy?

I'm not sure I want to know the answer.

Movement across my peripheral catches my eye and I drop my drink, twisting my head over my shoulder. A shadow slides behind the bushes of oleander that encircle the outside terrace. It could be one of the wait staff, or even a patron taking a piss outside to avoid the long lines of the bathroom. Or…

I press a finger to the com at my ear. "Alberto, do you have eyes on the east side of the building?"

"I can't see anything from where I am, but I'll move closer."

The hair at my nape prickles, and I reach for the gun at my hip as I move beside Isabella. My pulse quickens, my breaths instinctively coming faster. I find that practiced calm and draw in a steadying breath. Cool, collected and in control.

"Right, Raf?" Isabella's voice cracks my self-imposed composure.

With one eye still on the periphery, I turn to face her. "What?" I snap.

Her brows knit, a hint of hurt flashing at my brusque tone, but I can't explain myself right now. "I was just telling Jeff that the view from the rooftop of my apartment is the best in the city."

I grind my teeth together to keep from biting her head off. There could be a dangerous situation in the making, and she's still worried about getting laid. "Yes," I hiss.

"I'd love to come by and see it." A smarmy smile crawls across Jeff's face, and I clench my fingers into a fist, nails cutting into my palm to keep the string of curses from seeping out.

"Tonight probably wouldn't be the best night, right, Isabella? You have that date with Massimo tomorrow. You don't want to be up too late and keep your professor waiting." I offer the guy a shit-eating grin.

Isabella glares up at me, sky-blue eyes shooting daggers. It's not my job to help her get laid, and I don't feel even a tiny bit badly about that cock-block. She whirls at Jeff, shaking her head. "It's not a date. Massimo offered to take me on a tour of the city. And we're not going until later in the afternoon so you're more than welcome--"

That sixth sense, the one I've honed over the years sends alarm bells ringing. My head swings to the right an instant before I see it. The muzzle of a rifle peeking through the foliage of the deadly oleander.

"Get down!" I shout as I lunge for Isabella.

A loud, piercing bang cuts through the chatter the instant we hit the ground. I cover her body with my own, draping myself over her so that not an inch remains exposed.

"Are you okay?" I whisper-shout over the chaos.

"Yes," she breathes.

Confusion clouds the air as a second shot rings out, more distinct this time. Panic ensues. People scream and duck under tables, glasses shatter on the ground, and chairs are toppled as everyone scrambles for cover. The music that filled the air with rhythmic beats is abruptly silenced, replaced by the chaotic sounds of a crowd in terror.

"I'm going to get you out of here. Just stay calm," I shout over the commotion.

"Okay."

I drag her closer to the bar, positioning her against the impenetrable brick. Once I'm certain she's safe, I pull my gun out and point it around the corner. I can just make out a figure behind the bushes. The bullets continue to whiz through the air, a steady chorus beneath the screams and cries.

Pressing my finger to the com again, I shout, "What the fuck is happening out there, Alberto? Put this *bastardo* down."

"Sorry, capo, we couldn't get around—"

"I don't want excuses, I want the asshole dead."

"On it."

"Raf!" Isabella's cry sends my heart leaping up my throat. I spin around and see her crawling out into the open.

"What the hell are you doing?" I lunge for her and jerk her back a second before another bullet speeds by.

"Jeff's been hit." She points at the intern huddled

beneath a table, his hand pressed to his stomach. "We have to help him."

"You aren't going anywhere until the shooter is down," I growl.

"But I can help him!"

"And die in the process? Fuck no."

"Then come with me!"

"What good am I to you, if I'm dead, too?"

"Raf, please! I can't just leave him there." Her eyes are wide, pleading, and fuck me, I can't say no.

"*Cazzo*, Isabella, you really are going to be the death of me."

CHAPTER 28
HOLD ON

Isabella

Adrenaline rushes my veins as I crawl toward Jeff with Raf draped over me. It makes our movements painfully slow trying to move in unison with the barrage of bullets spraying the air.

"Stay down and stay close," Raf growls in my ear.

"I am. You're literally on top of me. How much closer do you want?"

A devious grin twitches at the corner of his lip, but it's gone before I can fixate on it.

"Just keep moving," I hiss. I'm cursed. There is no other explanation. How is it possible that I can't even have one night of fun without all hell breaking loose? And in Rome? Which of my father's enemies even knows I'm here?

I fix my gaze to Jeff, the pallid green of his complexion and the sweat beading his brow, and my heart wrenches. And now he's paying the price… I'd been stupid and selfish to think I could come here and there'd be no consequences. As the damned Kings' mafia princess, I didn't get to have normal, even across the whole damned Atlantic Ocean.

When we finally reach the table Jeff's huddled beneath, Raf pushes me under the tablecloth and arranges the two chairs in front of us like a makeshift barricade.

"Bella... what's happening?" he mutters.

"I don't know, but you're going to be okay," I whisper as I take his hand. "We all are."

"The bullet penetrated my abdominal cavity," he rasps out. "If it tore through my stomach, it could create a hole, leading to leakage of stomach acids and partially digested food into the abdominal cavity, which can cause severe inflammation and infection."

I press my palm to his flushed cheek and do my best impression of a reassuring smile. "Relax, Jeff. Now is not the time to be regurgitating textbook material. I'm going to do my best to stop the bleeding, then they'll tend to the wound when we get you to the hospital. You're going to be okay, I promise." I ignore the tremor in my voice and inhale slow, measured breaths to decrease the manic pace of pulse.

"I don't know..."

"I do, so just hold on."

The sharp rip of fabric tearing sends my heart leaping up my throat before Raf hands me a strip of white cloth he's stolen from the table. He's already ripping through another one with his teeth. "Wrap this over the bullet wound and around his waist to slow the blood flow."

"Right." I should know this, damn it. What kind of an emergency room doctor am I going to be if I get flustered in the chaos?

I draw in a deep breath and focus on all the years of studying, the endless labs and countless tests. I can do this. *Assess the situation, stabilize the patient, control the bleeding, prevent infection...* My professors' words echo in my mind.

"You got him?" Raf asks, eyes wild but voice as steady as a surgeon's hand. Damn it, why can't I be like him, so cool and collected?

I nod with an assuredness I do *not* feel.

"Good." He turns around in the cramped space and points his gun through the hole in the tablecloth. "Now, I'm going to make that fucker pay for daring to hurt what's mine." His words are hissed through clenched teeth, so low I'm not certain I hear him right.

A chill skates up my spine at the venom in his tone. I should be insulted that he just referred to me as his possession, but instead, only warmth fills my chest. Turning my attention back to Jeff, I squeeze his hand. "It's almost over. Raf's got this."

Jeff's head lolls back, lids sliding closed, as he leans against the table leg. I put more pressure on the wound. Blood blossoms over the white fabric, and anxiety eats away at my insides. He can't die… not another life I'm responsible for. Please, *Dio*, no.

Above the sound of my racing heart and whispered prayers, sirens begin to wail in the distance, growing louder as they approach.

Another shot rings out, this one closer, so damned close, my heart catapults up my throat. "Got you, *bastardo*." Raf twists his head over his shoulder, and those piercing eyes meet mine. "It's over."

My throat tightens, emotion clogging the airway, and hot tears prick my eyes. A spiral of emotion tangles in my gut, a thousand words stuck at the tip of my tongue. I want to thank him, I want to leap into his arms and let him devour me until everything else falls away.

Instead, I only nod and mouth a lame, "Thank you."

I pull the blanket up to my chin and curl into the overstuffed cushions of the sofa as I surf through Netflix's suggestions, none of which seem even remotely enticing. After a long shower and an hour-long call with Serena that left me blubbering, I planted myself on the couch in my pjs and haven't moved since. After the adrenaline surge from earlier, I'm exhausted, but I can't seem to get myself to sleep.

Every time my heavy lids dare close, fear snaps them wide open. I'm vaguely aware of Raf's presence drifting between the living room and kitchen, but he hasn't spoken much since our return.

I'm torn between wanting to be alone and craving his company, his comforting warmth and quiet steadfastness. He shuffles across the kitchen, and my lids slide closed. Then the slam of the microwave has my heart vaulting across my chest.

"Geez, Raf," I growl.

He saunters toward me, wearing only low-slung sweatpants, and carrying a heaping bowl of popcorn in one hand and balancing two mugs in the other. I'm suddenly wide awake again and can't seem to rip my eyes away from the expanse of perfectly tanned skin of his muscled torso. "Sorry," he whispers as he drops the items on the coffee table then folds down beside me. "Were you asleep?"

"No, I can't." I push myself up to a half sitting position and force my eyes up. "Did you find out anything about the shooter?"

"Not yet. Unfortunately, corpses tell no tales." He hands me the mug, scooting closer, an uncharacteristically wary look in his eye. "Hot chocolate?"

"Seriously?"

He shrugs. "Yeah, why not? It always helps me sleep."

"*You* have trouble sleeping?"

"When you've seen the things I have, *principessa*, you learn that nighttime isn't your friend. In the darkness, the deepest shadows stir, releasing the monsters that lurk within." He points at his temple, then his chest.

"It's a good thing I've got you to keep the monsters at bay then." I offer him a rare smile and inch closer. Most of our discussions are so combative I hardly allow myself to relax around him without the snark.

"I'm trying, *principessa*, but you sure don't make it easy."

"What fun would that be?" I angle my body toward his and take a sip from the mug. It's surprisingly delicious. "With such a talented guard at my beck and call, I figured you'd enjoy a little challenge."

"I'd enjoy it if my principal didn't crawl through a tornado of bullets to save some guy she wants in her pants."

"Ouch," I mutter. "That's not why I went—"

He lifts a hand, an appeasing smile settling over the hard line of his jaw. "I know it's not, but the fact that you want him doesn't make it any easier."

I take another sip, drawing courage from the sweet warmth in the mug. Or maybe I've just lost all common sense after being shot at for the umpteenth time in the past few months. Staring death in the face over and over again has a way of messing with your mind. And how much restraint am I really expected to have when this man, who's built like a Roman god, flaunts his perfect body around the damned apartment every day?

"Maybe it's because I can't have the man I really want..." I leave the remainder of the sentence hanging in the charged air between us.

His eyes latch onto mine, a torrent of emotions streaking beneath the impenetrable darkness. A sexy cross between a growl and a groan vibrates his throat, rumbling his powerful chest. He starts to snap that elastic around his wrist like mad before he slowly shakes his head, clucking his tongue. "I— we really shouldn't—" Still his hand creeps closer beneath the blanket until the back of his hand grazes my thigh, just below the hem of my soft sleep shorts. Rough knuckles skate across my skin, raising a host of goosebumps in their wake.

"No one would have to know," I breathe and reach under the blanket to position his hand across my upper thigh. His eyes widen, something like fear pulsing through those expressive irises.

That familiar ache blossoms at the mere thought of those fingers slipping beneath my panties. Only this time, I want *his* fingers inside me, not my own.

"It doesn't have to mean anything." Even I can hear the lie in my shallow words. I just hope he can't. As exasperating as Raf can be, there's no one I've ever felt safer with. His possessive streak is borderline psychotic, but sometimes I can't help but wonder if there's more to it.

"Ah, *principessa*," he whispers on an exhale, his lips only inches from my own, "how could it not?" And still his hand remains planted where I left it.

I tip my head forward so our lips barely touch. He remains perfectly still, so still I'm not certain he breathes until I sit back, defeated.

Maybe he doesn't want me… had I imagined it all?

"You know what? After the night we've had, fuck it." He tangles his hand in the hair at the back of my neck and his mouth captures mine with the urgency of a storm breaking, fierce and unrestrained, as if he's pouring every unsaid word into the kiss.

And all I can do is hold on.

CHAPTER 29
A BAD IDEA

R*affaele*

This is such a bad idea. A monumentally terrible, fucking idea that I am going to regret tomorrow, but I can't seem to stop myself as I drag Isabella into my lap and palm that perky ass like I've dreamed of. So much for the damned hair tie and negative reinforcement. Her naturally heady scent combined with that perfume she uses with traces of gardenias and sweet strawberries is all consuming. She's straddling me, rubbing up against my cock in those silky sleep shorts.

Dio, she feels perfect against me, the soft curves of her body yielding to the hard planes of my own. I dig my fingers into her ass, driving her against my cock and she releases a faint moan.

"Let it out, *principessa*, I want to hear every tempting little sound. If I'm condemning myself to hell for one night, let's make it worth it, eh?"

Her head bobs, and she grinds her center cross my arousal. "Just one night…" she murmurs against my mouth. "It doesn't have to mean anything."

Maybe it won't for her, but for me, this is breaking a cardinal rule, and what the hell am I without my rules? What kind of an effective bodyguard can I be if I'm more concerned with sinking my cock into my client than focusing on securing the perimeter?

"A one-time thing," I hiss as she captures my bottom lip. "And we never let this wildly inappropriate lapse in judgement happen again."

"Umhmm. Never."

"It's just the adrenaline, the shock of the shooting…"

"Right." She drops kisses across my jaw, moving toward my ear then she nibbles on the sensitive lobe, and goose bumps ripple down my arms. She reaches between us and cups my cock. "Damn, Raf, you're so hard already." She starts to stroke me over the thin material of my sweatpants, and I'm suddenly like a fucking teenager about to explode.

This woman's hold on me is like nothing I've ever experienced before. She's got me completely feral for her pussy. Before I come on the spot, I reach for her tank top and draw it up and over her head, forcing her hand off my cock. Fuck, no bra. A smile races across my lips, and I'm certain I'm grinning like an idiot. Her breasts tumble free, and I've never seen anything more beautiful. "*Cazzo,*" I whisper before I devour the delicate pink bud with my mouth, and her back arches against me, a moan spilling out. "*Sei bellissima.*" Her cheeks burn the most enticing crimson when I call her beautiful, and she buries her nose at the crook of my neck, licking and sucking. She's the most exquisite woman I've ever laid eyes on, and I cannot wait to see all of her. I'm torn between the desire to take my time with her to enjoy every minute and the burning need to drive my cock inside her sweetness.

I haven't even touched her yet, and I can feel her wetness through my sweatpants. She's soaked for *me*. My hands grip her hips, sliding beneath the waistband of her shorts and find bare cheeks beneath. *Merda*, no panties, either? This woman is going to be my ruin. That skin-on-skin contact has my dick rock-hard, and my fingers aching to sink inside her. Wrapping her legs around my waist, I rise and spin around, dropping her onto the couch and settle between her thighs. Then I fall to my knees and drag her shorts down her long legs.

I pause for an instant, taking her all in, and she visibly tenses at my scrutiny. "Don't do that," I whisper. "Don't hide from me. You are a goddess, and any man would be privileged to admire your beauty."

"Raf…" She laughs, a rosy hue coating her cheeks again. I can only imagine how she'll look when I coax the first orgasm from those pouty lips. "You're so cheesy."

"What? It's true. I should've known never to say yes to this job because I'm too damned attracted to you. Ever since I saw you at the club—" Shit. That wasn't supposed to come out.

"The club?"

Muttering curses in my head, I dip my chin. "The night your bodyguard was shot. I was there—"

"I know." A lopsided smile stretches across her face. "I mean, I remember you too."

The truth is, after that night, I simply couldn't get her out of my head. But she'll think I'm completely insane if I tell her. Not to mention the fact that for that reason alone I never should have gone after this job.

"I'm glad I left an impression."

"Me too."

And now, it's time for a subject change. My hands close around her thighs and draw them apart so I can take her in. She's so wet, her pussy glistens beneath the dim lights.

"You're gorgeous. I know it and you know it, *principessa*. And now, I want to know how you taste." I dip my head between her legs, my eyes fixed to hers. The vivid blue sparkles with excitement as she traps her bottom lip between her teeth.

I slowly run my tongue across her center, tasting her, memorizing her. I keep my eyes locked on hers, to take in the curve of her lips, the flush of her cheeks and *Dio*, it's so damned sexy. "Mmm, wet and ready for me, *principessa*, just how I like it. If only you were this obedient in all aspects of our relationship."

Her eyes narrow as she regards me. "Fuck you…" A playful smile curls her lips.

"You're about to."

She wriggles beneath my heated gaze, and I run my free hand up her torso to pin her to the couch. "You're not going anywhere," I murmur against her clit.

Her hips buck at the vibrations and I only work harder, twirling my tongue around the sensitive collection of nerves.

"Oh, Raf…" she moans, her head falling back against the cushion and finally severing our connection. "Fuck, is there anything you're not good at?"

A deep chuckle erupts, my warm breath spilling across the light smattering of dark curls. She gasps and her hands find my head, fingers running through my hair. She can barely contain herself from shoving my mouth into her needy pussy. I can feel the barely restrained pressure on my scalp.

So I give her what she wants, and I devour her.

Thrusting my tongue inside her, I fuck her hard and fast, licking and sucking as my finger circles her clit. I can feel her orgasm building as her breaths come more quickly, and she tightens around my tongue.

"Are you ready to come for me?" I remove my tongue for a second, but I replace it with two fingers and thrust deep inside her. Fuck, she's so tight. My cock is so damned hard it hurts as I imagine her wrapped around me.

"Don't stop." Her fingers curl around my hair, drawing me to her apex. "Please, don't stop. I'm so close."

"Oh, I'm just getting started, *principessa*. After this, I'm going to have you coming on my cock. I can't wait to feel that tight pussy of yours around my dick."

She lets out a gasp, cheeks flaring crimson.

"What? Has no one ever dared talk to the mafia princess like this?" I thrust my fingers deeper, curling to find the spot. Her pussy walls tighten around me, trying to wring out her pleasure.

She shakes her head, biting down on her lip.

Shit, did I go too far? "Do you like it?" Damn, why do I sound so flustered? I've never cared what a woman liked or didn't like in bed. I took what I wanted, fucked as I pleased, and was never nice about it either.

"I think I do," she finally whispers a long minute later. "I never thought I would but—"

I drop down between her thighs again and fuck her with my tongue. She tastes like heaven, like my redemption and salvation all rolled into one. My hand reaches up to find her breast, kneading the soft, delicate skin as I coax her nipple into a hard tip.

She groans again, fingers diving into my hair. "Raf, I'm going to come."

"Good girl…" I purr against her swollen clit. "Come for me, baby." With one final thrust of my fingers and a flick of my tongue, she unravels.

And *Dio*, I was right, the sight of her coming undone for *me* is enough to ruin me, body and soul.

I remain perfectly still, watching her as the waves of pleasure roar through her, brighten her eyes, flood her cheeks and make her squirm in delight. Her chest rises and falls in a rapid rhythm, her breasts bouncing with each ragged inhale.

My cock strains against my sweatpants, a second away from breaking through the flimsy barrier.

That pussy is *mine*.

Just one taste and I've claimed it.

No one will ever have her again.

Even through the haze of lust, I know how illogical I sound. I promised myself and her this would be a one-time thing. After tonight, I can never let this happen again. I just need to get her out of my system. One time and I'll be good, back to one hundred percent dedicated guard duty. And still, the idea of another man daring to touch her... *Dio*, it makes me want to strangle someone.

Once the heady vibrations subside, Isabella's body goes slack against the couch, a satisfied smile relaxing her typically tense expression. "That was—"

"Amazing? Incredible? Life changing?" I offer a smug grin.

"Unexpected." She throws me a smirk in return.

"And we're just getting started..." I shove my sweatpants down, taking my boxers with them in one go and my cock springs free. I nearly groan from the sudden freedom after being trapped by the constricting material.

Isabella's eyes dive down to my erection, and her eyes widen to perfect pools of endless blue. "That is not normal," she hisses out a long minute later.

Sometimes I forget my dick is larger than most. When I was a teenager, it was all I thought about when I found myself in locker rooms with other guys. Did I brag about it back then? Of course. But now I am a grown ass man and don't often measure my cock against other men. It's only when I find myself in situations like these that it becomes obvious. Some women actually find it intimidating.

By the look on Isabella's face, she's one of them. Her eyes are so wide, her brows nearly reach her hairline, and her mouth is curved into a capital O. No, this is more than intimidation, it looks like pure terror.

CHAPTER 30
STUPID AND DESPERATE

sabella

Any delusions of losing my virginity to Raf go right out the window when his cock is freed from his sweatpants, hard as fuck and enormous. There is no way in hell. My poor virgin vagina would be impaled by that thing.

I draw in a deep breath, forcing my pounding heart to regulate after that mind-blowing orgasm. And here I was thinking I was ready for more. Not only is it an incredibly stupid idea to have sex with my bodyguard but to let him claim my V-card is idiotic. And now that I've seen that dick up close and personal, I realize it would also be incredibly painful.

"Are you okay?" Raf's heated gaze searches mine, and now I feel like a total asshole.

He just had me coming like a porn star, and I need to return the favor, but there is no way that *thing* would fit inside me. I'd need to have sex with a few normally sized guys first.

Raf drops down in front of me, and I finally realize I haven't answered him. Midnight eyes sear to mine, an unreadable expression darkening his entire countenance. "What's wrong?" he whispers.

"Nothing." I make a big show of heaving in a breath. "I just needed a minute to recover."

A genuine smile flashes across his face, and fuck me, that rare glimpse is beautiful. Raffaele Ferrara is typically all business, dark brows furrowed, jaw set in a hard line, eyes intent on whoever or whatever has his attention, but that soft, unguarded smile is completely disarming.

"So, are you ready for more?" That wicked grin sets his dark eyes ablaze, like a thousand stars across a night sky. "Because if that had you breathless, my cock will have your heart stop." He wraps his hand around his impressive length and beads of cum glisten on the tip.

My tongue slides out, running across my lips as I imagine tasting him, and another swell of heat races below. But I swallow down the desire and smirk up at him. "Pretty cocky, aren't you?"

"It's not arrogance if it's true." He offers his hand and pulls me up off the couch, then tosses me over his shoulder. "Now let me prove it to you."

I barely make out the words as I squeal, hanging naked over the broad expanse of his shoulder. "Where are you taking me?"

"To my bed. I need more room if I'm going to fuck you properly. And like I said before, if we only have one night, we're doing it right."

A thrill of excitement races up my spine, momentarily drowning out the terror of that freakishly large cock. Maybe I can do this… vaginas are meant to stretch. It's a biological fact. And Raf's right. This could be our only chance if we stick to our stupid promise of one night.

Why the hell did I agree to that again?

Because you're stupid and desperate and want Raf so badly. My internal voice sounds an awful lot like my cousin, Alessia. So weird. I must be missing my family more than I thought.

A second later and we're already upstairs, rushing through the door to Raf's bedroom. We're moving so fast it feels like he's sprinting. Damn is he in good shape. He drops me onto the mattress and crawls over me, the fire in his eyes enough to burn down the entire city of Rome. His cock is heavy against my thigh as he settles his hips between my legs, and a raging firestorm streaks down to my lusty pussy. Never mind the fact I'm still buzzing from the last orgasm, but somehow, she's ready for more.

Stupid, greedy vagina. She has no idea what she's in for.

His lips capture mine and just like before, I'm lost in the moment, in the fire that consumes me from his touch. Raf's crazy sense of control and striving for perfection extends to every part of his personality. Even now as he's kissing me, he's putting everything of himself into it, just like he did when he devoured my pussy.

He works his way from my mouth, down my jaw to the column of my throat and the sensitive skin at my collarbone. He's everywhere, his tongue, his hands, his cock. He's like a starving man feasting on every inch of me, and damn, I've never felt so utterly adored.

I also feel kind of guilty because I haven't returned the favor at all. Besides pawing at him and reveling at the hard planes of his muscled back, I haven't reciprocated his heated touch. So I slide my hand between us and find his hard length. My petite hand can barely close all the way around him. *Cazzo*, he's like pure steel wrapped in silk. How something could be so hard and soft at the same time is a paradox I'll never understand.

Just the feel of him in my hand, his heat, his throbbing head has me all worked up again. As if Raf can feel it, he slips his finger through my wet folds, and my hips start to move beneath him.

Those piercing midnight orbs lock on mine, the rush of desire blowing out his pupils. "Are you ready for me, *principessa*?" He thrusts his hips, grinding his cock against my palm. "Because I don't want to come in your hand. I want to come in that wet, tight little pussy."

Well, damn, it's a good thing Serena suggested the pill before my trip, and better still that I actually listened to her advice.

But still, I don't stop stroking him.

A groan flees past his lips, eyes still locked to mine and damn, it's one of the hottest things I've ever seen. To see this powerful man at my mercy is intoxicating, it's beyond satisfying. No one brings Raffaele Ferrara to his knees… but me.

With his moans urging me on, I flip him over onto his back, and I'm more than surprised when he allows it. I crawl down his body with his heated gaze fixed to mine. Molten lava spews from those bottomless irises as I flick my tongue out and lick the bead of cum on his tip.

It's salty and sweet, with a musky flavor that's all Raf.

Taking all of him in my mouth alone is intimidating, but I have to try, a test of sorts. I wrap my lips around his thick crown, and a hiss echoes between us. "Oh, *cazzo*, Isa, that mouth," he groans.

I cup his balls, also enormous, and attempt to take more of him in. I'm not even halfway there when his head hits the back of my throat.

"That's it, *principessa*, you've got it. That's a good girl, you're almost there. I know you can take my whole cock in your mouth."

Apparently, I have a praise kink because heat is licking down my thighs at each sexy word. Hot tears burn my cheeks as I take him in deeper, but damn it, I need to prove that I can do this. I don't even understand why. Once my jaw relaxes, I'm nearly there. I start to twirl my tongue around his head and use my hand for the final few inches I can't quite swallow down.

"Good girl," he purrs and props himself up on his elbows to watch me. "*Merda*, you look so beautiful with my cock in your mouth. I could watch you all day."

I'm not sure what's come over me because I'm preening like a fucking peacock at his wicked praises. I've *never* been talked to like this. It has my feminist streak bristling, but my traitorous pussy is loving every second.

"Come closer." He reaches his hand out and cups the hollow between my thighs. "I want to feel how wet you are while you suck my dick."

I should be offended, but instead, I'm so turned on I only grind up harder against his palm.

"Do you like how I taste?"

I nod as I dive deeper, on a mission to fit him all in without gagging.

"Imagine how good I'll taste once I've been inside you."

Heat flushes my cheeks and surges straight down to my clit.

"Have you ever tasted yourself?" He drags his tongue across his chin, which still glistens with my arousal, and groans. "You will before this night is over. I can still taste you, and fuck you're so sweet, *principessa*. Better than that Nutella you can't get enough of. Just one taste and I'm hopelessly addicted."

His fingers delve into my hair, running through the wild strands, and he exerts a little pressure. Not enough that I'm gagging on his enormous cock, but I do feel his tip against the back of my throat.

"That's a good girl, you've got this. You're doing so well." He cups my cheek, dark eyes glinting as they regard me. "*Dio*, you're going to be my utter undoing."

I was thinking the exact same thing. This is only supposed to be one time, but how can I ever go back to before this? Now that I know what he tastes like, felt his heart crash against my own chest, seen the fire in his gaze as he watches me, nothing will ever be the same.

We can never go back, and we were stupid to believe otherwise.

And if I let him fuck me, that'll be it.

You know what they say about a girl always remembering her first time. It can't be with the man who's supposed to put his life before mine.

"I'm going to come if you don't slow down," he rasps.

"It's okay," I mumble against his dick. "Just do it."

He sits up, dark brows furrowed. "I'm not saying I won't be able to go again after, but—"

"It's not happening," I blurt around his cock.

"What? Why?" He pulls out and sits straight up on the bed. A string of saliva dribbles from my mouth, and a different sort of heat coats my cheeks. So fucking embarrassing. As if this moment isn't bad enough.

There's no way I'm admitting I'm a virgin, and I'm scared of his ginormous cock and more importantly terrified of getting attached to him.

"It doesn't matter. Do you want me to suck you off or not?"

Something like hurt flashes across those dark eyes, and his jaw stiffens. "That's not what I want, Isa… This isn't just about getting off."

"Then what is it about?" I grab the comforter from his bed and wrap it around myself, suddenly all too aware of how naked I am. "You said it yourself, it was a one-time thing, an outlet for both of us. So why does it matter how you get to the orgasm?"

His lips press into a tight line and that tendon feathers in his jaw. The fingers of his left hand clench into a fist as he starts to snap the tie around his wrist with the other. I can feel the anger roiling through him. Only I have no idea why he's so pissed. "You're such a fucking brat," he hisses and jumps off the bed. "I knew this was a bad idea. You're nothing but a child."

I gasp, red hot mortification surging up my neck. A slap in the face would've hurt less. "Fuck you," I grit out as tears threaten. He stalks out the door, that unfairly perfect ass clenched, and I tighten the blanket around myself, racing to the adjoining door to my bedroom.

What the hell just happened?

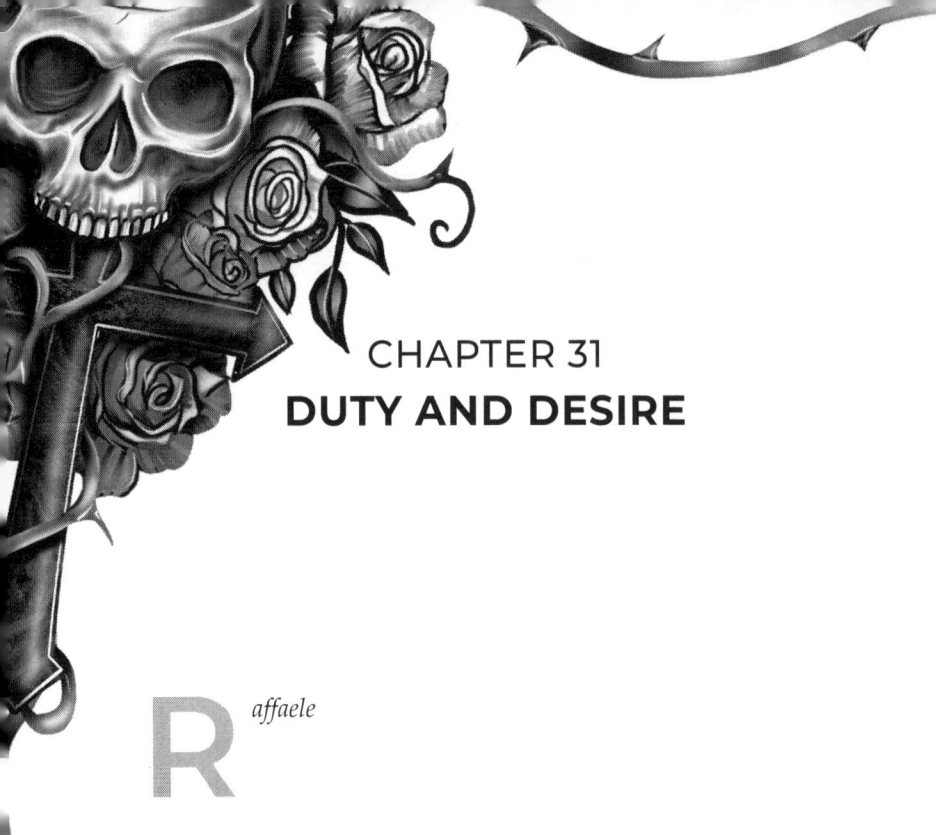

CHAPTER 31
DUTY AND DESIRE

R*affaele*

As we walk through the immense gates of the Colosseum, the grandeur of ancient Rome engulfs us, its history echoing through the vast, open air. But I can't even enjoy it, not fully. I scan the area instinctively, noting exits, potential threats, and the distances between us and other groups. But even as I perform my duties, my attention splits—mostly because of Massimo and that stupid smile on his face as he stands way too close to *my* client.

Fuck, even in my head the term feels wrong. It doesn't encompass an ounce of what Isabella has become to me. Even now, pissed and confused as all hell about last night, I can't keep my eyes away from her.

"Imagine the spectacles that once filled this arena, Isabella," Massimo says, drawing my attention to the pair as they saunter through the dim corridors. His voice is rich with passion, and it only pisses me off more. He paints a vivid picture of gladiators and roaring crowds, and I can almost hear the clash of swords and the shouts of thousands.

Damn him for being such a good storyteller.

Isabella's eyes light up with each word, her fascination clear, and I'm jealous, so damned envious that it's her professor getting to share this moment with her. This is *my* city, and she's *my* client. She moves closer to him, hanging on his every word. Occasionally, their hands brush, and though each touch seems casual, it grates on me like sandpaper. It's hard not to see every accidental touch, every smile between them as a calculated move by Massimo.

Dio, I will strangle the *bastardo* if that hand brushes her ass one more time.

My role demands invisibility and silence, traits I've mastered over the years, but today, it feels impossible. Not after last night's shitshow. After I stormed out like a *coglione*, I paced the block in front of the apartment for hours. I never dared roam too far, even with two guards stationed inside with Isabella and the usual three along the outer border of the apartment building.

I'd clearly lost my mind snapping at her like that. She didn't owe me anything, not a blow job, not sex. I'd been dying to taste her pussy for months; I did it because I wanted to, not because I expected anything in return. But in retrospect, I'm sure that's how it came off.

No, the real reason I freaked out is worse still.

I was fucking hurt.

Hurt that she thought so little of that pivotal moment between us.

I fully realize how insane that sounds since I was the one that insisted this would never happen again, but *Dio*, it was so much more than I ever could have imagined. Kissing her, touching her, tasting her, it was everything.

Over the past few months, Isabella has become so much more than just my principal. Every day, she peels back another layer—showing her resilience, compassion, and genuine nature—and it's slowly breaking down the professional walls I thought were solid.

Watching her now, laughing in the soft afternoon light with Massimo, something inside me starts to change. It's not just about duty anymore; it's about a deep need to keep her safe. Not just from the obvious dangers, but from anything that might dim that bright light in her eyes. Her happiness, her safety, it's become part of what drives me, and it's completely unsettling. I'm beginning to realize that my feelings for her might be the one thing I can't protect myself against.

The good professor and Isabella continue on to the next alcove, and I follow behind them, trying my damnedest to focus in spite of the suffocating rage. Every muscle in my body is tense, and my jaw is clenched so tightly I'm sure I could crack a tooth. I stay close, always watching, always ready, but today the threat feels personal, and it's infuriating.

As they wander slightly ahead to a quieter section, Massimo leans in to whisper something to her, his words clearly meant only for her ears. The intimacy of the gesture is like a shout, and I ball my hands into fists, fighting the urge to physically remove him from her presence.

Isabella must be paying more attention to me than she's pretending because she glances back, her lips pulling into a pout. Realizing I probably look like a psycho, I force my features into a neutral mask and focus on a detailed carving on the wall. "*Signorina*," I start, using her title to remind her —and myself—of our respective roles, "these markings here tell stories of great Roman victories, each one a chapter in the history of this city's glory."

Isabella joins me in the little nook while Massimo remains behind to continue reading the ancient text. The moment we're alone, I'm filled with the most overwhelming desire to pin her against the wall and—. No… Shaking my head free of the heated delusions, I delve into a discussion about historical strategies and the empire's legacies instead. Anything to refocus my thoughts. The professor isn't the only one with knowledge of this great city. *Ha!*

She watches me, carefully, a hint of awe in her expression, and satisfaction surges all the way to the tips of my toes. Because clearly, I'm a child. For a moment, I'm just her guard again, discussing, not defending. But the tension doesn't fully dissipate. It simmers under the surface, a silent standoff between duty and whatever the hell is developing between us.

Nothing is developing, *coglione*.

Last night was a mistake, a monumental, gigantic error.

As soon as we get back home, I have to apologize. Neither of us was even drinking so I can't blame it on alcohol, which would have made the whole awkward conversation that much easier. Instead, I have to suck it up and admit the truth.

Whatever that is...

As we continue the tour, I can't help feeling like a gladiator myself, caught in an arena forced to endure a battle with my own self-restraint. Every time Massimo looks at her or touches her, I find myself reaching for an invisible sword. If I could, I'd run him through with it like one of those ancient Roman warriors. Here, in the shadow of Rome's most famous battleground, I'm reminded that not all wars are fought with swords—they are sometimes silent, fought in the depths of one's own heart, under the weight of duty and desire.

We finally wind around the entire circle and find ourselves at the exit. Thank, *Dio*. Bloodied half-moon marks line the inside of my palm from the restraint it took to keep from shoving Massimo off my client and into one of the fighting pits.

"Well, that was amazing, Massimo. Thanks so much for

the guided tour." She's beaming at him, like he hung the fucking moon.

"It was my pleasure. But the night is still young, Bella. Would you like to have dinner with me?"

"Nope, sorry, not going to happen." I step between the pair, shaking my head. "All locations must be vetted by my team beforehand."

Isabella opens her mouth to likely rip me a new one, but Massimo cuts in. "Oh, come on, Raffaele, it's a small little trattoria on the outskirts of town. Isabella will be perfectly safe."

"That's what we thought about the *aperitivo* the other night and look what a disaster that turned out to be." I bristle and tower over the idiot, meanwhile cursing myself because we still know nothing about who was behind that shooting.

"That was an isolated incident. I've never seen anything like that in my ten years at the *Policlinico*."

"Well, Isabella's life is my responsibility so I'm sure you'll understand why I don't take my duty lightly." Glaring at him, I inch closer to Isabella, and I'm surprised she doesn't scoot away. She hasn't spoken more than a word to me since last night.

"How is Jeff?" Isabella blurts, cutting through the rising tension. "Have you visited him at the hospital yet?"

Massimo nods. "Yes, I went this morning. He's recovering well from the surgery. You did everything right last night in caring for the wound, Bella. I am very proud of you."

"*Grazie.*" Her cheeks flush that rosy hue that has my thoughts instantly flying to the night before. "Anyway, I'm still pretty exhausted from the adrenaline rush of last night so let's do dinner another night, okay?"

"*Si, certo*, of course I understand." He leans in and kisses her on both cheeks, and I barely restrain the growl building at the back of my throat.

As relieved as I am about not having to endure dinner with these two, I'm also dreading the talk we're about to have. Whatever this thing is between us, I must nip it in the bud or else my performance will suffer and ultimately Isabella will pay the price.

And I would never let that happen.

The quiet car ride was bad enough, and now here we are lumbering around the apartment in an even more charged silence. Isabella plucks a take-out menu from the fridge, reading through the assortment of pizza though I know damned well she's already memorized every item on the pamphlet. It's our go-to pizza place.

"You hungry?" I call out.

She doesn't even spare me a glance, only continues to stare.

Isabella gets the same thing every time, the Pizza Prosciutto e Rucola which is more of a salad than a true pizza if you ask me with all that arugula on top. She continues to stare at the menu, avoiding my gaze so I step closer. Still not a twitch in my direction.

"Do you want me to order something?"

No response.

Finally, I step in front of her and snatch the little flyer right from her hands.

"Hey!" she squeals.

"Ah, she speaks." I hold the menu just out of reach, so she stands on her tiptoes jumping up and down trying to grab it.

"Give it to me," she hisses.

"Why? We already know what you're getting."

She shoves me against the refrigerator, and I'm actually impressed by her strength. "You do not. You don't know *anything* about me, you ass." Her tone is biting, laced with some deeper emotion that sounds a lot like hurt.

I recognize it easily because I've been drowning in the same feeling since last night.

I pin my gaze to hers, still trapped between her and the fridge. "I'm sorry, okay?" Dragging my hand through my hair, I heave out a breath. "I fucked up last night, big time."

She stills, her entire body tensing. That vein across her forehead pulses, and I can practically see the gears spinning in that gloriously devious mind of hers. Still, she says nothing, waiting for me to continue.

"First of all, I never should have allowed any of that to happen."

Her eyes flash, and fuck me, I'm just digging myself into a deeper grave.

"Despite how much I wanted it to," I add.

The hard line of her lips softens a touch.

"Second of all, before I ran off like a *stronzo*, I wasn't implying I expected you to fuck me. I would never assume anything like that. I just thought that was what you wanted and then you caught me off guard, and—"

She stares up at me like I've lost my mind, which I kind of have because of her. This woman drives me absolutely batshit crazy. So I start all over again. "I have strict rules when it comes to my clients—"

"No shit?" Her eyes dance with a hint of mischief, the corner of her mouth tilting up ever so slightly.

"My rules exist for very good reasons, Isabella. They could mean the difference between life and death… *your* life. I never should have been so irresponsible with something so precious." I shove my hand in my pocket to keep from reaching out to caress her cheek.

Her lips purse, a faint exhale squeezing through. My head tips forward because I'm a complete masochist, desperate to take in her breathy sigh.

"I just don't understand why it's such a big deal…"

"You know how I am, how important the routine and procedures are to my success. How am I supposed to focus on that when all I can think about is the next time I'll get to touch you? Or feel your lips against mine? Just one night and the sounds you made are already permanently emblazoned in my mind, living rent free for all eternity. I haven't even brushed my teeth since last night just so I can savor your taste on my lips…" I force my tongue to still before I say something we can never come back from. Because just speaking the words is already making me hard. "Fuck," I grind out. "I never should have taken this job."

"But you did," she snaps, knotting her arms across her chest. "And now we're stuck together for the next two and a half months."

"Well, we'll have to figure out a way to make it work."

"I don't see how we can." Her words aren't biting like they have been throughout the conversation, instead, a hint of sadness laces them. And it cuts the deepest of all.

CHAPTER 32
IF I CAN'T HAVE YOU

I sabella

I heave out a breath as I step into the cool night air, the incessant, frenetic voices of the ER finally quieting when the doors slide closed behind me. A few weeks of this internship, and I'm already exhausted. I can hardly complain because unlike typical doctors who work the emergency room, I've been fortunate enough to keep to quite normal hours.

I could never do it.

I only hope my plan of becoming a pediatrician and opening my own practice will be slightly less chaotic. With the turmoil racing around in my mind, I hardly have time to notice my ever-present shadow. Or maybe I've simply become that used to ignoring the overbearing Italian.

After that night over a week ago, the situation between us has been frosty at best. And I hate it. I hadn't realized how much I counted on Raf not only as a guard, but as a friend. Without my family, Vinny and my crazy cousins, it's the first time in my life I find myself truly alone. I'm not lonely exactly because I am just too busy, but *Dio*, I miss Serena and Matty. I would do anything for one of our all-night tea sessions. And Vinny, I hope he's at least having some fun at King Industries. I am getting so desperate I would even settle for Alessia or Alessandro right about now.

Serena has been inviting me to Milano for weeks, but I can't ask for a weekend off when I just started working. And she is pretty much in the same boat with her new job. She keeps promising she'll come down, but we have yet to nail down a date.

Raffaele moves into step beside me, inching closer as we approach the parking lot where Sal always waits for my shift to end. "You want to grab something to eat before we go home?" he exhales on a rushed whisper.

"No, I'm tired."

He nods and slows his pace, dropping back a step. He's been nothing but professional, giving me my space but always lurking in the shadows. I hate how comforting his presence has become, even the stoic silence.

I wish there was a way we could go back to how things were, but I'm still so angry and embarrassed that I don't think I'll ever get past that night. Despite all the drama it has caused, I'm proud of myself for making the right decision by putting a stop to it. Raf has already wormed his way too deep, and if I had slept with him, it would have only made everything so much worse.

"Hey, Bella!"

I whirl around at the familiar voice and find Jeff jogging after us. I stop abruptly, scared he's going to bust his stitches if he keeps moving so quickly. "Whoa, slow down." I hold my hands up, stopping him. "You have to take it easy. You're still recovering."

Jeff waves a dismissive hand, a hint of crimson tinting his

cheeks. "I'm totally good. The doctors released me with a clean bill of health two days ago." He grins, his light blue eyes sparking beneath the final rays of sunlight dipping behind the backdrop of historic monuments. "Would they have let me come back to work if I wasn't fully recovered?"

"No, I guess not."

"So since I am all recovered, I owe you a thank you dinner for saving my life." He turns to Raf and offers a smile. "Both of you actually."

I can feel more than see Raf stiffen at the suggestion. Knowing my bodyguard, a dinner with Jeff and me would be the ultimate torture. Which is why I turn back to my colleague and smile sweetly. "I would love that."

"*Signorina...*" Raf mutters. He's back to the formal crap which drives me absolutely insane. "You know the rules."

I throw my hand up, shaking my head. "I do, no need to repeat them, Raffaele. I also know that there are a number of restaurants you've personally already vetted. So I was going to suggest one of those spots." Then I turn to Jeff, smothering the scowl that formed while arguing with my guard. "You don't mind where we go, do you?"

He shakes his head. "No, absolutely not. You should pick anyway since this is a thank you dinner."

"Oh, so it's not a date?" I glance over Jeff's shoulder at my sulking bodyguard, enjoying every minute of his irritation.

Jeff's light brows knit as he regards me before whispering, "Do you want it to be?"

I shrug nonchalantly. It's not that I don't find him attractive because I really do. It's only that the idea of pissing off Raf is my number one objective right now.

Jeff runs his palm across the back of his neck. "I was actually planning on asking you out the night of the *aperitivo*, but you know how that went..."

"Please, don't remind me."

"Okay, great, so where should we go?" Jeff directs the question at me before cocking his head back at Raf. "I don't want to step on your toes, buddy, so you pick."

"Buddy?" Raf barks. "I'm not your f—"

I dig my elbow into his side before he finishes the word. "There's a great little pizza place right by my apartment." I tick my head at the black Alfa Romeo in the parking lot. "My driver can take us."

"Perfect." Jeff's smile is so big I almost feel bad before I remind myself I'm not using him just to get back at Raf. I do genuinely enjoy his company, and it was his idea to take us out as a thank you anyway.

And Jeff is great. If I wasn't so damned obsessed with my bodyguard, he would be just the type of guy I should date.

I will date.

Mind made up, I wind my hand through Jeff's arm and lead him toward the car.

The second bottle of wine arrives, and my hand brushes Raf's as I reach for it.

"*You're* going to have a drink?" I stare at him, brow arched as he claims the bottle of Chianti and fills his glass.

"This dinner is in my honor, right?" He clinks his flute against mine and downs the deep burgundy wine in one go. His eyes are already beginning to gloss over, and for a second, I'm actually worried.

In all the months he's worked for me, I've never seen him wasted and from the looks of it, he's on his way there. "Maybe you should take it easy," I whisper.

"I'm fine, *principessa*, don't you worry about me." He leans closer, his warm breath spilling across my ear. "If there's one thing I can handle, it's my wine. You on the other hand—" He clucks his tongue, the sound vibrating across my eardrum, before sitting back.

"Whatever…" I grumble.

Jeff sits across the small table tucked into a corner of the pizzeria, oblivious to the tension as he finishes up on a call with his mom back home. He's already mouthed *I'm sorry* multiple times, but I think it's sweet. *Dio* knows my parents would have a fit if I didn't answer every time they called.

Raf leans in again, his hand finding my thigh beneath the table. I startle at the unexpected touch, but he keeps his fingers clasped around my leg despite the squirming. "You should probably let me know now if I need to buy some earplugs from the pharmacy before we get home. Because if you're planning on bringing that *coglione* home and fucking him, I will not be forced to listen to it." His fingers tighten around my thigh, the pressure growing so intense I'm scared he'll leave a bruise.

"You're hurting me," I hiss and wrap my hand around his, attempting to pry his fingers off. The pressure lightens, but he doesn't release me. "Raf!" I snarl.

Smoldering, dark eyes lock to mine, a raging tempest brewing below the sleek surface. "I need to know, Isabella. Are you going to bring him home?"

"I—I don't know." I hadn't planned on it, honestly, but there's something about the rage in his eyes that has my heart pumping.

His hand moves up my thigh until it reaches the hem of my sundress. I gasp as heat surges in its wake.

"Are. You. Going. To. Fuck. Him?" He punctuates each word by sliding his hand an inch closer to the building heat between my thighs.

"What do you care?" I hiss. "You said the other night was a mistake, that you regretted it."

"I never said I regretted it, *principessa*." His voice is nothing more than a serrated whisper. "There isn't a moment of what happened between us I would take back. It meant fucking everything." His hand reaches my throbbing center, cupping it gently. "Just because I can't have your pussy, doesn't mean it's not mine. Doesn't mean that the thought of anyone else touching you makes me want to rip my own heart out." His finger starts to move, stroking me over the silk of my panties.

A gasp works its way up my throat as my hips grind against the faint touch, desperate for more.

"I take it back," he snaps. "I'm not getting earplugs, and I've decided for you, you're not fucking that guy."

Jeff waves at me from across the table, motioning at his phone then mouths another *I'm sorry*. He points toward the door, and I nod absentmindedly, too caught up in the building heat surging toward my lower half. I barely notice as he stands and walks out the door of the small trattoria, leaving me tucked into the small niche at the mercy of my ruthless guard.

The chair legs squeal against the wooden floor as Raf brings his chair closer. His finger dances across the waistband of my panties then slides beneath the silk before slipping between my wet folds. A groan vibrates his chest as he circles my clit, and my breaths start to come quicker. "Fuck, you're so wet for me, *principessa*."

"How do you know it's for you?" I rasp, even as my hips start to thrust, begging him for more.

He glances across the table at the empty seat. "Because I'm the only one here." He shoves a finger inside me, and nerve-endings I didn't even know I had roar to life.

"Fuck," I groan as I quickly scan the trattoria. I don't know how it's possible that everyone seems too consumed with their own conversations to notice what's happening in our little nook.

"What's that, *principessa*? You want me to fuck you with my finger right here in the middle of this restaurant?"

"Umhmm." *Shit*, what is wrong with me?

He nuzzles my ear, then his tongue darts out, sucking on my lobe. "Or should I sneak under the table and fuck you with my tongue again?"

"No, you can't," I squeal.

He runs his tongue across his bottom lip. "Mmm, I've been dreaming about that sweet taste, Isabella..."

Before I can put together another sentence, he drops under the table, hidden beneath the white linen.

"Raf, no!" I whisper-shout as his scruffy cheeks rub against my inner thighs. "What if Jeff comes back?"

But it's too late. He's already replaced his finger with his tongue, and raw pleasure shoots up my core.

"*Madonna mia*," I pant as his tongue swirls around my swollen clit.

Then his finger is back, thrusting in and out of me in a frenetic pace as he sucks and licks me into oblivion. My head falls back, the restaurant blurring all around me. I'm vaguely aware I should not be doing this. Someone is going to notice. How could they not?

But pure pleasure roars through me, and all my fears melt away.

Raf's free hand crawls up my dress, finding my breast. He kneads the sensitive flesh until my nipples pebble. At least I have the sense to grab a cloth napkin and tuck it into the collar of my blouse, covering his hand.

Fire races from my pussy, up to my breasts and all the way down to the base of my spine. It flares, growing more intense with each sweep of his tongue, every maddening thrust.

My hand dives under the table, fingers curling around Raf's silky locks. I urge him closer until he devours me. A part of me is scared I'll smother him, but the other part is too overwhelmed with pleasure to care. His tongue continues the devastating twirls, flicking faster then harder. The fire builds, a wave of pressure surging, and I'm seconds away from exploding. I'm so damned close…

"Raf," I moan, "I'm going to come."

And just like that, he wrenches his mouth from my pulsing center and pulls his finger away.

I snarl a curse, the sudden emptiness rolling through me. I'm horny and needy as all hell, the orgasm just beyond my grasp. "What the hell, Raf?" I growl.

His head pops up between my legs, the tablecloth just covering his dark waves. "That is your punishment, *principessa*. No one can touch your pussy but me, no one can make you come but *me*. The next time you force me to endure a night like this, you'll know what a real punishment is." My arousal glistens on his chin, and he runs his tongue across it, lapping me up.

"You asshole," I hiss.

"And you're a spoiled little mafia princess." He smirks up at me. "But you're *my* fucking mafia princess, and if I can't have you, no one will."

Approaching footfalls sends my guard dipping back under the table only to pop up on the other side just as Jeff returns. Raf crawls out with a napkin clenched in his fingers and thankfully, my arousal no longer slickening his chin.

"I'm so sorry about that." Jeff slips his phone back into his pocket and sits down. "When my mom starts talking, there's no stopping her."

"No problem," I murmur, reaching for my glass of wine. I'm going to need another entire bottle.

"I hope I didn't miss anything."

Raf pulls his chair closer to the table, the sharp screech sending my heart slamming into my ribs. "Nope, nothing important at all."

"So should we get some dessert?" Jeff's bright eyes dart between us.

Raf shakes his head, a ridiculous grin on his face. "Oh, I

just couldn't eat another thing. I'm absolutely stuffed. My pus—pasta was exquisite, the best I've ever had." He runs his tongue across his bottom lip again. "Sinfully delicious."

All the heat raging down below surges to my cheeks, and I'm a second away from murdering the smirking bastard. How dare he withhold my orgasm?

The waiter returns, and I thank *Dio* he was busy five minutes ago. As Jeff orders *cannoli* for dessert, I lean toward Raf. "You think you're the only one who can play this game, *stronzo*?" I whisper. "Just wait till we get home."

CHAPTER 33
WHAT DO YOU WANT?

R*affaele*

Standing at the end of the walkway to Jeff's apartment as Isabella says her goodbyes, I force my lungs to draw in deep breaths then exhale slowly. Even from this distance, I can make out each quiet whisper, every drawn-out look, and each lingering touch. He's probably trying to convince her to spend the night. Too bad that'll never happen under my watch.

I'm beyond buzzed and still fully aware that I fucked up yet again tonight.

What's worse is that I can't seem to care. All my rules, my policies and procedures sailed out the damned door. Seeing my Isabella with another guy was just too damned much. Should I have feasted on her pussy at the restaurant in front of an audience, leaving her vulnerable? Absolutely not.

Do I regret it? Not one bit.

In fact, I can't wait to get her home and do it again. And if she behaves this time, I may even let her come.

The click-clack of heels on cement draws my attention at the scowling woman marching toward me. Fuck, she looks hot when she's pissed. Her cheeks are just as rosy as when she's on the brink of an orgasm.

"Get in the car," she hisses as she stomps past me.

"Yes, *signorina*." Dipping my head, I follow behind her like a good boy. Only a few times with her, and I'm already whipped. But I'll be damned if I admit that to her. If I hope to keep any sort of semblance of control, she must believe I'm still in charge.

I slip in front of her and open the car door, unable to keep the grin at bay.

"Stop smiling," she grits out as she slides into the backseat.

"What?" I scoot in beside her, then signal for Sal to head home. Our driver's dark eyes meet mine through the rearview mirror.

The moment he revs the engine, Isabella's hand lands in my lap. She cups my cock over my slacks, and I'm instantly hard, despite knowing full well what she's up to. Clearing my throat, I pivot toward her and start to unbuckle my belt.

Her eyes widen as she regards me, two pools of bottomless blue.

"I can play this game all day, *principessa*," I whisper into her ear. "I'm okay with you not letting me come because I'll just finish myself off when we get home. It doesn't change the fact that I'll have the image of your hand on my cock permanently ingrained in my mind."

"You're a liar," she hisses and slips her hand beneath my boxers. "I'm going to get you so worked up, you're going to beg me for release." Her warm breath skates across the shell of my ear, and I only get harder. Sure, I'd love to come in her hand, or better, that tight, wet pussy, but some of Isabella is better than nothing at all.

That's how stupidly addicted I already am.

Her warm fingers close around me, and I instinctively start to move against her palm. *Cazzo*, she feels good, even though I know she's only doing this to fuck with me. Her hand swirls around my length, fingers toying with my balls until she starts to pump faster. My breaths start to grow ragged, and I glance up at the mirror and catch a glimpse of Sal's watchful eye.

Fucking around with Isabella is one thing, but the other guards knowing about it is where I draw the line. I have no doubt Luca Valentino would cut off my cock at that inexcusable offense.

So despite how good she feels, I wrap my hand around her wrist and attempt to pry her off.

"Oh, I'm just getting started, Raf," she murmurs.

"Maybe we can finish this exquisite torture when we get back to the apartment?" I whisper before ticking my head up at the rearview mirror. Isabella's smirk grows downright wicked.

She brings her lips to my ear, her breath sending goose bumps rippling down my arms. "Are you afraid, Mr. Ferrara? Scared that *Papà* will find out you want to fuck his only daughter and heir?" Her devastating strokes quicken, and my heart struggles to keep up with the accelerating tempo.

I bite my tongue to keep the groan from spilling through my clenched teeth. "Isabella," I warn.

"What's the matter, Raf? You can't take a little payback?"

Her eyes glisten with mischief as she regards me with a devilish grin. She continues to stroke harder, precum slickening her hand so she easily glides up and down my hard length.

"I *want* you to come, *stronzo*. I want to hear my name on

your lips as you explode all over your pants so Sal can see exactly what we've been up to." She narrows her eyes. "How long do you think until he tells *Papà*?"

"Isabella," I growl as liquid lightning races through my veins. This woman has me strung so tight, I could come on the spot. Luckily, I have a little more self-control than that, despite the wine. "Think about it. If I get sent home, you'll be next. No bodyguard, no internship in Rome."

"Oh, you'll be sent home, all right. In a box."

I nod, swallowing hard as the pleasure blossoms to nearly uncontainable levels. "I'm fully aware of that possibility, *principessa*." I pause before the traitorous words slip out. "And I still can't stay away from you."

She starts to slow her pace, and the fire wanes to a more comfortable temperature. I take advantage to plead my case.

Leaning in close, my hand itches to cup her cheek, but I don't dare with Sal's wandering eyes. "Do you want me dead, Isabella, is that what you want?"

"No," she mutters.

"Then what do you want?"

A moment of charged silence passes between us. Her hand still strangles my cock, but she's stopped moving. I'm not even sure she's still breathing.

"Isabella?"

She snags her bottom lip between her teeth, eyes chasing down to my mouth. "What I've always wanted… I want you to fuck me," she finally whispers, gaze still not meeting mine.

As if those words have a straight line to my cock, the fading fire ignites once again, and I start to thrust against her palm. Grasping her chin between my thumb and forefinger, I force her eyes to mine. There are a million reasons why I should say no: my life, her life, my rules, just to name a few. I have every intention of denying her because it is the sane thing to do. But somehow, my brain malfunctions with her hand still rubbing my cock and instead, I blurt, "All you had to do was ask."

Her smile brightens and despite growing up in one of the most breathtaking cities in the world, it's the most beautiful sight I've ever seen. I keep telling myself this thing between us is only physical, an itch I just can't scratch. That once I've had her, I'll be able to move on and focus on my duties as her bodyguard.

But the mad thumping of my heart calls me a fucking liar.

It's more than just the desire to claim her, to possess her. The little mafia princess has awakened my cold, dead heart. And that is the most dangerous thing of all.

"Okay," she breathes before removing her hand from beneath my boxers.

I grit out a curse as she does. Another day of blue balls. Or maybe not... "When exactly were you thinking?"

A devious chuckle parts her lips. "Let's have another glass of wine when we get back to the apartment, and we can talk about it."

"Okay, I like that. Maybe we can set out some ground rules."

She rolls her eyes at me so hard my palm twitches. "No rules, Raf. We're doing this my way."

"But—"

Her hand flies up, and she presses her finger to my lips. My familiar scent races up to my nostrils, and fuck, I love that she smells like me. I never want her to smell like anyone else. If I could, I would cover her in my cum so that everyone knows Isabella Valentino is mine.

"Okay," I murmur against her finger. With a quick glance up at the mirror, I confirm Sal's eyes are elsewhere before sucking it into my mouth. Swirling my tongue around her finger, I watch her as her cheeks redden and her lips curve into a capital O.

I can't risk getting too carried away. I already know the sounds I can coax out of my *principessa* so I pull out that tempting digit before she starts to moan and blows it for both of us.

Just in time because I'd been so wrapped up in Isabella, I didn't realize we were nearly home. *Merda*, this is exactly why getting involved with a client is such a bad idea. Sal pulls the car to the sidewalk, and I adjust my pants to hide the obvious bulge. Jumping out of the limo, I race around to Isabella's side so our driver doesn't have to get out and see my erection up close and personal.

"*Grazie, Salvatore.*" With a quick wave, I escort my client up the walkway to the outer gate. She's already fishing through her purse for the keys, and I catch a slight tremble in her hand.

Once we're through the first gate into the courtyard, I press a hand to the small of her back. She whirls around, eyes bright with some unreadable emotion.

My hands slide up her arms, cradling her face. "You know, we don't have to do this… If you just got caught up in the heat of the moment or were doing it only to spite me, I'm not holding you to anything."

A rueful smile drives away some of the darkness in her expression. "No, I want to do this." Her arms lace around my neck, and she shoves me against the exterior wall of the courtyard, so that we're enveloped within the tangle of climbing vines. Her mouth crashes into mine, and everything else vanishes.

CHAPTER 34
IMPOSSIBLE

Isabella

I'm doing this. I am losing my virginity to Raf tonight. I'm done waiting, I'm tired of making excuses for why this is such a bad idea. I already know it is, but I'm willing to take the chance. Because as infuriating as this man is, I *want* him. Like I've never wanted anyone else.

And after waiting all this time, I don't want my first time to be with someone I have lukewarm feelings for. I want the fire, the overwhelming attraction, *and* the deeper connection I'd never get with Massimo or Jeff. I want Raffaele, the man who makes me feel safe and even adored.

I'm not stupid enough to think my bodyguard is in love with me, but there's something there beyond the jealous, possessive streak. I'm certain of it.

So before I can think better of it beneath the light of the romantic Roman moon, I press my lips to his and kiss him with the same fiery passion that he devoured my pussy at the restaurant only an hour ago. He groans against my mouth as I walk him backward until we hit the ivy-covered wall.

The scent of flowers fills the air, the trickle of the nearby fountain only adding to the idyllic atmosphere. I only hope the deadly oleander with its deceivingly innocent pink blossoms isn't nearby. Raf's hands move to my ass, pressing me harder against him so that our bodies are flush, and I can feel his rock-hard, enormous cock at my belly.

A shudder rolls through my body at the thought of it invading my virgin vagina, but I push back the fear, reminding myself it is made to stretch. A baby is way bigger than any dick, right?

Right.

The rumble of an engine vaguely registers in the back of my mind, but I'm too busy matching Raf's tongue stroke for stroke. The man can kiss, and that is a highly desirable trait in my opinion. Most men are more concerned with getting to the good stuff than taking time to properly kiss a woman.

So I bask in every sweep of his tongue, of the feeling of his fingers digging into the hair at the back of my nape, and I try to imagine what it will feel like to be fucked by this man. I briefly contemplate telling him about my virginal status before I decide it's a bad idea. I don't need him freaking out on me.

"No, I can handle my own luggage, Nicky." The familiar female voice echoes from just beyond the gate, and I jerk my lips free from Raf's. He immediately stiffens, back in body-guard mode.

I would know that voice anywhere. "Serena?" I call out from inside the courtyard.

"Surprise!" She leaps out from behind the oleander bush on the other side of the wrought iron gate with her designer duffle bag slung over her shoulder.

"Oh, my God, what are you doing here?" I squeal as I hit the buzzer to let her in.

"I came to surprise you, of course!" She races in, tosses her bag at Raf and jerks me into a hug. "I've missed you so much!"

I squeeze her so hard my arms begin to ache. "Me too!" Tears start to threaten, and I blink quickly to keep them from spilling over. *Control yourself, Bella.* It's barely been a month since last I saw my best friend and favorite cousin. "How did you know where to find me?"

Papà has been so paranoid he forbids me from telling anyone my new address. Obviously, I would have had to tell Serena eventually, but I had yet to figure out how since he was worried someone could have tapped my phone. Which is insane but part of him agreeing to let me come here meant following all his stupid rules.

"Oh, that was easy." She smirks. "I bribed Vinny to break into your dad's office and find the address."

"Not that I'm not enjoying this happy little family reunion," Raf grumbles, heaving Serena's enormous duffle over his shoulder, "but why don't we take this inside?"

"I see Rome hasn't done anything to improve his mood." Serena tosses my bodyguard a cheeky grin.

"Nope, not really. He's as grumpy as usual."

"You didn't seem to mind that a minute—" I shove my fist into Raf's stomach before he can finish his sentence. And yes, it was absolutely worth the momentary discomfort and likely bruised knuckles.

I motion toward the ancient building at the opposite side of the courtyard and loop my arm through Serena's. "Come on, let me show you my new place." I steer her around the fountain, the lanterns hung around the lush courtyard casting the area in a warm glow.

"It looks so charming," Serena croons. "Milano is nothing like this."

"Let me guess you got something super sleek and modern?"

"You know it, girl."

Raf marches ahead of us with the duffle swinging across his back and opens the front door.

"How are things going with you two?" she whispers.

"Eh, you know, the same." Guilt stabs at my insides at the blatant lie. I've never kept anything like this from my cousin. I always tell her everything. I can't even fully explain why I've kept whatever this thing between Raf and me is from her. It's not like she wouldn't understand or that she'd give me shit for it. Serena has made more than her fair share of bad decisions when it comes to men.

Raf leads the way through the apartment, pausing at the quaint kitchen and cozy living room like a good tour guide before heading upstairs. At the top of the staircase, he turns toward the guest bedroom which is at the opposite end of the hall from our adjoining rooms.

"Um, hold up, Raf, you can just drop off my stuff in Bella's bedroom. We always sleep together, right, cuz?"

My guard's eyes chase to mine, something like panic setting in. I freeze for a minute, having completely forgotten about my desperate plea for him to fuck me less than fifteen minutes ago. Serena's right though, even in her own apartment in Manhattan, we've always stayed in the same room whenever I slept over.

"Yup, that's right," I finally mutter.

The tendon in Raffaele's jaw feathers before he spins on his heel and disappears into my bedroom with her bag. Serena follows him to the doorway, peeking inside. "Cute." Her curious gaze immediately finds the adjoining door, and a mischievous smirk curls her lips. "You did not tell me about that." She points at the door, then back and forth between the two of us.

Luckily, Raf is too busy situating Serena's stuff in the closet to notice.

"Yeah, it's just a safety precaution."

"So no late night visits?"

"Nope." I pop the P because I know how much it annoys my cousin. As she grimaces at me, I weave my arm through hers once again and tug her down the corridor. "Come on, the tour isn't over yet. You have to see the rooftop. It's hands-down the best part of the apartment."

"Oh, I love the sound of it already. We should totally throw a party up there! We are going to have so much fun this weekend." She takes a step before stopping at the bathroom in the hallway. "Oh wait, just give me a quick sec, I have to pee." She dips behind the door, and the moment it's closed, I tiptoe back toward my bedroom.

Raf is still inside, Serena's luggage neatly tucked away. He stands by the window, staring out into the quiet night. His posture is stiff, the strain in his broad shoulders evident through his tight black tee.

"So..." I creep closer, crossing my arms over my chest. With the arrival of my cousin, I feel like something has shifted. I'm not sure if it's him or me, or maybe both of us. Seeing Serena brought reality back in a rush. "Maybe Serena's arrival was a sign or something," I whisper.

He steps closer, his dark hair gleaming beneath the dim lighting. "Is that what you think?" His voice is deceptively calm given the wild flutter of the tendon in his jaw.

"I don't know. Maybe." I step back and he traps me against the window, his tattooed, muscled arms caging me in. My breath hitches when I feel his cock, still hard, pressed against my bellybutton.

His midnight irises lock to mine, the surge of emotions beneath the glassy surface startling. "Do you not want this anymore?"

"No, it's not that—"

"Because it's all I can think about, Isabella. *You* are all I can think about from the moment I stepped into that boardroom all those weeks ago, hell, maybe even before. I can't get you out of my fucking mind. I've tried so damned hard to get past this obsession, but every moment near you pulls me deeper, and resisting feels more impossible each day."

I heave in a breath because my lungs have suddenly forgotten how to pump. My heart, too, seems to have given up on life.

"I'm not strong enough to fight this anymore," he whispers, his musky scent all-consuming. "And more than that, I just don't want to." He jerks the hair tie he's been wearing for weeks off his wrist and tosses it onto the floor.

"Bella, where'd you go?" Serena's voice filters from out in the hallway, and Raf jumps back, freeing me from the confines of his muscled arms. His lips twist, but he doesn't say another word. In all honesty, that confession was more than enough.

My heart is a mad battering ram as I shout, "In my bedroom, I'm coming!"

A devious grin tugs up the corners of Raf's lips. "No, you're not," he murmurs. "But you will be soon."

With that, he turns on his heel and walks out, leaving me way too flustered for my own good. *Cazzo*, this man will be my ruin.

CHAPTER 35
COCK BLOCKER

R*affaele*

A lethal mix of fury and jealousy pounds into me in time with the raging beat of the DJ's house mix. Isabella and Serena are encircled by a ravenous group of Italian men and if one more guy so much as brushes by her, I'm going to lose my shit.

Even the cool air of the open-air nightclub atop the surrounding hills of Rome does little to ice my temper. The past twenty-four hours have been absolute torture. *Dio* must really have it in for me. How is it possible that the moment Isabella and I decide to give into temptation, the grand cock blocker of all cock blockers shows up on our doorstep?

Not that I mind Serena as a person, but does she really have to insist on sleeping with Isa for the length of her stay? As if the nightclubs aren't bad enough…

Another breeze kicks off the hill, sending cool air across the old medieval fortress turned summer nightclub. Isabella sweeps the tumble of dark hair behind her ears, her forehead glistening with perspiration. Her cheeks are flushed, her lips glossy with a bright pink hue, and she's the most gorgeous woman in here. No wonder all the men are salivating around her like mongrels. Serena, too, is certainly beautiful with her long, curly blonde hair and eyes glittering with amusement, but beside my Isa, she pales in comparison. Any woman does. Regardless, between the two of them, it's been a long line of waiting men all night.

I'm not sure how much more I can take.

When a guy in a sports jacket and pink shorts makes his move toward Isabella, cramming his body between her and Serena, I can't control my legs from marching toward her. My fingers close around her upper arm and jerk her hard against me. The guy shoots me a scowl, and I throw him my middle finger in response.

"Raf," she breathes, a hint of a scolding in her tone, but still her body curves to mine.

"What? Did you actually want that *coglione* grinding on you?"

She shrugs, glancing over my shoulder at Serena who is now dancing with the *cornuto*. "I was just having some fun. Relax."

"Relax? You want me to relax?" I snarl. "Do you have any idea how hard it is for me to just stand by and watch as these assholes rub up on you?"

A satisfied smirk tips up the corner of her lip. "Are you jealous, Raf?"

"Yes," I hiss. "Is that what you want to hear? That simply the thought of any other man's hands on you makes my blood boil, and my fingers twitch to snap their damned necks?"

Her breath catches, perfect lips curving into a capital O.

"Does that scare you, *principessa*?"

Pressing her lips into a hard line, she slowly shakes her

head. I didn't think it would, and a pleased grin slashes across my face. I dip my head, my mouth brushing the shell of her ear. "Does it turn you on?" My voice is nothing but a jagged whisper.

Her eyes meet mine, defiant as all hell.

"I think it does." I walk her back a few steps until we're hidden in a small niche of the old fortress, roughhewn stone walls on three sides of us. "If I slid my hand in your panties, would you already be wet for me, *principessa*?"

She snags her bottom lip between her teeth, sucking, and I wish it was my lip in her mouth. Or even better my cock. I draw her lip free with my thumb, my mouth inches from hers. "You know it makes me wild when you do that, right?"

"Now, I do." A smug grin teases her lips.

I walk her back another step until her bare shoulders hit the stone wall. Caging her against it, I part her legs with my knee, rubbing my thigh against her apex. She's soaked, her arousal seeping through her panties and my jeans. I move against her, gently rubbing, but from behind it looks as if we're only dancing.

"Mmm, Raf," she groans as she grinds her hips against my leg.

"I don't know how much longer I can wait to claim you, *principessa*. The more I think about it, the worse of an idea it becomes." I dip my head to her neck and suck hard, earning a squeal. "Because I'm pretty damned sure that once will never be enough."

Her glittering eyes meet mine, something unreadable glistening just beneath the surface. "Who says it has to only be once?"

"Because twice would be my ruin and three times my total damnation. More than that, and I'm fairly certain I'd never survive."

A chill surges up her spine, the tremor vibrating through my own body.

"Well, that could be a problem then." She smirks. "I expected at least three times the first night."

A deep chuckle vibrates my entire chest, and my heart staggers before picking up its quickening tempo. "Demanding... I like that."

She rises to her tiptoes and glances over my shoulder, likely searching for Serena, before returning that hypnotic gaze to meet mine.

"Is Serena good?" I murmur.

"Yeah, she's still dancing with pink-shorts guy."

"Then let's get out of here. Let me take you home so we can finally—"

She presses her finger to my lips, slowly shaking her head. "I can't just leave her."

"Why not? She's got that guy and her own retinue of guards." None remain as close to her as I do with my charge, but then again, no one is as good as me.

"Serena's only here for one more night, Raf, then she'll be back in Milano. I want to spend this time with her."

Jerking back, I remove my leg from between her thighs, an unexpected pang lancing through my chest. I must have made a face because Isabella's smile softens, and she laces her fingers through mine.

"I'm not saying I don't want to be with you, too. You know things are complicated. If anyone found out about this" —she motions between us— "you know we'd both be screwed."

A smirk tugs at my lips. "So, you do care about me? And you don't want me returning to Manhattan in a box?"

"Of course, I do, you *stronzo*." She smacks my cheek before squeezing it gently. "Besides, you were right. *Papà* would send me right home, and my Roman excursion is just getting started."

A rueful smile spreads despite my best efforts. "Fine, but

the moment she's gone, I'm giving you a night you'll never forget."

"I'm counting on it." With her fingers still tangled with mine, she tugs me back toward the center of the dancefloor, and I follow like a complete idiot, because I'm already that gone for her.

Serena and Isabella walk arm-in-arm, giggling and gushing about the evening, as I lead them through the stone archway that spills out onto the dirt parking lot. Serena's guards are waiting in the limo to drive us all home, and I'm shocked by the loose tether they give their client.

Luca would never approve. Then again, I've heard his brother Dante is quite a different breed.

"Tomorrow we should have a party on your rooftop." Serena claps her hands, the haze of alcohol brightening her eyes. "Don't you know a bunch of hot doctors you could invite?"

Isabella chuckles, and I bristle at the remark, thoughts of her date with Jeff still at the forefront of my mind. "Sure, I could put something together quickly."

"You'd like that better wouldn't you, Raf?" Serena cocks a light brow in my direction. "This way sweet little Bella could be at home and protected?"

I nod slowly.

"Don't think I didn't notice how tense you were tonight." She throws me a knowing smile, and I wonder what exactly she's trying to get at.

"Oh, just ignore him," Isabella cuts in. "He's always tense. And I'm sure even with the party at home, he'll be grumpy."

Serena surges ahead to pluck a hibiscus from the nearby

hedge, and I lean into Isabella and whisper, "I'm grumpy because instead of watching other guys' hands all over you, I want my hands to be all over you."

A grin slashes across her face and her cheeks heat, sending wicked pleasure up my spine.

Before she can respond, Serena bounces back with the pink bloom tucked behind her ear. Behind her, two men walk up the cobbled pathway.

Every nerve stands at attention as the two familiar forms coalesce from the darkness. *Cazzo.*

What the fuck are my brothers doing here?

CHAPTER 36
FRATELLINO

sabella

A wave of power, raw and undiluted, descends over the suddenly tense atmosphere as two men in dark suits stalk toward us. I know the feeling well, I've grown up surrounded by it, the prickle in the air, the sudden shift in awareness. Behind the dark-haired men, march a retinue of guards that would put *Papà*'s team to shame. Raf stiffens beside me, every inch of his body exuding fiery tension.

"*Cazzo*," he grinds out.

As one hand clutches my elbow his free one slides down to his hip where his gun is hidden. Like the perfect hunter, his muscles are coiled, prepared to strike. My gaze bounces between Raf and the approaching strangers, a chill surging up my spine. I've seen my guard in a variety of dangerous circumstances, but I've never seen him like this. That tension surges from his body, leeching into my own until a tight knot twists in my gut. Serena is oblivious to the entire drama, chattering away about her pretty flower until her gaze lifts and locks on the first of the two men.

"Oh, *Dio*," she murmurs, before fanning herself. "And this is exactly why I have no plans of ever returning to Manhattan again."

The first man, with eyes as dark as midnight, pauses, his piercing gaze raking up and down Serena, taking in every inch of her scandalous, curve-hugging, ruby-red mini. The man is hot as hell with a decidedly dangerous edge. Maybe it's the tattoos peeking out from beneath his collar or that predatorial stare.

"Keep moving," Raf growls through clenched teeth as he attempts to steer me around the rising swell of black suits.

"Please don't tell me you're leaving already, *signorina*." The second guy, who looks strikingly similar to the first, only instead of the dark eyes and hair, he is blessed with deep emerald irises and tendrils of light chestnut that fall across his brow. "The party is only just beginning."

"That's exactly what I was saying—"

I grab Serena's hand and squeeze so tight I cut off the rest of her sentence. My cousin might be a little flighty at times, but she knows me well enough to pick up on my not-so-subtle hints.

A wall of men now blocks the pathway to the car, the two attractive ones who are clearly in charge taking turns ogling Serena, then glaring at Raf, or rather at his hand squeezing the shit out of my arm.

"Raffa," the taller one hisses, "all this time in Roma and not even a call?"

Serena spins at my guard, finally freed from the stare down with the gorgeous stranger. "You know these two?"

"Not anymore," he grits out.

The dark-haired guy steps closer, and Raf positions himself in front of me, a flesh and blood wall. "Come on now, *fratellino*, that's no way to talk about your brothers."

My jaw unhinges, and Raf's grip on my arm turns punishing. I let out an embarrassing squeal before biting my tongue to keep the string of curses from erupting next.

"Brothers?" A sharp, slightly unhinged laugh bubbles out from the hard line of Raf's lips.

In that moment, it occurs to me despite spending nearly twenty-four hours a day with my bodyguard for months now, I know nothing about him. He has brothers? Here in Rome? How could he not tell me?

"That's funny," he hisses, a violent edge to his tone. "Both of you made your choice long ago." He ticks his head at the green-eyed one. "Besides, Giuseppe told me you knew I was here weeks ago, Antonio."

Antonio, the taller one with the piercing coal-black eyes, sears the brother to his right with a glare before returning that hard gaze back onto Raf.

"Oh, so Giuseppe didn't tell you we ran into each other? Or that I called him prior to my arrival?" A devious grin softens the hard line of Raf's jaw. "What's wrong, Antonio? Are you losing control over your men? It's a fucking shame when you can't even trust your own damned blood, isn't it?"

Antonio erases the space between them, fury carving into his jaw. "*Vaffanculo,* Raffa."

"You first, Toni." Despite my bodyguard being the younger brother, he's the biggest of all three. And right now, looming over his siblings with his chest puffed out like a fucking peacock and the murderous rage set into his features, he looks damned terrifying.

And it makes me stand a little taller.

"Clearly, there's some family history going on here that we're not aware of." Serena steps between the brothers, her sparkly clutch in hand, and runs a perfectly manicured fingernail across Antonio's shoulder. "Let's not allow it to ruin anyone's night." Two of the guards surge forward, but Toni lifts a dismissive hand, and his men freeze midstride.

What only I know is that Serena's designer purse hides a loaded Glock 42.

"My apologies, ladies, my brother and I have been extremely rude." A practiced smile slides across Antonio's face as he takes a step back and adjusts the pristine white collar of his shirt. "Seeing our long-lost brother caught me a bit off guard." His dark gaze zips to Raf before settling on Serena once again. "My name is Antonio Ferrara, and this is my younger brother, Giuseppe." He signals toward the hilltop nightclub. "And this is our fine establishment."

Raffaele mutters a curse, dragging his fingers through the tangle of dark locks.

Antonio extends a hand, twin pools of darkness scrutinizing every inch of me. "And you must be my brother's new client."

"Don't touch her," Raf growls, the savage sound vibrating his entire torso. He drags me in closer so that I can feel every twitch of his muscle and the rapid staccato of his heart.

"Always so protective, *fratellino*... and that temper. I hope it hasn't gotten you into more trouble."

"Don't worry about me. I'm handling my business just fine."

"Clearly." Again, that hard gaze rakes over me, searching for what I'm not certain, but he sure as shit isn't going to find it in my cleavage. I glare right back, crossing my arms to cover the plunging neckline of my top. Raf likes to treat me like a fragile little thing, but I'm more than capable of handling myself.

From my current position, I've got a clear path to his throat. A direct strike with the edge of my hand, and he'd be choking on his own breath. Or I could go for the groin, simple and effective. Either way, even without a gun, I'm a pretty lethal weapon myself.

"Maybe we should all go back in there for another

drink?" Serena offers, her fingers still tight around her clutch. My cousin might play the part of a ditzy blonde well, but there's not a stupid bone in her body. "Make up for lost time?" She glances between the three siblings.

"Absolutely not," Raf growls.

Giuseppe steps closer, twinkling green eyes focused on his younger sibling. "Come on, Raffa. Don't you think it's time?"

"Hell would have to fucking freeze over twice before I sit at a table and share a drink with either of you."

Giuseppe laughs it off, but of the two brothers he seems the most ill at ease. Antonio must be the eldest, but not by much, all three siblings look to be in their thirties.

"Now, get the fuck out of my way so we can get out of here and never make the mistake of frequenting your fine establishment again." Curling me around his back, he steps into his brother, towering over his smaller frame.

"You're sure this is how you want to play this?" Antonio rasps.

"*Papà* was the one who started this game long ago, Toni. I don't want to fucking play at all. I'll be out of your damned city the first chance I get. Until then, you stay on your side, and I'll stay on mine. And tell *Papà* not to worry, I'm not here for him."

Antonio chuckles, the deep sound unnervingly similar to Raf's laugh, the fake one, not the real one that carries more depth and a swell of warmth. Once the fit dies down, he takes a step to the side and the curtain of dark suits parts, opening a pathway to the parking lot.

Raf tucks me under his arm, then drags me between the gauntlet of guards, and I jerk Serena along with us.

"*A presto, fratellino,*" Antonio calls out.

See you soon.

"What the hell, Raf?" I blurt the minute we hit the gravel parking lot. Salvatore starts the engine and one of Serena's guards opens the door to the back seat. Where were they a few seconds ago when World War III was about to erupt?

"I don't want to talk about it."

I dig my heels into the gravel and slow his manic footfalls. "I'm not taking another step until you tell me what is going on."

His stormy eyes mine, a tempest of emotions surging just beneath the dark surface. "Get your ass in the car, or I will throw you over my shoulder again. Is that what you want? I'm not fucking around, *principessa*." The jagged edge to his tone has the fire in my veins leeching out.

"At home then."

"Fine." He presses his hand to the small of my back and pushes me the rest of the way to the car.

What the actual fuck has Raf been hiding all this time?

CHAPTER 37
THE FIRST TIME

R*affaele*

A twist of red-hot anger and toxic fear pummel my insides as I slam the apartment door shut behind Isabella and Serena before sliding the deadlock closed. I've already informed all the guards stationed outside to be on high alert for my brothers, not to mention the fact that I had Sal drive around half of Rome before returning home to ensure we weren't being followed. The pair of typically chatty cousins move silently into the kitchen, and fiery guilt jabs at my chest.

Of all the damned clubs in Rome, how the hell did we end up at one my family owns? This is exactly why my rules are so important. If I'd done the recon as I typically do, I would have known the place was owned by the Ferraras. But *merda*, Isabella has me in such a chokehold, I'm letting things slide. She bats those long lashes at me and puckers those pouty lips, and I become a useless, spineless *coglione*. And it could have cost me her life.

I have to end this.

I cannot allow my feelings for her to cloud my judgement any longer. And as much as I hate the thought of it, I need to find my replacement. The sooner the better. Staying with Isabella only paints a larger target on her back.

And *Dio* forbid if my enemies discover I'm back in town. My own family is bad enough but the Sartoris, Mercurios, and DeLucas... My thoughts flicker to the shooter at RiverBar and invisible claws tear at my lungs. Could that attack have been because of me? If Antonio's sources had confirmed my arrival, maybe others had to.

Fuck.

I move around the apartment in a fog, securing windows, shuttering up panes, locking up every inch of the damned space.

"Raf!"

I spin around to find a pair of blazing sapphire irises. From the irritation puckering her brow, my guess is that was not the first time she called my name.

"What?" I bark right back because I already feel shitty enough for both of us.

"I waited for the entire hour-long car ride. I was way beyond patient, and now, it's time to tell me the truth."

Serena moves into step beside her cousin, nodding aggressively, with a glass of wine already in hand. "Yes, what she said." A smirk tugs at the corner of her lip, and her eyes begin to sparkle. "Also, are either of your brothers single, because damn..."

"Trust me," I snarl cutting her off, "you want nothing to do with either of them."

"Please start explaining." Isabella glares up at me, arms pressed against her chest as if she's trying to contain the anger. I recognize the motion well.

I have no intention of spilling my dark past to my current client, let alone her cousin. "I haven't spoken to my family in a decade," I huff out. "And that's exactly why I was so hesitant to return to Rome. My father and I had a big falling out, and he essentially disowned me. My brothers took his side. Shit happens. End of story."

"And that's it?"

"Yes."

"That standoff outside the club seemed like something much bigger than a little falling out." Serena takes a sip from the glass, swishing the red wine around her mouth.

Isabella inches closer, her eyes searching mine for an answer she will not receive. I would never—could never tell her what happened. The wounds are too raw, scars much too deep to ever see the light. Especially not now with the barrage of feelings my new client is eliciting. She finally diverts her gaze to Serena. "Will you give us a second, Sere?"

"Really?" Her eyes are wide as she stares at her cousin as if she's never been dismissed from a conversation in her life. Did they really tell each other *everything*?

"Yeah, I need to talk to Raf alone."

"Okay…" She spins on her heel and saunters toward the kitchen, topping off her wine glass before sinking down onto the couch in the living room.

Isabella's hand threads through mine, her long slender fingers fitting so perfectly between mine, that the gentle touch is actually painful. Because it'll have to be the last. I have no restraint around this woman. My entire life of control and carefully constructed policies and procedures go to hell around her. And that's not fair to her.

Lust is one thing. That I can control, but this has gone so far beyond lust…

She tugs me up the stairs, her footfalls quickening with each step closer to our bedrooms. Which one would she choose? The thought is so pointless, but still, it crosses my mind. If she selects her room, she's searching for comfort, a familiar surrounding, if she chooses mine, she's seeking to comfort me. The subtle difference is something most wouldn't account for.

Isabella turns at my room, and my heart quickens its pace. As pissed off as she is, she's more concerned about my state of mind than the fact that I lied to her all these months. Interesting and unexpected.

She backs me into the room, then pushes me down on the mattress. "It's just you and me now, Raf, and you owe me this. Tell me the whole story."

I blow out a breath, attempting to buy some time to come up with a decent version of the truth. All lies must be centered around a truth in order to be plausible. "I already told you," I mutter. "I did something unforgivable in my father's eyes and so he banished me from the family, from the whole damned city."

"And what was that?" That inquisitive gaze roams over me.

"I betrayed his trust."

"By doing what?"

"Siding with someone he considered an enemy."

Her dark brows furrow as she regards me. "Raf, I'm not an idiot. I know powerful men when I see them. What kind of business is your family in?"

I figured it wouldn't take her long to connect the dots once she saw Antonio and Giuseppe and their troop of guards. "Nightclubs and restaurants." I give her my most charming smile.

"Money laundering?" she retorts.

"Among other things." *Dio.* Why not offer more incriminating information, you *stronzo*?

She hisses a curse then drags her hand through her silky hair. "That was definitely not on your perfectly pristine resume, Mr. Ferrara. How could you not tell me?"

"Because it never would have come up if we hadn't

ended up in Rome. I've never had anything to do with the family business. I never wanted it."

"And that's why your father disowned you because you wanted out?"

I nod slowly because it's partially true. "I've always wanted to protect others. Whether that meant in the Carabinieri, the Army or in private security, it's my calling. It's the only way to mete out some justice, to tip the scales toward the right side in this dark world."

"And that's it?" She inches toward me so that her bare legs brush my knees.

"That's the gist, *principessa*. I don't believe all the dirty details are truly necessary, do you?"

She slowly shakes her head. Her eyes remain locked to mine, as if she could somehow ferret out the lie. "Then why did you seem scared?" Her brows pucker again, expression gone completely serious. "I've never seen you like that, Raf. Not even when we've faced a hailstorm of bullets."

I reach for her, my hands wrapping around the backs of her thighs before I can stop them. Drawing her closer, I loose a long, suffering exhale as I tip my head back to meet her worried gaze. "Because you've done something to me, *principessa*. You've stomped all over my rules, pitched my procedures to hell, and cracked open the fortress I've built around my heart. You make me feel vulnerable, and that scares the shit out of me, more than any bullet ever could."

Before I can stop the insane blathering, the words are out. I regret it instantly, but I can't even focus on my own stupidity for long because her lips are on mine before I can force my tongue to take them back.

Isabella straddles me, sinking down across my legs as her mouth captures mine, fierce and insistent.

"I'll never let anyone hurt you," I mumble against her lips, even as I remember I'm supposed to be finding my replacement. This is wrong.

But *Dio*, it feels so damned right.

She grinds against my cock, her mini skirt hiked up to her thighs as she nibbles on my bottom lip. I grab handfuls of her ass, kneading the firm but supple flesh. She's perfect and *mine*. I've never wanted—no, needed anyone more.

Especially after the brutal reminder that came along with running into my brothers.

I'm ready to toss it all to hell for her. To risk the wrath of Luca Valentino, to lose my job, hell, my damned life just for one taste of redemption.

My fingers latch beneath the waistband of her thong, and I drag the lacy thing down her legs, my mouth never leaving hers. I run my hand up the inside of her thigh and feel her already dripping for me.

A groan rumbles my chest, likely vibrating against her own as I press her flush against me, so her pussy soaks my jeans. I love seeing how wet I make her. I've barely even touched her yet. My cock is so damned hard it strains against my jeans, almost painful. I move her hand between us so she can feel my hard length. She grimaces, cheeks growing rosy, when she notices her wetness on the denim.

"Don't be embarrassed, *principessa*," I whisper against the shell of her ear. "It's so fucking hot. It drives me absolutely feral how drenched you are for me."

The blush fades as she nibbles on her bottom lip and begins to stroke my dick over the jeans.

"Trust me when I say it's taking all my willpower not to come just from looking at you." I curl my hand around her cheek and stroke her soft skin with the pad of my thumb. Her eyes glisten, pupils blown with desire.

"Raf, I—"

I cut off her words with my eager mouth, too hungry for those swollen lips. As I devour her, her hand slips beneath my jeans and closes around my cock. She's not the only one who's wet, her hand easily glides down my shaft, and I release a hiss. "Mmm, that hand alone is lethal."

I thrust against her palm and precum glistens on the tip. Fuck, I'm like a teenager, ready to blow. I really hope she's on the fucking pill because I want to feel her warm pussy clenching around my dick. But after the last time, I wait, biting my tongue. I don't want to spook her by saying something stupid again. Just when I'm certain I'm going to explode in her palm, she releases me and makes quick work of my zipper.

Stepping out of my jeans and boxers, I flip us around so she's flat on the mattress now, and I stand between her legs, my cock thick and ready. Her gaze drops between my legs, and that same expression sets in. Fear? Horror?

I just don't understand…

"Are you okay?" My voice is so ragged I barely recognize the rough timbre as my own.

Her head bounces up and down.

"Are you sure you still want this?"

She snags her bottom lip between her teeth and parts her legs for me, placing my hand at her apex. A thrill surges up my spine as I kneel between her thighs and glide my finger through her wet folds.

"Oh, fuck, *principessa*, you do want this, don't you?" I find her clit, rubbing slow circles and her head falls back on a groan, eyes closing. I want to fuck her so badly, I'm going to come in seconds once I'm inside her. Shit, which reminds me… "I need to grab a condom."

"I'm on the pill," she murmurs as I continue to tease her clit. "Serena made me."

Thank *Dio* for the fiery little blonde. The idea of feeling all of her without anything between us only makes me harder.

"I'm not seeing anyone else, obviously, so I mean, unless you are—"

"Fuck no," I hiss. Even if I had a second to myself there is no one else. There hasn't been, not really, not since *her*.

As I continue to circle her clit, I wrap my free hand around my cock and run my head across her slick entrance. Her eyes snap open, that fear flashing again, and I can feel her pussy tense around my finger. I pause, fiery heat racing through my dick which is just inches from burying inside her. It's the moment I've been dreaming about for months, but, *cazzo*, something feels off.

"Isa," I growl, my voice still laced thick with desire despite the confusion. "What's going on?"

"Just go slow, okay?" The faint line between her brows puckers, something unreadable streaking through those expressive blue eyes.

And then it hits me, like a mother-fucking freight train. How tight she feels around my fingers, how she panicked last time right before we got this close, how controlling her father is... No, it can't be. My heart cracks against my ribs, louder, harder, faster.

I fix my eyes to hers, capturing her in what I hope is a reassuring gaze. "Tell me why I should go slow, *principessa*."

Her cheeks heat, an intoxicating stain coating her cheeks.

"Isa, please."

She squeezes her eyes shut and grits out, "It's my first time, okay?"

CHAPTER 38
CLINGY AND ATTACHED

I*sabella*

Embarrassment steamrolls over me as I blurt out the mortifying truth. I'm a twenty-two-year-old virgin. Raf kneels between my legs, his cock still rock-hard and ready to go, his expression an unreadable mask. Those penetrating eyes are locked on mine as he searches for the truth in my gaze. Why would I lie about something like this?

When the silence reaches uncomfortable levels, I try to squirm free, but his hands clamp around my thighs, locking me in place.

"Raf, let go," I hiss.

"No." The surprise frozen into his expression has worn off, replaced by something else. A look I can't quite describe.

"What do you mean no?"

"You can't just drop a bomb like that and then try to run away." He crawls over me, pinning me to the mattress with his massive frame. His cock is heavy against my thigh as he braces his arms on either side of my head and locks me in that piercing shadowed gaze. The corner of his lip twitches as he regards me in a new way. Like I'm something fragile… or sacred? An endless minute later, he sets the wry smile free. "I told you that pussy was mine, didn't I? I just had no idea how right I was."

An unexpected laugh bubbles out before I smack him on the shoulder. "Oh, shut the fuck up."

He presses his forehead to mine and inhales a deep breath. "This isn't something to be embarrassed about. Actually, it's hot as fuck. I've never been with a virgin."

I chuckle again, the sparkle in his eyes relieving some of the tension. "You haven't?"

Raf shakes his head. "No, so it would be a first for me too." He brushes his lips against mine before pulling back. "Assuming you still want to?"

"Do you?" I squeak. Drawing in a breath to compose myself, I force out the words I've been practicing since our last failed attempt. "I don't want you to think just because you'll be my first, I'll get all clingy and attached or whatever…"

"Of course not." A smile still tugs at his lips.

"I'm not one of those sappy girls. I just want to get it over with to be honest."

"Ah, I see." He pins me in that dark gaze, a dangerous glint in his eyes. "And what if I get all clingy and attached? What if once I've claimed that pussy as mine, I refuse to let anyone else ever have it again?"

A chill crawls up my spine, spilling goosebumps up and down my arms. "You don't really seem like the clingy type. You said yourself you didn't do relationships."

"That's true." His lips pucker.

"But you are crazy controlling, jealous, possessive and slightly unhinged so I could see how this could become a problem." Now I'm the one grinning.

"Also, true."

"So maybe we should just forget all about this." I wave a dismissive hand and attempt to sit up, but Raf drops his entire weight on top of me, pinning me to the spot. I do my best not to giggle, despite the irritation furrowing his brow.

"I don't think so, *principessa*. You can't tease a man like that. Do you have any idea how long I've waited for this moment?"

"Not longer than me." I shoot him a smirk.

"Fair enough," he grumbles. Shifting his weight to one arm, he caresses my cheek, slowly running his thumb across my face. "I want this, Isabella, I want you. I've tried so damned hard to deny it, and maybe I should especially now, but it's too late for me. I would be fucking honored to be your first. So unless you've changed your mind, I'd like to give you that incredible night I promised." He captures my lips, searing his words with a fiery kiss that leaves my toes curling. "Oh, one more thing. I can't promise I won't go all psycho jealous after I've claimed that sweet pussy."

A stupid grin slides across my face. "Good. Because I can't promise I won't get all clingy and attached."

A deep chuckle rumbles his chest, reverberating against my own. He presses another gentle kiss to my lips before lifting up so he can drag my dress up over my head. "We're going to take our time and do this right. I need to get you ready for me. I don't want it to be unpleasant for you."

"Yeah, your cock is a little intimidating." I snag my bottom lip between my teeth as I take in the thick, veiny monster.

He slides down my body, parting my legs then settles between my thighs. "You're practically a doctor, *principessa*." His gaze turns savage as he takes me in. "You know that a vagina is meant to stretch, and I can already tell it was made for my cock."

Before I can summon a response, his tongue slides

through my wet folds, and my back arches against the mattress. "Oh, fuck, Raf."

"That's right, *principessa*." His head pops up over my dark curls, chin glistening with my arousal. "*Dio*, you taste so good I could eat you for every meal." He runs that tongue across his chin and groans, long and deep. "First, I'm going to fuck that tight little pussy with my tongue, then my finger, and then you'll be ready for my cock."

"Umhmm…" It's the best I can muster.

My fingers curl into his hair, urging him back to the pounding pulse at my core. With a chuckle, his tongue sweeps out and circles the taut bundle of nerves begging for release. The man is a work horse, licking and sucking, driving me closer to the edge with every passing second. He devours me like I gobble down a plate of pasta.

Dio, it's hot as hell.

As his tongue continues to lavish me his thick finger circles the sensitive nerve endings around my entrance. I want it inside me. I want to fuck his finger and pretend I'm riding that huge cock. Tilting my hips, I grind against his fingertip.

Raf's head springs up again, a wicked grin on his face, as if he's truly enjoying this. "Tell me what you want, *principessa*." He lifts his hand and sucks his finger into his mouth, swirling his tongue around. Then he pulls it out with a sharp pop. "Are you ready for this?"

My head bobs up and down.

"One or two?"

My breath catches, a rush of heat flushing my cheeks.

"Let's start with one then." With his dark gaze locked on mine, he slides his hand between my legs. Running his finger across my soaked center, he teases for a devastatingly long minute before dipping inside me.

He watches as I wriggle, my hips lifting to meet each

thrust of his finger. "That's a good girl. Do you feel your pussy tightening around me?"

I nod.

"Now, since my hands are a little busy, why don't you touch your breasts? They're aching, aren't they?"

My head dips again as I notice my nipples are so hard they could cut glass.

"Touch them for me and pretend those are my hands teasing them to tight little peaks."

I do as I'm told because damn it, they are aching to be touched. Closing my eyes, I pretend its Raf's calloused palms, his thick fingers toying and twisting. *Dio*, between that and his tongue and finger at my apex, I'm hurtling toward an orgasm. The fire is blossoming, building, and seconds away from detonating.

His finger thrusts more quickly, matching the fevered pace of my hips. "I'm going to try another finger, okay, *principessa*? I need you nice and relaxed and ready for me."

"Okay," I rasp out.

His mouth takes my clit as a second finger fills me. The rush of sensations is like a tidal wave. So much Raf, everywhere.

"I'm going to come," I pant.

"Hold on, just a little longer," he purrs against my clit, the vibrations alone sending me plummeting toward the edge.

"I can't," I cry.

"Yes, you can." He sucks and licks, his fingers thrusting harder, deeper, and I'm nothing but a raging ball of blazing sensations.

I hold off for another few seconds before that buzz ignites at the base of my spine.

"Come for me, Isabella," he murmurs against my clit before his tongue spins in another devastating circle.

With one final thrust of those magical digits, I soar over

the edge, crying his name. My fingers dig into his hair, reveling in the silky tendrils as a roar of ecstasy pounds through me. I ride the wave of pleasure as smoldering irises bore into me, enjoying every second of my release.

I'm nothing but a boneless, quivering mess a long minute later.

Raf crawls up the length of me, and I feel his cock still heavy against my belly. His eyes sparkle with mirth, pupils blown out with lust. "Don't you dare tell me you're tired already, *principessa*. We're just getting started."

CHAPTER 39
YOU'RE MINE

Isabella

Raffaele's eyes sear into mine as he hovers over me, the crown of his enormous cock nudging at my entrance. He drops gentle kisses along my jaw and slowly moves up my ear. With each brush of his lips, the pressure builds between my legs. He's trying to distract me, attempting to slip inside me. But despite how wet I am, he's huge and the initial penetration is going to hurt. I try to look at it clinically, logically. But in the end, it's still my vagina about to be split open by that monstrous cock.

"Isa?" His eyes find mine once more, the torrent of emotions streaking through those bottomless irises startling. "Are you ready?"

My head bounces up and down enthusiastically, but he must read the fear in my eyes because he pulls back, bracing his arms on either side of my head.

"Don't lie to me, *principessa*."

"I'm not." I worry my bottom lip between my teeth.

"There is no rush. We don't have to do this tonight…"

I wrap my hands around his perfect ass and drive him closer, so his head once again sits firmly poised at my center. "I want to… I want *you*."

"I'm not going anywhere, you know that, right?"

My head dips, but my heart soars. And as much as I feel the truth in his words, what if we realize what a bad idea this is? The fact that he agreed to the whole thing is a miracle, and I'm terrified he'll take it back.

And despite feeling a little guilty about abandoning Serena, I lace my arms around his neck and curl my legs around his back, baring myself to him. "I'm ready."

"Okay." The corners of his eyes crinkle, a wary expression flitting over the typically determined set of his jaw. "I'll go slowly, and if it hurts just say the word, and I'll stop."

Right.

He presses a kiss to my forehead then blows out a breath, wild eyes chasing to mine. "Just so that we're clear, I've never done this gently before. So I'll need you to guide me."

I nod as a tremor of fear surges up my spine. I'm not surprised, Raf doesn't seem like a guy who ever made love to a woman. He's probably as ruthless in bed as he is in real life.

"Just keep your eyes on me, *principessa*." His deep timbre soothes the building turmoil and once he captures me in that gaze, the remaining panic starts to recede. He kisses me softly at first, then his mouth becomes more demanding much like the second surge of fire kindling in my core.

I'm still buzzing from the first orgasm, but the thought of his cock inside me has those embers igniting all over again. His hand moves down my body, caressing my breasts, running down my abs and leaving a blaze in its wake. Then he angles himself at my entrance, and my entire body tenses again.

"Isabella," he whispers, the desire lacing his tone loosening my muscles a tiny bit. "You have to relax, or it'll never work."

"Okay, I can do this." I draw in a deep breath as he runs his head through my wet folds, and I focus on each little nerve-ending alight in pleasure.

"Don't overanalyze this, just feel," he murmurs against my mouth as he licks my tongue, then nibbles on my bottom lip. "Feel my cock against your soaked pussy, feel how ready you are for me and how hard I am for you. Think about how much I want you, how long I've craved to claim you as mine. How every single touch since the first day I met you has been complete and utter torture."

"Do it," I whisper.

His eyes widen, hooded lids snapping open.

"I want you to be the first man I feel inside me."

A surge of desire floods his expression, and I feel his ass clench beneath my palms as he thrusts. I gasp, all the air catching in my throat as his crown drives inside me.

"Are you okay?" Fear carves into his handsome face as he regards me, completely and utterly frozen.

My head dips. "More."

Raf glances down between us, and I follow his line of sight. The majority of his cock still stands between us. He can't be more than an inch or two in. "I'm going to ease in a little. But fuck, is this hard, because you feel so damned good."

A stupid grin crawls across my lips because despite the false bravado, I'm nervous. Only *Dio* knows how many women Raf has been with, and I have no idea what I'm doing. I'm just laying here, that's what I'm doing.

A sharp sting shoots up my pussy, and there it is, medically speaking. There goes my virginity, and he's not even fully seated inside me.

"You're doing really well, Isabella," Raf purrs as he

pushes further inside me inch by inch. "That's my good girl."

I lift my hips, trying to meet his slow thrusts. As the sting dissipates, the sparks of desire begin to reignite. And I want more of him.

"Mmm, you feel so good. Your pussy is just perfect, so tight, so ready for my cock."

He drives deeper, and I can feel myself stretching around his width. It goes on and on for an endless minute until I'm so full of cock I'm certain I feel him at the base of my spine.

"Almost there, *principessa*. I'm so proud of you."

For some reason I can't explain, I'm basking in the spotlight of his praises. And it feels like a challenge, to take that giant dick all the way.

"Almost there, just another inch or two." He eases the rest of the way in, and a groan purses his lips. "Good girl, I knew you could take my cock. How does it feel?"

"Good," I murmur.

"You feel like heaven... like the glorious afterlife. I must have done something right in this lifetime to deserve you." He sweeps his lips across mine. "I could stay like this forever."

Again, I'm smiling like an idiot and the good news is that the sharp sting has dulled. More than that, I'm ready for more. My hips want to move, want to feel his thick length gliding in and out of me, like I've imagined it hundreds of times.

As if he's read my mind, his finger slides between us and finds the pulsing nub at my center. With his finger on my clit, he starts to circle and my hips rock against him. It drives him impossibly deeper inside me, but instead of pain, I only feel the fiery sensations blossoming again.

"I'll go slow, but it's going to be hard because you feel so damned incredible. Just shove me off if I start to lose control." The feral look in his eye has me wanting him to lose control. So bad.

He thrusts, and his head hits something, buried in the far recesses of my pussy. It feels amazing.

"Again," I murmur, rocking my hips up to meet his.

"You sure?"

"Yes," I rasp out.

As his finger continues its shattering circles, his hips pick up the pace. In and out. In and in and in. Fuck, that feels good. I hitch my heels around his ass, driving him deeper, so deep that thick head kisses my spine.

"Oh, Raf," I groan, my head falling back as he hits that mythical spot once more.

"How does it feel now, *principessa*?" A savage grin curls his lips as he starts to move faster.

"Incredible," I purr. Why the hell had I waited so long to give into this? But also, I'm so glad I waited for *him*, for this moment.

I may not be in love with—wait… no, it can't be. My heart skitters on a beat. It's the rush of emotions, of hormones and adrenaline. It's not *that*. It can't be.

He makes me laugh like no one else while driving me crazy like no other. Just because I think about him constantly, I want to be near him at all times, and I've never felt safer around anyone else, it doesn't mean…

His eyes lance into mine, enormous pupils nearly eclipsing his midnight irises. "Are you ready to come for me again?"

"So ready," I pant, driving the spiraling thoughts to the far corners of my mind to deal with later.

He stills inside me, both his finger and cock freezing, and I barely restrain the frustrated whine from slipping out. "You're mine, do you understand, *principessa*? Now that I've had this pussy, claimed it as mine, no one else can have you. *Capisci*?"

I nod because at that moment as he holds my orgasm hostage, I would agree to anything. I don't consider the consequences of my promise because I can barely think at all with that delicious heat racing through my veins.

"I want you to say it, Isabella."

"My pussy is yours," I pant.

"You are mine." A pair of tormented, slightly unhinged eyes stare down at me from beneath a tumble of dark hair.

"I am yours," I echo. I want it to be a lie. I tell myself it's just for the orgasm, but a part of me believes every traitorous word.

And just like that, I plummet over the edge of sanity as he thrusts into me one last time. Blazing pleasure rips at my spine then tears through my veins, rushing through every inch of me. It's like nothing I've ever felt before, the depth of raging emotions, the intense ecstasy. I'm barely aware as Raf's cock jerks inside me, and my name parts his lips. Warmth spills down my leg as he fills me up with his cum, and I only squeeze him tighter, trying to wring out every last ounce of pleasure.

"*Cazzo*, Isa," he pants as he drops down on top of me, both of us glistening with sweat. His forehead dips to mine, and a heart-wrenching grin splits his lips. "That was not what I expected…"

Me neither. It was a thousand times better than I'd ever imagined.

And that is terrifying…

CHAPTER 40
A FIERY BLAZE

R*affaele*

I lay there, on top of Isabella for a long moment, my cock still buried in her sweetness, like a total *coglione* trying to catch my breath and calm my racing heart. And keep myself from just staring at her. She looks so beautiful, hair wild, cheeks rosy, pouty lips swollen, all mussed up from fucking.

She looks absolutely perfect.

She looks like *mine*.

I can't tear my gaze away from her. I want to commit this moment to memory, capture it and emblazon it in my mind where it will remain rent free until the day I die. This gorgeous, intelligent, amazing woman gave herself to me, to *me*. I don't fucking deserve her, but I will take her anyway because that is the type of man I am.

And if she'll let me, I'll claim her as mine over and over again until the sun rises.

Isabella squirms beneath me, tearing me from my scattered thoughts. *Dio*, I must be crushing her. "Are you okay?"

She nods, her legs still clamped around my hips.

"Do you want me to move?"

She shakes her head, and a breathy sigh spills out. We fit so damned perfectly together. A part of me was scared I'd hurt her. I'd never been with a virgin, and I was admittedly big, but that pussy had stretched to fit me effortlessly. It had never felt this right with any other woman, not even—

I cut off my dark musings of the past, refusing to compare the two. Isabella is not Laura, and she would never end up that way. I would put my life before hers a thousand times over before I let anyone touch her.

"Are you tired?"

She hasn't spoken now for a few whole minutes which is very unlike my chatty princess.

"A little," she finally murmurs.

It occurs to me I'm still inside her, and maybe she's uncomfortable. "Sore?"

"Not really."

Her expression is relaxed, but a little too blank for my liking. I can usually read her like a book, but right now, I have no idea what she's feeling. Does she regret it? Based on the orgasm, I'm fairly certain she enjoyed it, but was it all for show?

I bring a tentative hand to her cheek and caress her soft skin. "You're scaring me, *principessa*, I've never seen you this quiet."

A soft chuckle slips out. "I'm just thinking."

"About what?"

"What do you think?" A hint of mischief darkens the brilliant blue of her eyes.

"For once, I have no idea."

"Well now, that's interesting. I may have lost my virginity, but I've gained a new superpower—keeping my innermost thoughts from you."

Now, a faint chuckle rumbles my chest. "First of all, you didn't *lose* your virginity. You gave it to me." The thought has my chest tightening, my lungs struggling to function. Why would she give me that honor? "Now, it's mine forever."

Her eyes narrow as she regards me. "That's hardly fair. I gave you something so meaningful and what are you going to give me in return?"

My heart. My fucking soul. Everything.

I tuck the errant thoughts behind my teeth and keep them there. Because it's too much and too soon.

And wrong.

I remind myself for the hundredth time because in my experience one cannot be an effective bodyguard once sex is involved, and feelings? A thousand times worst.

"Whatever you want," I finally breathe.

She starts to move beneath me, her hips grinding against mine. My semi-hard dick is still inside her and if she keeps this up, I'll be flying at full mast again in only a few seconds.

"This is what you want?" The corner of my lip twitches.

Her hands slide to my ass, fingers digging in and urging me on. "For starters."

"Are you sure you can handle it? I might not be able to restrain myself now that I know how sinfully sweet you feel."

"I can handle it." She vaults her hips and rolls us over so she's straddling me.

My now fully hard cock dives deeper at this new angle, and a hiss surges through her gritted teeth. She repositions herself, and I can almost feel her pussy walls stretching around me. They're throttling my cock, so damn warm and wet. Isabella is the home I'd abandoned long ago, the one I didn't realize I still needed.

I sit up and capture one of her nipples in my mouth, dragging my hands down her spine to keep her upright and further deepening the angle of penetration. I devour one perfect breast then the other as she grinds into my cock.

"Next time we'll have to do this with Nutella. Licking the sweetness off every inch of you would be my absolute heaven."

Her eyes widen, mouth bowing into a tempting curve. "Oh, *Dio*, yes!"

She's slick as she slides up and down my shaft, so eager, so wet for me. My hands grip her hips, fingers curling into her flesh to guide her up and down. We start slowly, but after a few devastating minutes, I can't control myself. I quicken the tempo, the steady rise and fall turning manic.

I only came ten minutes ago, and already, I feel my balls tightening.

Her head falls back, dark hair cascading across her bare shoulders, and fuck, she's the most radiant woman I've ever seen. Her breasts bounce as she rides me like a pro, whimpering and moaning as I fill her with my cock.

"Are you going to come for me again, *principessa*?" This would be the third, a definite record for me in such a short period of time.

She groans in response before she slides one of my hands from her hips and positions my fingers at her clit.

"You want me to fuck you with my finger and my cock?"

"Yes," she pants. "I'm close."

So am I. Embarrassingly.

I press my fingers to her clit, letting her rub against me without so much as moving. Taking her nipple in my mouth, I suck long and hard before dragging my teeth over the sensitive tip.

"Oh, fuck, Raf…"

"That's right, *principessa*, I've got you. Come for me again."

And she did.
Like a good girl, for once.

As the first rays of sunlight slide in through the windows, my eyes jolt open. An indescribable feeling settles over me, one I haven't felt in years. Contentment. Isabella's head slowly rises and falls with the steady rhythm of my chest. She's naked, sprawled on top of me, and my arms are firmly encircling her torso, keeping her in place.

Besides on the jet with Isabella a month ago, I can't remember the last time I slept with a woman. Not sex… even though it's been a while on that count too.

My cock is still nestled between her legs, and on the way to becoming hard again. As if she's felt it, or maybe it's my increasing heart rate, her lids slowly open. She lets out a yawn as a lazy smile slides across her lips.

"Morning, *principessa*," I mumble.

She teeters to the side, but my arms tighten, keeping her firmly on top of me. "Morning." Her brows pinch as they regard me. "You look different today."

That's because she's never seen me like this… happy. But I don't dare speak the word out loud. We agreed last night it was supposed to be a one-night thing. I already had her twice last night, and my cock is quickly readying for a third —my total damnation. At this point, I'm a goner.

I'll have to ask Luca to send another guard as my replacement. I can't function properly if all I can think about is sinking my cock into that irresistible pussy, kissing those pouty lips, running my fingers through that silky hair, spending every minute… *fuck*!

A brush of soft lips drags me back to the present, and I

meet a pair of inquisitive sapphire orbs. "I should probably go downstairs and check on Serena."

"No." The sound is nothing more than a growl, more animal than human. I tighten my hold around her and run my hand down to her ass. I slip my finger down further, until I feel the wetness through her folds.

"Raf!" She squirms on top of me which only makes me harder.

"Just one more time," I whisper against those perfect lips.

"But that'll be the third one…"

I guess I'm not the only one keeping count.

"I was damned the moment I met you, Isabella Valentino. But if I'm destined to burn, at least I'll go down in a fiery blaze that lights up the Roman sky." I lift her hips and drop her down onto my erection.

Her head falls back, a groan parting her lips as I fill her to the hilt. And everything else vanishes.

CHAPTER 41
THREE IN ONE NIGHT

I sabella

"You're fucking glowing… don't you dare lie to me, Bella." Serena narrows her eyes at me through the mirror before her cheeks hollow, and she brushes a healthy amount of blush across her high cheekbones. When she's happy with the look she's achieved, she closes the compact and whirls on me. "Something happened with Raf, and I'm not letting you out of this bathroom until you spill."

I lean against the closed door, doing my best attempt at nonchalant. Which is clearly not working. "Nothing happened…"

"You little liar!" She cackles, trapping me against the light timber. "I can practically smell the sex on you." She pinches my cheek, an indulgent smile crawling across her face. "My little cousin isn't a virgin anymore."

"Shut up, Sere!" I hiss. I've always told my cousin everything, but for some reason, this feels different. Not to mention the fact that if this ever got back to *Papà*, Raf would be a dead man.

"What's the big deal? Raf is smoking hot and that body... If I had a guard like that, I would've broken him months ago."

"And that's exactly why Uncle Dante only assigns you seasoned professionals and mostly females."

She laughs again. "Pa does know me well." Turning toward the mirror to finish the final touches on her makeup, she finally releases me. "He's been in Milano twice since I arrived, and I'm sure that's no coincidence."

"Really? To check up on you?"

"He says it's some new business opportunity for the Kings, but I don't really buy it." She shrugs. "Enough about *Papà*. I want to hear every dirty detail." Serena stares at me expectantly, her eyes alight with curiosity. "So…"

"It was fine." I cross my arms against my chest as my heart starts to pound at the heated memories surging to the surface.

"Well, it sure sounded more than fine." A devious grin twists her lips.

"Oh *Dio*, you heard me?" Heat flares across my cheeks, burning all the way up to the tips of my ears.

"I *was* sleeping in the adjoining room."

I want to crawl into a hole and die. How embarrassing.

"And as first times go, it sure seems like you enjoyed it."

"It was fine…"

"Damn girl, you have no idea what fine is and trust me, that wasn't it." She fans her face dramatically. "That was mind-blowing! Three orgasms in one night? On your first time? That's unheard of. The man must be a master."

A ridiculous smile splatters across my face.

"When you're done with him, maybe I could take a test drive?"

A streak of jealousy roars through my insides, clawing at my lungs. The thought of his hands on Serena, on anyone, has red-hot fury pounding through my veins. "No," I blurt, the word spewing out like venom. "No way."

My cousin whirls on me, her light brows puckered. "Whoa, chill. I was just joking." She eyes me for a long moment before a knowing smile parts her lips. "Oh, shit, Bella. You're falling for him?"

"What? No, of course not." My voice comes out shrill and wild, a few octaves higher than my norm.

"Then why are you all twitchy?" She arches a perfectly plucked brow.

"I'm not falling for him, Sere. We both agreed this was a one-time thing. You know how Raf is with all his rules…"

"And if he wasn't?"

I shrug. "It doesn't matter. He's my bodyguard, and he's the only reason *Papá* let me come to Rome."

Two quick knocks at the door puts an abrupt end to our conversation, and a familiar voice seeps through the cracks. A voice that has my entire body lighting up at the deep timbre. "Isabella, can I talk to you for a second?"

That damned heat blossoms across my cheeks again as Serena watches me with a stupid grin. "You are so fucked, cuz," she whispers.

Shooting her the middle finger, I spin around and jerk the door open. Raf stands in the hallway, an unreadable expression playing on his unfairly gorgeous face.

"What's up?"

That cold mask drops, his eyes heating as he takes in my little black dress. It's my go-to with spaghetti straps, a plunging neckline and a hem that creeps up mid-thigh. "Um, I need to walk the perimeter with you before the guests arrive."

Ah, of course. It's back to business. Our one night—and morning—are up, and now, we're just bodyguard and client… My heart staggers at the whiplash. But I stiffen my lower lip and my shoulders as I follow him down the hallway.

"We'll have two guards at the door, then another three surrounding the building as always. I'll be with you—"

"As always," I cut in.

The hint of a smile tips up the corner of his lips, but it's gone as quickly as it appears. "And we'll have Manetti as backup. He'll be stationed on the roof." He motions toward the steps that lead to the third floor.

"Sounds like you have everything covered."

"I'm trying…" He opens the door to the roof and pauses, allowing me to go first.

My breath catches at the sight. Beneath the last rays of the sinking sun, strings of twinkling lights illuminate the space, weaving a magical tapestry of warmth. The lights hang in graceful arcs from one side of the rooftop to the other, enveloping the area in a soft, enchanting glow. With the breathtaking views of Rome's ancient skyline in the background, it's the most beautiful scene I could have ever imagined.

"It's—it's incredible," I murmur as I walk across the terracotta tiles.

Scattered across the rooftop are small tables draped in crisp linen, each one adorned with flickering candles that add to the ambience. In the far corner, a DJ table is set up, the entrancing beats already filling the air. Raf moves into step behind me, shadowing my every move. Once I've taken it all in, I stop beneath an arc of twinkling lights and find a pair of piercing midnight orbs.

"Who did this?" I whisper.

Raf's broad shoulders lift, straining against his uniform of all black. "Some of the guys helped, but I, uh, …"

"You did this?" My wild heartbeats stagger.

He nods sharply. "I knew how badly you wanted this rooftop party. You've been talking about it since we moved in, and I figured with Serena being here, now would be the time to go all out."

"Even though you were against it?"

"I'm against anything that puts you at risk." His eyes swiftly scan the rooftop before his hand lifts to my cheek. His calloused thumb brushes my skin, and a whirlwind of sensations ignite. "Including this thing between us…"

I bristle at his ominous tone, but I clench my teeth to keep from saying something completely inappropriate. Because Serena knows me too damned well. And I am falling for my forbidden guard. If I'm being honest with myself, it started well before the mind-blowing sex.

"Besides," says Raf, interrupting my musings, "after only a few months with you, *principessa*, I've already learned you always get what you want."

"That is true." I smirk and step into him, placing my hand on his chest once I've confirmed the rooftop is clear. His thundering heartbeat punches my palm, and that reassurance I so badly needed forces the words from my lips. "And what I want now, is another night with you."

A deep growl vibrates his chest, resonating through my hand. "Isa…"

"I know."

"No, you don't." He covers my hand with his big one, pressing my palm firmly against his chest. "And I pray to *Dio* that you never will."

With that, he releases my hand, takes a step back and whirls toward the door. I stand there for an endless moment, watching as he walks away from me.

And for once in my life, I wonder if this will be the first time I don't get what I want most.

The circle of grad students surrounding Serena and me grows larger and more frenzied with every passing hour. Maybe it's the DJ or maybe it's the waiters passing out shots of limoncello. Even my professor, Massimo, has joined us on the dance floor.

Which has Raf bristling as he watches me from the outer edge of the crowd. I can feel the tension radiating from the stiff set of his shoulders, the hard clench of his jaw. So I only grind my ass a little harder against whichever intern has the balls to dance behind me.

The manic tempo of the music begins to slow, and Professor Massimo inches closer, wedging himself between my cousin and me. Pushing his glasses up his nose, he offers a hand. "May I have this dance?"

Serena elbows me in the side when I take too long to answer, and my head bobs in reply.

With a smile, Massimo's arm weaves around my back, pulling me into his chest. The trace of citrus and cedarwood fills my nostrils as he draws me close. It's not bad, it's just not the familiar musky scent of Raffaele.

"This was a lovely idea, Isabella. The rooftop is the perfect spot for a gathering." His light eyes scan the skyline and the surrounding buildings, and an easy smile curves his lips. Twinkling stars dot the night sky, and a sultry breeze lifts the tumble of golden locks from Massimo's forehead. "I was hoping I could take you out again. Perhaps next weekend, once your cousin returns to Milano?"

My gaze flickers over his shoulder to where Raf stands, a sinister scowl etched into his jaw, as if he's somehow heard the question.

"Yeah, maybe," I finally reply, tearing my gaze away. "I'll have to check my rotation. It's been crazy at the E.R."

"I'm sure I can help with that." His smile grows wider. "I'll speak to Maria in the scheduling department."

A month ago, a date with the charming professor would've been exactly what I wanted, but right now, there is only one man that fills my every waking thought.

And he's stalking toward us with a murderous gleam in his eye.

CHAPTER 42
PUNISHMENT

R*affaele*

Breathe, cazzo. *Inhale, exhale. Inhale, exhale.* I force my lungs to continue their steady pace despite the suffocating anger coiling around my organs as I stalk toward Isa and the professor.

His hands are on *my* client.

His fingers dipping dangerously close to the curve of her ass.

And in a minute, I'm going to rip off every single one of those fingers for daring to touch what's mine.

Shoving my hands in my pockets to restrain the urge, I don the practiced smile as I reach the crowd of interns writhing around Isa on the dance floor.

It takes every last ounce of willpower to keep from jerking her out of his arms and tossing her over my shoulder. My fingers twitch in my pockets, my palm itching to spank that ass for disobeying me. I thought I'd made it perfectly clear. She is mine. And that means no one touches her without my permission. Which means no one would *ever* touch her. I tower over the *coglione* then lean into Isa's ear. "Excuse me, *signorina*. I need a word."

Goose bumps spill across her bare shoulders and race down her arms. The sight of her body's reaction to mine sends a swirl of satisfaction straight to my dick. "Right now?" she whispers, the faint hitch only discernible because I know her so well.

"Yes, right now." I barely restrain the beastly growl.

The professor releases her, and I can finally breathe, the steel bands around my lungs loosening. My hand instinctively wraps around her biceps, toting her through the mass of bodies. As soon as my flesh meets hers, my haggard breaths begin to normalize.

Merda, what has this woman done to me?

I've always had a possessive streak and been controlling to a fault, but this… this is beyond my typical madness. As I lead her across the bustling rooftop to the steps, I attempt to remember the last time I felt this out of control. The answer is on the tip of my tongue, but I refuse to acknowledge it.

Because I'm terrified.

Because the last time I felt like this, everything went to hell.

A desperate tangle of fear, anxiety and anger twists and churns in my gut. I hate the feeling, the utter loss of control. Fear is weakness, but fury, that I can hold onto. Channeling that anger, I quicken my steps until I'm practically dragging Isa down the stairs.

"Slow down, you're hurting me," she hisses once we reach the second-floor hallway and the thrumming beats of the DJ start to fade. She whirls around just a few feet from her bedroom door and glares up at me, planting her heels so I'm forced to stop. "What's going on with you?"

"You let him touch you," I roar, unable to keep the

tornado of emotions at bay for a minute longer. I tower over her, pinning her against the wall.

"Massimo?"

"Yes! That *bastardo* had his hands all over you. He was touching your hand, your ass, whispering in your ear… *No one* touches what's mine." I rake my hands through my hair, tugging at the wild ends until the pangs distract me from the overwhelming feelings surging in my gut. "You. Are. *Mine*," I growl, punctuating every word by erasing another inch between us. "Didn't I make that clear the other night?" I glance down the hallway, ensuring none of the other guards are around, then I dip my mouth to her ear. "Now, I'm going to have to punish you for your disobedience."

Those blazing blue irises ignite, shards of sapphire twinkling beneath the dim lighting. It's not fear, no it's something so much better. Curiosity. "How are you going to do that?" she whispers. "If I allow it…"

Sassy little thing.

And just like that I'm hard.

I slide my hand behind her back and palm her ass. A faint gasp erupts through those pouty lips. "I'm going to spank that perfect little ass until you scream my name." My fingers tighten around her curves, and I press her flush against my cock.

"I thought you said it was only one night…" Her lips are a hairsbreadth from mine, and I can barely think about anything else but capturing them.

"Oh, this isn't sex, *principessa*. This is punishment." I tilt my hips so my erection lodges itself beneath her obscenely short dress and rub my dick against her panties. "We might not be allowed to be together right now, but that doesn't mean I'll let anyone else have you either."

She glares up at me, defiant as all hell. "If I let you spank me, then you have to fuck me after. Or no deal…"

An unexpected chuckle spills out as those mischievous

eyes latch onto mine. "It's funny that you think you have a say in this."

"What's funny is that you thought I would just agree to my punishment like a good girl." She rocks her hips, rubbing her silk thong along the hard ridge of my cock.

Cazzo, even through my slacks, I can feel how drenched she is.

"I told you I always get what I want, Raf."

"Just this once…" I slide both hands down her ass and curl her thighs around my hips before lifting her off the floor and darting into her bedroom. I'm a fucking liar, and I'm well aware of it. I should have known once would never be enough, and now I'm just using whatever I can as an excuse to be near, on top of, inside this incredible creature who has my balls in a chokehold.

I lock the door behind us, rage still pounding through my veins, but something else weaves its way through the fury. Lust, longing and another L word I refuse to consider. With her legs wrapped around me in that indecent dress, I could easily throw her on the bed and slip my cock inside her. And *Dio,* I want that.

But I'm supposed to punish her.

Remind her that she belongs to me and no one else.

So I walk her to the window where a nice ledge stands at the perfect height with sprawling views of the Roman skyline, then I pull the tiny dress up and over her head. She's not wearing a bra, her full breasts tumbling free, and my cock is so hard I'm certain it'll bust the seam of my pants.

"*Cazzo,*" I hiss as I take her in.

Her cheeks are flushed, pupils so wide they nearly consume the brilliant sapphire. She's excited… my little, innocent princess has a naughty side just waiting to burst free.

"You want this, don't you?" I fix my eyes to hers, needing

the verbal confirmation. It's too easy for me to get caught up in the moment, but I want her to be sure. She was a virgin only a day ago, and despite how badly I need this, I would never force it upon her.

Her head dips, her flush deepening by the second.

"I need you to say it, *principessa*." I frame her face with my hands, locking her in my unyielding gaze.

"I want you to spank me," she breathes. "I want everything with you."

I've been shot at least a dozen times and yet nothing prepares me for those words. For the stab in the lungs, for the rush of air evacuating my chest and the piercing agony in my heart.

"I—"

Before I can utter a word, she places her hands on the ledge and bends over.

A groan fills my chest, vibrating low in my throat. She cants her head over her shoulder, and a naughty smirk tips up the corners of her lips. "Is this right?"

"Fuck, *principessa*, it's so right." I grip her hips, so desperate just to touch her. Once I've had my fill of running my hands up and down her torso and ass, I hitch my fingers through the waistband of her thong and drag it down her legs, dropping to my knees behind her.

Running my hand up the inside of her thigh, I push her legs apart. "That's a good girl, spread your legs for me." Arousal glistens from her dark curls, and damn it, I'm not sure I can wait to fuck her. This is going to be the quickest punishment ever.

From this angle, I can't help myself. I dip my head between her thighs and run my tongue through her wet folds. "Mmm," I purr against her clit. "Just like I remembered it. The sweetest pussy I've ever tasted."

Her knees tremble, the rapid rise and fall of her chest, the delicate bounce of her breasts doing illicit things to my cock.

I circle the taut bud with my tongue, teasing and nibbling until I can feel her orgasm building.

Then I stop.

She groans, muttering a curse.

"This is supposed to be a punishment, remember?" I'm not sure who needs the reminder more, her or me.

Pushing myself off the floor, I unbuckle my belt, then make quick work of my slacks and boxers in one go. The satisfying slough of clothes hitting the floor heightens my senses, electrifying my nerve-endings. I stand behind her, my cock so hard its painful. I inch closer, parting her ass cheeks with my thick head and running myself through her slippery folds. With her in this position, it would be so easy to take what's mine.

But she has to understand first. What it means to truly be *mine*.

"Are you ready, *principessa*?" My voice is nothing more than a serrated snarl.

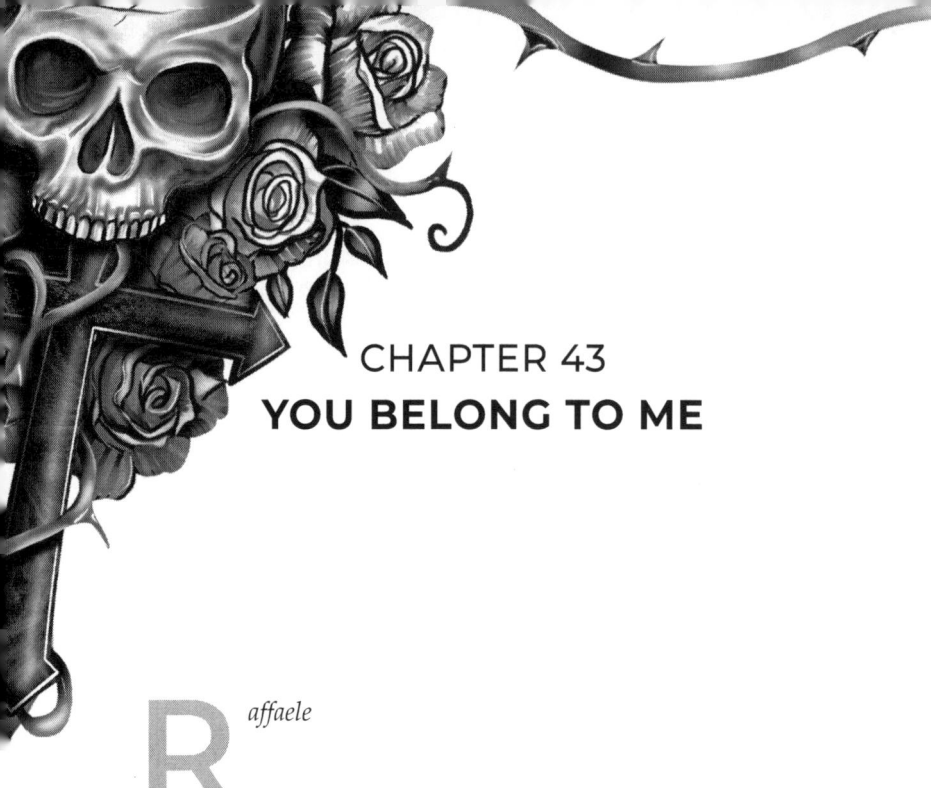

CHAPTER 43
YOU BELONG TO ME

R*affaele*

"Yes," Isabella pants.

And that breathy sigh is all the confirmation I need.

"This is for Massimo." I take a step away, and its practically painful to release her. With one hand rubbing her lower back, I pull the other one back and *smack*.

She jerks as my palm meets her flesh, the crack resounding over the frenzied pounding of my heart. I freeze, my hand still pressed to her warming skin. "Was that okay?" I murmur, something I've *never* asked in a moment like this.

"More…" she whispers, arching her back.

Dio, this woman couldn't be more perfect for me.

Before I pull my hand back again, I cup her pussy with my free one and run my finger over her pulsing clit. "Do you like that?"

Her hips grind into my palm as she groans a yes.

"One more spank, this one for forcing me to endure that

date with Jeff, and then I'm going to fuck that naughty streak right out of you. Understand, *principessa*?"

Her head bounces up and down.

"No more dates. No other men. If you ever let anyone else touch you, you will be punished again. And next time, I'll punish the *bastardo* too. And trust me, his retribution will be nowhere near as pleasurable as yours."

"I understand." Her ass pops up like she's looking forward to this.

And damn, so am I.

The sting across my palm surges all the way down to my dick this time. As I gently fondle her ass cheek after, rubbing the pain away, I curl my free arm around her waist and dip my hand between her thighs. She's impossibly wet.

"I want you inside me now," she whispers as she grinds her pussy against my palm.

"And you've earned it, taking your punishment like a good girl." There's nothing I want more than to take her from behind, but she's been bent over for a while now, and it can't be comfortable.

So instead, I take her hands and help her straighten, then wrap her arms around the back of my neck. Her cheeks are an enticing shade of crimson, and her bottom lip is swollen as if she's been chewing on it. She looks radiant, fearless, and *mine*.

I capture her lips, the hunger explosive. With other women, a view of their bouncing ass as I rail into them from behind is more than enough, but with Isabella, I need more. I want to taste her lips, to hear the sexy sounds I coax out with each thrust, to see the blazing desire in her gaze. I, too, want everything with her.

Cazzo... it's happening.

Her hand curls around my cock, jerking my attention to the fire racing through my veins. She pushes me back against the window ledge until my bare ass hits the cool marble. "Now I want to fuck you while I take in the amazing view." She straddles me, dropping down onto my cock like she's been doing it for years. She takes me in and in and in.

I should know better than to ever allow us in this compromising position. My ass is against the window for anyone to see. Luckily, my broad shoulders block most of the glass, hopefully keeping her out of sight. Still, it's risky and stupid, but I can't deny her.

Damn, she feels so good, tightening around me, drawing me in like I'm the drug she can't get enough of.

I suck one of her nipples into my mouth as my fingers tease and toy with the other. Already, her back is arching as she grinds into me, faint moans echoing between us. It won't be long now, not for either of us.

I'm embarrassingly easy when it comes to her. I feel like a horny teenager. It's weird and incredible… And I don't want it to stop.

She presses her palms against the glass, caging me in against the window and her breasts as she rolls her hips. And damn, it's the hottest thing I've ever seen. Or maybe with her, it all simply feels new and fresh.

"I'm going to make you come with all of Rome bared before you, *principessa*," I whisper as I nibble on her earlobe.

She releases a groan, and goosebumps sprinkle down her arms. "Yes, Raf… I'm ready."

Gripping her hips, I guide her up and down my shaft, making sure to hit that mythical spot that has her chest heaving over and over again. "Just a few more seconds, hold on for me."

Her pants become more ragged, but I capture her in my hooded gaze. "I'm going to fill you with my cum, and I don't want you to clean it up, understand? I want every *bastardo* at that party to smell *me* on you. I want them to know without the shadow of a doubt, that you belong to me."

Isa's head falls back as pleasure roars through her, her

pussy clenching around my cock and forcing my own orgasm. Her name squeezes out through my gritted teeth as I thrust through the explosive energy ripping through me.

"*Cazzo*," I growl as the powerful release sucks all the air from my lungs.

Isabella collapses onto my chest, her forehead resting on the tattoo inked over my heart. "Damn, Raf," she mumbles with a rueful laugh. "And to think, I've been missing out on this for years."

"Because you were meant for me." The dangerous words dribble out before I have the sense to stop them. My mind is mush after that all-consuming orgasm. My lips thin out, and I drop my chin to her head, hoping she'll let the confession slide.

We remain like that for a long moment, tangled in each other with all of Rome lit up behind me. I'm still buried inside her, and it feels good. Too good.

"We should probably get back to the party," she mumbles against my bare chest. Her lips are pressed against the image of the grisly skull, and as if she's noticing it for the first time, she pauses. "What does this tattoo mean?"

I squeeze my eyes closed, not ready to re-live that moment. "The precious balance between life and death," I finally mutter.

"It's beautiful." She runs her finger across the blood-red roses.

I lift her up, winding her legs around my waist and carry her to the bed. "*You* are beautiful." My cum dribbles down her inner thigh and for an instant, the satisfaction nearly outweighs the burgeoning memories of my dark past. "You're right, we should get back." I toss her the crumpled-up dress, then the panties before I step into my slacks.

She stares at her thong then throws it into her hamper in the back of the closet before tugging the skin-tight dress over her head.

"No panties, *principessa*, really? Are you trying to kill me?" I loom over her, my cock already hardening at the thought of her bare beneath that scandalous dress. "Now all I'm going to be able to think about is that pussy dripping with my cum, when I should be focusing on your safety."

"And the perimeter," she teases.

I shake my head, a rueful smile hitching up my lips. It's all I can do to keep from splaying her across the mattress and fucking her senseless until the damned party is over, and we can finally be alone.

Heaving in a breath, I wind my arms around her middle and pull her close. Dropping my forehead to hers, I breathe her in, her tantalizing scent wrapping around me like a warm blanket.

"What are we going to do, Raf?" she whispers, our breath mingling.

"We're going to have to find you a new bodyguard."

Her dark brows pucker as she regards me. "But I don't want anyone else. You said it yourself, you're the best."

"Normally, sure. But not like this. Not when you're taking up all the space in my head. Both heads." I smirk and drop a kiss to her full lips. "We'll figure it out tomorrow, okay?"

She nods and slips her hand through mine, turning toward the door. We walk like that down the hallway, but as the music grows louder, I'm forced to unwind my fingers from hers. I fucking hate it. I want everyone at this damned party to know she's mine, but I console myself with the fact that she's wearing my cum.

Twisting the knob, I hold the door open, allowing my *principessa* to walk through. A wave of noise slams into me, a mix of laughter, loud chatter and the DJ's pounding beats. I should be focused on the perimeter as Isabella pointed out, but instead, my eyes are fixed to her ass which has already started to sway to the music.

As I escort her to the middle of the dance floor, the male interns converge like moths to a flame, and that familiar jealousy surges once more. Nope, I'm not doing this again, especially not now with her pussy bare beneath the short dress for anyone to see. I'm too out of my mind to think about the consequences, so when Jeff walks up and asks her to dance, I jerk her back and spin her into my arms.

Fuck it.

Isabella Valentino is mine, and I don't care who knows it.

CHAPTER 44
DAMAGE CONTROL

Isabella

"So we're dancing together in public now?" I whisper against the shell of Raf's ear as his hands inch dangerously close to my ass.

"Just one dance." His voice is still ragged, just like it was a few minutes ago when I was riding his cock in my bedroom. The heated memories rush to the surface, and if I wasn't still wet from his cum dribbling down my leg, I would be soaked again.

Dio, what has this man done to me?

Just twenty-four hours and he'd turned me from an inexperienced virgin to a crazed sex kitten.

He parts my legs with his muscled thigh and the arm slung around my waist tightens so that I'm essentially riding his leg now. My sensitive bare skin rubs against his jeans, and the friction is almost too much. If we keep dancing like this, I'm going to have another orgasm in the middle of the dancefloor surrounded by my colleagues and professor.

I wouldn't be surprised if that is exactly what my devious bodyguard is up to. There's no better way to prove I belong to him. Which as caveman-like as it sounds, I can't get enough. The rough edge that laces his tone when he rasps out the word *mine* is hot enough to bring me to an immediate orgasm.

Someone bumps me from behind, and I spin my head over my shoulder to find Serena grinding up on Massimo's assistant, Carlo. I met the guy a few times, and he seems decent enough. Hot, too, but in a bookish sort of way.

"Hey, cuz!" Serena shoots me a grin as she spins around, rubbing her ass against Carlo's crotch. She inches closer, her nostrils flaring. "You smell like sex," she whisper-hisses before her mischievous gaze lifts to Raf behind me.

My cheeks flame, mouth curving into a capital O. Is that even possible?

"You know I'm all for you having a good time, but just be careful in public, okay? Your father would lose his shit if he found out…"

I swallow hard, all the excitement from a second ago trickling away. My head bobs numbly as I consider her warning. She's right. We're being stupid and reckless. I lift to my tiptoes scanning over the mass of bodies around me and can just make out one of the guards stationed at the southwest corner. Would they tell *Papà* about this completely inappropriate dancing? Even if they can't see the dirty details through the clump of writhing bodies, the fact remains.

Whirling around to face Raf once again, I take a measured step back, putting some much-needed distance between our bodies, but his hands still linger on my hips.

He immediately stiffens, dark brows furrowing. "What's wrong?"

"I don't want you to get into trouble for this…" I motion back and forth between us.

Raf hisses out a breath before finally releasing me. "This is exactly why we need to find you a new bodyguard as soon as possible."

"Raf," I groan. "You know how *Papà* is. It'll be a months' long process before he finds a suitable one, and he'll force me to return to New York in the meantime. I'll miss out on the rest of the internship."

"I can't protect you like this, *principessa*!" he hisses, lips pressed to the shell of my ear. "Don't you see? I'm so damned consumed by you that nothing else matters. You have my heart and my balls in a chokehold. I would risk it all just to touch you, to be near you, to sink my cock into the sweetness between your thighs, and that is *not* what you need from a bodyguard."

I open my mouth with a brilliant rebuttal, but a piercing shot rings out, halting the words at the tip of my tongue.

"Everybody get down!" Raf's shout is electric, slicing through the chatter and booming music. A heavy body pummels me to the ground, and all the air rushes from my lungs as I hit the terracotta tile with a smack.

Over the chaos, I can just hear Raf bellowing instructions to the other guards through the com in his ear. I didn't even notice when he put it back in after the mind-blowing sex.

More shouts ricochet across the rooftop as the crack of bullets vibrate the cool night air. My heart kicks at my ribs as I search the mass of huddled forms for my cousin. "Serena!" I call out from beneath Raf's muscled arm.

"Come, Isa, we have to move. Now."

"I can't, not without Serena."

He mutters a curse, then his dark gaze scans the rooftop before latching onto a familiar blonde. "There!"

She's crouched behind one of the lounge chairs which is tipped onto its side, the thick cushions providing some coverage from the barrage of bullets whizzing through the air.

Blanketing my body with his, we crawl across the tile, weaving between the legs of my fellow interns. Some are screaming, others crying, and still others frozen in fear and unmoving. Each one I pass, I nudge along toward the rooftop door. "Go! Get out of here!" I cry.

"Don't look," Raf hisses through clenched teeth as he steers me around a motionless form. Which of course only draws me gaze.

Shit, no! Carlo. Blood paints his cream turtleneck, his long, lanky form stretched across the tile floor. His vacant eyes stare into the heavens, and a wave of guilt crashes over me. Massimo's assistant is dead because of me. Another life lost, for what?

More shots explode across the rooftop, these much closer, and Raf forces me to keep moving. Three other guards have appeared, stationed on each corner of the *terrazo* returning fire.

We scramble toward Serena, and I lunge for her the moment I'm within arms' length. "Are you okay?"

I throw a quick glance in Carlo's direction as I squeeze her. It could have been her. She was with him only seconds ago.

"Yes, I'm totally fine," she replies. "You?"

My head dips before I turn to Raf and notice a tear in his shirtsleeve then the dribble of blood running down his tattooed arm. "Raf," I squeal. "You're bleeding!"

His eyes dart to his arm for only an instant before returning to meet mine. "It's nothing, just a flesh wound."

From when he used his body as a human shield. For me. No wonder the man has a map of scars across his torso.

Emotion tightens my chest as dark crimson blood consumes my vision, and I'm catapulted back in time to another shootout, with another bodyguard that seems like a lifetime ago. My heart pitches against my ribs, and darkness creeps into the edges of my vision. Frankie. I've barely thought about him in months. I shoved all the painful memories of my first bodyguard to the dark depths of my mind to deal with… never.

"Isabella…" Raf's piercing eyes are on mine, the wildness in those coal-black orbs forcing me from the dark spiral. His hands are clamped around my shoulders, fingers digging into my bare skin. "Do not shut down on me now. You are much stronger than that. I'm okay, I swear."

I suck in my bottom lip and blink quickly, chasing away the pools of blood consuming my thoughts. Then I hazard a glance at Raf's wound and attempt to look at it critically, logically, and unemotionally, like the medical professional I'm supposed to be. It's just a flesh wound. He's going to be fine. "Okay," I murmur.

The slap of heavy footfalls spins my head over my shoulder where one of the guards races toward us. He's one of the men usually stationed outside so I'm not sure of his name. I think it's Enzo. As he stops a few inches from us, I realize the storm of bullets has abruptly stopped, and a deadly silence has descended across the rooftop.

A few of the interns are still scattered across the space, hiding behind chairs and over-sized potted plants. Even the DJ is still crouched behind his booth. A few of the other guards are circling, checking for any wounded.

"The shooter took off, Raffaele," says the big guard. "Alberto spotted him climbing down the fire escape over there." He points to an adjacent building. "He's trailing him now."

Raf leaps up, a savage twist to his lips. "Good, I'm coming."

"No!" I'm on my feet, tugging at Raf's shirt. "Please, don't go." I'm fully aware of how pathetic I sound, but in this moment I just don't care. I'm not worried about me, it's him I can't bear the thought of losing.

He levels his stormy gaze on mine, a tempest of emotions brewing beneath the glassy surface. "I have to, Isa. It's my job." He runs his hand down my arm and squeezes my hand so quickly I barely feel it. "You stay here with Serena and the other guards; you'll be safe. I'll be back in a few minutes. I promise."

Serena moves beside me, swinging her arm across my shoulders. "Come on, cuz, let's get inside. Everyone must be freaking out; it's time for damage control."

I hear her words, but I can't quite process them, not with my eyes still fixed to Raf's. All I want to do is wrap my arms around him and force him to stay with me. But I know I can't. *Cazzo*, maybe he's right, and I do need another bodyguard.

"Okay," I whisper. "But be careful."

"Always."

Gently, Serena pries me away from Raf, and I can't help but trail his familiar form as he and Enzo race toward the door that leads back into the apartment.

Serena offers a reassuring smile and tucks me into her side. "He'll be fine, Bella. In case you hadn't noticed, he's kind of a badass."

A half-hearted chuckle tumbles out as she steers me toward the door. All the remaining guests are heading in the same direction, the guards ushering everyone through the archway.

"Isabella!" The shout comes from up ahead as we walk down the steps to the second floor. Massimo appears from the crowd of people huddled in the stairwell. "Oh, thank *Dio*, you are all right."

Does he know about Carlo? My professor is already pale, sweat glistening on his brow. The poor man is probably in shock, but I can't seem to find the words to comfort him. Not when I know Raf is out there chasing some psycho with a rifle.

"I am," I finally answer, leaning against the wall. "Is anyone else injured downstairs?"

"Thankfully nothing serious." His light brows pucker as he regards me. "What about on the roof?"

That guilt spirals through my chest, a steel band snaking around my lungs and heart.

Serena pokes her head over my shoulder, addressing my professor. "Carlo is dead."

"*Dio*, no." Massimo blanches, all the remaining blood rushing from his cheeks. "What is going on, Isabella? First the aperitivo and now here?"

"I'm not sure." The shooting at the bar was one thing, but in my own home? Has one of the Kings' enemies found me all the way in Rome? "But I sure as hell will find out."

CHAPTER 45
MAKE ME FORGET

R*affaele*

I glare at the *pezzo di merda* who dared to hurt what's mine, and raw fury pummels my veins. The asshole is cuffed to a chair, blindfolded and gagged in the basement laundry room of Isabella's apartment. When Luca had started his search for a place in Rome, I'd insisted on a basement just in case. I never thought I would actually have to use it.

We caught the shooter trying to escape a few blocks away from the apartment, then I dragged his ass back here. Now, I simply have to find the calm before I start the interrogation because I'm afraid I'll ring his neck before I can get any useful information out of him.

I need intel. I need him alive.

I remind myself over and over again as the raging wrath surges through me. My fingers are curled into fists, nails digging into my palms. All I want to do is rip his damned head off. He could have killed her.

And it would've been my fucking fault because I was so busy dancing with her, touching her, rubbing up against her hot little body, I hadn't been watching the perimeter. The *coglione* had been perched on the neighboring rooftop. The question was: why? Which one of the Kings' enemies had tracked her down here?

The other option… the one I dare not voice aloud is so much worse.

That it has nothing to do with her at all and instead, is because of me.

Have my past sins come back to haunt me? To steal the only woman I've dared care about in a decade?

"*Merda*," I grit out.

"I can do it if you don't have the stomach for it." Enzo appears beside me, flashing brass knuckles.

"No, trust me, I can do it," I growl. I'm worried I'll do it too well. "Take off his blindfold, I want this fucker to see my face, to intimately know the man who's going to deliver him to hell."

A whimper escapes from the *bastardo*'s bloodied lip. I allowed myself one shot just for fun when we finally caught up to him. Enzo loosens the dark length of fabric and drops it down around his neck. Like a noose.

Terrified eyes stare up at me, an unmistakable tremble in his lower lip. "Please, don't…" he cries.

I bark out a laugh. "Why should I show you mercy when you shot at a bunch of kids at a party? When you could have killed *her*…" I stalk closer, my sanity hanging on by a thread. "If you had shed even a tiny drop of her blood, I would have shoved my fist down your throat and tore out your spine. *Capisci*?"

"But I didn't…"

"Because you're a shit shot," I roar before I draw my fist back and slam it into his nose.

The satisfying crunch of bones breaking and the ensuing scream sates some of the fury. Blood streaks down his upper lip and into his mouth as he sobs.

"Who sent you?" I snarl.

He shakes his head back and forth. "No, please, I can't say. I don't even know—"

"Are you seriously going to deny me this?" I loom over him, my lips twisted into a savage sneer. "After everything you did, you cowardly shithead? I will get the information I need." I inch closer, fixing my eyes to his until he's trembling. "The rest is up to you. Either you give it to my now, and I make your death quick or you're difficult and you'll suffer every agonizing minute." I pause and reach for the knife in my pocket. Running my finger over the edge, I draw a thin line of blood. "I can make the torture last for a *long* time, *amico*." I bring the blade to his neck and press it to his Adam's apple until I see blood. "And I would much rather be upstairs tending to my client than stuck down here with you. So every moment you make me wait will only heighten my fury. Your call, *stronzo*."

He heaves out a shaky breath. "They'll kill me."

"You're dead either way. The question is how do you want it?" I exert more pressure until a steady stream of crimson dribbles down his neck.

"Please, you don't understand. They made me—"

"Who?" I snap.

"I swear I don't even know. It was a third party, an intermediary who brokered the deal."

"What was his name then?"

I pull the blade from his throat and jab it into the meaty part of his hand. He lets out a shriek and a string of curses as drops of deep ruby splatter the wall. I bend down again, searing him with a murderous glare.

"Give me a name."

"Arjan Kola," he bites out.

The name is familiar, but I can't quite place it. The Albanians have long been involved in the Italian mafia, more and more trickling over since the opening of the EU all those years ago. But what the hell do they have to do with Isabella?

"I need more, *bastardo*. I need to know who fucking sent you to shoot my… client."

"It wasn't her," he murmurs, mucus mixing with blood as it trails down to his upper lip.

"What?"

"I wasn't sent for her," he rasps out.

"Then who were you sent to kill?"

"You."

The blood paints the bottom of the basement sink in a bright red, the color much too vibrant for my weary eyes. I scrub my fingers mechanically, adding more soap until all the blood is off my skin. I kept my promise, making the shooter's death a mercifully quick one despite my desire to flail his skin off inch by inch.

He may have shot at Isabella, but he'd come for me. Her life had been in danger because of *me*. I drag my wet hand through my hair and huff out a breath. This is all my fucking fault. I never should have returned to Rome.

Once I'm done, I force my legs up the steps with guilt eating at my insides. The apartment is quiet upstairs, all the guests having left a long time ago. The Kings' team took care of the body, the local Italian authorities taking care of all the grisly details. I never realized how far Luca Valentino's power stretched, but when everything went to hell one of his men knew exactly what to do and who to call.

Thank *Dio* it's the middle of the night in Manhattan, and I'll have until tomorrow to deal with Isabella's father's wrath. Miraculously, I'd managed to keep the incident at RiverBar under wraps, but my luck would only go so far. Now is my chance to come clean to Luca about everything.

I reach the second-floor landing and pause at Isa's door. I peer through the opening and find her curled up beside Serena. I stand at the entryway, just watching her for an endless moment. After the hellish night, I just need to know she's okay.

Her eyes pop open, and a relieved smile creeps across her face. I texted her the moment we found the guy, knowing she would be worried. I'd insisted she go to sleep because I didn't want her waiting up for me. I had no idea how long it would take to crack the guy. Lucky for me, not long.

She crawls out from under Serena's arm and tiptoes toward me, the slight creaks of the old wooden planks ratcheting up my heartrate. Her hair is a wild mess, long, dark waves cascading down her bare shoulders. She has that sexy, sleepy look on her face, the one she wears first thing in the morning and *Dio*, she's gorgeous. My heart punches my ribs, the all-consuming feeling bloating my chest. *Fuck*. I'm in love with Isabella. Completely. Madly. Obsessively. Before she reaches the threshold, I lunge, unable to keep my hands off her.

My mouth crashes into hers as my hands curl around her hips before lifting her off her feet. Her legs wrap around my torso, arms lacing around my neck. A faint moan swirls between us as she kisses me with the same fire consuming my insides.

"I'm so glad you're okay," she whispers against my lips. "I was so worried…"

"Mmhmm, me too." It's all I can muster as our tongues tangle in a sweltering dance. Palming her ass to keep her pressed tightly against me, I walk us to my bedroom, locking the door behind us. This. This is why she needs a new bodyguard. Instead of spending the night tangled in her arms, I should be on duty.

Instead, I've relegated the job to Enzo and Alberto. They're good, but they're nowhere near as good as me. Still, I can't keep from kissing her, from touching her. With the fear of losing her so real, I can't not indulge in this one moment.

Then, I'll resume my duty.

"I need you, Raf," she murmurs as I lay her on the bed. "I was so scared—"

"Nothing's going to happen to me, *principessa*. I'm right here, with you." I crawl over her, bracing my elbows on either side of her shoulders and trapping her against the mattress. "I'll always keep you safe."

Her eyes meet mine, the blue practically glowing beneath the moonlight streaking in through the window shade. "Promise me. Promise you'll always be with me."

I swallow hard. "In any way I can." I don't want to lie to her, but I cannot keep this up. I can't be her bodyguard and whatever this is between us. It's not safe for her, not good for either of us.

"I just want to forget about tonight, Raf." She snags her bottom lip between her teeth. "Can you make me forget, please?"

The soft plea tears at my restraint, breaking down the walls I've fought so hard to build between us. *Dio*, I'm in love with her. I would do anything for her. But could I let her go, if it meant her safety?

Her hands find the zipper of my fly and before I can utter a sound, she's freed my cock. Of course I'm hard and ready for her. So I bury the unspeakable thoughts to the back of my mind, to deal with another day. Right now, my *principessa* needs to forget, and there's nothing I want more than to give her what she wants.

So when she slips her panties down her smooth legs and parts her thighs, I sink my cock into her, slowly, leisurely, enjoying every second as she tightens around me. Because with Isabella I've found my home, and it's not something I'm ready to give up. Maybe not ever.

CHAPTER 46
MY FIRST CLIENT

Isabella

I stare at my reflection in the mirror, at the puffy skin beneath my eyes, the frown tipping the corners of my lips, and the austere black dress I've selected for the memorial service. I may not have known Massimo's assistant, Carlo, well, but he was still a person, one that is now dead because of me.

Dio, I wish Serena could have stayed a little longer. Surely, she would have been able to talk me out of this guilt spiral.

Why did I think running away to Rome would magically erase all the problems that came with the title of mafia princess? I'd been stupid and so damned naïve. There is no escaping my destiny. Why am I even bothering with this medical degree?

Just being around my patients could put them in danger. And I want to work with children… *Dio*, this is so fucked up and unfair. I blow out a frustrated breath and tie back the dark waves of hair into a neat bun.

Soft footsteps echo down the hall an instant before Raf's familiar scent invades my nostrils. His knuckles graze the door, which is already ajar. "Are you okay, *principessa*?"

"No," I grumble.

He creeps in, dark eyes meeting mine through the mirror. Instead of his typical black tee and dark jeans, today, he's in a suit, the sleek charcoal fabric clinging to the sharp lines of his broad shoulders, then tapering down to his narrow hips. Raffaele Ferrara is gorgeous in any clothes, but in a suit, he's devastating. He drapes his body around mine, a comforting shield of warmth and pure muscle. Another sigh parts my lips as I lean into him, helpless to resist the pull.

"You know you don't have to go to the service," he whispers.

"Yes, I do. He died at *my* house... because of me."

His face contorts into something almost painful. "It wasn't because of you..."

"Of course it was." I spin around to face him, that guilt still so heavy even after an entire week it feels like I'm moving in slow motion. "Don't try to make me feel better. I'm a big girl, and I can handle the truth."

"It's not the truth," he grits out then takes a step back before he starts to pace the tiny bathroom. "Damn it, I should have just told you right away, but I was hoping I could get some answers first—"

"Told me what?" I grab his arm, jerking him to a stop.

He heaves out a breath before fixing his eyes to mine. "Before I killed the *pezzo di merda* who shot up your rooftop, he confessed you weren't his target." He paused, pain slicing into his features. "I was."

An actual gasp spills out, my breath hitching. "You? Why you? And how could you not tell me all this time?"

"Because I still haven't found out why," he growls and

drags his hands over his face. "I wanted to tell you the very next day, but I had the call with your father, and you know how that went."

"He threatened to kill you himself if there was one more incident."

"Right. And I couldn't come back to you without answers, answers you deserve. I'm supposed to be the best, Isabella. And now with you, the one person I fear losing most, I'm failing left and right."

The air sweeps from my lungs for the second time in so many minutes as I read the anguish in his piercing gaze. "You fear losing me the most?" It's not a confession of love, but it's something.

"Absolutely," he murmurs, his hand rising slowly to cup my cheek, rough and gentle all at once. "*Dio, principessa*, you've unraveled me. You stir something in me, a wild urge to shatter every rule I've ever lived by, just to be close to you. But it fucking terrifies me, Isabella. What if my questionable decisions put you in danger?" His voice breaks slightly, vulnerability flickering across his features.

I reach up, covering his hand with mine, the connection sparking a wave of warmth. "Raf, being with you," I whisper, "feels like the safest place I've ever known. Isn't that worth the risk?"

He searches my face, as if looking for an anchor in a sea of doubt. "Every moment with you is a risk I want to take, if you think it's worth it."

It's more than worth it. It's everything. In his eyes, I see the reflection of all my hopes mingled with his fears. We are two sides of the same coin, flipping endlessly, waiting to see where we land. But in this moment, I know. "It's worth it, Raf. You and me, we're absolutely worth it."

His mouth claims mine with the urgency of a tempest breaking the shore, wild and relentless, as if trying to communicate every unspoken emotion through this single kiss. He lifts me onto the vanity, wedging his hips between my thighs and stretching out my dress. I should be angry at him for keeping the truth from me for an entire week, but instead, all I can think about is how perfect his lips feel against mine, how my body naturally curves into his.

I'm desperately falling for my bodyguard. Hell, I've probably already jumped to my doom. Which reminds me... I force my lips away, despite every inch of my body screaming at me to remain trapped in his muscled arms. "So what did you find out from that *bastardo*? And why would someone want to kill *you*?"

The tendon in his jaw feathers, and I can almost hear the grinding of his teeth.

"Raf?" A wicked tangle of unease roils low in my belly. "What haven't you told me?"

"It's about my family..."

My thoughts flicker back to the night at the club when we ran into his brothers. At the fear, at the rage, that had consumed him not only during their discussion but for hours later after we'd returned home. So they had some sort of falling out, but a part of me knows there is more to this story.

"What about them?"

"My father is not a good man, Isa." His dark brows furrow as his wary gaze locks on mine. "He has enemies, men in this city who would stop at nothing to bring him down."

Understanding rolls over me in suffocating waves. I suspected it that night, but I preferred to remain blind than face the truth then. "He's involved in organized crime?"

Raf grunts, a snarl twisting his lips. "He *is* organized crime, *principessa*."

"Didn't you think that was an important detail to divulge the other night?"

"No," he grits out. "Because I never thought you would

get caught up in my mess. A mess I thought I escaped years ago."

"You have to tell me the truth now, Raf. How can this thing between us ever work if you're keeping secrets? We have enough hurdles to overcome as it is."

His head dips, and his fingers lace through mine as he tugs me from the vanity. "Fine, but not now. We have to get to the memorial, unless you've changed your mind?"

I slowly shake my head. Even if Carlo's death is indirectly my fault, I still played a role in his demise. After all, Raf was here at my insistence. He warned me he didn't want to come to Rome, but I'd insisted anyway. Because the spoiled mafia princess always gets what she wants.

"We'll talk in the car then." Raf takes my hand and leads me out of the bathroom.

I follow him through the apartment then out to the street where Sal awaits in the Alfa. I'm so relieved he chose the smaller, more inconspicuous vehicle today instead of the flashy limo. Anticipation rolls through me, growing with each step closer until we slide into the back seat and our driver closes the door behind us.

As soon as the engine rumbles to life, Raf slides to the edge of the seat. "Salvatore, play some music, something upbeat."

"Certainly, *signore*."

The loud music fills the car, and my guardian settles in beside me once more. Clearly, he doesn't want Sal listening to his confession. He remains silent next to me for a long minute, his knee jostling mine as his foot taps out a manic beat.

I slap my hand on his thigh, halting the erratic bouncing. "Just tell me."

He draws in a slow breath before pivoting his body toward mine, wary eyes following suit. "I never wanted you to know…"

"Know what?"
"How badly I failed my first client."

CHAPTER 47
A HORRIBLE NIGHTMARE

R*affaele*

Ten years and I still can't quite seem to find the words. Probably because I've never spoken them aloud in all this time. A part of me believed that if the truth never surfaced, I could pretend it was all simply a horrible nightmare.

"Your first client?" Isa whispers.

And just like that, the corners of my vision darken, and the back seat of the car disappears before another scene coalesces in its place.

I'm standing in a palatial suite at the Grand Hotel Flora, shirking a biting glare razed in my direction. Enrico Sartori. He sits atop a high-backed chair, a veritable throne of gilded mahogany and ornate tapestry. Before meeting the Capo dei Capi, *the head of all the mob bosses across Italy*, I thought my father was intimidating. The man lances a lethal gaze in my direction, the contempt in his eyes so palpable it has me, a full-grown man at twenty almost shitting myself.

A pair of warm chocolate doe eyes meet mine from across the room, and I force my shoulders back. You're a man, damn it, Raffa, act like one, for her. *Holding her hopeful gaze, I take comfort in her strength. Laura. My love. She's the one who bears the ultimate burden in this situation. I'm just the idiot that got her pregnant. And here I am trying my best to take responsibility for my actions.*

But Enrico Sartori obviously has other plans for me.

He clears his throat before beckoning me forward with one long finger. I creep closer, forcing my spine to stiffen. We had agreed that today would be the day Laura would tell her father the truth. I waited outside at her insistence, but now it's my turn to face Enrico's wrath.

"Raffaele Ferrara," *he mutters my name like a curse.* "You are the son of Alfredo Ferrara, are you not?"

I nod. "Si, signore."

"And I understand you work for the Gruppo di Intervento Speciale."

"Yes, for two years now." *I joined the elite group specializing in counter-terrorism, hostage rescue, and anti-terrorism operations both within Italy and internationally straight out of high school. Even then, it had been clear where* Papà's *operations were headed, and I wanted no part of it.*

"I see." *His fingers drum the lavish chair arm, matching the rhythm of my escalating pulse.* "And yet, somehow despite that tremendous responsibility, you managed to fuck my daughter enough to get her pregnant."

I bristle, heat warming my cheeks. "I love Laura," *I mutter before saying it again, more forcefully this time.* "I want to marry her and raise this child together."

"You are a fool, Raffaele. You have no idea what that means. To have a wife and nurture a child in the world we live in is impossible."

"Then let me take her away from this life."

A dark chuckle seeps past his clenched lips. "I'm afraid that's *impossible. I have enemies everywhere, and the only place my daughter is safe is right here with me."*

"I want a part in her life. I will not abandon her or our child."

His eyes narrow as he regards me. "I've already looked into your past, into your time with the GIS. You seem quite talented. My daughter could use someone like you on her security team." He pauses, cold eyes drilling into me. "That is all I can offer you for now. If you prove yourself capable of keeping my daughter safe, I will consider allowing you a future with her. Are you up for the challenge, Raffaele?"

"Yes, absolutely. It will be my greatest honor to keep Laura safe. I'll guard her with my life, and I swear I will never let anything happen to her."

The scene fizzles away but the painful memories bloat my chest, thickening my throat so I can barely swallow.

"Raf, please tell me." Isabella's voice draws me to the present, to those brilliant blue eyes, not brown.

I blink quickly in a vain attempt to banish the past to where it belongs. "*Cazzo*, Isabella, I failed her. I swore to keep her safe, but I couldn't. And my failings along with her ghost have haunted me for ten years now."

She laces her fingers through mine, squeezing, but still, I can read the dread in her eyes. "You failed who?"

"Laura Sartori. My first client." I pause, the words stuck at the back of my throat. "My first love."

Hurt slashes across Isa's face, and I hate that I put it there, but she asked for the truth, and I would give it to her, even if reliving those painful memories kills us both. She schools her face into one of compassion as the fleeting jealousy passes. "What happened?"

I grunt, the dark, frustrated sound erupting from my depths. "My fucking father happened."

She stares at me, eyes wide as I find the most gentle way of putting the most monstrous act. No, there is no way. It's impossible. "She was the daughter of the most powerful man in Italy at the time, and I was her bodyguard." I chew on the next bit, the part I haven't been able to speak for ten years. Not my father, not my brothers, not a single soul knew she was pregnant back then. I try to form the words but steel binds wind around my lungs, their hold suffocating. I can't... I can't even speak the unthinkable words. "But to him," I choke out, "she was only his enemy's daughter. A pawn caught in the dangerous games powerful men play."

"Was?" Isabella whispers.

My head dips to my chin, the weight of her memory crushing.

"Your father caused her death?"

I bark out a dark laugh, my heart a mad drumbeat kicking at my ribs. "He didn't just cause her death, *principessa*, he dragged the fucking knife across her throat."

"Oh, God." Her mouth pinches, brows knitting.

Bile crawls up my esophagus as blood taints my vision. So much blood. My hands covered in it.

"But why would he do something like that?"

"To teach me a lesson and bring Enrico Sartori, her father, to his knees." I close my eyes, a vain attempt to hide from the terrible confession. "Sartori may have been a monster, but he loved his daughter. That single act ignited a war that continues to this day."

Isabella inches closer, releasing one hand to caress my cheek. "I'm so sorry, Raf."

"Yeah, me too." Prying my lids open, I look into the eyes of the woman who means everything to me. Imagining those vibrant ocean blue orbs clouding over, that vacant stare, the cold touch of her skin, it would kill me. "I can't lose you," I whisper.

"You won't." She shakes her head, that fiery determination set in her jaw. "I'm not going anywhere, Raf." Crawling into my lap, she laces her arms around my neck and crushes me to her chest. For once, I'm the one who feels safe in someone else's hold. Tears threaten, but I will them back, resolving to mourn the woman, the family I'd lost another time. It wouldn't be fair to Isabella.

The car slows, and I glance out the window to the towering spires of the gothic church. On the verdant lawn beside it, lie dozens of marble headstones. The cemetery. Another pang jabs at my heart as I recognize the familiar hallowed grounds. Shit, I'd been so distracted I hadn't even realized which cemetery we were going to. The very same one where Laura and our unborn child are buried.

If it were anyone but Isabella, I would have Sal turn around and drive us straight home. The thought of returning here has my stomach dropping to the soles of my shoes.

We remain silent in the backseat for a long minute as I run my fingers through Isa's hair, until soft strands fall from the neat bun. I just need to touch her, to assure myself of her presence. Finally, she inhales softly and presses a chaste kiss to my cheek. "You don't have to go if you don't want to."

I lock my eyes to hers and offer the best smile I can muster. "If you're going, I'm going."

"So stubborn." Isa smirks before glancing over her shoulder to check on Sal. His head is down, likely scanning his cellphone. She brushes her lips over mine, still softly, but the light, comforting touch starts to mend the pieces of my shattered heart.

If I'm being honest, just being with her these past few weeks in Rome has healed wounds I thought were permanent. *Dio*, I love her. I should just tell her…

We've been putting off the inevitable for long enough. I would have to step down as her bodyguard and have Luca send a replacement. He'll be pissed off as all hell, but maybe, I can make him understand.

"Ready?" Isa spins toward the door, her hand closing on the handle before I can pry the words out.

It's probably for the better anyway. After that grisly tale, maybe now wasn't the best time to confess how much I loved her. I finally nod and slide out of the car so I can open her door on the other side.

Offering my hand to help her out, her fingers easily intertwine with mine when we hit the sidewalk. I know I'll have to release her soon enough, but I want to savor every moment. The ominous tolling of the church bell echoes as we walk up the steps of the old cathedral, mimicking the mounting dread in my gut.

Before we reach the grand double doors inlaid with gold and engravings of the saints, Isabella stops, her eyes whirling to mine. "You never told me who you think is behind the shooting," she whispers. "Is it your father or Laura's?"

My brows draw together as I regard her for an endless moment. "Enrico Sartori?" It hadn't even crossed my mind that he could be behind this.

She nods, sucking her bottom lip between her teeth.

Why would—? The words fall away as realization slaps me in the face. "Because it was my fault his daughter died."

CHAPTER 48
THE L WORD

Isabella

Grief constricts my ribcage, the pain of loss so potent it coats my tongue and cramps my belly as I walk across the verdant lawn of the cemetery. I didn't even know Carlo well and still, his death weighs on me for more than just guilt. In the world I've grown up in, loss of life is a constant and one can so easily become immune to it. I can't even count how many guards we've lost over the years, not to mention Frankie, who's death I still can't quite process because it's easier to live in denial.

Carlo was young, not even twenty-eight with a whole life ahead of him. He had parents who loved him, a sister who cherished him, cousins, grandparents, a whole slew of people whose lives were just irreparably changed. In one fraction of a second.

Dio, how is it fair?

I glance over at Raf who walks beside me, a grim expression wearing into his handsome face as we cross the now empty graveyard. He hasn't spoken more than a few terse words since his confession in the car. His sadness weighs on me, too. Dozens of colorful flowers mark the gravestones, too bright for the somber occasion. It was a lovely ceremony, filled with inspirational speeches and reassuring words, but in the end, Carlo was still dead.

Just like Raf's first love.

People would continue to die, and the world would keep churning, but *merda*, it's so depressing. Beneath the guilt, there's the knowledge that life is fleeting, and we should take advantage of every moment. Before it's too late.

"Raf, I—" I blurt as he spins toward me and says, "Isabella—"

"Sorry, go ahead." He stops in the middle of the empty cemetery, and it occurs to me this is probably the most morbid place in the world to say the three words that have been racing across the tip of my tongue.

So instead, I shake my head and mutter a lame, "No, you go first."

Raf takes my hand and leads me toward the shade of a classic stone pine, its distinctive umbrella-shaped canopy the perfect spot to escape the mid-day sun. His dark eyes chase to mine, and a tide of unfettered emotion sweeps through that brooding gaze. "I know you don't want to hear this, but we have to find you a new bodyguard."

I open my mouth to tell him just what I think about that, but he presses his finger to my lips.

"No arguing." He heaves out a pained breath, and I still my tongue to at least hear him out. His hands clamp around my shoulders, intense eyes dipping to trap mine in that haunted gaze. "Do you want to be with me? For real, *principessa*? Not this sneaking around, but really be mine?"

The rough edge to his tone has my insides quaking and

my heart slingshotting itself against my ribs. I don't trust myself to speak so I simply nod instead.

"As if continuing this thing between us as your bodyguard isn't risky enough, now we have the problem of the shooter to contend with." He sucks in a deep breath before continuing. "I've had no solid leads in a week, other than the name of the Albanian mercenary who hired him, and that guy has conveniently disappeared. I have your father's men ransacking the city for him, but it's possible he's left the city or worse, the country. Until we know for certain who is after me, I cannot risk your life by remaining beside you."

"So you're just going to abandon me?"

"No, of course not." His fingers tighten around my shoulders as he draws me closer. "But don't you see that I'm putting you directly in harm's way by being with you?"

"I'm always in harm's way, you *coglione*. I have been since the day I was born."

He bites his lip, a flicker of anger darkening his countenance as he holds onto me as if his life depends on it. "I won't be responsible for putting your life at risk, Isabella. Can't you understand that?" His grip is punishing as he reels me in so I'm flush against him. "I cannot bear it. I will not lose the first woman I've loved in a decade—" His jaw slams shut, the crack reverberating through the sudden silence.

"Love?" I choke out.

But the word is drowned out by the squeal of tires racing across cement. Before the first shot detonates, Raf has me behind the tree, pinned between its rough bark and his unyielding torso.

He's yelling through the com in his ear, one arm around me and his free hand wrapped around the butt of the gun that appeared out of nowhere. Bullets pierce the air, slicing through the solemn silence of the cemetery with deadly intent. Tombstones shatter around us, sending fragments of marble and stone spraying the air.

Raf's eyes fiercely scan the perimeter, his body a shield against the chaos erupting around us. "Stay down," he commands as he forces me to the ground, his voice a harsh whisper against the backdrop of gunfire. I nod, my own heart hammering in my chest as I clutch at his jacket, the scent of gunpowder mingling with the earthy dampness of the ground.

In the distance, I can see shadows moving, figures darting between the headstones, advancing towards us. *Merda*, where is Sal? Raf waits, his breathing controlled, his focus absolute. As one of the attackers comes into clear view, he squeezes the trigger, his arm steady despite the adrenaline that must be coursing through him.

The sound of the return fire is deafening, but Raf is unflinching as the body drops to the ground. "I've got you," he assures me, though the shrill edge to his tone has every hair on my body standing on end. "Where the fuck are you, Sal?" he growls through the com as another wave of men in black suits surge across the graveyard.

Over his shoulder, I catch sight of the navy Alfa tearing toward us. Sal slams on the breaks, inches from where we're crouched behind the tree. A door swings open and Aldo jumps out, spraying a line of bullets across the sea of headstones.

"Go, go, now!" Raf curls his arm around my shoulders, blanketing my body with his powerful one as we race toward the car. Both Aldo and Sal provide a barrage of bullets as cover as we sprint the few yards between us and dive into the back seat.

The door slams behind us, and Aldo darts around the car before jumping into the front. I heave in a breath with Raf's massive body still wrapped around me, a shield of rigid muscle. The wail of sirens pierces the air, growing louder now amidst the backdrop of slowing shots. As our driver peels out of the parking lot, my frantic pulse begins to slow.

Only once we're clear of the cemetery does Raf turn his attention to me, his expression softening just a touch. "Are you okay?" he rumbles, his concern palpable.

"Yeah, I'm fine."

"Good." Finally releasing me, he slides to the end of the backseat and glares at our driver through the rearview mirror. "Where the fuck were you, Sal?"

"*Scusi*. I just went across the street with Aldo for a *caffè*. We were only gone for a second."

"A second when all hell broke loose." He glares between the two men, the rage entrenched across his jaw terrifying. He turns that murderous gaze on Aldo and the man actually flinches. I've never seen him do that except with *Papà*, and he's been under my family's employ for decades. "You should know better. What would *Signor* Valentino do if he were here?"

"We'd be fucking dead before nightfall," Aldo mutters.

"No," I hiss and grab Raf's arm, urging him back. "Don't you dare tell *Papà*. I won't be responsible for any more deaths today."

His jaw ticks for a long minute before the fury simmers. He turns back to his men, the feral gaze in his expression enough to make me pee my pants. "You only get one warning, and that's more than I would have given you. Isabella is right. There's been enough death for one day. But trust me, there will be no second chances."

Both men nod, and a heavy silence blankets the car for the rest of the ride home.

Raffaele is moody and distant for the next two days, shadowing me around the hospital and the apartment without speaking. He hasn't said the L word again, and a part of me is sure I imagined it.

I've apparently grown feathers and a beak because I'm too much of a chicken to bring it up. Mostly it's because I'm scared he'll threaten to get me another bodyguard again. But also because I'm terrified to admit the truth, that I love him too.

I'm certain once I breathe the words to life he'll insist on leaving me for my own good. Which is just ridiculous. No one is as good as Raffaele Ferrara, and I want him as my bodyguard and no other.

Clearly, I'm insane.

I go through the motions at the hospital on autopilot, following up with my patients, filling out endless charts, smiling and nodding at concerned family members, but it all feels so futile. I will never get my doctorate, and even if I do by some series of lucky events, I'll never get to practice medicine.

I would be putting all my patients at risk, simply because of who I am.

The mafia princess.

Maybe it's time to face the truth instead of deluding myself and dreaming of a future I can never have.

CHAPTER 49
THAT WAS ME

R*affaele*

The sliver of a moon still sits high in the dark sky as I creep out of the apartment and dart across the courtyard. The thought of leaving Isabella has anxiety tearing at my gut, but I convince myself it's for the greater good. Plus, Aldo and Alberto are with her, along with the other three guys I have stationed around the outer perimeter.

She's asleep anyway and since it's her day off hopefully she'll stay that way until I return. I've thought about it for days, and this is the only way. It was Isabella who flicked the light switch I was too damned blind to notice. After the shooting on the rooftop, I'd been certain it was *Papà* who had sent the Albanian after me. Enrico Sartori hadn't even crossed my mind. But then I did a little research and as it turns out, my almost father-in-law has employed Arjan Kola on a few projects over the years.

It makes sense, I suppose. Enrico sees me back in Rome

with another woman and he snaps... I understand. I almost sympathize with the old man.

A whirlwind of dismal thoughts fills my mind as I hop on Sal's Vespa and tear onto the quiet streets. For days, I've considered what I would say to Sartori, how I could get him to admit about the shooting and more importantly, how to get him to change his mind about exacting his vengeance.

Or rather, maybe I should just point him in the right direction.

I was a fucking idiot back then covering for my father. I hadn't done it so much for him, but rather for my brothers. If Enrico knew *Papà* was the one who slit Laura's throat, I would have found myself an orphan.

At twenty, lying seemed like the best option. I had taken the full blame for Laura's death, but I'd lied through my teeth. I told her father I wasn't there when it happened, that I'd only found her body after the fact. He had no idea that I'd been there in that basement, holding her in her final moments as she gasped for air, watching the light drain from her lively, soulful eyes.

Memories of Laura flit across my subconscious, her smile, her voice, the scent of rose petals that always lingered on her skin. The vivid images are like a punch to the gut, and I'm left gasping for air as I maneuver the empty streets. Tears prick at the corners of my vision but the rush of air from atop the Vespa plucks them away before they can fall.

I've buried all thoughts of her for years now. I'd sworn off women, indulging in only one-night stands because I'd vowed never to endure that pain of loss again. But here I am, ten years later and stupidly in love with another woman with the potential of shattering my heart once again.

And worse, I've put her life at risk because of me.

I veer off the main road, beneath the dim streetlights to the *Parioli* district where elegant apartments and expertly manicured parks line the wide avenues. It's been ten years since I was here last, and still, everything remains just as I remember it.

Releasing the throttle, I slow the Vespa until the familiar palatial building takes shape. The classic Roman façade with climbing ivy is bathed in moonlight, giving the ancient white stone structure an otherworldly glow. A wrought-iron gate lines the perimeter with guards stationed on each corner of the grand estate.

I glance up at one of the large, arched windows where light already peeks through. Enrico had always been an early riser, and I suppose not that much has changed in the past decade. The moment I pull up to the sidewalk and cut the engine, two guards are on me, each with their hands a millimeter from their guns.

They bark at me in Italian, but once I've given them my name, the head guy walks off before pressing a finger to the com in his ear. I stand on the sidewalk, my heart like a battering ram against my ribs.

Will Enrico agree to see me?

Am I a fucking idiot to even risk being here right now?

No... I have to do this. For Isabella.

Heavy footfalls spin my head over my shoulder to the approaching guard. His scowl is so deep it looks as if it were permanently engraved into his face. "*Signor* Sartori will see you now." He motions toward the gate and one of the other guards unlocks it, then pushes it open. The sharp keening sound has every hair on my body standing at attention. He pauses at the opening, his dark gaze intent on the bulge in my jacket. "I'll need your gun, of course."

"*Certo.*" Reaching into the interior pocket, I pull out the Glock and hand it over. He doesn't say anything about my knife, so I don't offer it. The small blade is tucked into my pant leg where it permanently resides.

"Follow me." The guard ticks his head up the marble steps to the entrance.

Another member of the security team opens the front door and as I cross the threshold, the foyer is just as I remember it. The grand entryway boasts high ceilings and there isn't a speck of dust on the polished marble floors. The center of the hall is adorned with a dramatic staircase leading to the upper floors with intricate wrought-iron railings.

Standing at the top of the landing is Enrico Sartori.

He glares down at me, the silk robe, streaks of silver in his hair and ten years that have passed doing nothing to smooth down his hard edges or menacing demeanor.

"This is quite the surprise, Raffaele. You are the last person I expected to find at my doorstep at this hour of the morning."

He surprises me with the heavily accented English. The man I knew refused to speak anything but his mother tongue despite being fully versed in multiple languages.

"*Scusi*. I'm sorry for showing up without notice, but it's important."

"I assume it is." A sneer curls the corner of his mustache. "I thought you were a smart man, but it appears I was mistaken." He slowly descends, dragging out each step. Once we're nearly toe to toe, he glares up at me, the picture of confidence despite the foot of height I have over him. "Before you enter my living room, remove that knife from wherever its hidden."

It takes all my years of training not to flinch. Apparently, the man hasn't lost his touch in his old age. "*Certo*." I bend down and pluck the blade from my pant leg, then press it into his awaiting palm.

"You'll have it back at the end of your visit."

"Fair enough."

One of the guards leads the way to the sitting room, while the other follows a step behind me. In the grand living room, yet another sentinel awaits, standing beside the heavy velvet curtains.

Enrico folds down into a high-backed leather chair the color of my favorite scotch. Then his darting eyes lift to mine. "Why have you come today?"

I remain standing because for some damned reason it feels like I'm the accused, here to plead my case in front of a judge. Again, the words seem to allude me despite having gone over my speech a hundred times overnight when I should have been sleeping.

"Raffaele Ferrara, I don't have time for stalling..."

"I'm not. I only came to ask an important question."

"Then ask."

I knot my hands together to keep them from clenching. "As you may be aware, I arrived in Rome about a month ago with a client. She is to remain here only for another month then we will return stateside. Someone sent a shooter to her apartment last week, and I need to know why."

His silver speckled brow lifts into an arc. "Well, she's your client. Shouldn't you have the answer?"

"I caught the shooter, but the name he gave me was a middleman, nothing more than a low-life Albanian who negotiates contracts for hire." I pause, attempting to tread lightly in spite of the fury lashing at my veins. "You remember Arjan Kola, don't you?"

The flicker of a smile tugs at the wrinkled edge of his lip. "The name does sound familiar..." His eyes narrow as he regards me. "But as I recall, your father uses the man as well. What makes you think he isn't responsible for this, too?"

"Too?" I blurt.

"Mmm." He drums his fingers on the arm rest. "I've heard your father is attempting to expand the Ferrara empire into Manhattan. Were you not aware?"

I shake my head as ice rushes my veins. *Dio*, I remember

hearing him talk about that when I was just a kid. It was a fool's dream...

"In fact, I understand some Russians shot up a popular bar owned by the infamous Kings a few months ago. Perhaps, you've heard of it? The Velvet Vault."

My stomach churns, acid eating away at my insides. No. It couldn't be...

"The Kings have been making moves in your father's territory in Rome, Raffa, so it was only natural for him to strike back. You would know if you hadn't walked out on your family. Such a drastic move... I often wonder what could have precipitated that?"

Ignoring his question, I spit out the venom-laced words on the tip of my tongue. "You're telling me that it was my father who organized the shooting at The Velvet Vault?"

"That certainly seems like a logical conclusion, doesn't it?"

My thoughts whirl back in time to all those months ago. The attack had been on the front page of every New York newspaper, print and digital alike. And somehow that night, a mysterious text message had brought me to the very laundromat beside the exclusive club where I met Luca Valentino's daughter for the first time.

Cazzo, could *Papà* have coordinated that, too?

"But why?"

"I was never overly fond of you, Raffa, and especially not after you got my Laura pregnant, but you were never a stupid man." He leans forward, searing me with that dark glare. Even seated the old man is intimidating. "Don't you think it's convenient you found yourself with a job as bodyguard to the Kings' *principessa*?"

"No..." I growl. There is no way. No way *Papà* could have exerted his influence from thousands of miles away like that. *I* got the job because *I* earned it. Because I was the best choice. Again, my thoughts spin to the past, to that fortuitous day that I happened to be at the right place at just the right time when those mobsters tried to shoot up Isabella's car. *Cazzo*, had my father arranged that too? My head spins, nausea clawing up my throat.

None of this makes sense.

I repeat the words over and over again.

But they do… they make perfect sense. What better way to fuck with your enemy than by penetrating their inner circle? And with a completely unsuspecting fool?

There is only one part that doesn't add up.

"Then why did *Papà* try to kill me?"

"Ah, Raffa, that wasn't your father. That was me."

CHAPTER 50
COFFEE AND PARANOIA

Isabella

A big yawn spills out as I search the cabinets for the coffee beans. Raf usually grinds them up and prepares my morning *caffè* before I roll out of bed. This morning, I found a note on my pillow from my mercurial bodyguard beside an oleander blossom, the stem carefully wrapped in aluminum foil.

Beautiful and lethal, just like my principessa.

My heart had staggered for a beat as I traced the dark scrawling. It was uncharacteristically sweet, especially after how moody he's been lately. But besides the cute words, there was no explanation other than he'd be gone for a few hours and had left Alberto in charge.

I sent a few texts but got no response, just that annoying *Raffaele has notifications silenced* reply.

Well, I guess Alberto doesn't know how to make coffee.

Irritated, I keep rifling through the cabinet in search of that blessed liquid caffeine, then hiss out a curse when I find it empty. Dammit. At least there's Nutella. I jerk the jar open and dip my finger inside. As I suck on my fingertip, swirling my tongue around the sweetness, I remember Raf still hasn't followed through with his promise of licking my favorite treat off my naked body.

My new guard glances up from his perch by the front door, the clatter of banging cabinets catching his attention. Unlike Raf who's constantly up my ass, Albie has maintained a professional distance, only talking to me when I start the conversation.

"There's no coffee," I mutter.

He shrugs before returning his watchful eye to the window by the door. It looks out onto the quiet courtyard below, and I can't imagine what could possibly be so interesting down there.

"Have you heard from Raf yet?"

"No, *signorina*, still nothing."

The moment I saw the note, I'd asked my temporary guard if he knew where Raf had gone, but he'd been oddly tight-lipped about the whole thing.

The sharp ring of the outside gate buzzer sends my heart vaulting up my throat. Alberto rises, moving toward the intercom by the door. He barks a surly, "Who is it?" in Italian, and a surprising voice echoes back on the line.

"*Professore* Massimo, I've come to check on Isabella."

I run up, pushing by Albie and practically press my mouth to the speaker. Perfect excuse to go out for a coffee. And surely, my new guard won't be half as strict as Raf. Maybe I can finally try a new place in town. "*Ciao*, Massimo, it's Bella. What's up?"

"I was hoping you were free for a walk around the center of town since it's your day off. There is still so much you haven't seen."

"I would love that. As long as we can grab a *caffè* on the way?"

Alberto's dark brows furrow as he regards me, shaking his head. He lifts my finger from the intercom, so the speaker is no longer broadcasting outside. "Raffaele was very clear that I was not to let you leave the flat."

"By myself, sure. But I'd be with Massimo and you, right? I'm sure you can handle a little stroll along the *piazza*."

He shakes his head, but I can already see his resolve wavering.

I wrap my hand around his upper arm, finger running over his bicep through the tight tee. "I'm sure I would be perfectly safe with you. Raf thinks he's the best guardian in the world, but I think you're right up there with him. Don't you?"

"Well, yes, but—"

"He won't even have to know we ever left. Just a quick coffee and we can come back, okay?"

"Fine," he grits out. "But only coffee."

Nodding, I press my finger to the intercom once again. "Give me five minutes, and I'll be right down, Massimo."

"*Perfetto.*"

Massimo greets me with a warm smile when Albie opens the outer gate, holding it for me to walk through. I swear it turns downright giddy when he notices it's not Raf accompanying me. "*Buongiorno.*" He brushes his lips against both cheeks in the typical Italian greeting. "You look beautiful as always."

"*Grazie.*" I'm in a plain white tee and jeans, sporting the cute red Pradas Raf gifted me. And for some crazy reason, I stuck the poisonous oleander blossom in my ponytail. Thanks to the foil he'd wrapped the stem in, I'd managed the feat without ever touching the toxic flower. He'll probably yell at me when he sees it, but if he didn't want me to keep it, he shouldn't have left it on my pillow. "Your timing couldn't have been better," I say with a smile to my professor. "I'd just found out we were out of coffee before you showed up, so you're pretty much a lifesaver."

"That certainly is fortuitous."

"And sorry, but we'll have to put off our tour of the city when Raffaele returns. I've only been allowed a quick visit to the café around the corner."

Some of the light in his emerald-green eyes dims. "Oh, that is unfortunate. I was hoping to take you to the Fori Romani. The monumental public squares were constructed in ancient Rome over a period of about 1,500 years. They were the center of Roman public life during the Republic and later the Empire. They are truly an impressive sight."

"I'm sure they are, but we'll have to see them another day. If they've been around this long, they're sure not going anywhere." I'm actually proud of myself and hope Raf will be too. The old Bella would have run off with the professor without a second though. I've come a long way.

"*Va bene,*" he finally says, nodding.

I lead the way around the corner to the familiar café Raf vetted before we moved in. Alberto walks a few steps behind us, not crowding my personal space like Raf does. Weirdly enough, I find myself missing my controlling, obsessive bodyguard.

"At least let me take you to a nice coffee shop," Massimo offers. "This one is not so good. It's for the tourists."

I wave a dismissive hand. "I like it here actually. They even have caramel syrup that they add to my latte if I ask nicely."

His mouth puckers, but his head dips all the same. "As you wish, *signorina.*"

Once we're seated with a warm latte in hand at the back of the quiet café, we lapse into an easy conversation about the internship program. Neither of us mentions the shooting, and I'm more than relieved. I'm actually shocked. It was all the other interns could talk about last week. A part of me feared Massimo was going to tell me I was kicked out of the program because he'd somehow found out it was my fault.

I still can't wrap my head around the idea that it's somehow Raf's. Everything he told me still seems so unbelievable. I often found myself cursing my luck for being born into a family like the Valentinos, and we may be dysfunctional at times, but to go to the lengths that Raf's father went to?

That's insane.

My heart hurts for what Raf has endured. Despite the slight pang at the knowledge that he loved someone else so deeply. Does he love me? Had he meant to let that slip the other night and if he had, then why hadn't he mentioned it since?

A whirlwind of unanswered questions plagues my thoughts as I smile and nod while Massimo goes into the nitty gritty of the program and all the new ideas he has in mind now that he's the director. It all sounds great, but I can't seem to focus as I sip my latte.

Maybe it's because Raf hasn't answered any of my text messages, and I keep sneaking peeks at my phone.

"Is everything all right, Bella?" Massimo's eyes find mine, and I feel like a jerk because I've totally been ignoring him.

"Yes, sorry, I'm just distracted." My eyes lift over Massimo's shoulder where Albie stands.

"I can imagine after the incident last week."

I almost say which one? Until I remember the only one he knows of is the shooting on the rooftop, not the following attack at the cemetery. "Have you spoken to Carlo's family?" I ask before I take a measured sip.

"Yes, they are just devastated." He lifts the small espresso cup to his lips and drinks it all in one go. "Have you heard anything from the police? Because his parents have been given absolutely no information about the shooting."

"No nothing," I mumble. Never mind the fact that Raf has already paid off the entire Roman police department at my father's order. In our world, we take care of these sorts of things from the inside. I finish off my latte and offer Massimo a smile. "Thank you for this little outing. It was nice to get my mind off things." *Lie.* I push my chair back, the scrape of the chair legs against the tile, jarring.

"You're leaving already?" His hand twitches, something about the jerky movement attracting my attention.

"Yes, sorry, as I said, I have to get back home. Raf's probably waiting..." I don't know what possesses me to lie like that, but the words spill out of their own accord. "Actually, I should probably text him." My fingers fly over the screen with a quick message about being with the professor. I expect an immediate irate response, but I still get nothing.

"*Si, certo.*" He rises as I do. "Oh, I almost forgot, I have a letter from your instructor at NYU, Professor Dykeman."

"You do?"

"Yes. He didn't have your address, so he sent it to me."

"Why wouldn't he just have emailed?"

He shrugs. "There's something more special about receiving an actual letter all the way from home, don't you think?"

"I guess..."

Massimo leads me out of the café, and Alberto stalks behind us. "My car is just around the corner." He quickens his steps, a slight sheen coating his upper lip.

"When did you say Professor Dykeman sent the letter?"

"Ah, I just received it yesterday."

I nod, but there's something about the pinch of his expression and unnaturally hurried gait that has my hackles raised.

Raf's paranoia is clearly rubbing off on me. Why would I ever suspect my professor of anything nefarious?

We reach the corner, and Massimo points down a quiet alley where a small red Fiat is parked. He motions for me to go first, but I spin around and find Alberto's eyes narrowed. "Albie, I'm just going to get a letter from the professor's car." My gaze dips down to the gun at his hip.

The stern guard traces the movement then nods. "I'll be right behind you, *signorina*."

I'm being crazy, that's all. Not having Raf glued to my side has me off. *Dio*, I hadn't realized how much I relied on him.

Massimo slows as he reaches the car, and it's as if each remaining step is painful. He pulls out the car FOB and the trunk pops open. A man leaps up, firing off a round at Alberto before a gasp escapes from my gaping jaw.

From the corner of my eye, I see my guard fall, the thud of his body against the cement sending my pulse skyrocketing. "No!"

I try to run, but a sharp pain explodes across the back of my skull and darkness invades my vision.

CHAPTER 51
FOOL ME TWICE

R*affaele*

"Come on, Enrico, is this really necessary?" I struggle against the ropes binding me to the chair. Despite the fact that no fire crackles in the massive fireplace in front of me, sweat trickles down my spine. The moment the *coglione* admitted he was the one who'd tried to kill me, his guards tackled me. I may be good but five against one with no weapons is hardly fair. Now all I can do is glare up at the man whose hatred I completely deserve.

He trusted me with his daughter, and I fucked everything up.

I deserve to die. It should have been me all those years ago, not Laura.

Enrico looms over me, his silk robe brushing my knees, and his revolver pressed at my forehead. "I'll make it quick, Raffa, for Laura's sake, that's the best I can offer."

"I deserve death," I grit out. "And I would have gladly

given my life for hers a hundred times over. I relive the torture of that day every fucking night, Enrico. No punishment you could ever inflict could be worse than that."

He presses the muzzle more firmly to my skull, the hard metal digging into my skin. The most fucked up part is that I'm ready to die. I don't fear death... heaven or hell, whatever it may be. Sometimes, I long for the quiet, for the stillness.

But I can't leave Isabella.

I won't leave her unprotected.

"Wait," I grit out. Locking my gaze to Enrico's, I prepare to grovel, to fight, to burn down this whole damned house if that's what it takes to walk out of here alive. Not for me, but for *her*. "My client. Swear to me that once I'm dead no harm will come to her."

"I have no quarrel with the Valentinos or the Kings, and I intend to keep it that way. If the past few months have been any indication, it seems we will be seeing much more of them in Italy. I will bide my time, watching and waiting. If the need arises, I will strike, but not before then." He cocks the trigger, the ominous click ratcheting up my pulse.

Isabella fills my vision, those intense blue irises, full pouty lips, the way the corners of her eyes crinkle when she smiles. No... I was wrong. I'm not ready to die, not when there's still so much to do, to say to her. "Enrico, there must be another way. Please. I—I can't leave her." I strain against the ropes, the rough twine burrowing into my skin until it rubs it raw. "I'll do anything you want. Just let me get Isabella out of Rome and safely back to New York with her family. I swear to you I'll come back and shoot myself in the head if that's what you want. I just need to know for certain she's out of harm's way..."

A harsh chuckle spills from the hard slant of his lips. "*Cazzo*, Raffa, don't tell me you've done it again? You've fallen in love with your client?" He still looms over me, but the pressure on my skull relents a notch. "I thought you were smarter than that."

"No," I hiss. The lie tastes so bitter I can barely swallow it down. But the last thing I need is one of the most powerful men in Rome knowing my *principessa* is my ultimate weakness.

"*Bugiardo*," he growls. "You're lying through your teeth, Raffaele." He steps back and swings his gun around, pointing at the very living room we sat in over ten years ago. "You know, the only reason why I didn't kill you back then was that I knew you loved my Laura. I could see it then just as clearly as I see it now." He draws in a breath then expels it with a curse. "*Merda.*"

"My father clearly wants her dead, too." The words bubble out, a part of me just wanting this to be over with already.

"Too?" His eyes narrow and he stalks closer, his focus zeroing in on that one word that could change everything.

I hold my tongue for an endless moment, mulling over the series of life-changing events I'm about to unleash.

"Raffa?" He hinges at the waist and traps me in that murderous, weathered glare. "What do you mean too?"

I could lie my way out of it, tell him I was referring to him wanting me dead and my father wanting to kill Isabella. But why protect *Papà* any longer? His sins are unforgiveable, and the devil's finally coming for him.

Antonio and Giuseppe are another story. My brothers turned their backs on me, but do they deserve the retribution for my father's sins? A month ago, I would have said no. But that was before Isabella, before I'd started to breathe again, to want more out of life, to actually look forward to the future.

"My father killed Laura, in front of me, as punishment for siding with you, his enemy." The moment the confession is out, the pressure in my ribcage subsides. My heart pumps more freely, my lungs no longer constricted by the heavy burden of the lie I'd kept for all these years. And for what? To protect a monster?

A string of curses pours out of Enrico's mouth. He throws the gun across the room with a beastly growl then kicks the ornate coffee table, sending elaborate silver picture frames crashing to the floor. Then he comes for me. His fist collides with my nose, the sharp crack vibrating across my skull. Warm blood dribbles down my lip, and with my hands bound there's nothing I can do to keep it from trickling into my mouth.

The metallic tang makes my stomach roil, but I can't focus on it for long because another fist pummels into my cheek. I grit through the pain, refusing to growl my anger. I deserve this. I've kept the truth from this man for over a decade.

A punch to the gut, then another to the kidney. I buckle over, writhing in pain but I don't utter a sound. I take it, again and again, as Enrico spews all the pain and anger over the loss of his daughter on me.

It's my fault she's dead.

I should have stopped my father.

I'll take my punishment, but I will not die today.

Darkness creeps into the corners of my eyes, head lolling back as my mind attempts to protect itself by passing out. The hits stop for an instant and despite the dizziness and sudden nausea, I can make out Enrico's towering form pacing in front of my execution chair.

"Now what?" I rasp.

"I don't know," he grumbles. "My wife, *Dio* rest her soul, always said I was too soft."

I barely restrain a wild chuckle. There are many colorful adjectives I'd use to describe Enrico Sartori but soft is not one of them.

"In regard to you, I mean." He stalks closer, dark brows

furrowed. "You lied to me for years, swearing you had no idea who killed Laura. That sin alone deserves death."

I nod slowly. "My offer still stands, just allow me to get Isabella somewhere safe."

He clucks his tongue, then pulls a handkerchief from his robe pocket and wipes at the blood coating his knuckles, my blood. "And if I let you go, what will you do about your *Papà*?" He inches closer, and I can practically see the fury streaking through those cold, dark eyes. "Because you understand that he can no longer continue to live, *vero*?"

Right. Of course I knew what my confession would cost.

"I will do what I must to protect Isabella."

"Alfredo Ferrara's life is mine," he snarls. "For taking my daughter's life, I deserve the right to mete his punishment."

My head dips. "And what about my brothers?"

He pauses, lips pressed into a tight line. "If I leave any of them alive, I am only condemning myself to their eventual retribution."

My conscience begs me to speak up in their defense, but what can I really say to protect them? My own fate hangs in the balance. "They weren't there," I finally mutter. "Not when he did it."

His nostrils flare, a tangle of fury and pain slicing into his hard expression.

"Antonio is still learning how to run the Ferrara empire. He's young, tractable. Keep him alive and instead of creating an enemy, forge an alliance."

Enrico grunts, then runs his hand across his face. "With his father's murderer?"

"Antonio is pragmatic and ambitious. And unlike me, he wishes to sit the Ferrara throne. Give him the chance, I can almost guarantee he won't be a problem."

"And if you're wrong?"

"I'll take care of him myself."

A dark chuckle rumbles his chest. "That would force me to keep you alive too."

I shrug. "A fortunate side effect." I do my best to sit up straight despite the pounding in my skull. "You'll never have to see me again after this, Enrico. You'll get everything you've ever wanted. Revenge for Laura's death and me out of your life forever."

"There's still the matter of you having lied to me for all this time."

"I was young and stupid back then. I was destroyed by Laura's death. I couldn't sleep, couldn't eat, couldn't imagine my life without her and our child. I didn't want to start World War III on top of that." I draw in a breath, inhaling deeply to work past the pain. "And he was my father, Enrico. It took me years to come to terms with what he'd done. But by then, it was too late. I couldn't come back here…"

"And then you met *her*, the Valentino princess."

"And he came for her," I growl. "You know the saying, 'fool me once, shame on you, fool me twice, shame on me'. I'll give you a week to kill him, if not, he's mine." Narrowing my eyes, I stare up at the man who used to terrify me with nothing but pure conviction. "It's a win-win for you, really."

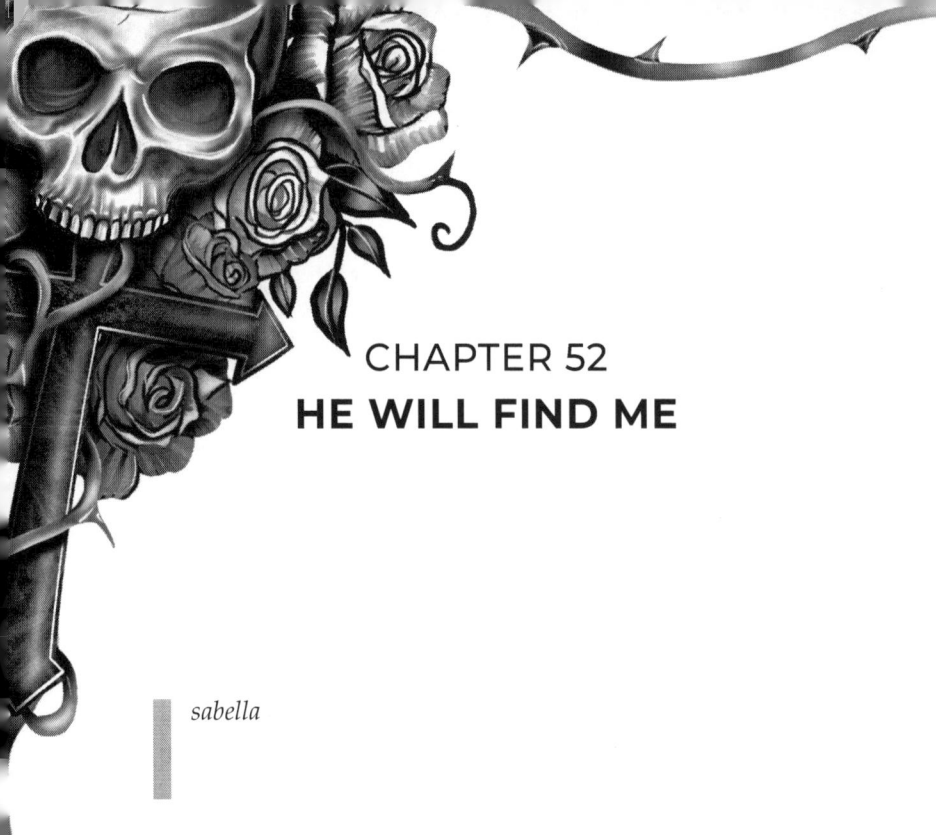

CHAPTER 52
HE WILL FIND ME

Isabella

My eyes snap open, and I jolt up from the stone floor, my heart racing. A dim lantern hangs from the far wall, barely illuminating the dark, empty space. I suck in a breath and attempt to still the mad pounding for fear someone will hear it and come for me. A familiar earthy scent clings to the room, invading my nostrils. The air is cool and musty, heavy with the scent of damp earth and the faint, lingering aroma of... aged wine.

A wine cellar.

We have one in the basement of our summer home in Montauk. Dim light filters through cracks in the cellar door, casting long, slanting beams across the cobwebbed darkness. I glance around the chamber and as my eyes become used to the poor lighting, I can just make out rows of empty wooden racks that stretch like skeletal fingers along the walls. Pushing myself up, a sharp ache swings my attention to the golf-ball-sized knot on the back of my head. That *bastardo*. I gingerly finger the sensitive area, then curse Professor Massimo and his damned pretty green eyes and chic glasses. What the actual hell? And who was that thug that jumped out of the trunk?

No way my professor is the mastermind behind this kidnapping.

Now, where am I?

I scan the room for my purse, which has my phone, but of course there's nothing. A hint of panic starts to roll in, but I shove it down, determined not to let it control me. Just breathe, Bella. You've been in worse situations than this, right? A live shootout would definitely be worse, and I've been in three in the past few months.

This I can handle. I have time to think. I just have to puzzle this out, be observant like Raf has attempted to drill into me all these months.

Raf... Oh, *Dio*, he's going to lose his shit when he finds out I've been taken. And then he's going to kill me once he finds me.

And I have every confidence that he *will* find me.

Walking around the large, musty chamber, I search for something, anything I can use as a weapon. Immense wooden casks lie on their sides in the far corner, swollen shut by years of neglect. Those wine barrels are a bit too unwieldy, but I don't disregard them completely yet.

I walk toward the massive double doors carved out of an ancient wood with iron hinges securing it to the roughhewn stone walls. Pressing my ear to the door, I listen for a sound, anything.

I waffle for a minute, debating between screaming my lungs out and pretending to still be unconscious. Maybe I should just wait it out. If I stand behind the door, then I can in theory get the drop on my kidnapper.

Yes. That's what I'll do.

Now I only need a weapon. I pass by an antique mirror, spiderwebs covering the patinaed glass and catch a glimpse of the flower still tucked into my ponytail. The oleander. A smile slides across my face as I eye the poisonous bloom through the mirror. "Thanks, Raf," I whisper. "Even when you're not with me, you're always looking out."

Careful not to touch the toxic petals, I pluck it from my hair, touching only the foil-covered stem, then slip it into my back pocket for easy access. I pace the length of the old wine cellar for a few more minutes before I begin to lose patience, and the anxiety starts to take hold once again.

I dart toward the door, unable to control myself. "Let me out!" I shout, banging my fist against the old timber. "Massimo! You can't keep me in here!" I stop and wait, listening again with my hand hovering just over the oleander blossom.

Nothing.

So I start to pound again.

"Get me out of here, you *pezzo di merda*!" I spit out a colorful mix of Italian and English curses that would have my mom cringing and my brother Vinny thoroughly impressed. The warm and fuzzy thoughts of my family have that panic rising again, but I shove it down hard. I *will* see them all again soon. *Don't even go there, Bella.*

The slap of approaching footfalls sends my heart catapulting up my ribcage. I dart behind the door and cautiously grip the oleander between my thumb and forefinger, careful not to let the petals graze my skin. My heartbeat escalates with each step closer, my pulse hammering in my ears like a relentless drum.

The door opens a crack, and I hold my breath, pressing my back against the rough slabs of stone.

"Isabella?" Massimo's voice only twists the fear into anger. I'd trusted that asshole, given Raf so much shit for his paranoia and my professor betrayed me! He pushes the door open all the way, and I lunge around the thick timber, then shove the lethal pink blossom right into his face.

He gasps, and I manage to get some of it inside his mouth. His eyes widen as I keep my hand clapped over his face until he begins to struggle against me. Thanks to Raf's tireless efforts and years of Krav Maga, I hold my own for a few seconds, keeping the toxic flower crushed against his face, before he overpowers me, and I stumble back.

I hit the floor, my tailbone smacking the hard stone and sending pain shooting up my spine. "Fuck," I grit out.

"*Che cazzo?*" he hisses, coughing and spluttering. "What the hell was that?" His mouth twists, and a pallid sheen starts to coat his skin.

I have no idea how quickly the poison takes effect, but he's already clutching his stomach, nostrils flaring.

His unfocused gaze tracks down to the crushed petals of the oleander, littering the floor. "No…"

I offer a wicked smirk. "Oh, yes."

His hand lifts to his chest, pressing his palm against his heart, and I wonder if he's starting to feel the toxins penetrating his coronary system. Erratic heartbeat, palpitations, and dizziness if I remember correctly. If left untreated, it can cause cardiac arrest. "What did you do?"

"What did you do?" I spit back. "Where am I?"

He staggers back, leaning against the door behind him, which he's failed to lock. I inch closer, waiting for the right moment to make my move. "I didn't want to do this," he whispers. "He made me… he threatened my family…" His breaths are coming hard and fast now, an unnatural pallor coating his suddenly sallow cheeks. "He had Carlo killed because I couldn't—" His words fall away as his knees give out, and he sinks to the ground.

I don't wait another second.

Lunging for the door, I squirm past him and dart into a dark hallway.

"Isabella, no!" Massimo's shouts fade in the distance as I blindly race down the corridor.

I have no idea where I'm going, but I need to get out of here before I find out who *he* is. My mind swirls with possibilities, my heart pounding in time with my quickening footfalls. Raf was wrong. He isn't the target; I am.

It is all about me. It always is.

I hit a dead end with a staircase as my only option. Guess, I'm going up. A rush of voices filters down the steps, and I mutter a curse. Spinning around in the direction I came, I internally berate myself for not having checked Massimo for a weapon. With my oleander gone, I'm completely defenseless now.

Well, except for the Krav Maga, which I've pretty much abandoned since the arrival of my new bodyguard. *You are Isabella Valentino, and you will not die today.* For some reason, my inner voice sounds suspiciously like Raf. For once, I agree with him.

I will not die.

The smack of heavy footfalls approaching pushes me to quicken my pace. Pumping my arms to force my legs to cover more ground, I dart down the corridor, passing the wine cellar and race in the opposite direction.

"Come on, come on." There has to be another door. There is no way the previous owners of this villa lugged those wine casks up that narrow staircase. There must be another exit. A few yards ahead, I can just make out the end of the hallway.

And a door!

I knew it! Sprinting now, as the footsteps draw ever closer, I push myself to the limit, until my calf muscles are screaming from the strain. I barrel into the door, attempt to yank back the metal bar across the wood, but it doesn't budge.

"No!" I hiss as I jerk at the rusted old metal. "Come on,

please." I pull harder, my arms straining, and I feel it. A slight budge. Then with a sharp keen, the bar slides out and the door creaks open. I jerk it back, and cool night air washes over my heated skin.

I race across a cobblestone courtyard, winding around a classic Roman fountain which spits water across my burning flesh. Lush gardens surround me, olive trees and tall cypresses encircling the grounds. I reach the end of the yard, and my breath hitches.

I'm standing atop a rolling hill with the flickering lights of Rome stretched out below me. *No, no, no. It's too far.* A wrought-iron fence encloses the perimeter, more guards lining every corner.

My stomach sinks.

"Miss Valentino, finally we meet in person." A male voice I don't recognize sails on the breeze, compelling the tiny hairs on my arms to stand on end.

I spin around, forcing my shoulders back and a steely set to my jaw as I face my kidnapper. A pair of inky orbs lock on mine, the startling similarity sending ice rushing through my veins.

There's not a single doubt in my mind, even before he speaks.

A sinister grin curls the man's lips, lifting the ends of his mustache. "I'm so happy to finally meet the woman who has stolen my son's heart after so many years." He steps closer, and a horde of black-uniformed guards move in a wave around him. "It's a pleasure to meet you, Isabella. I am Alfredo Ferrara."

CHAPTER 53
MY PERSONAL HELL

R*affaele*

"You're saving an innocent girl's life, Enrico." Unfamiliar emotion constricts my throat, the words coming out garbled and hardly intelligible as I shake the old man's hand.

He must notice it because he whacks me on the shoulder almost tenderly as he escorts me to the door. "Don't make me regret this decision, Raffa."

The sun is already high in the sky, the warm rays seeping into my skin. So much for being back at the apartment before Isabella notices I'm gone. My cheek is throbbing, and I can barely see out of one eye, but I'm alive. For a minute there, I didn't think I'd be walking out of this house at all. I doubt Enrico did either. I sold out my father for my own life. After what he did to Laura, I think the deal was more than fair. "I don't think you will regret it." After all those years of guilt, it wasn't until today that I finally realized it wasn't *my* fault Laura was dead; it was my father's. And he deserved the full breadth of Enrico's wrath.

My former future father-in-law smirks. "You've come a long way in ten years. Maybe love and the resulting loss has changed you."

"It has..." I step down the stairs and his piercing gaze follows me until I'm on the other side of the wrought iron gate. I whirl around to look at him for what will hopefully be the last time. "I wish I could have saved her, Enrico, for you, for her, but mostly for me. And I promise I won't let the same fate befall upon Isabella." I pause, deliberating on my next words. "I consider you an ally now, and I hope you do as well. But I know how this dark world works, and if that should ever change, and you come for *her*, I won't think twice about blowing your head off, past be damned."

A dark chuckle spreads his thin lips as he continues to regard me from the top step of his elaborate villa. "Laura would have been proud of the man you've become, Raffa."

A jab of pain lances through my chest at those words. I failed her so badly, but I resolve never to make that mistake again. My fingers are itching for my phone. I'd turned it on silent before I arrived, and I can't wait to check on Isa. "*Grazie*," I mutter before turning toward the Vespa.

I slide the phone out of my pocket and cringe at the string of text messages from Isabella. Especially the last one which says she's going to coffee with that damned professor. If he so much as lays a hand on her...

My fingers jab at the screen as I punch out a reply.

Me: I'm gone for a few hours and you're already with him?

I try to keep the tone light, but my insides are twisting at the thought. Where did he take her? How close did they sit? Did she go out with him just to piss me off?

I've been acting like a fucking idiot ever since the gun fight at the cemetery when I accidentally let the L word slip. It simply wasn't the right time, and I want everything to be perfect with my *principessa*. I feel so damned guilty. She's become a target because of me. How can I say I love you in the same breath as I'm the reason you're in danger?

I glance down at my screen, and still, there's no response. She can't be mad for leaving before she woke, could she?

Me: *You better not still be having that coffee...*

Nothing.

Me: *Isabella, answer me.*

Me: *I'm worried now.*

I reach the Vespa and a mix of fury laced with inexplicable foreboding tighten my chest. "Fuck the messages," I grumble before I jab my finger at the call button, Isabella's bright smile filling my screen.

It rings and rings before finally going to voicemail.

She better not be ignoring me. That pit of dread blossoms, my pulse quickening as I scan my call list for Alberto. Stabbing the call button, I hold my breath for the familiar ringtone, but it goes straight to voicemail.

"Fuck!" I growl.

With anxiety now eating away at my insides, I search my contacts for Aldo's number. He's supposed to be in charge in my absence. My heart is a thundering war drum by the time he answers.

"What's up, Ferrara?"

"Do you have eyes on Isabella?" I bark.

"No, she left with Alberto and her professor about an hour ago for coffee."

"And no one else went with them?"

"They were just going right around the block." His footsteps echo across the sidewalk, and I can just make out the rumble of an engine in the distance. The *bastardo* must have been outside taking a smoking break.

"Alberto's not answering his phone. Neither is Isabella," I snarl.

"I'll run over to the café and check on them."

"They better fucking be there, Aldo, or you're a dead man."

"I'll call you back," he mutters.

"No, I'll stay on the line." Paralyzing fear streaks through me, the blood icing in my veins. I'm torn between staying put so I can hear his answer and gunning the Vespa to get across town. I can't just sit here. I twist the ignition and the engine ignites, shooting us across two lanes of traffic.

Horns blare and shouts echo from the cars behind me as I weave across traffic. I have to get to Isabella. She has to be okay. Why would Massimo do anything to her? It can't be… There must be some logical explanation.

At this point, I prefer the idea of her in some tawdry motel with her professor than the alternative.

No… do not go there.

She's fine. She has to be.

"Ferrara, you still there?" I can barely hear Aldo's voice over the rushing wind.

I press the phone to my ear. "Yeah. Did you find her?"

"No one's here."

"You better have some fucking answers for me by the time I get home." I press the red button and shove the phone into my pocket as terror's claws rip into my heart.

This cannot be happening. Not again.

"Where the fuck is she?" I roar at Aldo and the remaining guards in the living room of our apartment, which has now become command central. I've already questioned every person on staff at the café where they were last scene. Everyone had the same story: Isabella left with Massimo and Alberto nearly two hours ago.

And now they had vanished.

I pace the small living room, my angry footfalls eating up the small space in long strides. Aldo is on the phone with the Kings' connections in Rome and two of the other guards are out on foot canvasing the neighborhood.

My thoughts flicker back to my meeting with Enrico and what he'd said about the shooting at The Velvet Vault. Isabella's bodyguard had been killed that night, leaving the position wide open. I still wasn't sure I believed Enrico's story. Why go through such lengths? But if *Papà* had…

"Still no sign of Alberto," Aldo calls out from across the room, jerking me from the dark spiral. He throws his phone on the couch and skulks closer.

"He's dead," I mutter. "Don't waste your time. Isabella is our priority."

"But if he was with her—"

"He's not anymore," I growl. "Clearly someone took her, and Alberto would have just been deadweight. The question is what role does Massimo play in this? Was he just at the wrong place at the wrong time or did he orchestrate this whole thing?"

"We haven't found a single thing on the professor. He's clean."

"And his assistant?" Maybe there's a reason he ended up dead on the rooftop.

"I didn't—"

"Get on it."

"Sure thing, Ferrara." Aldo trudges back to the other side of the room, like the other guards giving me a wide berth. As if my beaten, bloody, bruised face wasn't intimidating enough, the savage scowl has kept them at bay.

I glance out the window and suck in a calming breath. This frenzy isn't going to help Isabella. I have to stay calm, levelheaded. But all my training, all my procedures went to shit the moment I heard she was gone.

It has to be my father…

The last rays of sunlight dip below the horizon, and the setting darkness mirrors the black void that has become my chest. I thank *Dio* this is Aldo's fuck up as much as my own and he's as wary to call the big boss in Manhattan in the middle of the night as I am. If we don't find Isabella before dawn, I'll be forced to make the call that will rain down all hell upon us.

A personal hell I'll never escape if I lose the woman I love.

Dio, I love her, and I was a fucking idiot not to have said it sooner. What if I missed my chance? My fingers dig into the soft skin at my palm as the encroaching darkness threatens to consume me.

No, it can't be, I won't lose her. I shake my head, forcing the devastating thoughts to the furthest corner of my mind. I'll find Isabella if I have to raze the entire city of Rome in the process.

And I know just where to start.

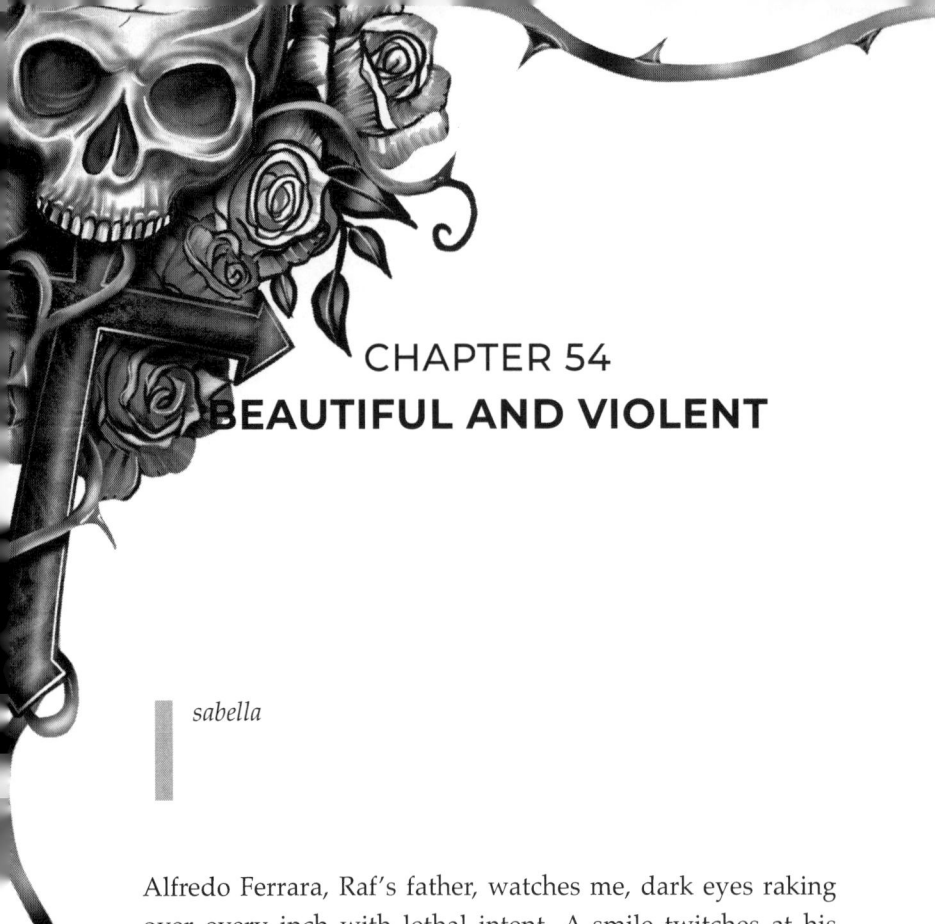

CHAPTER 54
BEAUTIFUL AND VIOLENT

Isabella

Alfredo Ferrara, Raf's father, watches me, dark eyes raking over every inch with lethal intent. A smile twitches at his lips, and again, I'm both revolted and amazed by the resemblance between father and son. With midnight hair threaded in strands of gray, strong Roman nose, and that dark, scrutinizing gaze, he's the spitting image of Raf in a few dozen years.

"You are certainly beautiful," he whispers as he stalks closer.

Steeling my nerves, I stand tall, eyeing the courtyard and the villa behind it for any possible path of escape. Once he's within a few feet, he pauses, that intimidating stare razing over me once more. I gather all the remaining saliva in my mouth and spit in his face. Then I offer a sweet smile as I jab my knee into his crotch while he's distracted.

He doubles over, and his men move on me like a black

wave. A beefy asshole wrenches my arm back, and I grit my teeth to muffle the shriek. Another guard grabs my free arm, so I'm sandwiched between the two big guys in black, their thick fingers curled around my upper arms.

"Beautiful *and* violent." He smirks as he straightens and pulls a handkerchief from his jacket pocket to wipe the spit from his brow. "I see how you've won over my son." He inches closer, wagging a finger at me. "I'm disappointed in him actually. I thought he would have learned his lesson after the first time."

My stomach roils as Raf's confession about his first love rises to the surface. This man murdered her right in front of him. I would *not* let that happen again.

"To be honest, when Antonio and Giuseppe brought back word of your arrival in Rome, I was thrilled. My plan couldn't have worked better. To have you, the great heiress of the Kings' dynasty right here in Rome was poetic. There was no need for me to go to such lengths to destroy your family all the way in Manhattan anymore."

"Your plan?" I blurt.

"Yes, *signorina*, my plan to insert my son into your inner circle."

My heart lurches, slamming into my ribs before dropping to the soles of my feet. "No…"

"Yes. I was the one behind the 'Russian' attack at The Velvet Vault. I was the one who orchestrated the removal of your bodyguard, and I was the one who ensured Raffaele would be there to take his place. Don't you think it was convenient how he showed up at the club that night, then again that afternoon along Park Avenue when those thugs shot at your car?"

My stomach churns, nausea working its way up my throat. Raf betrayed me? After everything we've been through… Oh, *Dio* I'm going to be sick. The things I let him do to me—

Curling my arms around my torso to keep from falling apart, I glare at the monster who took Frankie's life. "You are a *pezzo di merda*," I spit. Piece of shit. "And you'll never get away with any of this. *Papà* will come for me, and he'll tear you apart limb from limb."

"I'm afraid it will be too late by then." He smiles wickedly. "Guards, take *Signorina* Valentino back inside."

Men surround me on either side despite my kicking and squirming, and I'm escorted back toward the palatial estate perched atop the hill. They force me back through the cobblestone courtyard, around the beautiful marble fountain and up the white steps to the entrance of the Mediterranean home with terracotta roof tiles and tall stone pillars lining the entryway.

If I wasn't being held prisoner, I would marvel at the beauty of the villa beneath the sinking rays of the setting sun. Focusing on that is easier than giving into the panic starting to set in. If Raf really had been planted as my bodyguard, who would come for me? A part of me refused to believe it... His father could be lying, right? There is no way the all-consuming emotions between us aren't real.

I take a quick second to observe the three men escorting me through the home. One of them must be the weak link, and I'd have to find out which one ASAP. I'm led through the spacious entryway with dark wooden rafters soaring overhead, then forced down a corridor with walls covered in hand-painted frescoes. Did Raf grow up here? Despite the burn of betrayal, I can't help but picture a tiny version of my bodyguard scampering down these very halls.

"*Cazzo, Papà*, what did you do?" A male voice echoes down the passageway, and my head spins over my shoulder to find another Ferrara barging through the entryway. One of Raffaele's brothers. From over the broad shoulders of the guard shoving me forward, it's hard to tell which one. "Raffaele is going to lose his mind."

The rest of the conversation is muffled as one of the lead security guys opens a door and pushes me down a dark staircase. The familiar earthy odor once again assaults my nostrils. Oh, hell no, not the wine cellar again. I squirm and kick, trying to get free but the threesome escorting me form an impenetrable wall of muscle.

"Please," I whisper. "Do you know who I am? My father will pay you more money than you've ever seen if you just let me go."

The big guy holding my arm snorts. "Your father is all the way in America," he grumbles, his accent thick. "*Signor* Ferrara is right here, and suffering his retribution would be a far worse fate."

"*Zitto*, Alfonso, shut your mouth," one of the other guards hisses.

I'm shoved down the steps and hurried down the hall without another word. The big guy, Alfonso, heaves the cellar doors open, and my stomach revolts at the sight. Massimo is splayed out across the floor, vacant eyes staring up at the stone ceiling. Tiny fragments of crushed pink petals surround his mouth and nose.

I wish I had more of the toxic flower to use against these guys.

"*Merda*," Alfonso grumbles as he eyes the body then makes the sign of the cross. "What the hell happened to him?"

Hypocrite. "Cardiac arrest would be my guess." I offer the men a cheeky smile.

"You stay with her," the other guy commands. "I'll get the body out of here before the rats come."

Rats? I smash my lips together to keep from squealing. Ugh, I hate rats. It reminds me of the subway in the city, and all those disgusting little rodents crawling across the tracks. Right now, I'd give anything to be back there, even put up with the nasty little creatures.

I watch as one of Ferrara's men hauls my former professor off the floor and throws his motionless body over his shoulder. A wave of nausea threatens, but I swallow it down. I've seen worse, much worse. *Now is not the time to be weak*, principessa. I can practically hear Raf's voice in my head. Clapping my hands over my ears, I push away that voice and the pain it brings. I don't want to believe his father, but what if it's true? What if he planted Raf all those months ago and capturing me was all part of his elaborate plan?

No, it can't be... Then why would Raf's brother have said my bodyguard would lose his mind when he found out?

Alfonso eyes me from his post at the door, as if he's not quite sure about me. This could work in my favor. I saunter closer, batting dark lashes. "I killed him, you know." Ticking my head toward the door, I pause only a few feet away from the big guy. "My professor, I mean."

He blanches, mouth curving into a capital O.

"I'm not some defenseless little mafia princess, Alfo. And if you don't watch out, you'll be next." I erase the remaining space between us, and he flinches as he hits the door. "I wasn't exaggerating earlier. My father is one of the richest men in Manhattan, and you could be too. We've got a private jet and everything. Just help me get out of here, and I'll make sure Ferrara never gets his hands on you."

"My family..." he stutters. "He'll kill them all."

"Then we can bring them all to America. Wouldn't you want that? A new chance at life? More opportunities? I'm sure *Papà* would even hire you himself for saving his daughter, his heir."

The man's brows furrow, and I can practically see the gears turning in his head. *Come on, come on*. It won't be long until the other guy comes back.

"Please, Alfonso." I reach for his arm and cling on tight. "Don't do this. I can tell you're not like them. You're a good man." I stare at the gold cross nestled between the thick curls of dark hair peeking through his unbuttoned shirt.

"I cannot risk it, *signorina*. I have my family to think about." His lips press into a hard line, but I can tell he's wavering. I'm right. He's not happy here. And Raf says I'm not observant…

"I swear they'll be protected," I continue. "You have my word."

The slap of quickly approaching footfalls puts an abrupt end to our conversation. The heavy door squeals open, and a familiar face peers through the crack. It's Giuseppe, the younger of Raf's two brothers. His bright green eyes linger in my memory from the night at the dance club. He shoves by Alfonso and growls a quick, "Get out."

The man scrambles away, and my shoulders round, defeated. Still, I refuse to give up, not yet. Whirling around, I march to the row of empty shelves and nonchalantly run my finger through the layer of dust covering the wooden ledges. "My father is going to annihilate your entire family." I speak softly, keeping my gaze trained on the dusty imprint of where a wine bottle once lay. Then on a shard of broken glass. It's no longer than my finger, but it's still sharp and could do some damage.

"Maybe…" he mutters. "I'm Giuseppe—"

"I know who you are."

"I'm surprised you remember me." His footsteps draw closer.

"I only met you a few weeks ago," I reply.

"I'm glad to hear I left a lasting impression."

"Only because of the terrible story your brother told me after we ran into you."

"Ah, so he told you?" He's closer now, judging by the prickle at the back of my neck. "I suppose it's true then, he truly is taken by you."

I don't reply because I only want to ask if what his father

said about planting Raf is true. And I'm not sure I can bear the answer...

"What are you doing here?" I grit out as I gingerly reach for the glass and slide it into my pocket.

"I only came to check on you."

"To make sure your father hadn't slit my throat yet?" I whirl around, eyes shooting venom.

He staggers back a step. This time I hold off on using my new weapon. Massimo was a senseless kill, and this next one could be my last shot at escape. I must use it at the right time.

"I don't condone what my father did." His dark brows pucker, a frown twisting his lips.

"But you didn't stop him."

"I wasn't there..." Giuseppe pauses and draws in a breath. "And I regret it every day. What it did to him, what it did to Raf, to all of us... I'll never forget it."

A twinge of hope flares in my chest. "So what are you saying?"

"I spoke to Raf long before you two arrived in Rome, and even then, I could tell how important you were to him." The deep lines across his forehead pinch as he regards me, regret written across his face. "I might have failed my brother once, but I refuse to allow that to happen again."

"So, you'll help me?"

"I'll do whatever I can to ensure you do not meet the same fate as Laura and their unborn child."

My stomach plummets for what feels like the tenth time today. "What? Their *child*?"

"*Merda*," he rasps through clenched teeth. "You didn't know..."

"No." And now I wonder what else Raf is keeping from me.

"I'm sorry. I'm sure he would have told you when the time was right, if he told you everything else."

I snort on a laugh, wrapping my arms around my chest like a shield. "Or maybe it was simply all a ploy to get me to trust him."

Giuseppe shakes his head, that same regret darkening his features. "He would never use the memory of Laura like that."

I twist my fingers into a knot, that question lingering on the tip of my tongue. "Your father said he planted Raffaele as my bodyguard… is that true?"

He nods slowly. "He's been waiting to infiltrate the Kings ever since your uncle, Dante, started making moves in our territory."

"So Raf—"

He holds his hand up, shaking his head. "To my knowledge, my brother had no idea about any of it. He was as much a pawn in this as you are."

Patting the shard of glass in my pocket to confirm it's still there, I eye Giuseppe, torn between desperately wanting to believe him and not trusting my gut because love makes you stupid and blind. "I guess we'll find out when he comes for me."

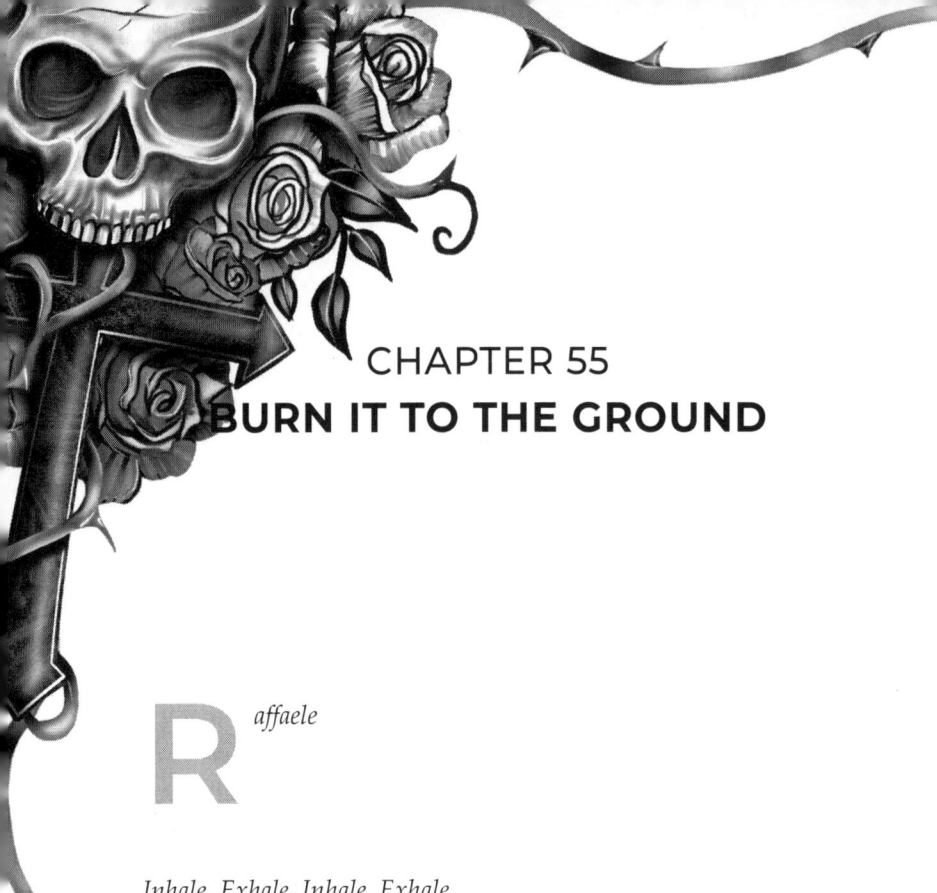

CHAPTER 55
BURN IT TO THE GROUND

R*affaele*

Inhale. Exhale. Inhale. Exhale.

I force the calm my body doesn't feel as I approach the gate to my father's compound on foot with my backpack slung over my shoulder. The elaborate Mediterranean villa sits on a hill with all of Rome stretched out below it. *Papà* used to say it made him feel like a king to own such a grand estate after his humble beginnings. To me, it's nothing but an extravagant reminder of the worst day of my life, and I'd be more than happy to burn it to the ground. And finally, today I will…

I never thought I'd be back. And now here I am, forced to return to the place where *Papà* stole the first love of my life to save the second, the woman I want beside me for the rest of my life. The thought, even in the privacy of my own mind is startling. I never thought I could feel this way again. I vowed he would never have Isabella, and I intend to keep my word. I can feel it in the depths of my bones; she is here.

And I will get her out, even if it means destroying my entire family in the process.

I scale the wrought iron gate, silently drop down onto the lush grass, then release my gun from the holster and clutch it tight in my fist. Then I creep along the outer wall, careful to avoid the roving guards. *Papà* is so predictable, his security hasn't changed in ten years. I circle the compound, searching for any sign of Isabella before I rain all hell down on my father and his men.

Where are you, Isa?

My heart takes turns kicking and punching at my ribs as I move silently around the villa. The wine cellar would be the most secure location to keep a captive. It's where I would take her. Hurrying to the back of the house where the door to the old cellar hides behind a tangle of bougainvillea, my fingers tighten around the grip, sweat slickening my skin. I take measured breaths, refusing to allow the knot of fear and fury lodged in my chest to control me.

I *will* find Isabella.

I will bring her home.

As I turn the corner, I find two guardians stationed by the entrance to the old cellar. That's unusual. The pair stands stiffly on either side of the rusted metal door, each one with a gun already in hand. It must be for Isa. Unless my father has gone rogue, capturing some other new enemy.

"*Hai visto la ragazza?*" The guard's words about a girl halt my breathing. "*È stupenda. La scoperei senza dubbio. Spero che il capo ci permetta di provarci prima di ucciderla.*"

Fury rushes my veins as I hear the man's disgusting words; he wants to fuck *my* Isabella. My feet are moving before I can stop them. I dart around the corner and train the barrel of my gun already equipped with the silencer at the second guard's head. I squeeze the trigger, and the guy crumbles to the floor before I lunge at the one who made the repulsive comment about Isa.

I need to feel the crunch of his bones against my fist, and the spurt of his blood on my knuckles before I kill him. I haul my arm back and let it loose. The crack of his nose sends a wave of satisfaction to the dark monster lurking beneath the surface. I hit him again and again, his head bouncing on the concrete.

"That's my *ragazza*," I hiss. "You will never defile her with your dirty hands."

He opens his mouth to speak, but I shove the barrel of my gun inside, cutting him off. I pull the trigger without a second thought, then leap up to my feet as deep crimson splashes my shoes. Wiping the blood off my hands on the guard's black shirt, I search his pockets for the key to the cellar. Finding the key ring, I slip it into my pocket before sliding the pack off my shoulder to search for the lighter fluid. Dousing the two bodies in the pungent liquid, I light the match and race for the basement door.

The moment the thick metal slams behind me, I hear the rush of footfalls outside. *Merda*. An old chair is propped up against the wall, so I grab it and wedge it by the door. Hopefully, it'll buy me a few more seconds. Killing those two men was not part of the plan, but I simply couldn't control myself after what that *stronzo* said about my Isabella. And this is why I'm spiraling because without that control I'm nothing but chaos incarnate.

Get your shit together, Raffaele.

Forcing in ragged breaths as I traverse the dark hallway, I attempt to still my racing heart to listen for approaching guards. Once *Papà*'s security team finds those bodies, they'll come straight for Isabella. I lengthen my stride, eating up the distance between us in seconds. It's as if an invisible tether is leading me straight toward her. She's close, I can feel it.

The double doors of the wine cellar appear at the end of

the corridor, and I slow, grisly memories of the past assaulting my subconscious.

"No, Papà, no, please, ti prego." I'm on my knees in that damned wine cellar, begging.

He sneers down at me, nothing but pure malice in his dark glare. "It's too late, figlio mio, her fate is sealed along with yours, traditore pezzo di merda."

I blink quickly to chase away the terrible images that come next. I'll die first before allowing that to ever happen to Isabella. I pause by the door, straining to make out a sound. Muffled voices seep through the cracks. Tiptoeing the final few steps, I press my ear to the old timber.

Two voices, one that has my heart thundering like mad.

Clutching my gun, I whip the door open and level the barrel at my brother.

"Raf!" Isabella cries, and all the air squeezes from my lungs at the sight of her. Alive. Her expression falters as she takes me in, excitement morphing into something darker. For a second, I forgot I must look like total shit with all the bloodied bruises.

It takes every ounce of restraint to remain still when all I want to do is run to her, pull her into my arms and never let go. Instead, I focus on my asshole brother and point the gun at his head.

"Relax, Raffa," Giuseppe murmurs.

"Relax?" I bark, swinging my gun around like a *pazzo*. "You fucking kidnapped her, you *pezzo di merda*!"

He holds his hands up and takes a step back, only inching closer to Isabella.

"Get the fuck away from her," I growl. I don't dare look down at the floor, at the spot where Laura bled out as I held her in my arms.

"Okay, okay." He backs off, creeping farther into the bowels of the cellar. "I had nothing to do with this, Raffa. You have to believe me."

"I don't have to believe *merda*. Now, don't move or I'll blow your fucking head off." I reach for Isa, but something unreadable flashes across her face, and she doesn't move. "Come here." The hard line of my jaw softens as I regard her. "Please."

"I—I just have to ask you something first."

"Isa, we don't really have a lot of time here."

"I know that." Still, she doesn't move, only crosses her arms over her chest. Her typical move when she's being stubborn.

"Okay, ask…"

"Did you know that your father orchestrated the attack at The Velvet Vault?" Her lower lip trembles, and a sliver of my heart just about snaps right off. "Did you know your father arranged to have you take Frankie's place? Were you in on it the whole time?"

A stab of pain lances through my chest, worse than any bullet wound. "No, absolutely not. *Dio*, Isa, how can you even think that?"

"Your father said—"

"My father is a fucking liar. He only said that so you'll doubt me. Which clearly worked." *Cazzo*, how could she have such little faith in me?

We remain there silent, locked in a battle of wills for much too long.

"You have to get out of here now," Giuseppe barks, snapping me from the tense silence.

My eyes jolt to his. "Oh, so now you're helping me?"

"I never condoned what *Papà* did to Laura, Raffa. You have to know that."

Blood consumes my vision, dark crimson staining the stone floor, my fingers, my nails. Squeezing my eyes shut, I force the nightmares back. "Well, you didn't do shit to stop him either or to stand with *me* back then. You just stood there and watched as he banished me from our family, from the entire damned city."

"I'm sorry. I regret it every day, *fratellino*." He creeps closer, a look so sincere in his eyes that I want to believe him. "I wish there was a way to go back and change things, but clearly, it's too late for that. But it's not too late to get you two the hell out of here."

I chew on the inside of my cheek as indecision wars in my chest. How can I trust him after all these years?

"Please, Raffa, there's no more time to waste." Giuseppe surges toward the door just as heavy footfalls echo in the hallway beyond.

"*Merda*," I hiss.

Isabella races to my side, her bare arm brushing mine, and the faint touch is enough to spur me to action. "He's right, Raf, let's get out of here. We can talk about all of it later."

My head dips, and I reach for her hand tentatively. Her fingers weave through mine, and a wave of relief rolls through me.

But it's short lived.

Giuseppe leads the way, darting out into the corridor. He pulls out a gun from his back pocket and turns toward the door to the courtyard. The one blocked by the torched bodies. "Wait," I hiss as I slide my backpack down and reach for the lighter fluid once more. Even if the rest of the villa survives, I need to erase the existence of this room. Maybe then, I'll finally be free of the ghosts. I douse the old wooden doors of the wine cellar then light a match, holding it tightly between my thumb and forefinger.

I pause, and my eyes latch onto Giuseppe's from over the flickering flame.

Something unreadable flashes across his face, but an impossible moment later, his head dips. I flick the match into the air, and the entire door goes up in flames within seconds.

"Go!" Giuseppe shouts.

CHAPTER 56
NO WAY OUT

Isabella

"I'll hold them off." Giuseppe shoves me toward Raf as the footfalls grow louder and dangerously close. "Go!" he shouts again.

Flames lick up the old wooden doors to the wine cellar, heating up the narrow space. Sweat slickens my brow, and my lungs struggle as smoke and the pungent earthy odor thickens the air.

Raf's gaze chases to his brother, and a charged moment passes between them.

"Please, Raffa, go now, before it's too late."

My guardian's hand tightens around mine before he jerks me to the right, in the opposite direction of the thundering footfalls. "Let's go." We race across the stone floor, toward the door I'd escaped from earlier. Gunshots ricochet across the narrow hallways behind us.

I point at the door at the end of the hallway, slowing. "Be careful, there are guards out there."

"Not anymore," he mutters.

We reach the end of the corridor, and Raf yanks the chair out of the way before drenching it in lighter fluid.

"You're really set on burning this place to the ground, aren't you?"

He nods, pure darkness etched into his jaw. "It's only a breeding ground for more nightmares."

"Okay. I'll help." I reach for the book of matches in his pocket and light a few before tossing them on the floor, igniting the trail of combustible fluid. A wall of heat erupts, crimson and ochre flames setting the hall ablaze.

He pauses for an instant to watch the fire, the flares reflecting across those intense midnight orbs.

I lace my fingers through his and squeeze. I want to tell him I know about the baby, tell him how pissed I am that he lied, but now is not the time. "I'm sorry for the hell your father put you through. And I'm sorry for doubting you for even a second."

His gaze locks onto mine, the intensity swirling within those dark depths enough to steal my breath away. "I would never betray you, Isabella. I love you. You own my heart and my soul, and nothing will ever change that," he whispers, voice thick with emotion. "It's not exactly the most well-timed confession, but I need you to know that just in case—"

I press my finger to his lips. "Don't you dare finish that sentence. We're getting out of here, both of us." I pause, just long enough to let a smile through. "And I love you. So you better find a way out of this."

A lop-sided smile crawls beneath my finger before he yanks it away. "I swear I will. As if I didn't have enough motivation before, now I need to make sure we get out of here alive so I can show the woman I love the real beauty of this damned city." A fiery glint lights up the shadows in his eyes.

A thrill courses through my body at his words. "Also, what the hell happened to your face?"

"I'll tell you about it later."

Bullets pepper the air down the hallway, muddling with the cloud of smoke, and Raf presses me against a wall, his arms covering my head.

"Watch out!" Giuseppe's voice echoes over the chaos as two guards race toward us.

The crackle of fire and the surge of dark smoke crawls closer, obscuring everything in its path. With one arm over my head and his body draped over me, Raf discharges his weapon at the approaching men. *Pop. Pop. Pop.*

The sharp blasts vibrate across my eardrum, and I can't help flinching at each shot. The sound of a body hitting the ground momentarily stills the panic. But there's still one more guy and with the fiery inferno blazing, I can't see shit.

A dark form emerges from the haze and pummels into Raf.

"No!" I shriek and stagger back from the force of the men's collision.

Giuseppe appears next, a bloody gash across his forehead. He jumps into the rumble, trying to wrench Raf free from the other guard's grasp. My hand instinctively reaches for the fragment of glass in my pocket. I could try…

The piercing bang of a gun sends my heart catapulting against my ribs. The three men are nothing but a blur of black clothes and pounding fists. "Raf!" I scream.

Giuseppe rolls over, crimson splattering his shirt. He clutches his chest, blood dribbling through his fingers.

"*Cazzo*, no!" I hiss.

Raf's hand tangles around the guard's gun and a sharp crack sends a chill up my spine. The guard cries out, his wrist going limp as Raf wrenches the weapon away before turning it back on its owner. I squeeze my eyes closed as Raf pulls the trigger. Then he's crawling toward his brother, and I drop down to the floor beside them.

"Giuseppe, you're okay. I've got you." Raf presses his hand on top of his brother's, putting more pressure on the wound.

"Go," he hisses. "You're wasting precious time." His glassy eyes lift to mine. "Tell him to get you out of here, Isabella."

"No," Raf grits out. "I'm not abandoning you."

"Yes, you are. Just like I abandoned you all those years ago, *fratellino*. Poetic justice, *no*? This is my penance and my punishment. Now, let me have it; it's what I deserve." He pries Raf's fingers from atop his hand. "Go now!" he shouts, eyes lifting to mine.

Curling my arm around Raf's I tug him off the floor. "Come on, he's right. Let's go."

Pure anguish is carved into my bodyguard's face as he rises. With one last look at his brother, his head dips, and he spins us toward the door.

Jerking the heavy metal thing open, he drags me outside. I nearly trip over the burnt corpses, but Raf manages to steer me around the piles of grisly charred flesh. A shot erupts, whizzing just over my head and my bodyguard pushes me to the ground. His massive body envelops me as a spray of bullets dot the night air.

All around us, the thud of heavy footsteps looms closer. The basement door is ajar, and smoke billows from the gap. Screams and shouts echo down the hallway where we'd just left Giuseppe.

We're trapped.

"Raffaele, stand down, you *stronzo*." I've only known the man for a short while and already I recognize Raf's father's voice. "There's no way out." It's not quite as polished and in control as it was when I met him an hour ago.

I'm not surprised. His son has managed to single-handedly cause quite a bit of chaos across the compound. I run my hand down to my pocket and feel for the shard of glass. It's not much, but it's a weapon, and I'll use it if I must.

Alfredo emerges from the shadows, a horde of guards surrounding him, each with a gun leveled in our direction. "I need the girl alive," he hisses at his men. There must be half a dozen encircling the head of the Ferrara household plus another few crawling around the perimeter. Smoke thickens the air, the acrid odor burning my lungs.

Raf leaps to his feet, pulling me up with him, then jerks me behind his broad shoulders. With one arm holding me back, he trains his own gun at his father. "I'm not standing down unless you let us walk out of here."

His father steps closer, moving beneath the light of a carefully hung lantern. A wicked sneer slashes across his face. "I'm afraid it's too late for that, Raffa. You've killed my men, destroyed my home... But I must say, I never thought you had it in you. This woman has brought out a new side of my youngest son."

A savage, murderous one, apparently.

The sinister smile broadens. "You've become quite impressive." He stalks closer and every muscle in Raf's body stiffens, coiled to attack. "In fact, I'd like to make you a deal. You're right, you know, this family rift has gone on for long enough. I'd like you to return to the Ferrara fold. You've proven yourself more than capable, and I believe it's time for you to step into your role in this *famiglia*."

Raf barks out a laugh, the twinge of madness in the wild chuckle setting the hair on my nape on end. "I would never work for you, *Papà*. I will *never* be a part of this family after what you did."

"Then you won't survive long enough to have your own."

The ridges of corded muscles across Raf's back strain,

tensing and coiling. "Kill me if it'll satisfy your desire for vengeance, but let Isabella go."

"No," I cry, curling my fingers around the hem of his shirt. "I'm not going anywhere without you."

"I'm afraid *Signorina* Valentino must be part of the deal, Raffa. You see, her uncle has orchestrated strategic moves in *my* territory. And Dante doesn't do anything without Luca's approval."

I almost snort on a laugh. He clearly knows nothing about my uncle. He's as unpredictable as they come.

"So Isabella is nothing more than a pawn?" he barks. "You plan to use her as a bargaining chip?"

Alfredo's head slowly dips. "That's correct, *figlio*. If Luca Valentino wants his daughter back, he needs to get his men the fuck out of my territory."

Raf twists his head over his shoulder, eyes meeting mine. We both know *Papà* would do anything for me. My mom and our family are the reason why he's taken a step back from the Kings and allowed Uncle Dante to run the operations. Which apparently, he's doing a shit job at.

"I don't trust him," Raf whispers.

"You think he'll double-cross *Papà*?"

He nods slowly. "That's the type of back-stabbing *bastardo* my father is."

"Okay… so what do we do?"

"Get ready to fight our way out of here."

"And, what have you decided, Raffa?" Alfredo's eyes lift over his son's shoulder to meet mine. "Or are you the one in charge, *signorina*?"

"She's in charge," Raf grits out, "but I won't force her to waste her breath on you." He takes a step to the side, and I mirror his movements. The guards' guns trace our subtle shift.

Fuck, there is no way out of here.

I don't know what the hell Raf has planned, but it better

be good or we're dead. Weirdly enough, the thought isn't completely debilitating. Losing Raf would be one thing, but both of us dying together? It wouldn't be the worst thing in the world.

Dio, when did I become so fatalistic?

"So, what will it be?" Alfredo hisses, taking a step closer.

Only a few yards separate us now. I gingerly sink my fingers into my pocket and close them around the jagged glass. My years of Krav Maga surge to the surface. If we could just get Alfredo closer, I'm sure I could land a hit to his jugular. He'd never see it coming. I'd practiced the move for years, only without the sharp weapon, instead just using the edge of my hand to strike the throat and incapacitate my attacker.

"Get him closer," I whisper to Raf.

"What? Why?"

"Just trust me."

The lines across his forehead furrow, but he takes a measured step toward his father and gun-toting lackeys. "There's something I have to say to you, *Papà*…"

He raises a dark brow and inches closer. "What's that?" He eyes the gun clenched in Raf's fist. "I'm not taking another step until you drop the weapon."

With a grunt, he tosses the Glock onto the grass only a few feet away. Then he whispers over his shoulder, "Get ready."

Another step and Raf and his father are nearly nose to nose. The circle of guards tightens around us, and I only hope this doesn't end up being a bloodbath.

"This is only for your ears." Raf leans close, and I can barely make out his words over the roar of my pulse. "The day you killed Laura and my child, you destroyed something in me, *Papà*, and now I'm going to destroy you. I'll see you in hell, *bastardo*."

Raf strikes at the nearest guard, wrenching his weapon

free and I dart around his broad shoulder, lunging at his dad with the shard of glass. Putting all my weight into it, just like my instructor taught me, I strike at his throat.

The sharp weapon pierces his skin, but I can tell by the amount of blood I didn't hit the jugular. The glass protrudes from his neck as he chokes and gasps. All hell breaks loose as the guards descend around us.

Alfredo clutches his throat, wheezing as he staggers, blood rushing down his pristine white shirt. Raf shoots one of the guards in the face, then rounds on a second. More shots erupt from behind us, and I whirl around in time to see Giuseppe crawling through the basement door.

He takes out two of the guards before he collapses again.

"Giuseppe!" Raf calls out.

He squeezes the trigger and brings down another guard racing across the lawn. Then his head lolls forward, and he drops to the ground with a shuddering breath.

No...

I spin back toward Raf, and in a whirlwind of movement I can't quite follow, he manages to subdue the remaining circle of guards until only one man beside his father is still standing.

"Drop the gun, you *cornuto*, and I'll let you live," he snarls at the remaining guy. His lip is split and blood spatters his cheek. It takes me a second to recognize the guard, Alfonso, from earlier.

"Let him go," I mutter. "He was going to help me escape. He only works for your father because he's terrified of him."

Alfonso's head bounces up and down. "*Si, é vero.*"

Raf swings his Glock at the guard. "Get the fuck out of here before I change my mind."

The man drops his gun and races across the courtyard.

Alfredo sinks to the ground, his hand still wrapped around the glass protruding from his neck. He glares up at me, then turns that hateful gaze onto his son. A long minute of silence thickens the air. The sudden stillness after the chaos of the shootout is unnerving.

Raf crouches beside his father, a feral smile lighting up the impenetrable darkness in his eyes. "I am going to enjoy every second as I watch the life drain out of you, *Papà*."

He gasps and blood trickles from his lips, dribbling down his chin.

"You deserve a special seat in hell for what you did."

A sickening gurgle seeps out from his thinned lips.

Raf pivots his gaze from his father, blazing irises finding mine. "You don't have to watch this."

"I'm not leaving you."

He nods slowly as I crouch down beside him.

And we wait…

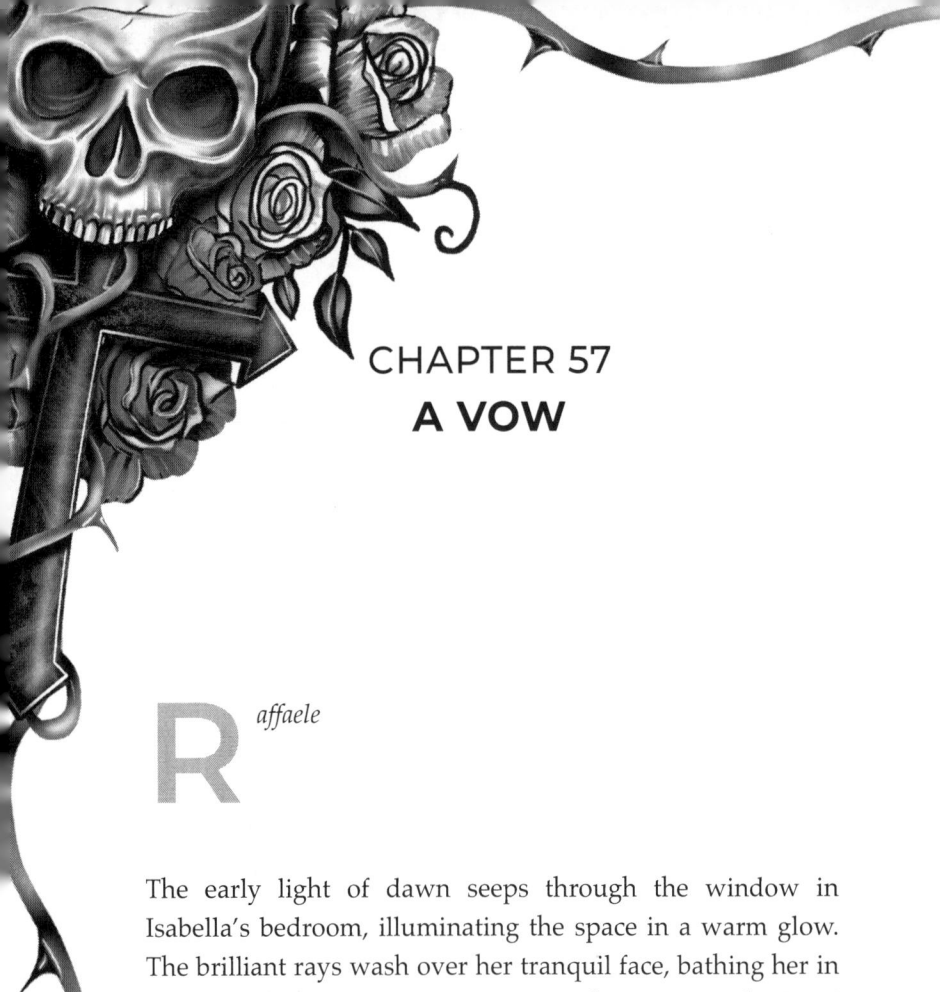

CHAPTER 57
A VOW

R*affaele*

The early light of dawn seeps through the window in Isabella's bedroom, illuminating the space in a warm glow. The brilliant rays wash over her tranquil face, bathing her in an otherworldly radiance. *Dio*, I love her. And to think I'd come so close to losing her only a week ago.

A flicker of movement sends my head spinning toward the door. A shadow creeps across the crack beneath, and I draw in a steadying breath, reminding myself it's supposed to be there.

Isabella's new bodyguard arrived nearly a week ago now, fresh from Manhattan. After the disastrous turn of events with my family, we'd told Luca everything. It was probably the second most frightened I'd ever been in my life. To tell the man who trusted you with his only daughter that you'd fucked up and it had nearly cost her life? And more than that, that you were in love with her?

It was not a pretty conversation.

But as Isabella loves to remind me, she always gets what she wants. I'm so damned lucky that right now, *I'm* what she wants.

After a very moving speech about how much she loves me, and what an invaluable bodyguard I've been, she somehow convinced her father not to kill me. The fact that an ocean still lies between us is a little bit of a comfort, and I'm dreading the day we return stateside in just a few short weeks.

Isabella shifts beside me, her arm tightening around my waist. "*Buongiorno,*" she whispers.

"Every morning is a good one when I wake up with you in my arms." A smile slides across my lips, unbidden.

"I bet that's what you say to all the mafia princesses you sleep with."

I roll her on top of me and tug up the hem of my t-shirt she's sleeping in so I can squeeze her ass. She's bare beneath, and her wearing my tee with nothing underneath is the sexiest thing I've ever seen. If I wasn't hard already when I woke up, I would be now.

She brushes her lips against mine, and the faint touch has blood racing to my cock.

I capture her lips before she can get away. "*Cazzo,* Isabella, you taste so good in the morning. I can't wait to sink my cock inside you."

"Shh!" she hisses. "He's going to hear you."

"So let him. We don't have to hide anymore, remember?" I trail my fingers up her spine, reveling in her soft skin. "And, though I'll always protect you, now I don't have to split my focus anymore. We'll have Harper outside to watch the perimeter."

"Finally." She laughs, the sound rich and bubbly, warming my insides. I spent the first four days with Andrew Harper twenty-four-seven, teaching him everything I know.

I still spend an inordinate amount of time with the guy according to Isabella, but how can I not? He's responsible for keeping the woman I love alive, and I plan on spending the rest of my life with her.

She doesn't know that yet, but she will soon.

She's young, and I'm not. I'm ready for it all. I promised Luca to wait a little while before I officially make her mine, but I'm not sure how long I can stick to my promise.

Isabella's mouth claims mine, and I momentarily lose all focus as she wriggles on top of me. She's straddling me now, her pussy rubbing against my shaft. She's already drenched, and I'm aching to be inside her.

Before we start our life together, I need to confess the one part of my tragic story with Laura that I'd omitted. I've been meaning to tell her since we left the fiery hellhole of my father's compound. Somehow, I can't ever seem to find the words.

But I have to stop being such a coward.

Despite my cock screaming at me, I grip Isabella's hips and stop their tantalizing roll. "There's something I need to tell you."

Her eyes widen as she regards me. "That sounds ominous."

"It's not... It just is..."

She sits back and attempts to roll onto the bed, but I dig my fingers into her hips and hold her still. "It'll be easier for me if you stay like this. Just the feel of you on top of me makes everything better."

"Okay..."

"When I told you about Laura and what my father did—" I pause, swallowing hard. "There was one important detail I failed to mention. Because it was just too horrible, too painful to speak... But I don't want any secrets between us because I plan on us lasting forever."

A smile parts her lips, and *Dio*, she looks radiant. "I love you, Raf, and if you're not ready to tell me—"

"No. I'm ready." I draw in a breath and will the words from my mind to my tongue, but it's frozen, paralyzed in the horror of re-living that moment.

"I already know," she whispers, her bottom lip quivering. "About the baby…" Her words trail off and I'm left gaping, unable to form a single cohesive sentence. "Giuseppe told me by accident that day in the wine cellar. He thought I knew."

My thoughts flash to my brother, to the one person in my family who tried in the end to make up for the past. He'd given his life to save us, and I'd never forget that. Emotion constricts my throat as memories of his bullet-ridden body coalesce at the forefront of my mind. If it hadn't been for him, Isabella and I would be dead.

"I didn't tell you because—"

She presses her finger to my lips then replaces it with her mouth. The kiss is gentle, comforting. "I understand why you didn't tell me. What happened to you, to Laura, it is just unspeakable. I'm so sorry, Raffaele. I'm so sorry you had such a shitty father, and such a terrible past ten years, but I'm going to do everything in my power to make the next ten so much better."

"Only ten?" I arch a teasing brow.

"I'm not sure I can put up with you for much longer than that."

I dig my finger into her sides, and she wiggles on top of me, rubbing up against my cock. "Well, you better get used to it because I'm not going anywhere."

She stills, a slow smile spreading her lips.

"I never thought I could love after Laura, Isa. I never wanted to open myself up to that sort of loss again. It's literally fucking terrifying. But with you… it's a risk I can't *not* take. You know how hard I tried to fight this, and now you know why. Still the idea of losing you—" My throat swells, the ache from only a week ago still too raw.

"You're not going to lose me, Raf." She frames my face with her warm hands, drawing me so close our noses nearly touch. "I'm not sure if you noticed, but I can hold my own. I love that you want to protect me, but I'm kind of a badass myself."

A wicked grin splashes across her face, only bringing out my own.

"Yes, you are, *principessa*." I press a gentle kiss to her lips before I dig my fingers into her sides once again. "Except against me of course. You're powerless to stop me from getting what I want. And what I want right now, is you."

She starts to laugh as I tickle, but the smothered fire from earlier starts to build again. I lift her hips and drop her down on my erection. She's so wet I slide right in, and we groan in unison as I fill her up.

"Oh, Raf," she moans, her hips starting to grind against me.

"I want you to have my baby," I murmur as I thrust.

Her eyes grow wide, but she doesn't stop the tempting roll of her hips.

"I want you to be my wife, Isabella Valentino, I want you by my side forever. It took ten impossibly long years for my heart to start beating again, and I never want it to stop again."

"Are you proposing to me, *Signor* Ferrara? Because I don't see a ring."

A deep chuckle vibrates my chest. "No, not yet, but it's a promise, a vow I intend to keep for as long as it takes for you to say yes. Anyway, I figure your father would cut off my cock if I didn't get his approval first."

"You're not wrong there." She smirks.

I sit up, wrapping my arms around her back and

bringing her body flush against mine. "So we better enjoy this moment then, just in case."

"I've been enjoying every minute with you, Raf." Her lips claim mine, softly at first, but in a second the blazing fire between us ignites. With one hand on her hip, I reach for the open jar of Nutella on the nightstand and stick my finger inside. It's become my new favorite morning treat when paired with my favorite, Isabella. I fist her hair, tugging her head back to expose that neck and run my chocolate-dipped finger down the length of her body. I lick my way down to her collarbone then toward the full swell of her breasts. She moans as I thrust deeper, her head falling back in pleasure.

"You're mine, Isabella Valentino."

"I'm yours, Raf."

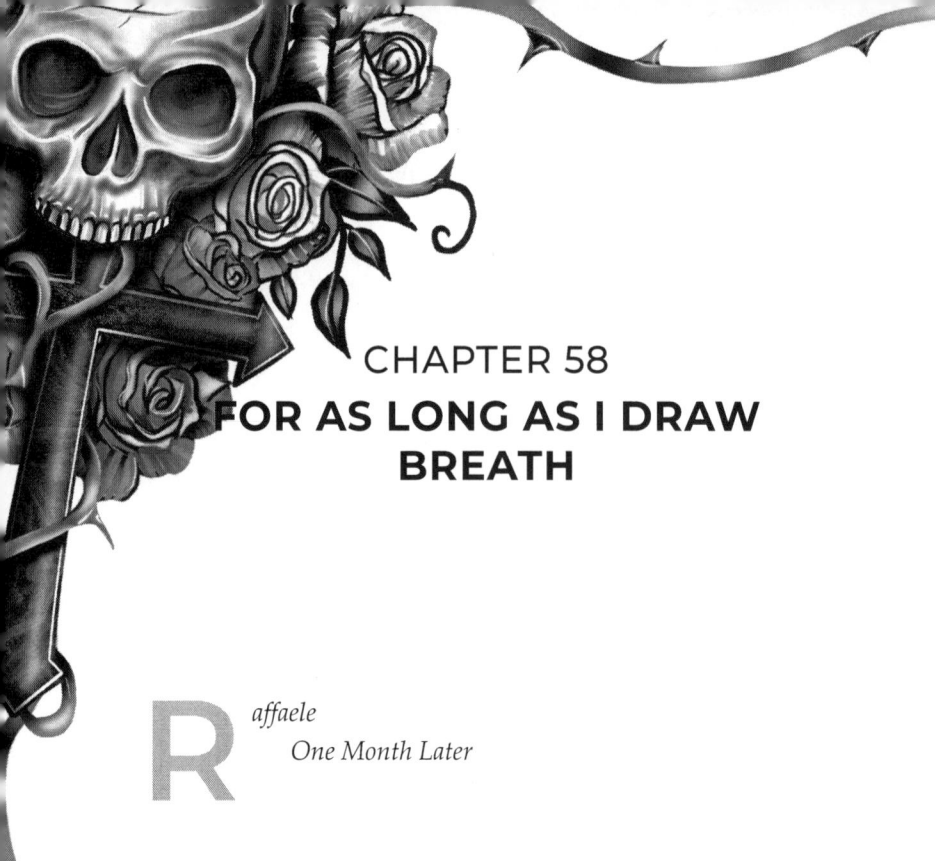

CHAPTER 58
FOR AS LONG AS I DRAW BREATH

R *affaele*
One Month Later

The jet door slides open, and a rush of warm, dense air engulfs me. Welcome back to JFK. Thank *Dio*, it will be fall soon, and we won't have to withstand the oppressive heat of the city for much longer. I step off the jet onto the tarmac with Isabella at my side, and a wave of Valentinos and Rossi's crash over us.

There's a lot of squealing and hugging and an onslaught of "I missed you so much!" I take a step back to allow Isa to enjoy the long-coming family reunion. Then I move beside her new bodyguard, Andrew, who's watching as she's swallowed up by the mob of cousins, aunts and uncles. Her new guard has been decent, but despite my tireless training, he's not quite as good as me. Yet. Andrew has enormous shoes to fill, so I can't quite blame the guy. At least with both of us on Isabella, I'm confident she's protected.

Isa and Serena gush about their time in Italy while Vinny and Matteo watch intently, eyes bright, while the twins, Alessandro and Alessia simply smile and nod. A hint of jealousy flashes across Alessia's face as she regards her cousins. She tries to hide it beneath a plastic smile, but I recognize it for what it is. I'm hyper aware of the way anyone looks at my *principessa*. From what Isabella's told me, it's an interesting dynamic at play between the Valentinos and Rossi's but at least they make it work. And in spite of the family drama and bickering, they seem to truly care about each other.

Unlike my own family.

After I burned my father's villa to the ground, I attempted to reach out to Antonio. Not that he'd extended me the same courtesy ten years ago, but now he was the one alone, in exile from the paltry remains of our family. I never heard back. Not a single call or text. I imagine he must be busy, having inherited the Ferrara empire, the new prince to the throne.

I have no doubt my brother will succeed as the new *capo*. *Papà* groomed him for the role since before he could walk. I'm just happy to be far away from Rome and the dark past the eternal city conceals. I finally have everything I've ever wanted in Isabella.

She cants her head back over her shoulder as if she's overheard my mental musings. Her eyes sparkle as she regards me, the depth of emotion in that glimmer enough for my heart to trip on a beat. She throws me a smile before continuing her conversation with Serena.

As I scan the crowd, a pair of piercing coal-black eyes meet mine. I force my gaze to stay the course, despite their lethal intensity. Because I'm certain of one thing, if I plan on truly making Isabella mine, I will have to stand up to Luca Valentino and prove I'm worthy of his daughter.

He ticks his head at the enormous hangar behind him,

the one that houses the fleet of King's Industries' airplanes and begins to walk toward a murky corner.

Merda. Well, this confrontation isn't entirely unexpected. I knew a quick Facetime call a month ago with his daughter beside me wouldn't get me off the hook that easily. Placing my hand on Isabella's back, I drop my lips to her ear and whisper, "I'll be right back. I've been summoned."

She follows my line of sight to where her father stands in the shadows. "Maybe you should take Andrew with you."

"No, I can handle your father, *principessa.*"

Her eyes widen, the incredulous look doing nothing for my confidence. "Good luck, *amore.*"

My love. "Thanks," I grumble, releasing her and moving around the circle of tight-knit family. To face my doom.

I keep my head held high and shoulders pinned back, despite the unease churning in my gut. I feel like I'm on my way to meet the executioner. I console myself with the thought that no matter how ruthless Luca Valentino can be, he'd never kill me in front of his daughter. He may be many things, but he is nothing like my own *Papà*. He loves Isa too much to ever put her through that hell.

"*Signor* Valentino." I offer my hand and a tight smile when I reach the corner of the hangar.

He ignores both, flashing me teeth in a frightening semblance of a grin. "I hope you understand that the fact that you're still alive has little to do with me and all to do with my overly trusting and naïve daughter."

I nod, breathing in and out slowly to temper the agitated thundering of my pulse. "Thank you for the consideration, and just for the record, she's not as naïve as you may think." His head snaps back but before I stick another foot in an early grave, I blurt, "You've taught her well. She's got a good head on her shoulders, she's smart, and quick on her feet."

"Of course, she is. She is *my* daughter."

"And I love her." I let the words hang in the air for a long moment, hoping he'll take them for what they are. The God's honest truth. "I want to protect her, I want to be there for her for as long as she'll have me. I know I messed up in Rome, but it's only because I was so crazy about her, I made stupid decisions. I should have walked away the moment I started to develop feelings for her, but I couldn't let her go."

"And you've since learned from your mistakes?"

I twist my head over my shoulder and motion at Isa's new guard. "Well, Andrew is still breathing, right?"

A dark chuckle rumbles low in his chest. "What do you think of him?"

"He's not me, but I've been working with him, so hopefully he'll get there."

"Good." Luca nods slowly. "I don't need to remind you that if anything happens to my daughter—"

I raise my hand, cutting him off. "You don't need to threaten me, *signore*. It's totally pointless. If anything were to happen to Isabella, I'd be dead right alongside her."

"You're that devoted to her?" He narrows his eyes, a skeptical gleam in his gaze.

"I love her with every shred of my being," I breathe, my voice firm and unwavering. "I would lay down my life for her without a second thought."

Luca watches me for a long, tense moment, then finally nods slowly. "If you're willing to protect her with your life, then you better be prepared to do so at any cost. She's not only my daughter; she's the future of this family."

"I understand the weight of my vow and what it means for all of us." I lock my gaze to his, despite the intensity surging through those stormy orbs. "I am prepared, *signore*. Whatever it takes."

Luca holds my gaze a moment longer before he extends his hand. I'm shocked by the unexpected gesture, but I keep my expression neutral. "Then prove it, Raffaele. Prove that my daughter's life *and heart* are safe with you."

I grasp his hand firmly, channeling all my resolve into that single handshake. "I will. You have my word."

Isabella

As Raf leads me into the living room of my parents' penthouse, blindfolded, I clutch onto his arm, stepping gingerly in the four-inch heels Serena insisted I wear to my welcome home party. The sounds of Frank Sinatra and faint chatter already fill the great room when I arrive.

"Can I take off the blindfold yet?" I whine.

"No not yet," Serena replies, "just wait a second."

From the sound of it, she's only a few steps ahead of me. And I can already hear Matteo snickering beside her. What are those two up to?

"I should be the one to give it to her. I found it." Alessia's voice cuts through the muttering.

"Fuck this, I'm giving it to her." Raf's hands curve around my cheeks, his familiar scent infiltrating my nostrils. "It was my idea anyway." He jerks the blindfold off, and I blink quickly, my pupils adjusting to the bright lights.

I stare into a pair of ink-dark eyes. "What was your idea?"

He ticks his head just over his shoulder where my brother Vinny, Matteo, Serena and the twins are all standing around a blown-up picture on an easel. It's a stunning modern apartment with soaring rafters, exposed brick and floor to ceiling windows.

"What's that?" I murmur.

Alessia bounds toward me and snatches a key ring from

Raf's hand. "It's your new apartment! It's only a couple blocks away from NYU, in a brand new, secure building."

Papà pokes his head into the circle and Mom sneaks in beside him. "Very secure. Raf assured me it's virtually impenetrable."

I turn to my bodyguard turned boyfriend. "You guys did this together?"

He nods, an indulgent smile on his lips. "After living with you for the past three months, did you really think I'd agree to anything less now that we're back in Manhattan?"

I spin to my dad in disbelief. "You're actually okay with us living together?"

Papà grunts, but my mom shoots him a placating smile. "It took some convincing," Mom interjects, "but Raf made some very persuasive arguments."

"I bet he did." I slide my arm around his waist, and he peers down at me, velvety eyes smoldering.

Raf leans in, brushing the sensitive shell of my ear with his lips. "I want to wake up beside you every morning for the rest of my life."

"Is *that* the proposal?"

He chuckles, the warm sound shooting heat between my legs. "Not yet, *principessa*, but soon. I need to make sure I can buy an engagement ring fit for the King's queen."

Shaking my head, I press my lips to his. "Just being with you makes me feel like a queen, *amore*. I don't need anything else."

Muttered groans fill the space as Raf pulls me into a kiss, a slow, deep one that has my father cursing in Italian and my toes curling inside my stilettos. I can feel the smile on Raf's lips, mirroring my own, as he finally pulls away.

"Come on buddy, let's liven up that music!" Serena's shout over the crooning Frank Sinatra impersonator only widens my smile. As the melodic tune twists to a thumping beat, I scan the crowded room filled with all the people I love most in this world.

Raf's hand closes around mine as he leads me to the center of the dancefloor. His lips brush my own as he whispers, "I love you, *principessa*. Always and forever, I am yours. I will guard your heart just as fiercely as your body for as long as I draw breath. That's my vow to you, my queen."

EPILOGUE

S*erena*

Plopping down on the couch beside Matteo, I let out a dramatic sigh and take a long pull from my brimming champagne flute. "Drink with me, Matty. If I'm forced to watch their nauseating cuteness for a minute longer, I'm going to vomit." I clink my glass to my cousin's empty tumbler and lift my gaze to Isabella and Raffaele slowly swaying on the dancefloor. The Frank Sinatra wannabe is back on stage, and the fun party music has long since died out.

Matty follows my line of sight, and his lips screw into a pout. "Jealousy isn't a good look on you, Serena."

I roll my eyes back so hard I'm worried they'll freeze that way, like my *Papà* used to warn me as a child. "I'm half-way to a hangover and jetlagged. Be gentle, asshole."

He barks out a laugh, shards of emerald lighting up across his bejeweled irises.

"And anyway, I am happy for Bella, thrilled, super

enthusiastic, over the moon, even. She's not only my cousin, she's my best friend. You know that."

"Oh, I do. I don't think you begrudge her boyfriend; I think you're scared of losing your best friend."

"Psshaw." I wave a dismissive hand between sips of champagne and ignore the unexpected pang in my chest. "Sure, Raf's hot as hell, but it's been Bella and me forever. No dick could ever come between that kind of love."

Matty's gaze turns pensive as he watches them on the dancefloor. "I don't think he's just any dick, Sere. Have you seen how he looks at her? I saw glimpses of it before they left, but now? That guy is whipped... He's not ever letting our little Bells go."

"We'll see about that. I've never met a man who sticks around after the fun stops."

"Well, I'm happy for them and for what it's worth, I think he's a good guy." He shrugs and sits back on the couch, folding one long leg over the other. "Probably better than most of us."

Now, it's my turn to laugh. A cackle bursts free, and I toss my head back, laughing so hard my cheeks burn. When the fit finally passes, I finish off my champagne, cooling my parched throat.

"I just hope he's good enough for her," Matty adds.

"I'm sure Uncle Luca will see to that."

"Without a doubt." He clinks his glass to mine, and we sip in perfect unison, pinkies held high like we did when we were kids playing tea party. "So are you seeing anyone in Milano?"

"I'm seeing plenty, Matty. I see nothing but gorgeous Italian men everywhere I look."

He chuckles. "Oh, Sere, you're going to be responsible for the downfall of the most industrious city in Italy."

"But the collapse will be ever so worth it."

My phone vibrates my clutch which is pressed to my leg,

distracting me from thoughts of hot Italian men to… hot New Yorkers. I pull out my cell to find a dozen guys who swiped right on my photo. Looks like Bella won't be the only one getting laid tonight. I must have been smiling because Matty snaps his fingers an inch from my nose, grinning.

"Another night of Tinder?"

"Don't judge, jet lag makes me horny."

"Does anything not make you horny, cuz?"

Ignoring him, I flag down a passing waiter in a tux, reaching for two more champagne flutes. I hold onto one and offer the other to my cousin. He's been oddly quiet tonight. Maybe I'm not the only one a tiny bit uncertain about our future now that our baby cousin has a boyfriend. It's been the five of us, our cousin crew for as long as I can remember. None of us have ever had a serious relationship, and with us all in our mid-twenties, that says something about how screwed up we all are, in one way or another.

The craziest part is how happy our parents are. Sure, some of them may have had screwed up starts, but there is no question in my mind that my dad would do anything for my mom and that goes both ways. The same is true for all the Valentinos and Rossi couples. I mull over the random thought as I continue to sip on the fizzy bubbles.

"What about you? Are you seeing anyone?"

He shakes his head. "How can I with my two favorite wingwomen out of town?"

"What about Ale and Alessia?"

Matty shrugs before finishing off his champagne. "You know what it's like going out with the two of them, they're constantly at each other's throats—"

"Like a typical old married couple."

"Yeah, exactly. It's even worse when it's just the three of us. I've even tried getting Jackson to come out now that he's turned twenty-one, but he hates all the crowds."

"Wow, resorting to your anti-social little brother? Sounds like you're screwed." I bump my glass to his with a smirk.

"Here they come…" Matty whispers, jerking my attention to our quickly approaching cousins.

The twins are bickering about something as usual, Alessia twirling long strands of her bleach-blonde hair around her manicured finger. She sinks down beside me with a grumble. "Shouldn't Bella be paying more attention to us than him? We're the ones she hasn't seen for months…"

"*Dio*, Alessia, not everything in this world revolves around you," her brother snaps before folding down onto the couch beside us. He cradles his whiskey and coke in his palm, taking a measured sip which draws my attention to his upper lip.

"Is that a scar?" I scoot forward on the cushion and reach for his mouth, but he bats my hand away.

"He claims the ladies love it," Matty singsongs.

"Shut the fuck up." Alessandro scowls into the tumbler.

"How'd you get it?"

"It was from that night at The Velvet Vault all those months ago…" His words fall away, and I don't blame him. Uncle Marco had been livid and threatened to take the club away from him if he couldn't handle it himself. The Vault is Ale's pride and joy and seeing it destroyed like that turned my already moody cousin into a full-on recluse for a few months, according to Alessia.

"So when's the grand re-opening?" I opt to lighten the mood.

"Soon, I hope."

"Well, let me know so I can fly back into town for it."

He nods just as Bella rushes over, teetering on those fabulous heels I'd bought with her at Barney's in the spring. "What are you guys doing just sitting here?" She flicks her hair over her shoulder, motioning toward the dancefloor.

Alessandro throws her a lazy grin. "Not sure if you've noticed Bella, but they're playing old-timey romantic music and none of us have dates."

"Since when has that stopped you and Alessia from giving everyone a show?" Matteo smirks at his cousin, a shit-eating grin lighting up his eyes.

"You're disgusting." He throws a decorative pillow at Matty who easily deflects the cushiony missile.

Ignoring them, Bella drops down between Alessia and me. "Come on, Sere, we don't have much time to hang out if you're heading back to Milano on Monday already."

"I don't think your new broody, bodyguard boyfriend is going to appreciate my hands all over you on the dancefloor." I waggle my brows just to get a laugh out of her.

She's too easy.

"Oh, stop." She giggles, that smile lighting up the entire room. It was hard enough being away from her this summer, but now that I've decided to stay in Milano indefinitely, I don't know what I'm going to do without my best friend.

Only my parents know the plan, and I'd hoped to tell everyone else this evening. But Bella just seems so happy, and I hate to put a damper on her night. I'll have to tell them all tomorrow. Maybe I'll even throw one last epic party in my loft…

"Come on!" Bella's already tugging me off the couch before I can reach for my flute. If I'm going to be forced to endure slow dancing with my best friend, her boyfriend and Frank Sinatra, I'm going to need some more alcohol.

"Promise me we're hanging out tomorrow?" Bella pushes out her bottom lip into a dramatic pout that has me proud. She learned from the best, after all.

"Absolutely, all day." My gaze flicks up to meet a dark one. "As long as Raf here will let you out of his sight."

Bella wraps her arm around his waist, and he gently tucks her into his side, and even my jaded ass can see how well she fits there. "Don't worry." Raf smirks. "You won't even notice I'm there."

"*Amore...*" My cousin smacks him playfully on the chest. "I'll have Andrew—"

He presses a finger to her lips, and her eyes heat at the touch. "There is nothing I'd enjoy more than spending the day walking across Manhattan and watching your cute little ass swaying to an invisible tune."

"Oh, *Dio*, he's obsessed," I laugh.

"Told you." She feigns annoyance, but I know Bella better than anyone and dammit, Matty's right. This is for real. Figures our little princess would marry the first man she fucked.

My phone buzzes again, drawing my attention to the clutch tucked beneath my arm. Pulling it out, I glance at the new message. Another Tinder match. Maybe I won't be going home just yet. Before sliding my cell back in the purse, I take a quick peek at the guy. Italian_Stallion69. I barely suppress the wild cackle from bursting free. He's in a black hoodie, with sunglasses, his face covered in shadows but damn, there's just something about him, despite the ridiculous name. I swipe right and stuff my phone into my new Prada.

"Booty call?" Bella's eyes twinkle as she glances up at me.

"Maybe..."

"Well, don't stay out too late tonight. I want to go to your mom's yoga class at nine."

"Deal." I pull her into a hug, squeezing the shit out of her. "I miss you already, cuz. I don't know how I'm going to survive with you so far away."

"We'll make it work. I'll come to visit, a lot, I promise." After the situation with Raf's family had been resolved, they had come up to Milano twice, but that was when they were only a three-hour train ride away. Now how often would I see her? Once, maybe twice a year if we're lucky.

"I love you," I whisper, unexpected emotion suddenly making it hard to get the words out.

"Love you more!" She squeezes me tight before finally releasing me. Raf stands behind her, his protective stance obvious even in this family setting.

"Okay, see you in the morning!" I waggle my fingers and spin around before the tears spill over. Damn it, what's wrong with me? Who knew I'd start to get all emotional and shit at the ripe old age of twenty-four?

One of the guards closes the penthouse door behind me and I rush to the elevator, jabbing my finger at the button. The doors finally glide open, and I dart inside, exhaling a sigh of relief as I lean against the sleek metal wall.

My phone vibrates again, and I draw in a breath as I fish it out of my purse. New message from Italian_Stallion69. My finger hovers over the *View* button for an endless minute. I should just go home and get some rest, right? Or I could drown all my anxieties and fears with a hot stranger and just forget for one night…

Fuck it.

I press the button and the message pops up.

Italian_Stallion69: Meet me for a drink?

This guy doesn't waste any time. I like that.

Me: Where?

Italian_Stallion69: You pick. I'm not from here.

Oh, a tourist. Even better. Then there's no chance we'll meet up awkwardly a few months from now. And luckily, there's the perfect bar down the block from here.

The elevator doors glide open, and I find my driver parked out front. He opens the door, but I wave him off.

"I'm not going home yet, Nicky. I'll text you when I'm ready."

"Yes, Miss Valentino." He dips his head and slides back into the front seat of the Audi SUV.

I don't know what I'd do if my father was as crazy as Uncle Luca who always forces an entire security team on Bella. I would lose my shit to have someone following me every second of the day.

With a quick wave at Nicky, I continue down Fifth Avenue toward the Pierre Hotel. It's sophisticated and luxurious, the perfect spot to wow a tourist, plus if things don't work out with the Italian Stallion, I won't have to worry about getting harassed by dirtbags.

The grand façade of the elegant building is just ahead, and I pick up the pace, an odd stillness across Fifth Avenue. Most of the stores are closed at this hour, the sidewalks barren. A limo pulls up alongside me, likely going to The Pierre or the St. Regis Hotel nearby. It slows, and the hair on the back of my neck rises.

The black stretch limousine stops just a few yards in front of me, and the back door whips open. I can just make out the distinctive gilded canopy of The Pierre next block. I almost make a run for it, but he's too fast. A man leaps out of the car, reaching for me. My heart catapults up my throat as an arm curls around me. I wiggle and squirm and kick, but the steel band around my torso only tightens, squeezing the air from my lungs.

"Let go of me!" I scream as I try to slide my purse from under my arm into my hand. Not only do I have my phone in there but also my gun. The asshole wrenches my clutch from my fingertips, and I hiss out a curse.

He tosses me into the backseat of the limo before I can shriek out another string of expletives. Another man sits on the far seat wearing a black hoodie, smoldering velvety eyes locked on me. He's completely still, jaw locked in a hard line.

"Do you have any idea who I am?" I shout as the guy who just nabbed me dives into the car. "When my father finds out I'm gone he's going to paint the city in your blood," I hiss.

The man in the back slides to the edge of the seat and pushes back the dark hood. The overhead light reveals the harsh contours of his savagely handsome face. "Do you have any idea who *I* am, *tesoro*?"

My stomach drops, a tight knot twisting my insides. "Fuck," I grit out.

Antonio Ferrara.

Get ready for Serena's story in Savage Prince, coming in April! Can't wait till then to find out what happens? Join my Patreon and follow along as I write the next story, chapter by chapter!

In the meantime, join my Facebook reader group, Sienna Cross's Heartbreakers to get the FREE prequel novella and get a glimpse of when Isabella and Raf first met!

While you're waiting, go back and start where the story began with Isabella's parents, Luca and Stella in Ruthless King!

Love is gentle, love is kind, but my love kills.

Sold to the mob.

Four words I never thought I'd utter.

Worse, it was my father who did the unthinkable.

When the creditors come to collect, I'm handed over to the most ruthless man in New York City--Luca Valentino.

The head of the notorious Kings is as gorgeous as he is lethal. Dark, possessive, and violent. Nothing like the boy I grew up with, my dead brother's best friend.

And now I'm his…

The longer I spend in this gilded cage, the more certain I become he will ruin me for anyone else.

ALSO BY SIENNA CROSS

<u>Ruthless Heirs</u>

Ruthless Guardian

Savage Prince

<u>Kings of Temptation</u>

Ruthless King

Savage King

Brutal King

Wicked King

ACKNOWLEDGMENTS

I'll let you in on my dirty little secret… Sienna Cross is my pen name, one I've been dying to launch for a while now. I never would've even attempted it if it wasn't for the support of my husband. He's the only one in my family who knows about naughty Sienna. Thanks for pushing me to do all the things, honey!

A special thank you to my awesome V.A., Sarah, who has been such a huge help and also vault when it comes to keeping all of this a secret. And thank you to the incredibly talented Samaiya for the gorgeous art (you really make the story come to life!) And of course my beta readers and Sarah (again!), and my ARC team, you're all amazing! Some of you have been with me for years and I really appreciate all your feedback (thanks for keeping the secret too!)

And the biggest thank you to my readers! I could never do this without you :)

~ Sienna

ABOUT THE AUTHOR

Sienna Cross was kidnapped by mobsters, saved by her super-hot step-brother, then forced into an arranged marriage with a billionaire. From there, things got really interesting... She loves to write about dark, morally-gray alpha males and the captivating women that bring them to their knees. For all the inside info, join Sienna Cross's Heartbreakers on Facebook, like her page, and follow her on Instagram and Tiktok. She has a thing for stalkers ;)

www.siennacrossbooks.com

Printed in Great Britain
by Amazon